LILLYBETH AND HINSBERTH

THE EDGES OF THINGS

A Novel

WRITTEN AND ILLUSTRATED BY

R. S. MARKEL

To the Lavelle girls,
Always remember to follow
your dreams!

— RS Markel
2015

Amazon Create Space
ISBN-13: 978-1492382034
ISBN-10: 1492382035

Library of Congress Control Number: 2013916437

http://www.rsmarkel.com

⚜ ACKNOWLEDGEMENTS ⚜

I am forever grateful to those who have helped *Lillybeth and Hinsberth* along their Journey, those whose quirks, conversations and advice have in some way influenced the words chosen for this book. I must include a special thanks to my wife, Cheryl, and daughter Annaliese, for tolerating the long hours of writing and editing, for providing suggestions and ideas and motivation and support. I love you both.

With gratitude,
R. S. Markel

DEDICATION

For Annaliese.

TABLE OF CONTENTS

LILLYBETH
AND
HINSBERTH
THE EDGES OF THINGS

A Novel

WRITTEN AND ILLUSTRATED BY

R. S. MARKEL

LILLYBETH IN FLIGHT

"...It is free now, to go wherever the sky takes it."

THE WIND OFTEN CHANGES

CARRIED ON THE WIND, it flew well enough.

"Lillybeth! Here, hold on. Tightly, but not too tight," said Hackleberg to his endlessly curious duckling as he presented her the small wooden handle wound with string.

Lillybeth took hold of the gift from her father and felt a gentle pull as the kite sailed further aloft and swayed about over the heights. The kite was of Hackleberg's own design, and as he watched his daughter grow a warm smile and the kite soar in the soft, clear blue of morning, he felt rather pleased with his latest invention.

"The kite is *so* beautiful, Papa," Lillybeth declared. "Thank you."

Hackleberg donned a proud smile and stood a little taller.

"Keep it steady. There is certainly a bit of a breeze up there," he suggested.

Lillybeth gazed in wonder at the soaring kite. The bright red diamond shape grew ever smaller, losing itself in the vast ocean of the cloudless summer sky.

Lillybeth's mother Millybeth stood nearby. With one eye on her daughter she began to grin, revelling in her daughter's delight even while chatting away with a small group of friends all huddled together in the sun dappled field of grass. As their voices chimed in the morning air, every now and then a small pair of curious eyes glanced in Lillybeth's direction.

Presently the kite began darting about, only an instant after Lillybeth noticed the feathers lift from her wings and the tall grass bend low.

"Papa! The wind!" she exclaimed excitedly.

"Yes, becoming a bit stronger I would say," Hackleberg noted nonchalantly as he turned to his daughter, who, even while bracing herself against the breeze, had a familiar far-away look return to her eyes. Hackleberg knew she probably did not hear his voice. She was onto something; putting things together.

"The sky…" Lillybeth whispered to herself with a note of awe, and she set her gaze upward. For the longest time she peered into the seemingly infinite blue. She felt the wind. From where did it come? Where did it go? What was its nature? After a long moment spent in silence watching the kite, all at once Lillybeth excitedly announced, "Papa! The sky! We must explore the sky!"

Hackleberg and Millybeth shared a familiar glance, for they knew their daughter well enough. Plans for an expedition regarding this new curiosity were almost certainly taking shape in her tiny head. Always inquisitive, always searching, exploring, discovering; Lillybeth could only rarely be found clean and tidy on dry ground.

While Lillybeth's imagination soared off into the clouds, the kite abruptly dove, first one way, then the other, and the line suddenly drew taught. It pulled and pulled as if trying to fly away. The sudden tugging on her wings immediately returned Lillybeth's attention to the present.

"Papa!" she exclaimed.

The wind grew stronger. Placing one foot forward, Lillybeth planted herself firmly against the gale.

"Just a bit of wind," Hackleberg stated calmly.

But all at once a more vigorous gust came swiftly over the kite, and Lillybeth was immediately taken from her feet. Tumbling forward, she clasped the handle tightly and held on. She slid fast over the ground.

Millybeth suddenly turned from her friends and was startled to see her daughter slip away on her belly into the grass.

"LILLYBETH!" exclaimed Hackleberg as he bounded after her.

In an instant Millybeth was right behind him.

From behind his mother's wing, the other witness to the scene, only a bit larger than Lillybeth herself, suddenly darted toward where she disappeared into the foliage.

"Hinsberth!?" his father exclaimed with a start.

After only a few steps, Hinsberth caught himself and stopped.

Gaining speed, Lillybeth twisted and turned and struggled mightily to dig her feet into the soft dirt. In vain she tried to raise her head, but all at once another forceful gale seized the kite and Lillybeth's bill abruptly found the ground, bringing the disagreeable journey to a sudden halt. The handle tore from her wings. She lifted her head from the dirt, only to see the handle rising fast into the air, and along with the kite, speeding off into the distance.

She had lost her father's gift.

Hackleberg and Millybeth finally caught up to her, and each taking hold of a wing, they helped their daughter from the ground and tried to clear her bill of dirt.

"You are fine," Millybeth stated in a reassuring tone, satisfied after a brief examination Lillybeth was not harmed by the unexpected voyage through the brush.

Lillybeth tried to speak but her mouth was full of earth.

"Papa... the kite... I'm sorry," she finally sputtered in a muddy tone, pointing a wing skyward.

Together they watched the kite until it disappeared into the bright glare of the azure sky. Hackleberg knelt down to look directly into Lillybeth's eyes, and noticing her sudden intention to fly off after it, he placed his wings on her tiny shoulders.

"Let it go. I can always make another," he said in his most comforting manner. He paused a moment, looked upward, and added, "The wind must have wanted it. I had a sense that particular kite was not destined to be tethered. It is free now, to go wherever the sky takes it."

Lillybeth peered deep into the distance to the spot where the kite vanished from sight. She wiped her eyes. The kite was free, she thought, to fly wherever it wished, and she suddenly felt lighter. The wind calmed.

"Will it ever return?" she asked hopefully.

"Well — truthfully, I cannot say. Certainly the wind often changes," Hackleberg replied thoughtfully. "I suppose anything is possible."

Lillybeth's eyes widened, and she drew a deep breath. She knew not from where the notion had come, but it arrived with the utmost certainty: *something* must be up there.

As the sun drew slowly higher those in the field began to depart, but not one of them imagined such a seemingly innocuous curiosity from one of the smallest amongst them was to beget events so peculiar — events destined to change forever the lives of so many, and allow for so many others to simply live...

❖ ❖ ❖

Lillybeth Andalin Smythe was somewhat slighter than most ducklings her age, primarily ruddy brown of feather and more often than not donning what may have at one time been a bright canary colored shirt, but having tasted sediment from nearly every puddle on The Farm the color was faded and dull and like most of her wardrobe, it was in dire need of a fresh laundering. Always over one shoulder was a strap bound to a well worn satchel hanging to one side and packed tight with all the bits and bobs, from marbles to compass to strands of twine, she believed necessary to be prepared for anything unexpected. Her feet were characteristically adorned with a pair of durable and often muddy shoes tied tightly across their middles. During her frequent outings she almost always gave the impression a journey into the unexplored regions of distant lands was an imminent possibility. She was ordinarily with an expression of deep inquisitiveness, maybe even puzzlement at times, as well as a sense of distance, or perhaps fantastic possibilities in her clear, dark eyes.

Along she would go, carving curvaceous paths through the deep and murky waters of The Farm's ponds and streams, absorbing the sensations of chilly water and sloppy mud, and observing the variety of interesting creatures — large, small, and so tiny as to be nearly invisible — all walking, crawling and twitching about.

Such things, she thought to herself, *are* things. As far as she could tell, an ant was an ant, all somewhat similar to each other, but one could certainly tell where one ant ended and another began. The same it was with trees and flowers, and stones and pebbles.

But not so with the sky. She had flown about The Farm, never too distantly, and had noticed no matter how far she had flown, or in what direction, she had never even a faint impression of becoming closer to the edge of the sky, the point where it ended and something else must certainly begin. It seemed a great and irresistible mystery.

Presently, as she wound her way homeward, Lillybeth was inattentive once again; preoccupied by her conjectures regarding wind and sky, until suddenly startled by a timid pat on the wing.

Turning, Lillybeth came to gaze upon her young and feathered acquaintance, Hinsberth Smerckington, who, although keeping his condition as much to himself as he believed proper, also possessed a rather curious disposition, in addition to a hitherto hidden but nevertheless real ambition for adventure into the unknown. After a number of lengthy, anxious deliberations to determine just the right moment to make his approach, Hinsberth had gathered his courage and decided to respond personally to Lillybeth's earlier declaration of an impending investigation into the nature of the sky.

Hinsberth was well regarded by those on The Farm as having, despite his youth, rather sound judgement, a trait Lillybeth was certain was not only inherent but also carefully honed to a high degree by his father. Level headed and stable of mood, Hinsberth was also invariably polite and well mannered. His appearance reinforced the impression of dignified dependability, as over his feathers he commonly wore a tightly drawn but tasteful blue vest bound in the middle by a matching trio of inconspicuous gold buttons. In his wardrobe hung no less than three identical versions, and little else.

Ever since Hinsberth had first met her, as she ambled along tracking a pill bug on a footpath just near their homes, he could not have enough of curiously observing the decidedly odd Lillybeth. He had historically watched Lillybeth's "shenanigans", as some on The Farm would characterize them, from afar. Hinsberth often wondered if she had ever taken notice of him, but he was not at all certain. Although when he considered the matter, he noted that in contrast with her usual attire, she had recently begun wearing a petite yellow bow to one side of her head.

Over time Hinsberth found himself developing a sincere fondness for Lillybeth's ability to wade through her day with little awareness of or regard for convention, and for how she was always kind and helpful, even enthusiastically so, whenever the opportunity presented itself. So on this occasion Hinsberth made an uncharacteristically hasty decision — committing himself to joining Lillybeth in whatever events were destined to unfold.

As they stood facing each other, Lillybeth, somewhat nervously, regarded Hinsberth from tip of bill to webbed toe, and then for a long moment she just stared at him; concerned her bill was still covered with dirt and unsure of what to say, for what seemed to Hinsberth the better part of a hour.

Hinsberth had only just summoned the courage to share his intention to accompany her when Lillybeth inquired in her notoriously precise manner of speaking, "Whatever is it, Hinsberth?"

Hinsberth was caught; he was not prepared to explain himself, since doubt about the correctness of his decision — given the results of Lillybeth's previous expeditions — was never altogether absent from his mind.

Consequently, his reply came forth in a rather befuddled manner, "I am... not sure. I mean — I was considering..."

"Considering what, do tell?" Lillybeth interjected, and at once she realized she might have rudely startled Hinsberth with the interruption. For the naturally pensive Lillybeth, the intricacies of formal conversation were a frequent source of frustration.

Historically Hinsberth's voice would fail him by the second, or perhaps third spoken exchange with Lillybeth, and this day would not prove an exception. He took a moment to compose himself and then stated candidly, with undue speed in a singular exhalation, "I wish to accompany you on this most important investigation."

It was all he planned to say, and having it out, he continued on awkwardly, "I heard you — this morning — mention exploring the sky to your father. I am sorry for listening in... Your kite was very beautiful."

Lillybeth — her face normally etched in an faraway, quizzical expression — suddenly and inexplicably changed, if only for an instant. Her eyes briefly sparkled and she seemed more than a bit surprised, perhaps even delighted, at least to Hinsberth. Lillybeth was entirely unaware Hinsberth had been listening to the conversation she had with her father before the wind whisked the kite away. She was rather flattered knowing Hinsberth had bothered to pay attention.

After a long silence and just as Hinsberth began to question whether he had perhaps somehow offended her, Lillybeth shifted her eyes nervously and stated in an unusually soft voice, "Your company is very welcome."

Never before had anyone other than her mother and father demonstrated any interest in joining Lillybeth on her explorations, and she was not at all sure how to proceed. Further complicating the matter, without warning her rather cantankerous belly began inventing new kinds of knots. So in the characteristic manner she had developed to avoid being governed by her often loudly speaking stomach at the expense of her broadly thinking head, Lillybeth swiftly turned her focus to the task ahead.

"Given the nature of this particular expedition," she began studiously, "I believe we must begin to prepare at once, for the secrets of the sky must be well hidden."

"I agree completely," announced Hinsberth wholeheartedly, more than pleased at the chance to utter those particular words. He could not help but to grow a warm grin. "So — how do we begin?"

Lillybeth was more than delighted over Hinsberth's wish to join her on the expedition, even if she could not manage to offer the precise words to say so.

"Well, first of all — I believe we need a plan..." replied Lillybeth thoughtfully.

And for the remainder of the morning until growling bellies compelled a return home for the midday meal, the pair of ducklings worked happily together, drawing up ideas for a voyage into the greater heights of the sky.

As the sun marked the arrival of noontime, they stood and faced one another, at some distance apart, and bid a rather formal goodbye. Parting ways, the ducklings turned and with broad grins they waddled lightly homeward.

❖　❖　❖

The following day dawned equal to the previous in clarity and brilliance. The two ducklings convened as planned, in the cool air and warm light of early morning, beside the Old Barn — a tall, weathered building with a high, rounded roof which at one time may have been red or brown, but now had the patina of aged wood. The Old Barn was sited in a small grove of trees, not too far from The Pond, The Farm's largest and most revered body of water. With its nearly central location, quaint sandy beaches and gentle banks, The Pond was a hub for Farm activities and a favored meeting place for social gatherings of all kinds.

As Hinsberth waddled up behind the Old Barn he spotted Lillybeth, always the early riser, standing by herself, her eyes once again gazing skyward, seemingly as if in wait for something to happen.

Seeing Hinsberth approach, Lillybeth grew suddenly tense and her breath became shallow, but she offered in her most formal manner, "Good morning, Hinsberth," and she added quickly, "We will need some supplies."

"Yes, a very good morning," Hinsberth agreed. "Supplies, certainly... but what?" he inquired, thinking hard, looking around and hoping to be of help.

"Such a flight cannot be accomplished with only our normal abilities," suggested Lillybeth, thinking aloud with one wing folded across her middle and the other resting upon it, supporting her bill. She was rummaging with her eyes through the old detritus scattered here and there and mostly hidden in the tall grass.

After a time spent searching, Lillybeth found an item of interest, and she stated in a whimsical manner, "We will need to fly higher, much higher than ever before!"

She held a small bottle in both wings, and rolling it around slowly, she examined it closely from every angle.

Bringing it up to one eye, she exclaimed, "And this may help us!"

She turned to look upon Hinsberth through the bottle.

Hinsberth looked at her confoundedly, "I see. But if you may excuse me... How exactly will such a thing help us?"

"Well... perhaps it would allow us to see further? Or carry water, or we could use it to hold the air — air from the very top of the sky. Or... Oh, Hinsberth, there are so many things we could do."

Lillybeth lowered the bottle from her eye and deflated a bit.

She could at times be rather moody, Hinsberth reminded himself.

In an instant Lillybeth perked up again as another idea took hold. "Yes, perhaps you are right. Maybe the bottle is not what we need. But — it does seem curious. I put the bottle over my eye, and I can still see you. Not perfectly mind you, but you are still there, a little hazy perhaps."

"And you look like you, but holding a bottle over one eye. But I fail to see..." Hinsberth replied, trying his best to follow Lillybeth's reasoning.

Lillybeth was becoming flustered. She wanted to keep Hinsberth's interest but sensed he was quite unsure what she was trying to say.

"Well, at times the sky is hazy, with clouds and fog and mist, as when peering through this bottle. Perhaps the bottle and the very top of the sky are made of similar things," she explained. "The light passes through but we know the glass is there because of the glare and shadows."

Hinsberth paused a moment.

"But the bottle is hard and brittle and the sky is not. It is so soft we only feel it when it moves. Or when we move," he suggested thoughtfully.

"But perhaps around the sky, holding the air and clouds and wind is a *giant* bottle. And we are trapped inside, looking out... wondering," Lillybeth suggested. "Perhaps the sun, the stars and the moon are sliding over the surface of a huge glass!"

With great enthusiasm for this latest idea, Lillybeth let the bottle fall to the ground and she waved her wings in a great arc above her head, as if rounding them over the whole of the sky.

"I am not so sure I like the idea of being trapped," said Hinsberth gravely. "Do you think perhaps the sky has no edge? It may just go on and on."

Hinsberth wished to agree with Lillybeth, but he had his doubts the sky could, at its very top, be made of something so solid and impenetrable as glass.

"Your idea about the glare in the sky just might have something to do with the clouds and fog, things in the sky. If the sky were a great bottle with the sun and moon and stars above it, they would always look fuzzy."

Lillybeth paused for a moment. She felt flattered by Hinsberth's thoughtful considerations of her ideas, for he seemed so genuine in his interest.

"Yes. The clouds certainly must be below the stars. Or perhaps you are right; the bottle and the top of the sky are not the same things at all. I do not favor the notion of being trapped in a giant bottle. But, there is only one way to know for certain. We need to find the edge, the very top of the sky," she explained with a growing wonder.

With the purpose of the expedition becoming firmer in her mind, Lillybeth grew silent and the vast realms of possibility returned to her eyes.

Hinsberth thought Lillybeth's idea to find the top of the sky seemed rather grand, but also daunting. What unimaginable construction might be up there, holding the tiny lights of the stars in place at night, and guiding the sun and moon along their daily travels? It did seem a great mystery, one almost certainly not easy to solve, for the past was replete with dauntless explorers of one kind or another, and at some point the sky must have also beckoned them to find its secrets. But not wanting to dampen Lillybeth's excitement, Hinsberth kept his trepidations to himself.

The pair continued picking their way through the treasures lying about, every now and then separating an odd object or two for potential use during the expedition.

After rummaging together silently, Hinsberth, hoping to find some reassurance, asked "Is not the ground one edge of the sky?"

"Yes, quite certainly," replied Lillybeth.

After a long pause as she considered Hinsberth's question more deeply, she began to reason aloud, "But the top of the sky could not be ground; no light would come through. And we would look up and see more trees, ponds, farms and maybe even the tops of heads of some like ourselves, perhaps thinking the same as we, but only upside down instead of right side up."

"Or the opposite," offered Hinsberth speculatively. "Maybe it is we who are upside down."

Lillybeth looked skyward.

"Well, there may be only one way to know for certain."

"You may be right. We will have to see for ourselves. Perhaps we should gather our things and prepare for tomorrow?"

Lillybeth nodded.

And with that, the pair carried off several odds and ends and left behind the Old Barn. Together they waddled buoyantly down the narrow trail toward home. The well worn footpath was bordered on one side by an old picket fence rippled with peels of white paint and on the other by an unbroken wall of tall, verdant grass, and upon reaching the point where the fence became one with the earth, the two adventurers shared a rather less formal goodbye than the day previous and even managed a pair of twitchy smiles. Parting ways, they went off with light steps and hopeful thoughts for the expedition to come.

❖   ❖   ❖

Lillybeth wound her way homeward, but this day her path seemed oddly fresh and new, and for the first time she paused every now and then to notice the beauty of her surroundings: the bushes and trees huddled tightly together, with leaves and stems swaying gently in the soft breeze, and the sweet, calming scent of the newly blossoming wildflowers colorfully watching over the trail. She listened closely as she went — her feet scuffled softly over the tamped soil of the footpath and the metallic items she carried chimed delicately together in rhythm with every step.

Finally Lillybeth rounded the final bend in the trail and came to a clearing in the tall grass. To one side was a quaint, tidy house, with a lightly pitched roof wearing a quilt of garden plants, herbs and flowers. The front of the house was marked by a well finished, gently curving door of polished wood adorned with a tight quartet of small window panes, and beneath the windows rested a brightly painted planter box, within which a single flower stood guard, cheerfully greeting any visitors. Its companions sprayed forth blooms of color from out of planter boxes mounted to either side of the door, and all were arrayed in a welcoming manner and giving the impression of having been noticeably arranged and carefully tended.

Lillybeth went up to the door and pulled with intent on the large round handle mounted to one side, which replied with a dull thud. After a brief, muted symphony of metallic whirring, the door creaked open and Lillybeth bounded inside.

"Might I inquire where you have been?" came her mother's voice. She had spotted Lillybeth's sack of newly discovered treasures. Millybeth was always curious about the most recent incarnation of the unintentional mischief her daughter was so prone to instigate. "Out behind the Old Barn I suppose?"

"Yes, with Hinsberth. He has decided to accompany me!" Lillybeth answered excitedly.

"Why, that is very kind of Hinsberth," said Millybeth happily. She was pleased to hear her daughter would not be traveling alone, for Lillybeth had rather unusually not yet invited she or Hackleberg to join the flight, and now she understood why. Millybeth was excited Lillybeth had made a new friend.

Millybeth was also a bit of an explorer, and never short on encouragement for Lillybeth's activities, believing them paramount to her learning about the world. Millybeth's youth was an adventurous time, for she was always out with her family exploring The Farm and surrounding lands, and it had seemed there was always something new and surprising awaiting over the next hill, hidden within the next grove of trees, or beyond the far horizon, and she wished the same richness of experience for her daughter.

Like Lillybeth, she often donned durable and rugged attire. For between Lillybeth's collections of mud, insects and the occasional amphibian, and her husband's frequent experimentation with mechanical detritus from wherever it could be found, it seemed an appropriate choice to be ready for any possibility.

Never one to sit idle, Millybeth was scuttling about with busy wings, and stopping frequently to fidget with one of Hackleberg's strange looking, wiry gadgets, which sat on a small, round wooden table brightly lit from above by a series of circular windows embedded in the roof garden.

"Your father and I, we have flown from here to there," she began while shuffling her wings from side to side, "to many places, but never have we seen anything like an edge to the sky. Mind you, if you fly high enough, it is cold up there, and the winds can be quite stern. You may wish to carry something to keep yourselves warm."

"We have these..." Lillybeth mentioned as she dumped her finds unceremoniously onto the floor, and not an instant later through the front door stepped Hackleberg, his tall, lean figure wrapped from head to toe in odd looking bands of different colors. His entrance was accompanied by a cloud of dust, and he was coughing profusely.

"Ah, yes. Lillybeth, I am glad you are back, and just in time. I have gathered a few items for your journey tomorrow," said Hackleberg.

He then lifted his wing and deposited upon the table a collection of old clothes, shoes and boots along with some shoestring and twine. "These should help keep you warm and dry," he declared in his typically giddy manner.

Hackleberg fancied himself an amateur inventor. He was perpetually on the lookout for things and ideas to mend or improve the family quarters or whatever problem seemed to be nagging his irrepressible mind. Like Millybeth, he encouraged his daughter's pursuits in finding the hidden workings of her world, an endeavor he believed as important as having enough of the right food, enough time with friends, or enough sleep: in short, all the things he did not always attain for himself.

In keeping with his convictions, his clothing had been assembled purely for utilitarian concerns, the different layers keeping different parts cooler or warmer as Hackleberg had carefully designed to be most efficient. He tended to ignore, however, that his eminently rational choices nevertheless resulted in a high level of discomfort.

Lillybeth spent the remainder of the day arranging the items gathered from the Old Barn and by her father. She carefully examined every piece... she tried to assemble them together... she rolled them about in her wings.. she tried to stuff everything into her satchel.. and she spent a long moment lying on the floor, flat on her back, imagining soaring high into the upper reaches of the sky with Hinsberth at her side.

❖　❖　❖

The following morning dawned cooler and overcast, with the pleasantly ample and sweet scent of moisture wafting thickly through the air. But by the time Lillybeth had finished her preparations, speckles of sunlight began to pierce through the otherwise uniform blanket of grey. Lillybeth sat on the floor under the skylights and organized her things, arranging them in her own particular order, and then she placed them carefully into her satchel, putting the leftover pieces in a large cloth sack, which she bound tightly at the top with a piece of string.

Ready for flight, she went excitedly outside.

"It is a grand morning for a little adventure," declared Hackleberg, spotting his daughter and her purposefully packed belongings.

CHAPTER 1

Millybeth and Hackleberg were in fitful repose on a pair of seats of Hackleberg's own design; being quite efficiently constructed yet somehow discomforting. Between them sat a small table and on its top was their favorite morning meal. It was a ritual they enjoyed frequently: sitting in front of their home, eating a bit of breakfast and discussing the planned course of the day. On this particular morning there was a tinge of excitement in their voices, for they were rather pleased Lillybeth was to be accompanied on her adventure and were hopeful a new friendship was unfolding.

"Do you believe Hinsberth is ready?" inquired Millybeth.

"I do not think him an early riser," replied Lillybeth. "But today we cannot wait for the normal proceedings."

"Most certainly," stated Millybeth, playing along as if there could be no question about the importance and significance of her daughter's plans. "Please let us know as soon as you two have returned. We are excited to hear the results. One never knows what may happen when delving into the unknown."

Lillybeth went over to her parents, and they wrapped their wings around her so only her head was above the mesh of feathers. They held her for a moment, and then Lillybeth turned to begin the short walk to Hinsberth's home.

As she scurried along the crumbly trail still darkened in shadow, Lillybeth examined her sack of gear, holding it in front of her with both wings, double checking to make certain she had remembered to pack everything needed for the voyage.

"Hinsberth!" she called out, unable to hide her excitement after arriving before the brightly painted house Hinsberth and his family called home.

"Yes?" came a polite voice from behind.

"Oh, I see. You are ready then?" Lillybeth said as she turned around, just in time to see Hinsberth emerge from out of the lush, colorful gardens fronting his home.

Hinsberth had been gazing skyward, trying to peer through the clouds and evaluate the conditions for flight. He felt just a bit weary from awakening earlier than was customary. He had a sturdy pouch tied round his middle, packed tightly with an assortment of warm clothing, including his favorite (and only) argyle sweater, and a few small pieces of dried fruit.

Without objection, Lillybeth impulsively stuffed a couple of items from her satchel into Hinsberth's pouch to help even the load, and then draped the strap of her satchel around her torso so it would not interfere with the movement of her wings. She presented two small, knit helmets which they put over the tops of their heads, tying them securely with the attached bits of string.

They were both twitchy with anticipation.

"The edge of the sky," Hinsberth murmured quietly to himself. He felt a tinge of anxiousness mingling with the weariness and excitement. By chance, he thought, whatever could go wrong?

As they readied themselves for departure, more breaks appeared between the clouds, and they steadily grew wider. The sun grew more brilliant, throwing its rays brightly over the mottled landscape and bathing the two would-be explorers in light.

"Be careful, and be sure to record what you find. I for one do not want to be left out of important new discoveries," declared a polite, cultivated voice.

Hinsberth's father Eldsworth was standing in the open doorway to his home, closely observing the ducklings with a charmed smile. "And naturally, a proper good morning to you, Lillybeth," he added.

"Yes, a very good morning," replied Lillybeth, a little nervously.

Eldsworth was of an ever so slightly rounded sort; his attire was invariably sharp and polished and he was known for being always polite and proper. He was also never without a bit of hesitancy in exercising his notably dry sense of humor, if only because on occasion, when he did find something amusing, he could come dangerously close to losing his faculties altogether. He shared this characteristic with Lillybeth, and had developed a particular fondness for her as a result.

Eldsworth placed importance on the restraint of behavior and on the upholding of a balanced and civilized manner through a proper sense of fairness, justice and etiquette. Consequently, he endeavored to bring up Hinsberth with a similar sense of civility. And his example was readily accepted, as Hinsberth was in many ways not unlike his father. However Eldsworth's nature was rather opposite of, if considered broadly, his strong willed, independently minded and very beloved wife.

"Ah, good morning!" exclaimed an immoderately loud, sonorous voice, and not a moment later out into the morning air stepped Hinsberth's mother, Marista Rosalita Lopenzo Smerkington, called by everyone only "Marista" for necessary brevity. Round her sizable head was a bright amber scarf and bound to it on one side flashed a plate sized silken flower of the deepest crimson. Her substantial torso was wrapped neatly in a flowing gown splashed with a large and bright floral pattern, tied round with a length of spiralled yarn. Her attire made Marista appear even larger than she was. Her garment was long enough to float freely near the ground, and it made a slight swishing sound as she moved, and with every step the ends swirled round and traced intricate patterns through the air.

"It is indeed," Lillybeth agreed bashfully.

"Well, well, then. *What* are you two waiting for?" Marista inquired, her voice booming through the garden.

With a big, broad, warm smile for her son and his newfound friend, she waved the ends of her wings at them, as if they were tiny insects needing to be shooed away.

"Go. Go now. The sky is waiting," Marista added.

When it came to her son, or her rather large family in general, Marista was very protective, and with her physical size and voluminous voice, she could be very intimidating toward any who found themselves judged to be unacceptable company.

Lillybeth anxiously returned Marista's smile. With Marista's apparently enthusiastic approval for Hinsberth joining the expedition, Lillybeth felt much more at ease.

"Do not forget your sweater," Marista reminded her son, as she peeked into the contents of his sack.

"I have it," Hinsberth said meekly.

Marista and Eldsworth gave the ducklings a warm embrace, and finally the time had come for departure. Lillybeth and Hinsberth shared an excited glance, and they turned and proceeded down the trail to find a suitable clearing for taking flight. Hinsberth's parents watched the pair of ducklings make their way down the trail, thinking it charming seeing the two of them together, off on their little adventure. Certainly, they thought, the duckling's stomachs would have them returning home before the midday meal.

❖   ❖   ❖

CHAPTER 1

The two explorers prepared to go aloft.

"Helmets?" called Lillybeth.

"Check!" replied Hinsberth. And so it went.

"Sweaters?"

"Check!"

"Socks?"

"Check!"

"Food?"

"Check!"

"Goggles?"

"Ah — yes — well…"

"Next time then?"

They descended a small slope to arrive beside a clear, shallow pond fed by a burbling creek. Above was a broad window open to the sky, encircled by leafy tree canopies. For a moment they flexed their wings and kicked up their short, stubby legs, readying themselves for flight.

"This looks to be a proper spot," announced Lillybeth, coming to a stop and gazing upward into the improving clarity in the sky. "Are you ready?"

"Ready!" replied Hinsberth with a little quiver in his voice.

Also noting a bit of shakiness in Hinsberth's legs, Lillybeth tried to reassure him, "Surely nothing to worry about," she stated calmly. But her stomach belied her own nerves.

"Yes. Surely," agreed Hinsberth, at least in principle.

"Alright then, on the count of three, shall we?"

Hinsberth held up his bill and made a slight nod, committing himself to the flight, but still unsure of what might be up — way up — at the top of the sky.

They started running as swiftly as their tiny legs would carry them, with wings flapping fast and cargo bounding up and down.

"Three... two... one... go!" bellowed Lillybeth, and they rose into the air, flapping hard and climbing fast.

The pair spiralled higher and higher into the air, their dwindling shadows circled slowly over the patchwork hues of the ever more distant earth.

Lillybeth looked down and watched the ground below slowly fade into the distance. She could see The Farm, The Pond, and the roof top gardens of their homes poking through the verdant green mats of grass. As they climbed higher familiarity drifted into obscurity; The Farm slowly became a smaller and smaller portion of a massive landscape which stretched wide into the hazy distance.

Hinsberth glanced around. Soon after takeoff he had fallen some distance behind; Lillybeth flew a bit higher and Hinsberth sagged slightly below. He was feeling the early start. Even so, in little time the pair had soared beyond the sight of home and entered the realm of the clouds. Tiny droplets of water skirted onto their feathers and flew rapidly off their backs, and the earth below and the sky above vanished into the mist.

As she took in the featureless world within the clouds, a thought sprung into Lillybeth's mind — she and Hinsberth seemed to be the only things of consequence in this curious place, their bodies immersed in a sea of unbroken grey. Although flapping purposefully under the effort of flight, Lillybeth imagined she and Hinsberth were not actually moving at all, perhaps the sky was moving past them as they only hovered in the same spot, frozen in place in the middle of the sky. She wished to share this notion with Hinsberth, but it was not long before the opportunity had passed, for the two duck-lings were still climbing fast and suddenly they spiralled out of the top of the cloud into brilliant, unencumbered sunshine. Above them, stretching into infinity, was an expanse of pure, shimmering blue.

As they climbed higher still, the air grew colder, but the ducklings were feeling elated and energized by the ethereal beauty of the crys-talline sky, and for the moment they did not notice. Flying onward, Lillybeth suddenly realized she had lost sight of Hinsberth; he was no longer behind her. She turned to one side but saw only a sheen of blue stretching ever upward above a gossamer sea of vivid white. She turned to the opposite side. With a start she noticed Hinsberth directly at her side, their wing tips almost touching. An unpleasant tightness suddenly gripped Lillybeth's stomach. She had never been particularly comfortable listening to such rumblings and did not care to have them, preferring instead to give her attention to musing about the workings of the world. But there they were; her stomach spoke as fervently as ever, in a language she did not understand.

Thinking quickly, Lillybeth anxiously glanced over to Hinsberth, and called out, "Let's go!"

Startled by Lillybeth's invitation to cease the relentless climb and enjoy an opportunity to stretch their wings, Hinsberth suddenly be-came aware of how close he had drifted toward her and he swiftly banked to allow some distance.

Again flying a comfortable distance apart, the ducklings sought to relish in the newfound energy granted by the rarefied air, and they playfully darted about as fast as they could: rolling, curving and tum-bling in great arcs, weaving in and out of the cloud tops; perforating them with ephemeral dimples, for a brief time marking them with what seemed the footprints of some mythical cloud walking giant. But soon their breath grew short and a deep fatigue swiftly set in. The two ducklings slowed and drifted back together.

Once Hinsberth was near enough to hear her voice, Lillybeth exclaimed, "We still need to go higher! We must have a closer look!"

She did not mention her concern but she was becoming a bit bothered by the sky, for stretching into the heights above them was the same featureless blue seen from the ground, even at their present lofty height. Lillybeth began to wonder. How could the edge of the sky not be any closer? At the very least should not the color be changing? Perhaps it was a little deeper blue, and the sun was certainly as luminous as she had ever seen.

"Somewhat of an effort," Lillybeth shouted breathlessly, acknowledging she and Hinsberth were slowing down, unable to climb as fast as before.

"Agreed," Hinsberth quipped. "Also becoming — a little chilly — for my taste," he added slowly, a few words at a time between labored breaths.

Before going aloft, they had donned their helmets and sweaters, but the air at altitude was quite cold. With a growing concern over the fate of the expedition, Lillybeth glanced upward once more, searching for any sign of, say, an all encompassing glass sheet, or some other unimaginable, mysterious boundary.

As they continued climbing, and despite in present company wishing to demonstrate a penchant for bravery, Hinsberth felt ever more anxious and uncomfortable. He was increasingly chilled and light headed. The brilliant summer sun seemed unusually bright, and he was rather bothered by the glare.

CHAPTER 1

"I am not seeing anything above!" shouted Hinsberth with a raspy voice in the thinning air. "How much higher?" he inquired, hoping to soon descend.

"I am not sure…" Lillybeth replied, straining to look upward. She cut her response short, for the first time noticing her own discomfort in struggling for breath. She glanced downward, to rest her neck for a instant.

"Hinsberth!" she exclaimed, pointing her wing emphatically downward.

Hinsberth's bill fell open.

Where were the vivid greens and browns of earth? The clouds below had merged into a bubbling stew, and toward the horizon, majestic white towers billowed upward, threatening to blot out the sun.

The sky, having earlier appeared so playful, had swiftly become a danger. Lillybeth knew these clouds and their frantic growth meant wind — strong and dangerous. Her stomach turned to knots as she also became aware neither she nor Hinsberth had been paying much attention to the direction their bills had been pointing.

"Hinsberth!" Lillybeth shouted. "Where are we?"

As the sky darkened ominously, Hinsberth looked at her with wide eyes. He glumly shook his head.

"I am not sure…"

Lillybeth tried not to appear panicked. She reminded herself of the effort expended in preparing for the expedition, and she did not wish to make a sudden or hasty descent. But the edge of the sky seemed no closer than it had from the ground and the sky only became colder with height. Their bodies seemed to grow heavier by some strange, invisible force as the air thinned into inconsequence and flight became impossible. It was as if the sky desired to keep hidden its secrets, permanently masking them behind an unbroken veil of brilliant blue or the impenetrable darkness of night.

A sudden, strong headwind snapped Lillybeth back to the present predicament. Tired and anxious, Hinsberth had fallen below and well behind, and Lillybeth, lost in her thoughts, was unaware she was still drifting upward... until a succession of emphatic gusts came suddenly against her, like giant waves breaking against an unseen shore. Even while flapping as fast as she could Lillybeth could make no progress against the wind. Her wings quickly fatigued, and she was suddenly tossed backward through the sky.

"HINSBERTH!" she cried out.

Between the shuddering waves of air, she could barely hear Hinsberth shouting from below, but the wind stole his words, whisking them off into the distance.

The wind suddenly halted as quickly as it had begun, and Lillybeth abruptly tried to sail down to Hinsberth so they could descend together through the brewing storm. She held her wings steady, bending and warping them to guide herself to Hinsberth, but as she fixed her eyes upon him, she was distraught to notice dark, swirling clouds had gathered beneath him and their bubbling tops were surging skyward!

Hinsberth was alarmingly distant and he traced a chaotic path across the sky as the wind buffeted him rudely about.

"GO DOWN!" Lillybeth repeatedly called out.

She looked on in dismay as the final passageway to earth narrowed and disappeared and Hinsberth continued flapping frantically. He was trying to climb, trying to reach her.

CHAPTER 1

Lillybeth's stomach dropped.

Without warning, she was struck by such a blast of wind that she was thrown helplessly through the sky. Shaken but regaining her bearings after the gust passed on invisibly through the air, she glanced round in a panic for her friend. She spotted him even further away, and to her alarm he was in danger of being swallowed whole by the rising cloud.

"HINSBERTH!" she called out in desperation.

Why would he not listen to her?

"GO DOWN NOW!" she bellowed into the wind with all her strength.

But finally, as Lillybeth watched helplessly, Hinsberth's fatigue overcame him and he dropped like a stone into the storm.

LILLYBETH & HINSBERTH

*"Regaining her focus, Lillybeth recalled the advice she had
given Hinsberth as they prepared for the expedition:
One must remain calm in the face of danger."*

IS SOMEONE THERE?

LILLYBETH WAS ALONE. Tossed about in angry turbulence, it took all her strength to remain in the ever smaller pocket of clear air. She could not believe she had lost Hinsberth, but there was no kindness in the present sky and no time to consider what to do. The storm was nudging Lillybeth from below, insisting on sending her further aloft. She desperately tried to descend, flapping downward into the updrafts with all her might. She kept her eyes fixated on the spot where Hinsberth had tumbled into the clouds.

"HINSBERTH!" she bellowed at the top of her voice, hoping he might somehow be able to hear her. Suddenly she was struck by the notion she might never find her friend, and the mere thought engulfed her in an overwhelming surge of distress.

Nonsense, she thought. She had to find him.

Regaining her focus, Lillybeth recalled the advice she had given Hinsberth as they prepared for the expedition: One must always remain calm in the face of danger. She quickly assessed the circumstances. Could Hinsberth have fallen all the way to the ground? Or was he trapped by the vortex of wind somewhere inside the storm? And how far had they drifted away from The Farm?

Without warning, she was jolted from her considerations by a blinding flash of light and the crack of a resounding thunderclap.

Once again she regained her bearings. Great streaks of light flashed between the clouds and the air cracked into shards, trembling and rumbling angrily as it did so. She had to decide quickly. She considered diving straight into the wall of cloud to search for Hinsberth, for she felt certain if he had fallen through, he would be stranded on the ground, unable to fly. She peered into the convulsing cloud. It was as dark as a moonless night. She gathered her courage. There was no time for hesitation. She tucked her wings tightly, pointed her bill downward, and set off to take her chances in the mouth of the tempest.

❖   ❖   ❖

It was raining harder now. The sky shuddered with the all too frequent peals of thunder and the roof began leaking continually under the onslaught of rain. The drip... drip... drip... of water into a carefully placed ceramic bowl ticked the time away for Millybeth and Hackleberg. They sat in anxious silence, sharing fearful and worried glances.

Nearby, over the rolling hills of sodden grass, Hinsberth's mother Marista stood motionless, staring out a window so spattered with rain as to be nearly opaque, hoping to see a pair of ducklings on the approach.

Suddenly, a particularly bright flash ripped through the sky accompanied by a sharp crack of thunder like a hammer blow on the roof of the world, and the house shook with the report.

Not one to withhold her opinions, Marista tore herself away from her attempt at preoccupation and exclaimed loudly to Eldsworth, "I think it is time to go NOW, to see if we can find them!"

"Yes — yes," agreed Eldsworth, still reeling from the crack of thunder and tense with worry.

Eldsworth considered the circumstances for an instant and then he suggested, "It might be prudent to check with the Smythes. Perhaps the ducklings beat the weather to a nice cup of warm tea at Lillybeth's."

Eldsworth had not finished speaking when Marista grabbed a pair of umbrellas and marched in a heavy, determined manner toward the door.

"For you," said Marista, handing Eldsworth one umbrella, which he held low and firm just above his head.

Marista pushed her flower down over her forehead. She opened the door, looked out, and then the two ducks boldly plunged into the storm.

The rain was pouring down so heavily that Marista and Eldsworth could barely discern what lie ahead of them, and stepping onto the trail they were immediately splattered with mud. They had only taken a few steps when, with a surprising bump they encountered two large shapes.

Before them, uncovered in the rain, wet as could be and presenting the strong impression of having departed in haste, stood Millybeth and Hackleberg.

"Excuse us. Our apologies, but we are not quite able to see where we are going in this torrent," Hackleberg offered calmly, as if out for a peaceful morning stroll.

"So you too, concerned over the whereabouts of our little ducklings?" inquired Marista, knowing very well why Lillybeth's parents were standing just outside their doorway, fully exposed to the worst storm in memory.

Marista and Eldsworth maneuvered their umbrellas to help protect their neighbors from the rain.

"Yes, this weather is quite a surprise," said Millybeth anxiously while trying not to appear as deeply panicked as she felt.

She was not able to hide her worries for long.

Millybeth quickly directed a serious gaze onto Marista and Eldsworth.

"Do you agree we should go and search for them? I think they could not have gone too far — they planned to go straight up. But this storm may have blown them in any direction."

Eldsworth agreed immediately, "Precisely. Hinsberth is a decent flyer, mind you, but at the moment, I would rather know exactly where he is."

Hackleberg said nothing, but merely raised his wing, brandishing four pairs of goggles, which in their roughness were obviously of his own design. Marista and Eldsworth hastily stowed their umbrellas on the porch, and the four ducks quickly slipped the goggles down over their tufted heads. Together they went swiftly down the footpath, splashing mud with every step. Finally, wind blown and mud-spattered, they arrived at the pool of water marking the clearing where Lillybeth and Hinsberth had taken flight.

"Three... two... one... GO!" bellowed Marista; her voice overwhelmed even the thunder, and the four ducks launched themselves into the wind and rain.

❖   ❖   ❖

Meanwhile, somewhere high above The Farm, Lillybeth struggled downward against the gale. She was in the clouds, she knew not where. She was cold and fatigued from fighting the wind. The wind whipped rain felt like icy shards. The gusts were so insistent, the notion of letting them take her where they wished began to fill her thoughts.

She grew distant and began daydreaming. She imagined the wind calming, the storm dissipating into soft, puffy billows, finding Hinsberth, flying home…

Lost in her dreams, she let herself be carried by the wind.

❖ ❖ ❖

Buffeted by the wind and pelted by rain, the duckling's parents streaked through the sky, holding tightly together and calling out for Lillybeth and Hinsberth. They flew low, so they could see both the dark, ragged base of the storm and the sodden ground below. Bearing the brunt of the storm, they hoped the ducklings had been fortuitously grounded in a place sheltered from the weather.

The goggles, although a grand idea of Hackleberg's, were prone to fogging up, restricting their sight and mounting the feelings of frustration.

Even after flying many broad circles above where the ducklings departed, they found no sign of either of them. Undeterred and hopeful, they continued on, tracing out a winding path in the air over The Farm. But still they found not a sign of the ducklings, and the disappointed glances between them eventually prompted a reluctant turn toward home.

Alighting just outside Hinsberth's house, the four ducks gathered on the covered porch and wiggled their feathers dry, then dejectedly entered the small but comforting home.

For a long moment they stood silently together, only dripping on the floor.

"It was certainly worth a go," Eldsworth offered glumly, and then noticing the worry etched on the faces of his company, he added in a feigned tone of optimism, "We may have to wait until the storm settles. Lillybeth and Hinsberth are both quite capable. If they have not flown in, we can set out again when the worst of the wind and rain has passed."

Marista, never one for hiding her thoughts and harboring a great concern over the fate of her son and his companion, stood up, flared her wings onto her hips and began addressing loudly everyone in the room, "Let me tell you, I give them no more time than until this detestable storm breaks. And if they are not here, safe at home, then we go and search again, and not alone. Of that you can be sure."

Millybeth and Hackleberg held misgivings over the course of action Marista implied. They would need assistance for a larger search, and the most expedient means for organizing such an effort was to approach the Mayor's Office. The couple turned their eyes downward and carefully examined their toes while trying to imagine how their request might be received. After the round of recent mishaps, they did not at all fancy approaching the Mayor's Office yet again and asking for help. But the course was set; they would do whatever was necessary to see Lillybeth and Hinsberth safely home.

❖　❖　❖

Lillybeth could not see. The cloud had blackened around her and sky had become sea, she was immersed in water and ice. She struggled for air. Where had the wind taken her?

"HINSBERTH!" she bellowed, fearing it might be her last chance.

Then all at once she was spun round by a great swirling gale, flipped head over feet, and in a flash of sunlit sky, she was suddenly right side up in the clear air beyond the storm.

Rattled and shaken, she took a moment to compose herself and regain her wings. She set her gaze downward to search for anything familiar on the rain soaked earth far below. She noticed the verdant green fields in oddly regular geometric shapes, the groves of trees, the narrow lines of fencing in stone and wood, the occasional rooftop and the thin ribbons of road slicing through the landscape and streaking off to the distant horizon. Lillybeth thought the scene, at least in its generalities, was similar to home. But not one of the specifics were recognizable. She descended quickly, all the while hoping Hinsberth might have been caught in the same wind.

Nearing the ground, Lillybeth levelled out and sailed low and fast just above the ground. She saw no sign of Hinsberth.

She had lost her friend.

A sickening, sinking feeling gripped her stomach. Uncomfortable with the unpleasant messages from her middle, she tried to suppress a rising sense of despair by flying faster and faster over the landscape.

The scent of moist soil wafted up to fill the humid air. The thunder still caused the sky to tremble. As she flew onward, she called out for Hinsberth. She called loudly for her friend again and again, but each time she heard no reply, and her heart tore deeper. Her voiced cracked. She could call no more.

Suddenly, while soaring swiftly over an otherwise uniformly green field, Lillybeth abruptly slowed. She turned about in a tight circle over a strange site. Some of the foliage below had been flattened in a peculiar manner, into a series of circles, arrows and odd geometric shapes all pointed in the same direction. Quickly deducing the patterns to be a sign for flyers such as herself, Lillybeth turned in the direction of the arrows. She flew fast over the broad level field and then over a tall forest. As she sped over the forest edge, she grew in hope, reasoning that perhaps the patterns would lead her to someone who could tell her not only where she was, but whether another young duckling had been seen nearby.

❖   ❖   ❖

In a signal of staunch determination, Marista lifted her wing and seized the flower which always graced her head. She pushed it even lower over her forehead. The onslaught of rain continued unabated, lightning still split apart the sky and the shocked air still rumbled the house, but Marista could wait no longer.

"Everyone! Time to go!" she announced while marching steadfast toward the door.

With her bill pointed defiantly toward the sky, Marista threw open the door and walked out uncovered into the torrent.

All at once her companions glanced at each other in surprise, and they quickly rose to their feet and went swiftly to the open doorway. They knew there was no convincing Marista of any further delay, and they darted outside to catch up to her.

The four ducks splashed along in single file on a muddy and narrow trail leading down a gentle slope, which at its base opened to a larger clearing ringed by a thick circle of trees. To one side was an assortment of older, worn and presently rain soaked buildings. There was a large house, which in its prime must have been painted white. The outside was embraced all round by a great porch adorned with ornate columns and rails. Near to the house was the Old Barn. The roof had garnered a large hole from age, but oddly, the very bottom wore a bright new coat of paint.

Toward the far end of the roughly circular clearing resided a cluster of many tiny homes, all nicely arranged, with fresh paint and surrounded by well kept gardens. Many were topped with flowering plants, making them appear almost as a natural or expected part of the landscape. Near to the middle of the clearing was The Pond.

The four ducks followed the trail toward The Pond and then circled around the shore. They paced themselves quickly toward an ornate and sizable house located on the far end of The Pond, beside the normally trickling stream which fed The Pond its water. On most days the stream burbled pleasantly between its stony banks. On this day, however, the heavy rain transformed the stream into a river and the torrent was threatening to swell over the banks and inundate the nearby residences.

There were many anxious and watchful eyes observing the rising water and four wet and muddy ducks waddling down the trail to the Mayor's Office. Standing under awnings, sitting on porches and looking out through rain spattered windows, many feathered heads uniformly traced their every step.

Marista was the first to reach the heavy and smoothly polished door to the Mayor's Office. She immediately lifted her wing and took hold of the large, rounded knocker mounted centrally on the door. Marista knocked, hard, not once but continually, until a rather ample duck in formal dress swung the door inward and blocked the width of the passage with her girth. She gazed at the foursome without making a sound, nor any attempt to hide her obvious vexation at both the timing and the sight of the wet and muddy visitors.

As Marista opened her bill to speak, from behind their silent host came a full, smooth, deep and carefully articulated voice, "Millybeth and Hackleberg, I presume?"

The greeter stepped aside and an even larger duck appeared, stepping slowly but purposefully toward the doorway, dressed even more formally and in a very official looking manner.

Marista closed her bill.

"Well, let them in," the larger duck ordered, coming to a stop still some distance from the doorway, perhaps so as not to catch a chill. The duck who had opened the door silently stepped aside. On the floor in the foyer was a very ornate, even extravagant rug, deep red in color and laced with gold embroidery, and as the newcomers entered, they huddled nervously together and dripped profusely upon it.

The larger duck was Mayor Swellington, a once self appointed and later elected administrator for the ducks on The Farm. His self nomination for the position was not objected to by the vast majority of residents, since many of them were content to be without such a hefty burden of responsibility, and furthermore, it was the Council, consisting of a number of esteemed volunteers from among the residents of The Farm which convened to make decisions of truly high importance. The necessity to convene the Council was quite rare and the Mayor's Office preferred to manage the day to day operations of The Farm.

Mayor Swellington resided in the large house which also served as the Mayor's Office with his wife of many years, Quilly Pompon

Swellington, or "Quillypom" as she was commonly called, and who more often than not administered the Mayor's administrating. It was known by the older ducks of The Farm that they had several duck-lings, all of whom while still fairly young had abandoned The Farm, for reasons which could only be the source of speculation. The Mayor rarely talked of them, and a melancholy mood had settled over he and his wife ever since.

Peering into the foyer, Mayor Swellington fixed his sight on each visitor in turn. His eyes widened in surprise, and perhaps a little dismay, as he recognized Eldsworth and Marista.

Mayor Swellington cleared his throat, breaking the discomforting silence. He then spoke in a deliberate, commanding voice, "Hackleberg and Millybeth, I expected. Regarding their daughter no doubt. Eldsworth and Marista, what might be the purpose of your journey here in these foul conditions?"

Millybeth spoke first, hanging her head with the realization she had come perhaps one too many times to ask for help regarding her mischievous duckling, "Apologies, Mayor. You are correct. It is indeed Lillybeth. She and Hinsberth took flight this morning on an otherwise harmless little adventure. Lillybeth is quite curious as you know. We did not think they would actually be out for long, the weather seemed fine, just a few spots of cloud, we really did not expect..."

Mayor Swellington immediately turned to Eldsworth.

"You allowed Hinsberth to accompany Lillybeth?"

Eldsworth nodded, "Yes, but I fail to see..."

Millybeth felt her stomach tighten and her head suddenly felt warm. "And why not?" she interrupted Eldsworth with her question to the Mayor.

"Why not, indeed," replied the Mayor in a condescending tone, turning his gaze back upon Millybeth.

Sensing the conversation might become even more inimical, Hackleberg quickly interjected, "We feel it may be wise to organize a search. They may have been blown in any direction by the storm, but hopefully they are still nearby. They had planned to go straight up, the four of us went for a look, but we found not a trace. The weather is settling down, perhaps only a few of us in each direction could…"

"Yes — yes," interrupted the Mayor carelessly.

He turned his head over one shoulder and bellowed back into the long hallway leading to the rear of the house, "Quillypom, my dear, please prepare to round up some of our generous neighbors, and have them volunteer to help us find a pair of missing ducklings, preferably without delay."

Even before the Mayor had finished announcing his request, Quillypom appeared and was already assembling, with the utmost speed and efficiency, her overcoat, an umbrella, a pencil and a small collection of neatly organized papers.

Tall and slightly frail, Quillypom was almost always donning formal looking but characterless attire, black in color and bound tightly up to her neck. She normally seemed stern or without expression, her eyes sullen behind a pair of wire framed spectacles worn near the end of her bill. When she moved, her manner was quick and deliberate, giving an impression of bureaucratic precision, but little else.

Having gathered her things, she shuffled swiftly out past the visitors without saying a word.

After watching Quillypom depart through the doorway, the Mayor announced as if speaking to the air, "I might advise that some be prudent regarding the company they keep."

Millybeth and Hackleberg choked down every word, for they wished to appear both gracious and thankful to the Mayor as they would receive the help Hackleberg requested.

Marista, however, being who she was, had enough. No one would tell her son who he could befriend. Her wing rose slowly upward, and she pushed the large flower brandishing her head even lower over her brow, bringing forth a furrowed visage. Silently, but with palpable intention, she stepped forward and stood tall, bill to bill with the Mayor. Her massive wings flared out and came to rest on her hips.

Her deep, dark eyes glared at the Mayor, and he felt as though they were piercing the very core of his being. Not able to stop himself, he stepped backward.

"Let me tell you something," Marista boomed, "My son can befriend anyone he pleases. And nobody — nobody except him has anything to say about it."

Marista stood unmoving, face to face with the Mayor long enough to give him an opportunity, daring him to speak. He remained silent.

Marista then turned, grabbed Eldsworth, and marched outside.

Together, Millybeth and Hackleberg watched Marista and Eldsworth pass swiftly through the doorway. They glanced at one another and shared a silent message: that even under such unfortunate circumstances, they had most assuredly gained a pair of rather valuable friends.

❖   ❖   ❖

Hinsberth was rattled. After striking the muddy ground uncomfortably hard, he found himself at the edge of a large pond, encircled by trees, dense groves of cattails and long grass. The sun shone intermittently as the clouds raced overhead. The storm was swiftly receding into the distance; only the ominous, deep rumbling of distant thunder recalled the storm's fury.

Hinsberth had fallen completely through the storm. The chaotic winds inside the maelstrom spun him round, and tossed and buffeted him about for what seemed an eternity. The sting of wind whipped rain and tiny shards of ice could still be felt. Hinsberth was only relieved to have reached the ground whole and intact; from bill to toe, nothing seemed broken.

Ruffled and bruised, Hinsberth felt rather resentful toward the vagaries of nature, firstly for separating he and Lillybeth and secondly for treating him with such disregard. Nevertheless, his main concern was the whereabouts of Lillybeth, for he was suddenly overwhelmed with worry over her safety. He was determined to take to the air once more and set out to search for his friend, but the seriousness of his injuries became apparent after the powerful and immediate emotions of being in danger wore off. Hinsberth was too exhausted and too sore in his wings and legs to fly. After hobbling a few steps, he knew he was not in any condition to search for Lillybeth, so he sat down upon the moist ground, rested his back against a tree trunk and turned his gaze upward, hoping to recognize a familiar silhouette soaring against the backdrop of blue and white.

After quite some time, Hinsberth noticed the sun beginning to sink low in the sky, and he became disenchanted with sitting idle. Still unable to fly, he gingerly rose up, doddered his way down to the muddy shoreline, and after dipping his toe he descended into the cooling waters of the pond. He swam to the far shore, glanced around and decided to go and explore. He hoped to stumble upon someone who might help him find his lost friend. He clambered onto the shore and after taking a moment to straighten his wet and ragged attire, he hobbled up the bank and into a dense grove of trees.

The songs of unfamiliar birds sparkled through the canopies; the sweet smelling soil wore a coat of fallen leaves which made a hollow crunching sound as he went. It seemed an agreeable place.

Hinsberth limped up the slope, away from the banks of the pond, and as he crested the summit he was at once startled by a sudden, disagreeable impact on his senses, for there was a terrible odor wafting through the heavy, humid air, and a loud, disturbing noise of the strangest character, as though hundreds of voices were speaking all at once.

The hill sloped down to border another pond, only unlike the last, this one was not at all alive. The barren banks consisted only of mud and stone, the water was an opaque, murky color, and it emitted an appalling scent. An equally murky and muddy flow entered the lifeless pond from one side, the source flowing from somewhere beyond the next hill. The ground was strangely devoid of flora. Nothing seemed alive. Despite the repugnant nature of the air and the apprehension he felt over the strange voices, Hinsberth suddenly imagined how interested Lillybeth would be in the rather odd place he had stumbled upon, and the notion drove him down toward the shore of the lifeless pond.

Coming to the shoreline, Hinsberth at once concluded it would surely be wise to fly over the disagreeable looking water, but his wings were not yet up to the task.

He dipped the end of one toe into the water and found it surprisingly warm. His toe, when extracted, felt odd, with some dismal substance clinging to it. For an instant he withdrew from the pond, concluding the best course of action was to leave behind this lifeless place. But his long held desire for adventure and the sudden, strong and hopeful notion of salvaging the expedition for Lillybeth with an important discovery had the better of him.

Despite his trepidations, Hinsberth suddenly leapt into the water, and immediately began to thrash about. The water was full of muck and not very deep, and for a time Hinsberth thought he might be in very grave danger. The foul odor weakened him and he worried he would not have the strength to free himself from the clingy muck and regain the slippery bank. The strange sludge in the water weighed him down heavily and he felt as though it was seeping beneath his feathers.

But popping into his mind was Lillybeth's voice, and a piece of advice she had given him: When exploring the unknown, one had to remain calm in the face of danger. At once Hinsberth composed himself and ceased thrashing about. He pushed gently through the water with his feet, floating into the deeper water. Once there, he tried to splash himself clean. The water, however, still possessed a horrible nature, and Hinsberth decided to proceed as quickly as possible to the far shore and gain solid ground. In little time he had pushed and pulled himself onto the slick and muddy bank. He was now more than a little exhausted and rather frustrated, for his circumstances seemed only to have become worse. He was feeling uncomfortably warm after his unpleasant dip in the pond, and in addition to feeling stiff and sore from his injuries, he was now covered with the most unpleasant muck. Once secure upon solid earth, he turned onto his back and lay still in the mud, resting for a moment, and then, although painful, he tried kicking his feet and flapping his wings in an unsuccessful attempt to dry and clean his limbs. Frustrated with himself, Hinsberth lie motionless in the mud, considering what to do next, when his attention turned to the haunting noise of the voices talking all at once, seeming as if in some kind of distress.

Where Hinsberth now lay, the voices were louder and more distinct, and he realized he must be that much nearer to the source. With the possibility of discovery beckoning and with the hope of finding some help, and despite feeling depleted from being battered by the storm and a bit ill from the foul air and his regretful dip into the pond, Hinsberth pushed himself out of the mud. He slowly rose to his feet, and hobbled awkwardly up a steep slope toward the voices.

Rounding the barren summit, coming into Hinsberth's view was a most peculiar sight: Below the hilltop on which he stood, several huge, rectangular buildings were arrayed in the small and otherwise empty valley below. Each building was much larger than anything on The Farm, but they appeared in disrepair, perhaps neglected and constructed from dull metal and unadorned wood.

Upon the hilltop, the voices were frightfully loud, and becoming concerned for his safety, Hinsberth stood silent and still, not wishing to draw any attention to himself.

After observing for a time and noticing the murky streams seeming to flow from the muddy slopes near their bases, Hinsberth became certain the strange buildings were the source of the disagreeable water, the foul air and the distressed voices. He believed this an important discovery, but not one having the mysterious and illuminating nature he and Lillybeth had hoped for.

Hinsberth still wished to salvage the expedition for Lillybeth with a further discovery, so again he summoned his courage and decided to take a closer look.

❖   ❖   ❖

The search party was swiftly organized as Quillypom dispassionately made her predetermined rounds. She went from house to house, visiting each and every one in the tight cluster fronting The Pond. When she told them of the two missing ducklings, Quillypom had no difficulty finding volunteers willing to help. Many of the residents who recognized the four ducks waddling to the Mayor's Office suspected such a call might be forthcoming.

The search party decided, under Quillypom's direction and with unsolicited approval from the Mayor, to go aloft four to a group, in each of four directions. Marista and Eldsworth joined one group, and Hackleberg and Millybeth joined another.

"Everyone. Please return by sunset to report your findings. If you spot either duckling, you must return with them at once," Quillypom announced firmly as the search party prepared to take to the air.

Millybeth and Hackleberg meekly approached Quillypom.

"Do you think we will have enough time?" Millybeth asked quietly. "Nightfall will not be long."

"I agree," Hackleberg added. "If they have been carried a great distance by the storm — if they are far from The Farm..."

"...it will be difficult to find them on the ground, or in the air when darkness comes," Millybeth stated with her eyes awash in worry.

Quillypom made a slight nod. She too knew time was short.

"I will plan for another, larger search. For now, we need everyone to be in the air as soon as possible," she stated. She avoided looking into

Millybeth's or Hackleberg's eyes.

Hackleberg and Millybeth returned to the search party. Overcome with worry and feeling obligated to the volunteers and responsible for causing all the trouble, they meekly thanked everyone for their assistance.

"Everyone, our Hinsberth is also lost," Marista boomed. "Thank you. Thanks to everybody for helping."

And with that, they were ready for flight.

"It is not your fault," Eldsworth quietly offered in an aside to Hackleberg and Millybeth.

Marista and Eldsworth's sentiments only added to Hackleberg's and Millybeth's growing affection for their new friends. It was early evening when the search party finally sped off across the sandy beach and took to the air. They flew fast, spread into a wide pattern across the sky, as far apart as possible while still in range of each other's voices. Darting through the air, they called out continually for the two ducklings.

❖   ❖   ❖

Lillybeth flew at full speed in the direction pointed to by the arrows in the field. She passed over a patch of farmland and a tall, thick grove of trees — the boundary of a forest which continued into the distance as far as she could see. If Hinsberth had become stranded here, she thought in dismay, she would never find him. Lillybeth hoped her friend was still in the air, where there was a much greater chance of spotting him from a distance. She thought about trying again to call out for Hinsberth, but as she flew over the deeper forest, she began to feel increasingly anxious and ceased making much noise, as she was not familiar with the place or its inhabitants.

Finally, with trembling nerves and losing sight of the ground through the thick growth of trees, in disappointment Lillybeth decided to turn around and fly back to the fields.

Along her path over the forest, she had not seen any sign the arrows indeed pointed to anyone who might be of help, and she wondered what they were for.

The sun was lumbering low in the western sky and falling relentlessly toward the horizon. Lillybeth knew darkness would soon follow. Along with her worry over Hinsberth, she became concerned about finding home. She also began to wonder what consequences might await she and Hinsberth back at The Farm. She knew by now their parents would have approached the Mayor's Office and organized a search.

As she exited the air above the forest Lillybeth made a steep descent. Flying low, she returned over the symbols in the field.

Suddenly, she came to a stop in midair with her wings outstretched. After a day of duress she was hardly able to believe her eyes at the sight of apparent good fortune: in the field below she saw one of the arrows was being reshaped. Four ducks were inside the arrow. In unison they were busily stomping down the foliage with tools attached to their feet. Lillybeth, having stopped so abruptly, dropped like a stone into the field, provoking a loud crunch from the pressed stalks and shrieks of surprise from the stomping ducks.

After striking the ground, all at once the repressed worry, fatigue and hunger set in and Lillybeth slumped down with her feet outstretched and her back supported by the wall of upright plants. Her wings flopped down to rest loosely at her sides.

The stompers were startled and surprised by the sight of the haggard young duckling... her tattered clothes.... her helmet flopped forward over the upper half of her eyes... her side pack unbuttoned with the flap askew... all in all she appeared quite the worse for wear.

The four ducks shared a baffled glance and then they turned to gaze quizzically upon Lillybeth. They stood in silence, waiting for her to speak. They did not have to wait long. Not an instant passed before Lillybeth suddenly began sputtering words in a rapid, exasperated fashion after taking a single, huge breath, "We were flying up, we wanted to find the edge, the top, but it was really quite cold, and then a storm came in, so windy, and Hinsberth, he was so tired, I should have known but he fell into the clouds and..."

"If you please, perhaps a bit slower. You said your friend... Hinsberth is it? He fell into the clouds?" inquired one of the ducks. She stepped toward Lillybeth, bent down and reached out to help her helmet into a more suitable position.

She was a tall, lean duck with kind eyes and an informal manner.

"Yes — *Hinsberth*," replied Lillybeth.

"And what is your name?" asked another of the ducks curiously.

Lillybeth, too desperate and impatient for an exchange of platitudes replied, "Lillybeth," as if they should have known already.

The tall duck who had approached Lillybeth introduced herself in a soft and patient voice, "Pleased to meet you, Lillybeth. My name is Filipa, and this is Pommelstom, Trewnslough and Hershelbaum," she said while pointing to each of her companions in turn.

Pommelstom appeared slightly younger than Filipa, but they otherwise shared a number of similarities including Filipa's kind and informal manner. Pommelstom was also tall and lean and like the others, plainly but competently dressed in a warm and durable looking uniform. Trewnslough was slightly smaller, more abrupt in manner, and twitchy, as if always ready to go on a moment's notice. Like the others, Hershelbaum seemed enthusiastic but he was perhaps more inclined to keep his thoughts to himself and to think things over in silence.

All four were well supplied, with identical, carefully designed side packs brimming with an extensive assortment of tools.

After the introductions, Lillybeth said politely, "Pleased to meet you," for Filipa's calm demeanor was gradually having an effect on her, slowing her down, but she still managed to suddenly blurt out, "WE HAVE TO FIND HINSBERTH!"

❖　❖　❖

With careful, quiet steps, Hinsberth approached the nearest building. His stomach was all in knots; he was very much unsure of the safety of his surroundings. The building itself made him feel very unwelcome with its unadorned form, dull appearance and sharp corners. He decided to use the utmost caution. He hid behind things as he went: a ragged and lifeless bush, an isolated clump of dried out grass, and a worn, rusty cart with three flat wheels. He left behind a meandering trail of muddy footprints on the damp but hard pressed earth. In each of his temporary hiding spots, Hinsberth would peek ahead, positioning himself to expose only his eyes for a view toward the building, hoping for a revealing glimpse into the nature of this decidedly strange place.

Presently Hinsberth was tucked behind a sizable stone. He pulled his helmet down tighter over his head to add a needed sense of protection. Here the voices were even more distinct and he suddenly recognized the familiar source in an instant. Emboldened, he darted out from behind the stone, splashing mud as he went. Breathing hard, he stumbled into the nearest wall and pressed his back flat against the hot surface. All at once he turned and bent low to peer inside one of the many holes perforating the wall, but only darkness could be seen.

"Hello?" he whispered softly, rather unsure what sort of reception he might receive with his muddled, and to his standards, entirely unacceptable appearance.

He waited a few moments but received no reply.

The voices inside were loud, distressed. They echoed over the barren ground.

To ensure his own voice could be heard, he said a little more loudly, "Hello, my name is Hinsberth."

But no greeting, nor salutation nor any other reply came forth. Hinsberth wondered if the pigs on The Farm were also sometimes recalcitrant. Hoping for help and some direction toward home, and while managing a proper degree of restraint, Hinsberth inhaled deeply and bellowed at the top of his lungs, "Hello! I am Hins…"

Before he could utter the final syllable of his name, a loud clang like a hammer blow against the top of an empty tin bucket burst forth from the wall directly in front of him, and he fell, stunned, backward onto his bottom.

"Is someone there?" came a hushed, nervous sounding voice from somewhere deep behind the wall.

Hinsberth rose from the ground. He took a moment to brush his feathers free of dust and straightened his clothing as best he could, desiring to make his appearance at least minimally presentable.

"Yes," Hinsberth answered.

Pleased to have finally made contact, Hinsberth waited a moment to give the voice a chance to speak, but not hearing any further reply he continued on in an agreeable voice, "If I may, I would like to introduce myself. My name is Hinsberth. To whom am I speaking?"

"Sorry for kicking my foot," said the voice from inside, still hushed, and barely audible over the cacophony of other voices.

"No need to apologize, although you certainly did take me by surprise," Hinsberth replied.

He leaned over and peered inside through the other perforations set low on the wall, but it was too dark or full of straw to see anything.

"You surprised me as well, that is why I kicked," said the voice.

"Well, now that we have surprised each other, might I know to whom I am speaking?"

There was a pause, and then the voice whispered, "I have never heard a voice coming from out there, where you are, before."

Hinsberth thought this an odd reply.

"Yes, well, I — was being somewhat secretive. I am not familiar with this place. I am from The Farm."

"Your name — is Hinsberth?" inquired the voice.

"Yes — yes, Hinsberth," Hinsberth confirmed.

"I don't remember my name," said the voice.

"Are you not serious?" queried Hinsberth in surprise, and at once he thought he may have offended his host. He quickly added in a concerned tone, "You cannot remember?"

"I cannot remember."

"I see... Well then, I have a very good friend on The Farm named Milchester, quite well mannered and with a sound sense of humor. Would you mind if I called you Milchester?" asked Hinsberth, befuddled but thinking fast.

While Hinsberth had a number of friends on The Farm, Milchester was not one of their names, but Hinsberth did not think any harm could come from giving this voice a proper name, and a unique one at that.

"Yes — please. To have a name again is... very welcome. Thank you, Mister Hinsberth," said Milchester.

It was the first time in Hinsberth's memory anyone had referred to him with any kind of title, and he rather fancied it and certainly did not offer any objection.

But as he stood facing the wall separating he and Milchester, the discomfort of an ostensible illness crept into Hinsberth's awareness. A growing feeling of weakness and of being at a higher temperature than his considerably warm and stuffy surroundings had him wishing to sit and rest.

Before setting himself down, Hinsberth limped over and gathered several sticks lying about in the nearby mud. He poked the sticks into the soft ground and took his favorite sweater and propped it upon the sticks to face skyward for any familiar eyes to spot. He then waddled back to the wall, turned to face outward, and flopped down wearily, letting the wall fully support his weight. He stretched his feet in front of him.

"Are you still there, Mister Hinsberth?" Milchester asked hopefully.

"Yes," replied Hinsberth. "Just resting for a spell, with all this activity I seem to have unfortunately caught a bit of a bug."

"What activity, Mister Hinsberth?" inquired Milchester curiously.

Even though he found it draining of his energy, Hinsberth had to speak quite a bit louder since he was facing away from Milchester, but nevertheless he felt obligated to explain how he had arrived at where he now sat, and he proceeded to recall aloud the day's events.

Milchester listened intently; he turned his ears to hear only Hinsberth's voice, and his tale made him happier than he could remember. He imagined Lillybeth and Hinsberth's flight: soaring through the sky, the chill of the air in the heights, the terrifying danger of wind and storm. For a long moment he was somewhere else.

As Milchester listened and dreamed, Hinsberth continued his recounting of the day's events until the rapidly worsening fever began to overwhelm him.

❖　❖　❖

"If I may Lillybeth, in order to help, might I ask who Hinsberth is and what, exactly, has happened to him?" inquired Filipa.

In reply Lillybeth immediately began recalling the events of the day, at such a brisk pace and intensity and with such broad and rapid gesturing it was difficult for the others to follow the precise sequence of events. Nevertheless, by the time a breathless Lillybeth wound the story down to the final drop to where she now sat, Filipa and the others had understood enough to determine how they might be able to help.

Lillybeth sat listening attentively as her companions began conversing amongst themselves using words she had not heard before; "updrafts" and "downdrafts", "precipitation" and various names for different kinds of cloud. She understood they were trying to determine the nature of the storm she and Hinsberth had encountered and where within it Hinsberth may have dropped out of sight. Lillybeth described where she and Hinsberth had begun their flight, and how they had spiralled up into the sky, and Filipa and her friends spent quite some time discussing these details and trying to decide where to begin the search.

Finally the conversation came to an end and Filipa turned to Lillybeth, who was still seated against the upright stalks, "We think we know where Hinsberth may be, if he is indeed unable to fly. It is a large area, and we will have to fly with some distance between us to cover enough ground and have a good chance at spotting him. It will be dark soon and we may not find him before nightfall, and if we do not find him before dark, we can return to the field, it is fairly safe here. Or, if you wish, we will fly you home to The Farm. In the morning we will be able to find some additional flyers to help with the search."

Lillybeth believed these were generous offers and she felt a strong sense of gratitude toward her new acquaintances who were so willing to help. But she did not consider herself particularly skilled with words when trying to convey notions of a heartfelt sort, so she remained silent and fidgeted with her sack of expedition supplies.

As Lillybeth silently mulled over the choices Filipa offered, she also considered how worried her parents would be if she did not return home. She was already well beyond the time they expected her to arrive, and she knew they were out looking for her. She knew Hinsberth's parents were also terribly worried, and her stomach suddenly plunged beneath her toes as she imagined they might hold her responsible for Hinsberth becoming lost and perhaps injured. A feeling of the most terrible sort gripped her middle as she imagined they might forbid Hinsberth from accompanying her ever again.

"I need to go home *and* find Hinsberth!" Lillybeth abruptly blurted out with noticeable distress in her tiny voice.

"You can only choose one this night," said Filipa calmly. "But I do have another idea. One of us can go to The Farm, to let them know you are safe with us and that we are helping to find Hinsberth."

Lillybeth was tired and torn, and utterly confused over what to do. Her head sunk downward, and she covered her face with her wings.

Noticing Lillybeth was in some difficulty, Filipa sat down next to her and gently put forth a wing across the duckling's small back, and then she announced, "Let's go now. We will try to find Hinsberth before the light becomes too dim."

Lillybeth perked up slightly and nodded her head in agreement.

Filipa and Lillybeth rose to their feet, and Pommelstom, Trewnslough and Hershelbaum quickly stowed their tools. An instant later, five ducks were in fast flight over the field, racing against the night.

❖   ❖   ❖

The soft light of dusk had settled in over The Farm, and two of the search parties had descended out of the darkening sky to report to Quillypom. With heads hung in disappointment, they revealed they had not seen any sign of the missing ducklings.

"I see," said Quillypom simply.

Quillypom was not surprised the two remaining parties had yet to return. She knew the duckling's parents well enough to know they were still searching and would continue to do so as long as possible.

The bustling activity in the Mayors' Office had come to an end for the day and the Mayor, seeking a potential opportunity to show his clout, joined in the discussions about the search and the two lost ducklings taking place just outside his home.

"If the remaining parties return without the ducklings, another search is to be assembled just before dawn," Quillypom declared loudly as she was organizing her papers.

The returned flyers and a number of concerned onlookers immediately approached Quillypom to volunteer for the morning's effort. After queuing up and receiving instructions from Quillypom, they all stayed put, waiting for the remaining search parties to return and hoping to see two young ducklings in tow.

❖　❖　❖

"Milchester," Hinsberth began with a weakened voice after finishing his story, "I am beginning to feel rather ill. If I may, I would like to rest for a moment and then I should be off. It is becoming late and it would be appropriate for me to depart, to find Lillybeth and return home. Perhaps another day I can…"

"Please, Mister Hinsberth, please do not leave," Milchester pleaded. "I have very much enjoyed your story. Might you tell me more? If you are ill, I can help. Wait just a moment…"

Hinsberth listened as there was some scrambling and scratching about inside. Hinsberth was surprised by his new acquaintance displaying such an unwarranted desire for him to stay and continue recalling his adventure, especially with this being merely his first day on a real expedition.

After some time listening to the scratching and scuffling noises emanating from behind the wall, Hinsberth felt his back become suddenly colder. My, he thought, what an odd sensation to be so feverish, and yet so cold in only one spot. When the sensation of cold began trickling in a line downward toward his tail, Hinsberth suddenly realized Milchester was pushing a container of cool liquid under the wall separating them. Slowly he leaned forward and turned to look over his shoulder, and on the ground he spotted a small bowl cobbled together from bits of straw and mud and stamped centrally with the dull outline of a pig's foot. In its bottom sloshed a tiny bit of water.

"Well... thank you very much," Hinsberth said appreciatively.

He brought the bowl to his bill and drank its contents.

"I had not realized how utterly parched I am. Thank you again. I do not wish to be a bother, but might I have a bit more?" asked Hinsberth politely, masking how truly desperate he was for water.

"Yes — certainly. I have more, Mister Hinsberth. Push the basket back and I will refill it," replied Milchester hastily, hoping to provide an agreeable service and entice Hinsberth to stay.

Milchester and Hinsberth spent quite some time exchanging Milchester's makeshift bowl. Every bit of water helped Hinsberth feel slightly better, if only for a time. But as the veil of night spread slowly over the sky, Hinsberth's fever increased dramatically and he began to lose his spirit. As the last thin slice of the sun vanished beyond the far horizon, Hinsberth knew he would have to spend a long and dangerous night, fully exposed, feverish and too weak to move, in this troubling place with Milchester as his only companion.

❖ ❖ ❖

Millybeth, Hackleberg and their fellow searchers darted across the fading sky. The darkened hues and long shadows of evening were making it impossible to spot anything as small as a duckling on the ground or against the dim backdrop of grey clouds and fading light. As the conditions worsened, the search parties increasingly hoped the ducklings had already been found and were waiting to greet them back on The Farm.

Their companions could sense Millybeth and Hackleberg's desire to continue the search for as long as possible, for their pace had not slowed since their feet left the ground. Although they were well beyond the time Quillypom had requested for them to return with a report, they flew swiftly onward without objection.

It was a similar story for Marista and Eldsworth. Darting through the sky they called out loudly for the missing ducklings. Their companions were willing to continue the search for however long it might take to find Lillybeth and Hinsberth, but every now and then they sent worried glances across the void of sky between them, silently conveying their increasing doubt they would find anything in the dim light. The night was spreading like a dark blanket across earth and sky, but the searchers knew their voices could still be heard, and they propped their hopes upon the notion the ducklings might still hear their calls.

❖　❖　❖

Unbeknownst to the search parties from The Farm, Lillybeth and her companions were fast approaching where Filipa and her friends believed Hinsberth might be. Following Filipa, they banked sharply off the straight-ahead path they had flown since leaving the ground. With eyes fixed toward the ground, the five ducks wound back and forth across the sky while calling for Hinsberth. But after a time darkness hindered their sight, and having not found any trace of Hinsberth, Filipa waved her wing to signal a descent. They immediately dropped and alighted together in a small open field bordered by widely spaced clumps of trees.

Filipa turned to Lillybeth and spoke softly, "I am so sorry, but it is becoming much too dark. We will not be able to spot Hinsberth on the ground. We can stay here tonight, and begin the search again first thing come morning."

Exhausted, hungry and disappointed, Lillybeth hung her head, too tired even to cry. She was thankful for the help her new friends had given her, especially on such short notice and without any apparent concern for the sudden interruption in the course of their day. Naturally, she expressed her sentiments by standing silently. Nevertheless, Filipa and her friends understood the message by the unmistakable look in Lillybeth's eyes.

Filipa nodded to Lillybeth as if to tell her not to worry, and she plunged a wing into her bag of tools. She pulled out a compact, cylindrical, tightly bound package. Firmly holding a piece of the outer wrapping with one wing, she unexpectedly tossed the cylinder into the air, and it flew up, stretching a line to Filipa's wing. She pulled hard on the line and with a sudden pop it burst open into a dome shaped tent, many times its original size, with a flat bottom and a small arched opening. The dome floated down to rest on the ground, and then her companions performed the same feat, until there were five domes huddled together in the grass.

"I always carry an extra," Filipa mentioned with a reassuring grin.

Filipa pulled containers of food and water from her satchel and everyone else followed suit.

Wishing to demonstrate her own thorough preparations and knowledge of advanced gadgetry, Lillybeth dipped a wing into her bag and pulled out a small, rusted flashlight. After fidgeting with it for a few moments, in frustration she held it in one wing and gave it a solid nudge with the other, bringing forth a dim light and smiling bills.

Nestling between the domes, they took in a bit of nourishment before retiring for the night. As they ate, Lillybeth's friends began to discuss the events of the day and what they would have to do come morning.

As they spoke, Lillybeth listened attentively, discovering Pommelstom was Filipa's younger brother, and at once she noticed the slight family resemblance.

All four of Lillybeth's companions, although not entirely similar in appearance, nonetheless gave similar impressions — polite, enthusiastic, open to possibilities. They jointly consoled Lillybeth over her worrying about Hinsberth and her feeling of responsibility for so suddenly losing her friend, and they comforted her with hopeful predictions for the coming dawn. As the night wore on, they wearily agreed to retire to their tents to rest before resuming the search at first light.

Before crawling into her dome, exhausted but ever curious, Lillybeth inquired, "Why the symbols in the field? I thought they were pointing to something important, but I followed the arrow and it led me over the forest. When I turned and came back, you were all there. I thought the arrow might lead me to someone who could help, which turned out to be true, but not in the way I expected."

Filipa smiled, "You are mostly correct, they do point to something important. The Migrators. The symbols point the way for the Migrators."

"The Migrators?" Lillybeth inquired.

"Tomorrow," replied Filipa.

❖ ❖ ❖

Nightfall had made further efforts futile, and as difficult as it was, while overcome with worry and disappointment, Marista, Eldsworth and their search mates decided to return to The Farm. They were fatigued, not from the effort of flight, but from the strain of the search. Having flown swiftly back to The Farm on the hope that good news awaited them, Marista and Eldsworth finally slowed down as they descended to land. The loud brushing sounds of their wings announced their arrival to those patiently waiting on the ground.

On The Farm, the search party appeared suddenly, dropping out of the moonless night into the dim lantern light.

Millybeth, Hackleberg and their companions had alighted moments before, having made a similar decision to return home. Those on the ground immediately encircled the new arrivals, but no words were exchanged as everyone quickly realized it was only the members of the search party who had returned.

Everyone gathered around the duckling's parents to offer encouragement and to repeatedly make mention of the more extensive search planned for morning. Quillypom had already more than doubled the number of volunteers, most of whom had offered to go immediately home for a meal and sleep in anticipation of the early start.

Huddled tightly within the dim pool of light granted by the lantern she carried, Quillypom asked each of the searchers in turn for details regarding where they had flown and what they had seen, and with every response she made adjustments to the morning's plan. She busily marked out possible flight paths on an old paper map which crinkled as she drew upon it, and she assigned and reassigned the volunteers for what she believed would be the most efficient search.

After talking briefly with Quillypom, whose ordinarily sullen expression flashed with an uncharacteristically warm smile as she offered them encouragement, the duckling's parents thanked their friends and neighbors for all the help and the heartfelt sentiments. As if struggling to pull away from something they could not bare to be without, they reluctantly departed from the glow of lantern light, and went slowly together down the dark, muddy, and winding trail toward home.

Upon arriving at the home of Millybeth and Hackleberg, they sat down in the soft grass just outside the entrance door, and there they stayed, silently staring off into the starlit sky, huddled together in the cold night air, hoping to hear the scuffling sound of four small wings beating their way home.

MILCHESTER

"Thank you. I have never been a friend before..."

A GOOD FRIEND

DAY HAD GIVEN WAY TO NIGHT, and Hinsberth was feeling alternately cold and chilled and hot and feverish. Milchester generously continued speaking to him, but Hinsberth was less and less frequent with his responses. Hinsberth's voice grew weak; Milchester strained to hear his words.

"Mister Hinsberth, do you need anything more?" inquired Milchester sonorously, with growing concern for his newfound acquaintance.

"Am feeling rather cold," came Hinsberth's reply, after a worryingly long moment.

At once Hinsberth heard more scuffling and scratching, and an instant later a bundle of straw pushed under the wall and into his back, and then another, and another. Hinsberth struggled with arranging these gifts from Milchester, but gradually he was able to cover himself with a warming blanket of straw, with only his head and the ends of his wings exposed to the night air. He folded his wings over the straw covering his belly. With this gift of comfort and warmth, Hinsberth began to drift in and out of a fitful sleep, and while awake he became distantly aware that he might be delirious, for at times he thought

himself to be at home, warm in his bed with his mother gently strok-
ing his head and the smell of a fresh breakfast tickling his nostrils. As
the night deepened he was less able to tell whether he was lucid or in
the world of dreams.

"Milchester?" Hinsberth tried to alert his companion. "Are you still
there?"

"Yes — I will not sleep until you are well," replied Milchester reassuringly.

After another long pause, Hinsberth announced in a weary but
rather sincere voice, "Milchester, you are a good friend."

For a brief moment, Hinsberth thought he heard Milchester sobbing, but he was uncertain, for the voices continued on hauntingly
into the night.

Milchester had to right himself and clear his throat.

"Thank you, Mister Hinsberth. I have never been a friend before."

Hinsberth was bothered. He was no longer sure he could trust his
ears. Some of what Milchester had revealed — not having a name nor
any friends — for such a polite, generous and helpful fellow, seemed
immensely difficult to reconcile.

As Hinsberth stared into the dark, starlit sky, he spoke slowly, between labored breaths, "Milchester — can you come outside? I have
not seen — anyone outside here. I cannot see in. It would be nice
— to speak to you directly. If I am found soon — I would want to
recognize you — in the future — when I return for a visit. I know you
would — very much enjoy meeting Lillybeth."

Hinsberth then fell again into unconsciousness.

Milchester sensed Hinsberth's illness was becoming more severe.
His worry grew. He quickly assembled and pushed baskets of both

food and water under the wall to either side of where Hinsberth's back slumped against the cold metal, but there were only so many places Milchester could reach with his hind feet being constrained by thick metal bars.

Milchester raised his voice to awaken the faltering Hinsberth.

"Mister Hinsberth! I have food and water, please have some. It may help you."

Milchester was rather relieved to hear Hinsberth moving; he detected the faint sound of straw brushing over the metal wall.

Milchester reasoned that the sound of his voice might protect Hinsberth from any wanderers of the night, and so he began to tell Hinsberth all he knew of his tiny, confined world. As Milchester spoke, his voice grew tense, and Hinsberth, feverish and on the edge of consciousness, had the most terrible and vivid nightmares. He imagined the young piglets being taken from their mothers and having their tails and ears painfully clipped. He saw them being poked, prodded, and abandoned to see out their days alone, trapped in cages barely larger than themselves. He envisioned them standing day and night, unable to move, their legs growing stiff and sore. Never to be let out, they longed desperately to walk... to run... to MOVE! In the stifling air they cried out, pining to wallow in cool mud, yearning for even a glimpse of what lay beyond the burning metal walls...

Milchester's voice tensed further as he described the food, for in their confinement food was always available, but something did not taste or seem right about it. Everything seemed focused on the food. They were caged facing it, unable to turn from it, and they grew with it, fast and large, the weight worsened the aches and stiffness and the horrible sores and illnesses which took many of them away. For disappearance — to be carted away to an unknown but likely horrific fate — always defined their future. Once they had grown heavy or ill, they would be taken, never to be seen again. Over time they became resigned to their inescapable destiny, seeing out their days in a detached, melancholy stupor, despondently waiting to disappear.

Milchester had to right himself, and after a pause he described how over time, he had tried to find solace by retreating from the world into his imagination. He wondered about life outside, about different worlds, but his spirit had slowly sunk as he resigned himself to the possibility of never knowing what might have been, if his world had been different, if his birth had taken place somewhere else, in some imaginary, distant land where life roamed free...

As the night grew old, Milchester told Hinsberth of the stories he invented to grant himself a few coveted moments of escape. He painted a portrait of the fantastic lands he visited in his imagination, sun drenched and beautiful, and of the interesting and bizarre creatures inhabiting them. He spoke of his burning hope that perhaps one day, somehow, he would visit such a place.

As he listened, Hinsberth fell into sadness and confusion over what he heard. The severity of his fever left him unable to offer anything in the way of conversation or consolation. But Hinsberth's meek requests for water were always dutifully and quickly satisfied, and Hinsberth found himself developing a strong and sincere admiration for his new friend. He wondered how Milchester, trapped in his tiny prison, having lived a life amenable only to sadness and despair, could retain not only a deep and seemingly indomitable spark of hope, but also be so generous and loyal and kind, in a place possessing not one of these to any degree?

CHAPTER 3

Hinsberth sank once more into unconsciousness as the first signs of dawn appeared low on the eastern horizon. Milchester, having remained awake over the course of the night, finally, in utter exhaustion, slumped against his cage and drifted off into the world of his dreams.

❖   ❖   ❖

Lillybeth spent a long night gazing upward at the featureless dome ceiling, waiting impatiently for morning. She welcomed the ever so tenuous brightening which signalled the coming of dawn. Her helmet, satchel and sack were in place, at the ready for becoming airborne once again. She plunged a wing into her satchel and pulled out her flashlight. After fidgeting with it for a time, she became somewhat cross and gave it a solid nudge. The tiny bulb managed just enough light for Lillybeth to spy the whereabouts of her gear. She quickly organized her belongings and once satisfied, she proceeded outside through the small arched opening.

Lillybeth gazed wearily upon the five tents spread before her, and then up at the purpley black sky still spotted with stars. Standing alone in the peaceful silence preceding daylight, Lillybeth shivered in the cold air.

And she wondered…

As she stood gazing at the stars, her thoughts turned to Hinsberth, and she hoped he was there, somewhere nearby, perhaps at that moment his eyes even shared the light from those very same stars. For the sky looked the same everywhere, to everyone — somehow boundless...

She had to find him.

Lillybeth's eyes widened and she swiftly turned her attention to the task at hand. Her camp mates were soon stirring, awakened by the slowly brightening light of morning, and a sudden, bellowing, "WAKE UP!" from Lillybeth's bill.

❖   ❖   ❖

On The Farm, the faint beginnings of a new day did not go unnoticed. The duckling's parents had taken turns during the night; one remained alert while the others tried to sleep, but sleep was evasive and the night and their worry for the ducklings had them exhausted. But they were undeterred, the desire to find their ducklings was more than enough to propel them swiftly onto their feet and onward to The Pond to prepare for the search.

Before departure, Hackleberg scurried into his home, and an instant later he emerged with his head bound under a tightly tied helmet. Across his eyes he wore a goggle mask, but instead of the usual glass plates, two round protrusions extended outward, the ends of which were fixed with lenses.

"Binocugoggles," he said simply, after receiving the familiar quizzical expressions universally greeting him.

The others nodded as if to say, "Ah yes, of course." Then together they went quickly to The Pond.

The morning was young and dark, but upon reaching their destination they could see the assembly of the search party was only just beginning. Several volunteers were rushing about in the dim but warm glow of a few scattered lanterns. Quillypom was there, with paper and pencil, conveying her plan to the flyers. Other volunteers served up small rations for breakfast and organized supplies. Hoping to immediately ascend into the air, the duckling's parents wasted no time in joining the effort.

❖   ❖   ❖

In the cool, dew laden grass some distance away, Lillybeth watched in curious amazement as her camp mates took hold of the straps they had used to burst open the domes from their miniature packages and pulled on them hard and fast. The domes collapsed with a strong pop, somehow transforming themselves nearly back to their original shapes. The final fold and tie had to be accomplished manually, and Lillybeth took note of every detail, wanting to demonstrate, from all the tinkering alongside her father, a well earned aptitude for all things mechanical.

Lillybeth noticed Filipa eyeing her tent for packing. Seizing the opportunity, the duckling went quickly to the dome. She took hold of the strap and, as she had seen the others do, she yanked it hard with her tiny wings. In a flash, the dome bounced off the ground and flew rapidly toward her, and before she could react, it set upon her and began refolding. Lillybeth collapsed to the ground with a thud, wrapped tightly with only a wing, her head and one webbed foot protruding from an otherwise neatly formed package.

After spending a time carefully separating duckling from dome, Filipa and her friends began conversing amongst themselves. Lillybeth listened from a slight distance, still feeling a bit compressed and a little flushed from the rather unwelcome embrace of the folding tent. She watched closely as Pommelstom picked up a stick and carved some rough drawings into the soft dirt, and the others huddled over the drawing. They whispered earnestly to one another until they were all nodding in agreement, and finally, Filipa turned to Lillybeth.

Filipa explained to Lillybeth how they had determined the boundaries of a new area to search for Hinsberth. Lillybeth did not completely understand as she was only partially paying attention. She was ready to go and find Hinsberth and was not particularly concerned with the details.

Presently the morning light was brightening noticeably, and with it, the ability to see into the distance. The sun had not yet risen above the horizon, but with tents packed, snacks consumed, and a general plan for the search, the five ducks ran a short distance and took off, rising rapidly into the still cool air with the heavy beating of wings, flying fast into the tranquil light of early dawn.

❖ ❖ ❖

On The Farm preparations were moving slowly. So many willing volunteers had arrived, Quillypom had difficulty maintaining any form of organization. Everyone present held a sincere motivation to help with the search, but with so many helpers, progress was slowing perceptibly.

Marista was becoming impatient, and with characteristic bluntness, she clapped her wings together and shouted loudly, "Everyone! Everyone! over HERE!" to focus attention on herself.

She then proceeded to rapidly sort the volunteers, nudging them about with her massive wings into their assigned groups. Quillypom found Marista's booming voice and determined manner to be rather valuable under the circumstances. She followed Marista from one group to the next.

Finally the search party was ready to depart. By now the sun had crept above the horizon and was spraying warm rays and long shadows across the landscape. Marista returned to Eldsworth's side and they, Millybeth and Hackleberg and the rest of the flyers waited impatiently for the signal to go aloft.

❖ ❖ ❖

Darting through the soft morning sky, Lillybeth, Filipa, Pommelstom, Hershelbaum and Trewnslough flew fast and low, spread widely apart, skimming just over the tree tops of an unfamiliar forest.

Once beyond the forest edge, they descended to fly low over the ground, rising and falling with waves of verdant rolling hills interspersed by lush valleys harboring a thousand hues of wildflowers, with hills and valleys alike all sparkling with morning dew.

Soon they were flying over another, denser forest of tall trees. The great spires of twisted branches and viridescent leaves skirted by in a blur below them.

Unexpectedly, the flyers came upon a large void in the trees, and were startled to find the land below suddenly barren and desolate. Lillybeth glanced down curiously, for she had immediately noticed an unpleasant, humid and foul air rising from the broad patch of lifeless earth.

The flyers looked downward upon a trio of large, unadorned buildings in the otherwise empty field of mud. To one side was a dismal pond fed by several equally murky streams. As they darted over the buildings, the thickening and disagreeable air and calamitous noise from below made Lillybeth rather anxious, and she quickly accelerated to be away from them.

The five ducks continued swiftly on past the clearing.

As they flew over the deeper forest, Lillybeth's thoughts were abruptly overcome by a singular imperative — to turn around. At once she resisted the idea, given the unpleasantness of what was now some distance behind.

But had she seen something?

Lillybeth desperately tried to sort out from where the notion had come, but failing to do so and to the complete surprise of her companions, she suddenly peeled away in a steep bank and reversed course.

Befuddled, Filipa and her companions watched Lillybeth accelerate away. They called out to her but she was swiftly out of range.

With her stomach suddenly tying itself in knots, Lillybeth darted in over the buildings. She could barely breathe. She wondered what she was doing... Was it only her curiosity again? But as she circled fast around the barren landscape she noticed something familiar, on the ground far below, a vaguely familiar pattern. Yes, she thought, I know this pattern.

By now her companions had nearly caught up to her, and they followed Lillybeth down as she rapidly descended to investigate.

Upon landing, Lillybeth's stomach jumped into her throat, and despite trying hard to repress them, the strain and exhaustion finally overtook her and the tears came fast and heavy, transforming everything in her sight into blurry, unrecognizable blobs. But without question, she knew what she had found.

It was Hinsberth's sweater!

But where was he?

Wracked with sobs, she looked up and around but could not see anything through the flood of tears.

Lillybeth's companions did not need any explanation, they

understood immediately what she had found. They quickly scattered themselves over the landscape, looking for any clues to where Hinsberth had gone after planting his sweater beacon.

"Over there!" Hershelbaum suddenly shouted above the din.

He had spotted a curious lump of straw and feathers lying on the ground, mounded against the side of the nearest building...

...Hinsberth was far away, sleeping, dreaming a peaceful scene, of looking up into a brilliant morning sun and noticing a shadow — a familiar shape leaning over him, busily brushing away a blanket of straw, with a tiny face etched all at once with worry, joy and anguish. He tried to lift his wing, to wipe her tears, and whispered... "Lillybeth."

❖   ❖   ❖

Working fast, in little time Filipa, Pommelstom, Hershelbaum and Trewnslough assembled a flat rectangular platform from parts and pieces taken from the tents. They tied a rope to each corner and attached the ropes small harnesses they took from their satchels and strapped around their middles. They placed the unconscious and feverish Hinsberth gently in the center and covered him a blanket.

Filipa and Pommelstom lifted Lillybeth onto the platform. She sat upright next to Hinsberth, to watch over him and ensure he remained securely in the center.

In a swift and deftly coordinated takeoff, the four ducks flapped with all their might and slowly lifted into the sky. Flying low over the tree tops, they carried Lillybeth and Hinsberth as fast as they could toward The Farm.

Lillybeth held Hinsberth's wing with both of hers as they flew toward home. Hinsberth did not wake. Lillybeth could tell he was in the grip of a terrible illness, his wing was burning hot to the touch and his breathing shallow. She feared Hinsberth was injured during his plummet through the storm. But now, there was nothing more she could do. She tightened her hold on his wing.

After a careful, nerve-wracking flight, the four flyers and the platform appeared in the azure sky over The Farm. The search parties were not due back until midday to report to Quillypom and consequently the volunteers on the ground were unsure what to make of the approaching contraption, but many began to worry. If the flyers needed to improvise such a device, perhaps either one or both ducklings were injured and unable to fly... or worse. Arriving over the small sandy beach bordering The Pond, the four flyers, with wings beating furiously, dropped almost vertically, hovered for an instant and then lowered the platform carefully to the ground.

Immediately a large group of Farm residents gathered around the flyers and their precious cargo.

A heavy sigh of relief echoed through the assembly as Lillybeth rose from the platform. She looked dishevelled and moved slowly but otherwise appeared in adequate health. Gingerly stepping off the platform, Lillybeth was surrounded by fellow Farm residents. But she turned her eyes away, for she immediately felt a powerful wave of guilt grip her middle as she came to realize the extent of the trouble she seemed to have caused. At once she feared others might already be blaming her for the otherwise unnecessary efforts.

But her thoughts never strayed far from her friend, and Lillybeth immediately turned round and tried to help retrieve Hinsberth from the platform, but being smaller than most she was quickly pushed aside by the large wings pushing forward to take hold of Hinsberth and lift him from the platform.

One of the residents on a swift approach to the landing site was Doctor Lochswyn, a tall, slender, elder duck dressed in simple, modest clothing and thin framed spectacles. Doctor Lochswyn handled most every issue of a medical nature for the residents of The Farm. She was well studied and had many years of practice, and she was very well regarded by the residents of The Farm. She was also considered somewhat of an eccentric, as she generally dined only on small bowls of her own particular brand of porridge and was not known to eat most anything else. Within her well appointed and meticulously maintained home, she kept two small patient rooms fully stocked with medical devices, books and botanical remedies she had collected over the majority of her years. Upon hearing of the arrival of a pair of ailing ducklings, she went immediately to investigate whether her expertise was needed.

"Excuse me!" Doctor Lochswyn called out, as best she could above the many fervent voices as she pushed through the crowd toward Hinsberth. "Excuse me. But it might be best not to move the little one. He may be injured, and we do not know what is ailing him."

The crowd quieted so the Doctor could continue to speak, for her voice did not carry well.

"Please, do not move him," she insisted again. "If I may, might I suggest we carry him, without too much jostling, to my office. We should try not to wake him. Let him rest. I can examine him in my office and with any luck, help him there."

A swift wave of discussion washed through the crowd as everyone quickly agreed with Doctor Lochswyn's proposal. At once Doctor

Lochswyn led Filipa, Pommelstom, Trewnslough and Herschelbaum to her home — one of the older, brightly painted houses facing The Pond. The house had many windows and was fronted by an neatly arranged, expansive garden brimming with colorful medicinal plants.

As they could not all fit through the entrance door, Filipa and Pommelstom carried Hinsberth gingerly inside. Then the four flyers lifted him slowly from the platform and placed him on a tall, comfortable looking bed located centrally in the largest of Doctor Lochswyn's patient rooms.

Lillybeth struggled to enter to be by Hinsberth's side, but as she scrambled through the crowd of onlookers toward the door Doctor Lochswyn suddenly appeared and announced, "Please, please! Everyone remain outside. I must have my patient isolated for the time being for proper care and diagnosis."

In noticing Hinsberth's high fever Doctor Lochswyn was quite concerned about contagion.

Sadly disappointed over having been suddenly barred from the Doctor's home, Lillybeth stood despondently in the garden and hung her head. She felt helpless. After a time she began to meander through the crowd, glancing around hopefully for her parents, but she knew they were out searching for her. Curiously, as she was generally in the thick of any event, Lillybeth noticed Quillypom was nowhere to be seen.

After a brief time, Doctor Lochswyn again appeared in the doorway to her home and called out for "Lillybeth Smythe."

Lillybeth grew anxious wondering why she had been summoned. She turned back toward Doctor Lochswyn's and waddled through the crowd to the door. She was led into the house, placed in a room separate from Hinsberth, and asked to remain there until Doctor Lochswyn returned.

❖   ❖   ❖

Immediately after discovering the ducklings had been found, Quillypom dispatched The Farm's swiftest flyers, whom she had retained on the ground for the purpose of contacting the search parties if the need should arise.

Some time later, the first members of the search party returned home. They were all greatly relieved when told the ducklings were on The Farm, but celebrations were muted, as everyone became quite concerned when told both ducklings had been admitted to Doctor Lochswyn's.

While still in flight the duckling's parents were startled by the messenger's approach. When given news of the duckling's return and admittance to Doctor Lochswyn's, they were all at once relieved and overcome with worry. Without giving the messengers a chance to complete the usual formalities, Millybeth, Hackleberg, Marista and Eldsworth immediately reversed course and began speeding toward Doctor Lochswyn's as swiftly as their tired wings would allow.

❖   ❖   ❖

Lillybeth sat alone in the spare patient room in Doctor Lochswyn's home. The room contained two large, elaborately patterned pillows for sitting upon and, in the center, a table which doubled as a patient bed. The sun shown brightly through a pair of small windows facing The Pond. Lillybeth felt fine, although certainly exhausted and distressed over Hinsberth. To her dismay, her fervent imagination began presenting a spate of unpleasant explanations for why she had been told to wait for Doctor Lochswyn.

To distract herself, she waddled over and stood by a window to observing the activities outside. She spotted Quillypom on the far side of The Pond, near the Mayor's Office. Quillypom was looking across at the conversation taking place between the flyers who had transported her and Hinsberth back to The Farm and a few volunteers.

The flyers were introducing themselves to the volunteers, who seemed rather curious about the tools and devices Filipa and her friends carried in their satchels. The flyers proceeded quickly through demonstrations of some of their gadgets, seemingly in a hurry to return to the tasks they had left idle the previous day in order to help find Hinsberth.

Suddenly Filipa snapped the platform back into a small, tidy cylinder and packed it away. Her companions stowed their tools. They all nodded respectfully to their new acquaintances, shook a few wings, and then took swiftly to the air.

Seeing them leave, Lillybeth became upset. She shed a few more tears; feeling a little heartbroken over the fact that they did not come to say goodbye. She was very grateful to them and felt frustrated with her inability to properly convey her sentiments.

Wiping her eyes, Lillybeth again caught site of Quillypom, and surprisingly saw her doing something she never imagined. From a distance Quillypom also seemed rather upset, maybe even blotting a few tears from her eyes. A bit befuddled, Lillybeth left the window and sat down on one of the pillows to wait for Doctor Lochswyn, but was abruptly startled back onto her feet with the thumping of heavy footsteps striding purposefully through the entrance to Doctor

CHAPTER 3

Lochswyn's home.

She could hear Doctor Lochswyn and a few other voices protesting, but then Lillybeth heard the familiar, voluminous voice of Marista, daring for anyone to "Just try and stop me" as she barged into the room where Hinsberth lay unconscious.

Lillybeth ran to the door, flung it open, and there stood Millybeth and Hackleberg, who instantly smothered her in a flurry of feathers and tears.

Doctor Lochswyn quietly stepped down the hall into the rear of the house, to allow the families a private moment to reunite with their ducklings.

After a brief time Doctor Lochswyn returned and asked politely, "If I may, might I please have some time to examine Lillybeth and Hinsberth alone?"

"Certainly. We will sit just over here. It will be fine, yes?" answered Marista pointing her wings at the patterned seats.

Doctor Lochswyn was not particularly interested in belaboring the point, especially with Marista.

"Yes, yes — that is fine," she agreed reluctantly.

After seeing Hinsberth, Marista and Eldsworth were terribly out of sorts, for they had never seen him so ill.

"Please, what is wrong with my son? Why does he not wake up?" pleaded Marista, her ordinarily booming voice overcome with worry.

"I am sorry," began Doctor Lochswyn. "At the moment, I am not sure what is ailing Hinsberth, and I am unsure whether he may be contagious. I wish I could say more, but I need to examine him thoroughly."

Doctor Lochswyn paused for a moment. She watched Hinsberth

breathe and her brow furrowed. She went into the patient room, and working quickly and methodically, brought out a number of blankets, a few wet towels and some ice. She placed them with great care over Hinsberth.

She then turned to Millybeth and Hackleberg and announced, "I will also need to examine Lillybeth, just to be sure."

While her parents nodded in agreement, Lillybeth glanced toward the door, trying to deduce the viability of a quick escape. But her parents immediately shuffled her into the spare patient room and she was forced to endure an anxious wait.

❖   ❖   ❖

A world away from The Farm, Milchester began to stir in his cage, slowly awakening from his tremulous sleep. Having remained awake most of the night and feeling rather detached and groggy, he nevertheless immediately thought to check on his ailing friend.

"Good morning, Mister Hinsberth, are you well?" he said in a hushed voice.

Receiving no reply, he raised his voice, thinking Hinsberth was perhaps still asleep, "Mister Hinsberth, I know I promised and I am so sorry for falling asleep. Are you well?"

He paused a moment, but hearing only silence beyond the metal walls, he raised his voice still further.

"Mister Hinsberth, are you awake?"

He heard not a stir nor any answer, and with a stomach suddenly full of knots, he brought his voice nearly to shouting.

"Mister Hinsberth, are you well? Are you there? Please answer!" he pleaded.

CHAPTER 3

The pigs nearby recoiled from Milchester's cries, believing yet another had lost the presence of mind and would soon be taken.

By now Milchester was overcome with worry; he thought of predators and of how very ill Hinsberth had been, and as his fervent imagination began to besiege him, he struggled mightily, as hard as he could, to turn in his cage, to see behind. He rammed his head and body into the bars, but there was just not enough space.

He felt ill. He began to panic.

"Mister Hinsberth!" he shouted again, "Are you there? Please answer!"

Tears blinded his eyes.

"Mister Hinsberth! Please!" he choked.

Then, overcome with desperation, he shouted for Hinsberth at the top of his voice and he kicked his legs with all his might through the rear of his cage to the wall, shattering the air.

"Mister Hinsberth! Please answer! Please! No... My friend! MY FRIEND!" he cried out to the sky.

"My friend..." he whispered to himself, and with nothing but silence returned, Milchester, exhausted, his aching body wracked with sobs, sunk weakly onto his knees. He knew he was once again, and this time would almost certainly be...

forever...

alone.

DOCTOR LOCHSWYN

"And one more thing, little Lillybeth,...
Whatever has happened to Hinsberth is not your fault..."

THE PROMISE

I N THE ELEGANTLY FINISHED and sunlit patient room, surrounded by walls of shelves lined with pots of medicinal plants
and bottles full of tinctures and remedies, Lillybeth shifted about
incessantly while seated on the bed as Doctor Lochswyn prepared to
examine her.

"How do you feel?" the Doctor inquired.

She wheeled about the room on a rolling stool and after selecting a
few implements, she rolled over to a restless Lillybeth.

"A — a bit tired," replied Lillybeth, with a quivering voice. She was
uncertain as to why Doctor Lochswyn had asked her to submit to an
examination. Was she ill? Had she caught something from Hinsberth?
Was Hinsberth going to recover?

Millybeth and Hackleberg settled on the generously stuffed patterned pillows facing the patient bed. They watched the proceedings
with trepidation.

Lillybeth sat up as tall as she could and let her eyes roam about the
room, even while responding to the doctor's queries.

"What is *that*?" she suddenly blurted out loudly, pointing to one
of the Doctor's more odd looking plants, growing large with bright

green, spiky leaves.

"Oh, that is just an herb. It helps to heal abrasions of the skin," replied Doctor Lochswyn matter-of-factly.

She was rather focused on checking Lillybeth's temperature with a thermometer placed under one of the duckling's wings, which had to be repeatedly replaced and reset as Lillybeth pointed to and asked questions about almost everything.

"*Wow*! What do you use *that* for?" Lillybeth inquired, suddenly bending over the end of the table and grabbing one of the many implements mounted on hooks along the bed's wooden frame.

"That is for stripping leaves off twigs," Doctor Lochswyn replied, waving a wing carelessly toward the rows of plants while continuing, with admirable patience, to try and examine Lillybeth.

While lifting Lillybeth's feathers and checking her skin, Doctor Lochswyn sent a brief sympathetic glance to Hackleberg and Millybeth. Lillybeth's parents returned a knowing look, silently conveying the message that, yes, she really is like this most of the time.

Lillybeth was taking more implements from their hooks and she tried to cobble them together, in an attempt to make some manner of workable contraption.

"Ouch!" Lillybeth squirmed as she pinched her wing in one of Doctor Lochswyn's more imposing tools.

After spending much more time on the examination than was usually the case, Doctor Lochswyn was satisfied Lillybeth was not ill. She sat up tall, took a deep breath and carefully returned her instruments to their rightful places.

"Well — good news. Lillybeth does not appear to have any sort of illness," Doctor Lochswyn announced, to the visible relief of

CHAPTER 4

Millybeth and Hackleberg. "However, if I may ask you to watch her closely, just in case. I want to be notified immediately if she shows any sign of fever."

Millybeth and Hackleberg nodded in agreement.

Lillybeth prepared to jump from the table, but Doctor Lochswyn caught her. "Please, if I may have just a moment longer. I understand you may be fine, but I would like to know everything you remember about Hinsberth, from the morning you met to fly off together until you arrived back at The Farm."

Lillybeth was quite content to tell Doctor Lochswyn everything she could recall about the expedition, especially since she believed her words might help heal Hinsberth in some way. She began with a detailed description of their preparations, speaking slowly and deliberately, but she gradually accelerated into a breathless pace, gesticulating broadly with her wings when recounting the storm and the desperate search for Hinsberth.

The Doctor sat fixated, listening closely, trying to pick up clues.

"Do you think Hinsberth was ill *before* you departed?" she inquired after Lillybeth finished her tale.

"I think he was tired. From what I understand, he is not an early riser," replied Lillybeth, who was usually wide awake before the break of dawn.

Doctor Lochswyn asked a few more questions about the time and place where Lillybeth and her helpers had found Hinsberth, searching for any clue which might help determine the nature of his illness.

Lillybeth described the place they had found Hinsberth as being most disagreeable, describing in some detail the foul buildings, the foul air and the haunting voices. She recalled that when they found

Hinsberth he was already feverish and covered with straw, probably to keep himself warm during the night.

Lillybeth's recollections intrigued Doctor Lochswyn and she suddenly wheeled over to a low-hanging shelf which acted as a small desk and began scribbling notes on a pad of paper. Lillybeth watched the doctor curiously for a moment, then gingerly hopped down off the table, and waddled over to her.

Standing at Doctor Lochswyn's side, looking up at her and watching her busily writing, Lillybeth suddenly whispered, "Doctor Lochswyn?" just to have her attention, and then, unable to hide the worry in her quivering voice, she inquired, "Is Hinsberth going to be well again?"

Doctor Lochswyn paused a moment. She sent a reassuring glance over her spectacles to Millybeth and Hackleberg, and then turning back to Lillybeth she replied forthrightly, "He does have a bit of a fever. But I for one believe, and if I have anything to do about it, that he is going to be just fine." She paused only a moment, and then added, "One more thing, little Lillybeth," she leaned in close and took Lillybeth's tiny wings into hers, "Whatever has happened to Hinsberth is not your fault, and I do not want you to leave this office if you have even one shred of belief to the contrary."

Lillybeth dropped her gaze to the floor.

"Thank you, Doctor Lochswyn," she said in a quiet, sincere tone.

Lillybeth could not help but feel herself warming to the doctor, for she felt as though a large weight had been lifted from her insides.

Millybeth and Hackleberg graciously thanked Doctor Lochswyn for her efforts and patience, then together with Lillybeth they quietly departed from the room and gently closed the door, with Doctor

Lochswyn still scribbling away inside. They ventured across the hall-way and joined Marista and Eldsworth in keeping vigil over Hinsberth as he lay feverish and unconscious.

"How is Lillybeth?" Eldsworth immediately inquired as their friends entered the room.

"Everything appears to be fine. She is a little tired, naturally, but does not seem to have any illness," answered Millybeth.

Always the gentleman, Eldsworth seemed genuinely pleased about this news, despite his deep concern over the health of his own son. Marista also seemed relieved after hearing Lillybeth was well, but she was noticeably more subdued as she watched Hinsberth, laboring in breath, his small head covered with cold, wet towels and his body subsumed under layers of thick blankets and bags of ice.

Doctor Lochswyn had also placed a thermometer under Hinsberth's wing, and every so often she would gently knock on the door, enter the room, and measure his temperature.

As they sat together watching over Hinsberth, Millybeth whispered to Eldsworth and Marista, "We are quite sure he is going to be just fine."

Hackleberg and Lillybeth nodded in hopeful agreement, but Marista and Eldsworth were not so certain. The deep expression of concern on Doctor Lochswyn's face had not gone unnoticed.

❖   ❖   ❖

Early that evening there came a knock upon Doctor Lochswyn's door, and soon Quillypom entered along with several of the doctor's neigh-bors from around The Pond. They had generously and unexpect-edly prepared meals both for Doctor Lochswyn and the two families keeping vigil over Hinsberth.

Doctor Lochswyn generally did not allow anyone to remain in her home with the presence of an ill patient, and this night was no exception. Although she did not agree to having the visitors stay for the meal, she did thank them profusely for their generosity and she allowed the two families to dine in the empty patient room, even joining them for a time, sitting down, naturally, with a freshly prepared bowl of her own brand of porridge.

Before the guests departed, Lillybeth received an awkward, discomforting stare from Quillypom as the visitors bid a good night and offered well-wishes. Quillypom seemed to be desiring to say something to her, but Lillybeth had the strong sense Quillypom believed the circumstances were inappropriate, and even though Lillybeth was grateful both for the thoughtful visit and the generous food, she was rather relieved when Quillypom and her companions finally made their way out the door.

After finishing their meal, Marista, Eldsworth and the Smythes returned to be with Hinsberth, and Doctor Lochswyn went to retire for the night down a narrow corridor to her bedroom at the rear of the house. She was known to be very strict about preparing for sleep at exactly the same time each night. Marista, Eldsworth, Hackleberg and Millybeth were surprised, however, as before bidding all a good night, Doctor Lochswyn did not request for them to leave, although neither did she declare they were welcome to stay. So at Marista's urging they settled down for the night, to keep watch over Hinsberth and wait with hope for the coming dawn.

❖   ❖   ❖

CHAPTER 4

When morning finally came on the first faint glimmers of sunshine, the families were awakened by the curious but somehow enticing scent of Doctor Lochswyn's morning porridge. But the strain of the previous day had taken its toll and they drifted again into slumber. A short time later they were awakened again by the doctor's now familiar gentle knock on the door. Doctor Lochswyn quietly entered and checked Hinsberth's progress over the night. She examined Hinsberth closely. The furrow over her brow deepened. Hinsberth was still unconscious and his fever remained stubbornly high. She replaced the cold towels and ice. Marista's eyes drew open and at once she was on her feet to help settle Hinsberth under a fresh set of blankets.

Marista moved her seat to be closer to Hinsberth. She sat down and caressed the side of his face with a single large feather from her wing. Eldsworth stirred and then joined Marista. He placed his wing over her back. Millybeth and Hackleberg awakened a moment later with the desire to do something to help. After a hushed conversation Millybeth offered their idea: "Would you fancy a little breakfast? We can go home for a moment and prepare Hinsberth's favorite. Perhaps the smell of a good, tasty meal will wake him."

Marista and Eldsworth accepted Millybeth's suggestion wholeheartedly.

"Yes… yes. A good idea, certainly," said Marista. "If there is one thing which might help him now, it would be food."

Hinsberth was not a bashful eater.

"Indeed. A most generous offer," added Eldsworth politely.

Doctor Lochswyn nodded in agreement, and, in thinking about food, she had the idea that perhaps *everyone* would benefit from a healthy meal, for she did not consider Hinsberth her only patient.

"If you would like," she announced, "I can offer some of my porridge. It would not take but a moment to brew another batch."

She was disappointed when everyone, although admitting the porridge must be quite delicious, very respectfully declined, for there was still the matter of that strange and powerful aroma.

❖　❖　❖

Millybeth, Hackleberg and Lillybeth strode swiftly home to prepare a special meal for Hinsberth. They went quickly into the kitchen and brought out the ingredients for Hinsberth's favorite meal: blueberries and algae on a bed of pond grass.

While busily assembling the ingredients, and given it was still early morning, they were surprisingly interrupted by a rap on their door. Millybeth answered, and was greeted by a familiar face, in a tightly pressed uniform and a small, square hat, standing nervously and impatiently on the front step.

Noticing Millybeth's faint air of recognition, the visitor quickly stated, "I am — I am from the Mayor's Office."

Then, without looking Millybeth in the eye, the Messenger read, in a brisk and formal manner, from a very small square of paper she nonetheless held tightly in both wings, "The Honorable Quillypom Swellington has requested that one Lillybeth Smythe come to join her at the Mayor's Office as soon as she is able."

Millybeth's bill fell open.

Without another word the Messenger turned and waddled swiftly away. Lillybeth had heard her name and was nearing the doorway as Millybeth closed the door and turned to face her.

"It seems you have been rather formally requested to meet with

Quillypom, as soon as you are able," Millybeth stated in a befuddled tone.

All at once, Lillybeth's stomach turned to knots, and the weight lifted from her insides the previous day returned, only suddenly bearing down even harder than before. Lillybeth instantly thought she must be in considerable trouble over the inconveniencing of all those involved with the search, and she imagined being punished in some terrible manner by those holding her responsible for Hinsberth's ailment. It was not the first time, after all, she had caused a measure of difficulty for the Mayor's Office.

But for the moment Lillybeth buried her concerns and returned to the present task, and she, Millybeth and Hackleberg worked closely together to assemble a well presented plate of Hinsberth's favorite meal. Upon agreeing it was satisfactorily garnished, they placed it on their finest serving platter and went carefully to Doctor Lochswyn's for delivery.

"A fine dish," said Marista, receiving the Smythes at the patient room door. "Thank you. I hope Hinsberth will wake soon so he can do more than savor the beautiful scent."

"We hope so too," agreed Hackleberg wholeheartedly.

Millybeth bent low to look earnestly into her daughter's eyes, "Your father and I will remain here, and you may go on to the Mayor's Office. I want to hear all about the purpose for the visit when you return."

"She has an appointment with the Mayor's Office?" asked Eldsworth, surprised.

Marista took notice of Lillybeth's rather anxious nod.

"Don't you worry," Marista told her with such conviction that a significant number of the butterflies in Lillybeth's stomach became fervently grounded. "You be sure to let me know if they give you any trouble."

Hackleberg quietly thanked Marista for adding to the moral support. He was just as curious and almost as anxious as Lillybeth in wondering why she had been summoned.

❖　❖　❖

Before departing Lillybeth went to make a quick check on Hinsberth. She stood silently, looking over his seemingly peaceful, sleeping face for a long moment. She noticed his breathing was shallow and quick, and even without touching him she could feel the heat rising from his body. She turned toward the door, and reluctantly proceeded outside to begin the short walk to the Mayor's Office.

The morning air was pleasantly warm and just a little moist; the sky shone all over in brilliant blue except for the occasional meandering cloud. The spirit of a fine summer morning gave Lillybeth a needed measure of calm.

In little time Lillybeth stood before the Mayor's Office door and she knocked tentatively with her wing, for she could not reach the large, rather official looking knocker. However, her raps on the door went unheard. Fortunately the door soon opened and she was let in by the same Messenger who had earlier delivered the request from Quillypom, as she was departing on yet another errand. Lillybeth thought the Messenger's uniform looked unbearably uncomfortable.

Lillybeth wandered inside and was led by an attendant into a small room off to one side of the foyer, where she sat down and waited to be called upon. Since the day was still rather young, Lillybeth waited alone in the room. The ornate, formal looking furniture was un- doubtedly built for much larger bodies, making her, as with the door knocker, feel somewhat undersized. Her mind set to wandering, and she let her eyes roam over the room to take in all the intricate details of shape and form; light and shadow, hoping to find something of in- terest. Along the walls were tables and shelves with piles of books and papers, but nothing which seemed worthy of further examination. She could hear muted voices in conversation, echoing from down the hall which led narrowly to the rear of the house. Lining the hallway were a number of large, heavy doors; entrances to the rooms where the Mayor's Office staff managed the affairs of The Farm.

Before long Lillybeth heard footsteps thudding purposefully down the hallway and soon after Quillypom rounded the corner.

"Good morning, Lillybeth," she stated with a tinge of forced cheer.

"Yes, good morning," Lillybeth replied, playing along with the for- malities, but not having any idea why Quillypom would suddenly be- gin acting kind to her. Quillypom had usually treated her, and most other ducklings, with a flat indifference.

"Follow me, please," Quillypom requested, again with a tight smile.

Quillypom led Lillybeth down the hall to her office. It was a large room with a row of tall windows on one wall and finished com- pletely in find wood. Quillypom closed the door behind her, and the thick, heavy wooden door, also brandishing a knocker too high for Lillybeth's reach, shut with a solid thud. A stout wooden desk stood like a fortress near the center of the room. A single small chair sat in front, facing timidly toward the overseer of the desk. Quillypom strode briskly over to take her seat and was surprised to see Lillybeth still standing just inside the doorway.

"Come now. Take a seat," she requested, suddenly forgetting her cheerful manner.

Lillybeth straightened her shirt and waddled over to hop up onto the chair facing the desk. She tried with some difficulty to repress imagining herself shackled in a stockade in front of the Mayor's Office, hearing the cackling laughter of Quillypom echoing out through the windows as she gleefully stamped approval of Lillybeth's punishment.

Seated in her chair, Lillybeth's eyes barely cleared the broad top of Quillypom's desk. She sat tall so her eyes could at least meet Quillypom's.

Quillypom was noticeably uncomfortable with having young Lillybeth sitting in her office, and she spoke in a very slow manner, as if talking to someone much younger, making Lillybeth feel all the more awkward: "Of course, I speak for the Mayor and myself when conveying how pleased we are that you and Hinsberth have been returned safely to The Farm, and we wish Hinsberth a return to good health as soon as possible. But with the efforts involved in the search, the Mayor has requested a full account of all related activities, from the very beginning of the events which precipitated the necessity to organize the search party."

Lillybeth was unfamiliar with such a formal, and in her judgement, round-a-bout manner of speaking, but she understood Quillypom's request: she wished for all the details of her and Hinsberth's misadventure. By now, Lillybeth had repeated the tale a number of times but she nevertheless began to recite it again, with her usual growing round of excitement and becoming ever more animated as she spoke.

Quillypom, however, seemed to be rather impatient.

"If you do not mind, I have, from various sources, acquired the details of the early stages. If I may ask you to begin from the time when you encountered those who returned you and Hinsberth to The Farm?"

"Certainly," replied Lillybeth, somewhat relieved at not having to recount the entire tale, but also somewhat surprised as she had only just begun to excitedly wave her wings, pushing the air around her head while describing the chaos of the storm. She thought her performance at least adequate enough to hold some interest.

Lillybeth explained to Quillypom how she had flown over the symbols in the field, and then met her four very helpful friends. As she did so, Quillypom listened more earnestly. Earlier she had been scratching notes on a pad of paper, but now her pencil rested loosely in her wing. Desiring to be helpful, Lillybeth recalled the events with as much detail as she could remember.

Quillypom only interjected once to inquire for a more precise description regarding the condition of Lillybeth's four helpers. She not only wanted to know how they appeared physically, but she asked Lillybeth to recall everything they had said, and the manner in which they had said it. Quillypom seemed perhaps vaguely concerned for their well-being, an impression which made Lillybeth feel more at ease.

Lillybeth was quite content to describe Filipa and her friends, for she still felt tremendous gratitude toward them and considered them her friends, even though they had forgotten to come and say goodbye. But even so, Lillybeth had no idea why such details were important to Quillypom's report.

Quillypom became impatient once more when Lillybeth began to excitedly describe, in rapid and animated fashion, the amazing popping domes and other inventive gadgetry Filipa and her friends possessed.

"Yes — yes, very interesting," Quillypom interrupted with a distracted tone, giving the impression she was not indeed very interested. Quillypom's head rested tiredly on one wing. Before Lillybeth could continue Quillypom announced: "You have been most generous in offering your recollections this morning, and I believe I now have sufficient material for the report. I can accompany you back to the entrance, if you desire."

"Thank you. I remember the way," replied Lillybeth.

She found it odd the details of how Hinsberth was found would be omitted from Quillypom's important report. However Lillybeth did not at all mind having to spend that much less time with Quillypom. Although, Lillybeth had once again noticed a faint, sorrowful air behind Quillypom's stern mannerisms, just as when she had accidentally spied on her through the window at Doctor Lochswyn's. And upon leaving Quillypom and passing into the hallway beyond the heavy wooden door, Lillybeth found herself feeling a surprising sympathy for her. Waddling down the hallway toward the foyer, Lillybeth sensed a subtle, somber, perhaps even vulnerable mood behind all the rigid formalities of the Mayor's Office.

❖   ❖   ❖

As Lillybeth wandered back to Doctor Lochswyn's, she pondered over the curious conversation that had just taken place, at least for the first few steps, for her thoughts quickly turned to Hinsberth, and she strode a little faster.

Once inside the doctor's office she came to a sudden stop just outside the patient room, for she heard hushed voices but could not quite make out the words. She glanced around the casement, and could tell by the sight of Hinsberth's breakfast sitting untouched on a small table next to his bed that he was still unable to wake. She stared at his breakfast, and seeing it lonely and bereft of purpose, its aromatic scent competing for attention with Doctor Lochswyn's all too familiar porridge, made her heart sink.

She waddled into the room. All eyes fell upon her.

"Why is he still asleep?" she asked Doctor Lochswyn in a whisper.

"His body is trying to fight off the fever, so it is enticing him to rest. Resting saves his strength for healing," answered Doctor Lochswyn, who, even in a whisper, almost always presented a subtle but contagious optimism.

Doctor Lochswyn's brief explanation regarding Hinsberth's unconsciousness seemed to satisfy Lillybeth, at least for the moment. He is healing, she thought, and the notion made her feel a little lighter. She surmised that perhaps the more Hinsberth slept, the stronger and healthier he would be upon awakening. One or two knots unravelled from her stomach.

As the sun dipped beneath the horizon, another round of well-wishers arrived with a number of gentle raps on the doctor's office door, generously bearing another meal and, unexpectedly, a few small gifts for Hinsberth.

The families knew by now most everyone on The Farm was aware of the plight of the ailing duckling, and they were grateful for the continuing visitations, support and sentiment.

The gifts and food were well received, and the routine proceeded similarly to the previous night. Doctor Lochswyn hastened the guests on their way, and then she dined on an exacting dose of her special porridge with the families in the spare patient room.

After the meal Millybeth and Hackleberg had an exchange of whispers, and then Millybeth turned to Marista.

"We would like to invite you to our home for the night. It may be rather beneficial for you to have a bit of rest in a proper bed," she offered sincerely.

"We can divide the night into short intervals, and each of us can take a turn staying awake to watch over Hinsberth," Hackleberg quickly added.

"No — no, it is fine. I will stay here with Hinsberth. But thank you, it is a generous offer," replied Marista.

"I think it is a good idea," agreed Eldsworth. "*You* need some rest," he said to Marista with a firm tone.

"Oh, no. Do not worry about me," Marista said, waving her wings. "I can go without sleep for weeks, months, or even years!" She could not imagine leaving Hinsberth's side.

"The Smythes certainly have a good idea. Please, I think it would benefit all of us to have more rest. If Hinsberth awakens, we need to be well for him," Eldsworth declared.

Marista paused. She could see the concern in Eldsworth's eyes, and she reluctantly agreed with his reasoning.

"If you insist. But only for tonight."

After gathering their things and waiting for Marista to whisper a long, tearful goodbye to her sleeping son, Millybeth, Hackleberg, Marista and Lillybeth left the doctor's office and in the waning light of dusk they made the short journey to the Smythe's home. Eldsworth remained behind, at Hinsberth's side.

CHAPTER 4

❖   ❖   ❖

As the warm glow of a new dawn spread over The Farm, the rays gently and silently snuck through the windows and crawled ever so slowly up the large, puffy bed where Lillybeth, Millybeth, Eldsworth and Marista were enjoying a very necessary round of unencumbered sleep. They were all together on the stout bed, drooping off the edges and only partially buried under a weighty, busily patterned and un-apologetically worn quilt Millybeth had sewn when she was only a duckling. Hackleberg was not present, having taken the early morning watch over Hinsberth at Doctor Lochswyn's.

Suddenly there came a number of loud, sharp taps on the entrance door. Once again, a Messenger from the Mayor's Office had arrived at the Smythe's home.

Millybeth, disappointed to be awakened from such a restful sleep, fell from the bed and stumbled about with squinting eyes toward the front door. She was surprised to see the Messenger standing on the threshold before her. The Messenger paused briefly, noting Millybeth was only partially conscious.

The Messenger had obviously departed in haste; her normally tight and formal looking uniform was in a state of disarray, her feathers ruffled and one shoe was missing. She appeared to not only have suddenly awakened, but had run or flown to the Smythe's home as fast as she could, as she was now trying to recover her breath. For a moment, she searched for an out of place pocket, and finally she managed to retrieve a message to present to Millybeth. The wrinkled paper was inscribed with hastily written print angled sharply across one side.

The Messenger read in her typically nervous and speedy manner: "The

Honorable Quillypom Swellington has been notified by Hackleberg Smythe that one Hinsberth Smerkington has requested Lillybeth Smythe to come to the doctor's office at once."

The Messenger had not yet finished reading when thuds, bangs and other unidentifiable scuffling sounds marking a sudden commotion burst forth from the bedroom, and an instant later Marista, Eldsworth, and Lillybeth came excitedly to the doorway.

Lillybeth had only heard "Hinsberth", "Lillybeth" and "doctor's office" and she was quickly out the door and striding at full speed toward Doctor Lochswyn's. Everyone else, including the Messenger, followed her lead and quickly caught up. The Messenger was overtaken by her own curiosity and the excitement expressed by the recipients of the message she now felt privileged to have delivered.

Upon arriving at Doctor Lochswyn's, their excitement was quickly tempered. Doctor Lochswyn only allowed Marista, Eldsworth, and Lillybeth to enter as Hackleberg came out, and they knew at once Hinsberth was not in the best of health. In fact, he was no longer awake at all. His breathing was even more labored than before, and Marista and Eldsworth were quick to be by his side, each holding one of his wings. Then, unexpectedly, Hinsberth's eyes opened again, just as he had done before when Hackleberg was with him, prompting the request for the Mayor's Office to send the Messenger to the Smythe's home.

"Lillybeth?" Hinsberth inquired, with a barely audible voice.

Lillybeth waddled into the patient room, taking a moment to glance upon Marista and Eldsworth, who silently nodded permission to approach their son. As his parents stepped away to grant a moment of privacy, Lillybeth came to stand alone at Hinsberth's side. Seeing him buried under ice and blankets and hearing his labored breathing made her heart sink. The tears found her eyes and she quickly tried to wipe them away to keep them from falling on Hinsberth.

"Lillybeth?" Hinsberth whispered again.

He knew she was there. He struggled for a deep breath.

She leaned in closer to better hear his voice and gently placed a wing over the towels covering his head.

"Lillybeth," Hinsberth whispered, "You are an odd duck."

At once Lillybeth felt a tinge of embarrassment and also a little confusion over Hinsberth's words, and for the moment she could only think to straighten her shirt.

But Hinsberth continued speaking, quietly, slowly, between breaths, "You are odd — odd enough — to make it happen."

"Make what happen? Please, I do not understand," Lillybeth whispered in her most quiet voice, so as not to startle him.

Hinsberth was barely present now, seemingly asleep again, his eyes closed. He seemed so ill; Lillybeth's heart broke.

"Promise me," he pleaded.

"I promise," sobbed Lillybeth.

Hinsberth managed only one word with each shallow breath, "Promise — you — will — free — Milchester."

He paused a moment to gather his strength and then spoke once more, "Promise — you — will — free — them — all."

"I promise."

MILLYBETH

*"This," she mumbled to herself looking at the pair of
deeply slumbering ducks, "will not be easy."*

CHAPTER 5

THE PLAN

HINSBERTH WAS UNCONSCIOUS, and the unmistakable signs of worry had etched themselves deeply onto the face of Doctor Lochswyn. When she spoke of him she was always optimistic recovery would come about soon, but the look in her eyes and the long spans of time spent in the spare room scouring her books for ideas only dampened the spirits of Marista, Eldsworth and the Smythes.

Since the Messenger accompanied them to Doctor Lochswyn's and noticed the abrupt shift from an excited to a sombre mood, news of the decline in the health of the ailing duckling spread quickly over The Farm. Consequently, visitors were even more numerous, and they brought with them get well messages, food and gifts.

Lillybeth spent her time just outside Doctor Lochswyn's house, sitting in a cozy patch of garden, thinking intently and watching an inchworm slowly plod its way around a delicate plant with a deep green stem and broad, reddish leaves. She was hoping Hinsberth would wake again. She was baffled by Hinsberth's last few words, and she desperately wished to know what he meant when he asked for her promise. Would she be able to fulfill her promise to Hinsberth before he awakened? Would he be disappointed in her if she failed? But she could only wonder, who is Milchester? And who are "them", and from what are they to be freed? Perhaps, she thought, Milchester was a friend of Hinsberth's on The Farm. But why had Hinsberth never before mentioned Milchester or "them"? And why had he waited to tell her of them until a time when his words could only be so few? Lillybeth thought Hinsberth may have been under the sway of his fever, perhaps even delirious. That would certainly explain at least some of Hinsberth's words, for *she* certainly did not think herself odd. And she had never heard of anyone called Milchester, although it seemed a fine name.

As the inchworm arched onto the back of the leaf and out of sight, Lillybeth's mind suddenly lit with an idea: The Mayor's Office! Lillybeth knew that Quillypom must keep records for many if not all of the inhabitants of The Farm, certainly for all of the ducks, and perhaps in those records she could find mention of someone named Milchester.

Lillybeth jumped up.

"I will return in a moment," she called into Doctor Lochswyn's window, and then she immediately set off with quick feet toward the Mayor's Office.

A moment later she stood before the large, polished entrance door. After spending a time searching about, she commandeered a large garden pot and, after exerting some effort dragging it over the plants, she placed it directly in front of the door. She flipped the earthen pot upside down and hopped onto its top, giving her the height needed to reach the thick, round knocker. She raised the weighty knocker as far as her wings could stretch and came down with it three times against the solid wooden door, hearing each thumping knock echo inside.

In short order the Messenger slowly opened the door and poked her wide eyes round the aperture. She seemed rather stunned until she spotted Lillybeth standing on her pot. Lillybeth immediately hopped down and waddled inside straight past the Messenger. At once she noticed a great many faces leaning out of doorways and windows and staring in her direction, all with the same wide eyed expression as the Messenger. All the excitement over her arrival seemed a much friendlier greeting than she received during her previous visits to the Mayor's Office. She waddled down the hallway to Quillypom's office with an added bounce in her step.

Soon she was at Quillypom's door; thankfully left ajar after Quillypom had checked to see who was responsible for the sudden, loud interruption. Lillybeth popped her head round the casement and saw Quillypom working diligently at her desk, scribbling with a pencil while shifting back and forth through a stack of paper.

"My, is she a fast reader," thought Lillybeth as she watched Quillypom at work. Feeling tentative, Lillybeth was not at all certain how to address Quillypom and catch her attention, so she chose a somewhat indirect method and began very noisily clearing her throat. This apparently startled Quillypom — her head popped upward from her desk and she began looking around her office. Her eyes quickly settled upon the tiny feathered source of the disturbance — the small head peaking around the doorway. Lillybeth gave her a meek if hopeful smile and Quillypom sat back in her seat with an expression mixed of puzzlement and amusement. She quickly waved for Lillybeth to enter.

At once Lillybeth waddled into Quillypom's office and hopped into the same chair she had occupied during her previous visit. She sat tall, but still only her eyes and the top of her head peeked over the desk.

"Ah, Lillybeth. How may I help you?" inquired Quillypom in a stern voice, as if she did not at all appreciate the interruption.

"I am not sure exactly," said Lillybeth. "I need to find someone."

"Find someone? Did you lose someone?" asked Quillypom flatly.

"No. I only have a name — someone who may be from The Farm. I wish to find if anyone on The Farm has this name," replied Lillybeth sheepishly. She was quite unsure whether the latter question was a not so subtle poke at her most recent misadventure.

"What is the name, if I may ask?" inquired Quillypom with a feigned curiosity.

"Milchester."

❖   ❖   ❖

At the doctor's office, Marista and Eldsworth were spending a long, worrisome day at Hinsberth's side in the patient room, when they were stirred by a knock at the door. Doctor Lochswyn lifted her tired eyes from her books and rose wearily from her chair. As she passed the doorway to the patient room she motioned to Marista and Eldsworth to tell them she would answer for the caller.

Upon opening the door Doctor Lochswyn was surprised to find two unusually dressed ducks standing before her, one slender and tall and the other identical in shape and appearance but from a much smaller mould. Despite the warm weather, they wore blue and white striped knit sweaters, and on their feet were bright red shoes with shiny brass buckles. Draped loosely about their necks were silky, pale amber scarves, and adorning their heads were matching felt berets;

tilted forward and to the side to hover just above their dark, smoky eyes.

Doctor Lochswyn opened her bill to greet them, but before she could speak, the taller visitor stepped inside and stood before her, uncomfortably close for Doctor Lochswyn's liking. She started speaking in a highly stylized, articulated voice, "We have heard about the poor duckling. Hinsberth is it? Oh, but I am so sorry, I am Monique. Monique Plummage. And this — is my daughter," Monique announced, and then with her voice overcome with pride, she added, "Her name is Anati."

Monique had spent her life on The Farm, and Doctor Lochswyn knew well of her and her family, having treated each of them at one time or another, although it had been quite some time since the last visit. Monique's desire to be at the center of Farm activities was rivaled only by Quillypom's, but the similarity between the two extended no further. While Quillypom was often compelled to lead and direct and manage, Monique was rather fond of just being in the thick of things, and she almost never missed an opportunity to be so.

Again Doctor Lochswyn opened her bill to speak, but Monique had the momentum and she continued: "Such a beautiful place you have here. I love the garden — very elegant. And the colors, so nice and... Oh, but Hinsberth! Yes, I want to speak to you. You are the Doctor, no? I know we have met before, but it has been some years, from when Anati was ill as a tiny duckling. She was so young, no? And always so beautiful. Hinsberth, though. I heard he was ill, not recovering, and maybe even becoming worse. And I was thinking..."

Monique stepped even closer to Doctor Lochswyn, and while gazing directly into her eyes she whispered quietly, "Can we step inside this little room over here?" even while already passing around Doctor Lochswyn and into the room with Anati trailing close behind.

Doctor Lochswyn, entirely befuddled, followed Monique and Anati into the spare patient room. She was not at all sure what to make of the two visitors.

Monique continued speaking in a hushed voice: "So I was thinking, about the poor duckling. You know we all want him to be better. Everyone has been talking about poor Hinsberth, hoping for him to get well. So it reminded me. Someone we used to know, when I was young. He was a, how do you say?... a little eccentric, not quite so normal like us. But smart, very smart. He started a place, and I think — I think if you take Hinsberth there, he can help."

Finally Doctor Lochswyn had a chance to speak.

"Firstly, as you may remember, I am Doctor Lochswyn, and I am certainly very happy to have the chance to become reacquainted with you and Anati. Secondly, I appreciate your concern and desire to help. But I do not think Hinsberth is in any condition to be moved, as you are aware he is quite ill. But I am curious to know more about this eccentric character you mentioned. Is he also a student of medicine?"

Monique's voice grew louder as her eyes took in the room, "He dabbled in medicine, I remember. But he was part of a group of friends and their families who studied many things together. They performed all kinds of experiments and were interested in many subjects. They were all very committed to their work. My mother; she was very creative, very artistic. A painter. She was part of their efforts for some time. I have the feeling he, or one of his colleagues, would be able to help, to find a cure for poor Hinsberth."

The notion someone might have some unusual and perhaps

undocumented knowledge about medicine greatly intrigued Doctor Lochswyn. She was always interested in learning new things of a practical nature to help her patients, and she felt a growing frustration over Hinsberth's persistent fever and unconsciousness. She had tried giving Hinsberth drops of soup and tea made of various herbs and tinctures in addition to the basic methods of applying ice and cold towels. She did her best to keep him hydrated and nourished. But Hinsberth's condition was deteriorating and Doctor Lochswyn was running short on ideas.

Marista and Eldsworth heard the muted voices emanating from across the hall, and Marista decided to peek in on the conversation and find out who was visiting.

Marista entered the room and noticed the two visitors with Doctor Lochswyn. She recognized them immediately.

"Ah! Hello Monique! And, oh, Anati, you look so beautiful!" she exclaimed sincerely. It was clear to all just how much Marista appreciated any visitors.

Doctor Lochswyn knew the conversation was free to proceed without introductions.

"Thank you. Thank you so much for coming. You both look so beautiful. And Anati, how much you have grown! You look just like your mother," Marista said in a loud animated voice. She extended her wings to Monique and Anati.

Monique smiled graciously and embraced Marista.

"It has been too long! We are so happy to see you. We had to visit as soon as we found out about Hinsberth. We felt so terrible, especially when we heard his fever was becoming worse."

"You are so kind to think of Hinsberth. We have been so very worried about him. We do not know why he does not wake up... Doctor Lochswyn has been very kind. It means a lot to us that you are here," said Marista sincerely.

"Of course, we will always be here for you. I have to tell you, we meant to bring gifts, but we forgot them. Can you believe it? Because — because I thought of something. I had an idea that maybe could help," declared Monique, lowering the volume of her voice and looking down her bill straight into Marista's eyes to show she was quite serious.

Doctor Lochswyn interjected, "Monique believes there is another practitioner of medicine, an acquaintance of her mother, who once lived on The Farm but has since moved away. She believes if we take Hinsberth to him, he or one of his colleagues may be able to help find a cure."

Marista's eyes grew wide and she pushed her flower and scarf further up toward the top of her head. She turned to look at Doctor Lochswyn and spoke with a hopeful tone, "Do you think this is true? Do you think someone else may help? Please, tell me. I trust whatever you say. You have been so good to Hinsberth, and so good to us."

Doctor Lochswyn replied in a thoughtful manner, trying to ensure consideration of all the alternatives and as always, focused on the interests of her patient: "It is very possible there are other techniques of which I am unaware to treat Hinsberth's illness. The methods I have employed have so far been unsuccessful. While he may eventually heal on his own, he might also become worse. I will not be the least bit offended if you wish to try another path. But if you do so choose, I would only ask I be allowed to observe or participate. If another course of treatment is successful, it may be something I can offer to other patients with similar conditions. If not, I might at least be there to help or to prevent any harm or misdoings."

Marista and Monique nodded in agreement and in appreciation of Doctor Lochswyn's openness to alternatives and possibilities. However, Doctor Lochswyn and Marista were still not fully decided and they wished to know as much as Monique could tell them about this curious expert in medicine, and where they could find him. So Monique, with a renewed enthusiasm and a bit of embellishment, told Marista everything she had revealed to Doctor Lochswyn. Monique was sincerely excited that perhaps her idea, only recently hatched, might bring forth some hope.

"Yes, yes, but what is his name?" inquired Marista after Monique had finished her tale.

Monique donned a far-away look as she summoned distant memories.

"I think... I think — his name was Chaffield. Yes. Chaffield Fowler."

❖ ❖ ❖

At the Mayor's Office, Quillypom was leaning back in her chair with her eyes turned up at the delicately tiled ceiling, running through her memory in search of a name.

After a moment, she turned to Lillybeth and said, "No — I cannot recall there being anyone named Milchester on The Farm. However, little Lillybeth, we do keep records for all residents, and you are welcome to search them for this mysterious Milchester."

"Yes, please!" exclaimed Lillybeth.

"Very well," said Quillypom, hoping to soon return to her work.

Quillypom rose from her seat and strode purposefully over to a huge, ornately carved cabinet filling the corner of her office. She opened a pair of doors hinged on the front, exposing a set of three large, solid and identical drawers. Taking hold of the thick wooden handle attached to the center drawer, she pulled it open with some degree of effort, for as the drawer reluctantly slid open it made a loud creaking noise — the contents within were revealed to be of substantial weight. Quillypom retrieved a hefty volume from the drawer, and carried it with both wings back to her desk, thumping it down directly in front of Lillybeth, temporarily shrouding her tiny head in a small cloud of dust.

Quillypom was taken aback as with a thud Lillybeth opened the book of records right there on her desk and stood up on her chair and started looking over the pages, searching for the name "Milchester."

Quillypom had for years approached her work with the utmost seriousness, believing it to be an important service to The Farm, and over time she had come to dislike interruptions and inefficiency of all kinds. In keeping with her ideals, she had often taken to working alone in her office, quickly shooing away all visitors except those having the most important reasons for their presence.

But as she reflexively lifted her wing to point Lillybeth to the door, she caught herself. She stopped her wing from rising over the top of her desk, and she stayed this way, frozen for a long moment, and then she let her wing drop. She watched her little visitor busily read over the pages, so innocently focused, so unaware and outside of Quillypom's world. And as she sat fixated on Lillybeth; as if from a great distance, a faint, familiar feeling suddenly washed over her. Quillypom unexpectedly stood up, and in an instant she quickly excused herself from the room as a single tear rolled down her cheek.

CHAPTER 5

Lillybeth gave not even a quick glance as Quillypom departed; she was consumed with checking each and every page within the hefty volume. The pages were penned thickly with rows and rows of names, locations and ages at the time of entry, along with an occasional scribble or two from Quillypom regarding some unusual item or organizational issue.

After quite some time, Lillybeth reached the end of the listings and lifted her head from the book in disappointment. She turned to the row of windows and folded her wings with the realization there may very well not be anyone named Milchester on The Farm. She wondered where could this Milchester be? She lingered for a moment, standing on Quillypom's desk chair, considering her next course of action. Where else might she be able to look for Milchester? And where was Quillypom?

She wished Hinsberth would wake again. She needed an explanation. How could she fulfill her promise without even knowing how to begin? Nevertheless, she did not wish for Hinsberth's recovery to be slowed by an interruption to his sleep. She remembered how Doctor Lochswyn had explained, in her rather knowledgeable manner, that Hinsberth's body was trying to heal by enticing him to sleep.

Lillybeth jumped down from the chair, and with Quillypom having not yet returned, she departed from Quillypom's office, leaving the door ajar, just a little more than when she had found it. Lillybeth strode down the hallway, and without seeing any of the excited faces who had earlier greeted her, she waddled disappointedly outside under the guidance of the Messenger.

❖ ❖ ❖

Returning to Doctor Lochswyn's garden, Lillybeth sat down and looked for the inchworm whose company she had abandoned for her visit to the Mayor's Office.

But in an instant, into her head sparked another idea.

Lillybeth swiftly popped inside the doctor's office. She saw Eldsworth in the patient room watching over Hinsberth and she heard the voluminous Marista in the spare room in conversation with Doctor Lochswyn and an unfamiliar voice.

"Mister Smerkington?" Lillybeth whispered to get Eldsworth's attention as she poked her head round the casement. "If I may ask, do you know of anyone by the name Milchester?"

Eldsworth was startled by Lillybeth's voice. He seemed to have been listening attentively to the muffled voices in conversation across the hall.

"Oh — hello Lillybeth. Might I ask you to repeat your question? I must admit I was off in another world for a moment."

"Do you know of anyone named Milchester? Hinsberth had told me of someone named Milchester who might be in some trouble," explained Lillybeth earnestly.

"Milchester? No — I do not believe I know of anyone by that name. Hinsberth never mentioned anyone named Milchester that I can recall. I am sorry I cannot be of more help. You may want to inquire with Marista, she certainly has her fair share of acquaintances on The Farm. She is in the other room with Doctor Lochswyn."

"Thank you," whispered Lillybeth in a hushed voice. She was fearful of disturbing Hinsberth. She turned and crossed the hallway to poke her head into the spare room. Inside stood Doctor Lochswyn, Marista, and two unfamiliar but very elegant looking visitors. Lillybeth immediately noticed one of the visitors was perhaps only a bit older than herself, and similar enough in appearance to the other that they were almost certainly mother and daughter.

Doctor Lochswyn, Marista, and the mother seemed to be embroiled in rather serious conversation, and Lillybeth was hesitant to interrupt, choosing instead to stand silent while holding onto the door casement and leaning in, listening to the proceedings.

"I think I remember him... I remember the name certainly. Mister Fowler, indeed an interesting and unusual character," recalled Doctor Lochswyn.

"But they left The Farm at some point? Why?" Marista inquired.

"Yes… they did. I believe some of their ideas were found disagreeable by the older residents at the time. They had some concerns about The Farm, but I cannot remember precisely what they were," recalled Monique vaguely.

"Mayor Swellington was also on The Farm at that time. I believe he knew Mister Fowler well, but they did disagree about certain things, always respectfully, though, if I remember. Mister Fowler had some ideas about building out The Farm. He and his colleagues wished to experiment and they eventually moved to settle in a distant place, more amenable to what they were trying to accomplish. This was sometime after the final migration, if I recall," noted Doctor Lochswyn, who was apparently not only knowledgeable about medicine, but also the history of The Farm.

Lillybeth listened closely, but with the unfamiliar names she could not piece together what, exactly, Doctor Lochswyn and the others were speaking about.

Marista turned to Doctor Lochswyn.

"So. Do you know where they are? Do you know where Mister Fowler and his friends finally settled?" she inquired. She was eager to find him, eager to have her son back to good health.

"Not exactly, there had been some distancing with The Farm over the years. The Mayor in particular does not seem entirely fond of maintaining much contact. Quillypom as well. As you know they do have a bit of influence, so much so that I believe they changed the views of the Council over time, for now they seem to discourage any relations," explained Doctor Lochswyn.

"My mother. She did as she pleased. She took me to visit Mister Fowler's when I was young. If you can allow me some time, I think I can remember, or at least try to find out where they are now," Monique offered.

Suddenly Anati tugged on her mother's sweater and pointed in Lillybeth's direction. Lillybeth froze, she was uncertain if this was intended to be a private conversation. The combination of the serious expressions on their faces and their hushed voices made Lillybeth worry she had been caught unintentionally eavesdropping, and the stockade might still be in her future. She nervously raised her wing and waved hello with as friendly an expression as she could muster.

"Come in. Come in, sweet Lillybeth," called Marista. "Don't you worry, we were only talking about something which may help my precious son."

Marista's gregariousness and her often forceful presence always had a way of reassuring Lillybeth, and she entered the room much more at ease; the images of the stockade fading fast. However, the daughter stared at her with a peculiar expression and as a result Lillybeth felt a bit uncomfortable. She glanced down to notice her shirt was inside out.

"Monique, this is Lillybeth, Millybeth and Hackleberg's daughter," announced Doctor Lochswyn.

"Oh, yes. I have heard so much about you," said Monique.

Monique's reply caused Lillybeth a great deal of surprise and also gave her a measure of concern; any notoriety she had on The Farm could only be a result of her misadventures, especially those which for one reason or another came to involve the Mayor's Office.

Presently Doctor Lochswyn introduced the daughter, "Lillybeth, this is Anati, Monique's daughter."

"Very nice to meet you!" said Lillybeth enthusiastically, very much hoping for a chance to make a new friend.

"Yes, thank you. It is nice to meet you," said Anati distractedly, as she glanced around Lillybeth to the open doorway.

Then she bent down slightly to Lillybeth's height and said quietly, "You know, everyone is talking about poor Hinsberth. We have come here to help."

"Well, I am happy you wish to help. We have certainly received a lot of food and gifts," noted Lillybeth.

"You know Hinsberth well?" asked Anati, standing tall again.

"Yes, I think so. I mean… I did not know him too well before, our — adventure. But since then we have spent a lot of time together. While he was awake, anyway," Lillybeth stammered anxiously.

"I would like to meet him when he is well again," Anati declared. "Do you think you could introduce us?" she asked, staring right through Lillybeth with a pair of alluring eyes.

Lillybeth suddenly felt ill. Nausea and a rush of heat had without warning flooded her head, and the room began to spin. She fumbled over a reply, "Yes — yes, Hinsberth is a very — friendly sort. I — am sure he always likes to meet new friends."

Lillybeth could no longer look into Anati's eyes. She turned her gaze to her feet, desperately hoping someone would say something which would allow her to leave the room so she could go and gather her thoughts.

"Monique, I think we have discovered a new pair of friends!" exclaimed Marista, grinning at the two ducklings.

"Yes, I certainly agree," said Monique. "I hope we can come to be together much more often, especially as Hinsberth recovers."

"I will talk to Eldsworth, we will discuss your idea. My thought is we give that rotten fever one more day, and if my son does not wake, then we go and visit Mister Fowler," declared Marista determinedly.

The conversation went on but Lillybeth abruptly excused herself and departed outside to the front garden. Marista became a bit concerned as she watched Lillybeth go, she knew the duckling well enough to know how fragile she could be, especially with how tired she was and while bearing the strain of the last few days.

Anati and Monique, however, shared a stern expression. They had concluded Lillybeth was not at all well mannered, with her out of sorts appearance, her well known history with the Mayor's Office, and her foiled attempt at eavesdropping.

The discussion soon came to an end; Doctor Lochswyn had agreed to Marista's wishes. They would allow the fever one more day, and if Hinsberth did not improve, and if the flight could be made accommodative to his condition, they would all make the journey to Mister Fowler's. Doctor Lochswyn also suggested, that at least for the moment, they keep the plan to themselves.

CHAPTER 5

❖   ❖   ❖

Lillybeth had become more silent than usual. She and her father were working side by side in his workshop — a large, tightly constructed shed nestled in the lush field beside their home. With its gently sloping roof supporting a veritable garden of herbs and flowers, the workshop was almost hidden in the tall grass but for the narrow, brushed footpath leading to the pair of wide front doors.

The workshop's interior was almost overrun with tools and parts and pieces of projects and inventions in various states of progress or neglect. Scraps of wood and metal and other useful materials Hackleberg had collected from around The Farm hung from the walls and were stuffed into every nook and cranny. Drawings and diagrams could be seen spread over every table, bench and shelf. On an otherwise empty wall were pinned three large sketches. On one was a drawing of a large balloon and gondola, the second was an odd looking submersible made of a hodgepodge of disparate parts, and the third was a type of rocket. Inside the workshop could be seen pieces of these inventions; a rocket casing and nose, a small prototype of the gondola, a makeshift propeller.

Earlier that evening, while they were keeping vigil over Hinsberth, Marista had quietly revealed to Hackleberg and Millybeth the plan to take Hinsberth to see Mister Fowler, and she implored them not to spread the news any further. Millybeth and Hackleberg immediately insisted on joining their friends for the journey. Marista told them of Doctor Lochswyn's request for Hinsberth to be kept warm, comfortable and protected from any change in weather, and Hackleberg naturally offered — with Lillybeth's assistance — to begin construction of an airworthy 'Transporter' to carry Hinsberth.

Everyone agreed that after the Transporter was completed, they would make an early morning departure for Mister Fowler's, when they were least likely to be seen. Because of the expected weight of the Transporter, passengers and cargo, Hackleberg estimated they would need at least four adult flyers to carry it aloft. It was quickly decided the duckling's parents were to fly the Transporter with Doctor Lochswyn inside watching over Hinsberth. Monique was to fly out front and provide navigation, with Anati at her side accompanying Lillybeth.

Upon arriving home, Hackleberg swiftly fashioned a design for the Transporter using inspiration from the platform Filipa and her friends constructed to return Lillybeth and Hinsberth to The Farm. He endeavored to shape the Transporter to resist swaying in flight, so Hinsberth would not be unduly jostled about.

Lillybeth was not privy to the earlier conversations over the plan and was bothered by the all the secrecy surrounding their efforts. She had gathered from what she had heard at the doctor's office that there was some disagreement between a Mister Fowler and his colleagues and the Mayor and Quillypom as well as some of the older ducks on The Farm. Lillybeth always found it difficult to understand such insensibilities. They certainly did not seem pertinent to helping Hinsberth.

As she and Hackleberg labored away in the workshop, Lillybeth thought to mention to her father what Hinsberth had asked of her during his brief moment of consciousness.

"Have you ever known anyone named Milchester?" she inquired nonchalantly.

"No. I do not think I have ever heard of anyone with that particular

CHAPTER 5

name," Hackleberg replied.

"What does 'free' mean? Supposing there were a Milchester of some sort, what do you think freeing him might mean? Or freeing 'them'? Who might they be?" Lillybeth wondered as she was sitting upon a shelf in a corner of the workshop, strapping a small harness around a wooden supporting post mounted to the wall.

Hackleberg lifted the goggles from his eyes and sat up. The Transporter was strung like a giant spider's web from every corner and filling most of the space in the workshop, and he came out from beneath the broad contraption, to look into his daughter's eyes.

"I am not sure who Milchester might be, or who 'they' might be, but from what you have said, it sounds as though Hinsberth was requesting you to free someone — some acquaintances of his, perhaps from a difficult situation. Since there does not seem to be a Milchester here on The Farm, I am not precisely certain to whom Hinsberth was referring. I wonder if he was dreaming? You mentioned that when he spoke to you he was very sleepy and had closed his eyes."

"Yes... Perhaps," said Lillybeth. "But he *was* rather serious about it. It took some effort for him to speak and I think he was well aware of what he was saying. I cannot fathom what it is he wants me to do, and I am quite bothered about it."

"Maybe, when he wakes up again..." said Hackleberg, stretching an elastic line over the top of the platform and fastening it on one side, "...we will find out."

Hackleberg uttered his last reply with conviction. He was well aware there was a shared, unspoken notion that the worst may yet happen — that Hinsberth might never wake up again, a possibility too inconceivable for Lillybeth to let rise out of her subconscious.

"I had the sense that Hinsberth believed by then it might be too late," said Lillybeth with urgency.

Hackleberg took note of his daughter's concerns, but without any answers, they could not do or say much more about the subject, and so the pair continued working quietly, side by side, well into the night.

❖   ❖   ❖

By morning, Hackleberg and Lillybeth had nearly finished the Transporter, and had strung it like a giant spider's web between the stouter trunks and branches in a grove of trees just near their home. Lillybeth was busily tugging on it here and jumping on it there, checking for rips or tears. Only once did she become entangled; for an instant she was caught hanging upside down by her feet, since Hackleberg was watching her closely. From his wings dangled a number devices for measurement. Every now and then he would hold a device up to his eye, or at wing's length, and mumble to himself, and then ask Lillybeth to perform an adjustment, and quickly switch to another. When after some time had been spent tugging and pulling and straightening and tightening, Hackleberg seemed assured the contraption he and his daughter had so swiftly constructed was of a sufficient sturdiness that it was ready to fulfill its purpose.

Needing some rest, they spent a long moment admiring their work, with feet splayed out and backs resting heavily against a particularly accommodating tree trunk. They slowly nursed a fresh breakfast, and afterward the pair decided it was time to make the short journey to the doctor's office to let their accomplices know the Transporter was ready for flight.

In accordance with Hackleberg's rather particular, detailed and thoroughly thought-out plans, the rectangular base of the Transporter was broad and made of a strong canvas. Each corner was finished with a metal ring to strengthen the mounts for the straps connecting the harnesses worn by the flyers who were to carry it aloft. Over the base was attached a sizeable dome, formed by two flexible masts mounted crosswise and meeting centrally, bound tightly together at the highest point. The dome was covered in several layers of fabric strangely similar to Hackleberg's clothes, and in each of the four directions resided a small round window, so those in the Transporter could communicate by sight with the flyers.

After savoring the rest and food, Hackleberg and Lillybeth laboriously stuffed the Transporter into the workshop and then waddled inside to clean up and prepare themselves for the short journey to Doctor Lochswyn's. But immediately upon stumbling wearily through the rear door, and not without some protest, they were both sent begrudgingly to bed for some well earned sleep by an uncompromising Millybeth. Millybeth had already decided she would be the one to go to Doctor Lochswyn's and report on the swift accomplishments of her husband and daughter. After ensuring Hackleberg and Lillybeth were soundly asleep, Millybeth departed at once for the doctor's office.

Arriving a short time later she and Doctor Lochswyn, Eldsworth and Marista huddled together in the spare patient room.

"Hackleberg and Lillybeth have finished construction of the Transporter," Millybeth whispered, trying to maintain an air of secrecy. "Hinsberth will be fine, he should be kept warm and dry and protected for the journey to Mister Fowler's."

Doctor Lochswyn, Marista and Eldsworth were rather surprised, for they had not expected the Transporter to be completed so quickly. They looked at Millybeth with astonishment.

Millybeth explained: "Hackleberg and Lillybeth spent the majority of the night working, and, as you might expect, they are at home, asleep."

"It is amazing, they work so fast. If you believe we can safely carry Hinsberth, I think we should depart at once," declared Marista.

She endeavored not to show it, but Marista was deeply worried. Hinsberth had been more or less unconscious now for several days and Doctor Lochswyn appeared to have run out of ideas.

Eldsworth, also desperate to see some sign of Hinsberth improving, agreed, "I think we should go now. If everyone is able, of course."

"I believe Hackleberg and Lillybeth can make the flight, but we will have to let them sleep again afterward," Millybeth offered. "Anati can fly in front of Lillybeth, to lighten her load."

Doctor Lochswyn did not offer any objection. She began busily rummaging through her shelves and cabinets, gathering everything she thought she may need for the voyage. She was jittery with nervous excitement, not only because of the hopeful possibility of learning a new medicinal trick or two, but also to be going on a bit of an adventure, something she had not done for quite some time.

To proceed with the plan, they would promptly need to gather their fellow accomplices. Eldsworth immediately set off into the air to retrieve Monique and Anati, and Millybeth departed for home to revive Hackleberg and Lillybeth.

Monique and Anati lived in a large house sited high on the slope of one of many rolling, grass covered hills near the edge of The Farm. Eldsworth flew fast until he spied the particularly ornate house which the Plummages called home. Painted brightly in a palette of many colors, the house was rather easy to see, even from a distance.

Eldsworth descended in a silent glide and alighted in front of the house with a flurry of intentionally hushed steps. Trying to maintain an air of secrecy, he looked around to see if anyone was watching, which naturally there was not, and then he lightly stepped up to the door and knocked quietly. After a brief moment, the door opened and Monique stood before him. Immediately upon seeing Eldsworth, she quickly surmised the purpose of his visit.

"Apologies for arriving so early," Eldsworth announced. And then in a hushed voice he added, "But we are ready to go."

"Yes, yes. I think I remember now where we are going. I will wake Anati, and we will be back to you just as soon as we can," Monique said wearily. "Or, you may wait here, no?" she added, waving Eldsworth inside.

Monique led Eldsworth into a large, open foyer with a wooden floor. There were odd sculptures, large and small, placed neatly on tables and the floor, and a grand one elevated on its own base in the center of the entryway. Eldsworth, too anxious to sit still, waddled about and studied the sculptures as Monique went back into the house shouting loudly, "Anati! Anati! We need to go!"

Eldsworth heard a tiny voice reply to Monique, and in the sharpness of the tone there seemed to be some kind of disagreement, and then came the much louder voice of Monique demanding, "NOW!"

"Anati! Come now, we need to leave!" Monique bellowed again as she charged back down the hall to Eldsworth. "She will be here. It takes her a little while. She is a little dramatic, no?"

"Well, I think she has a bit of independence; probably fine for her age," Eldsworth replied.

"I see. You are kind. But as for me, she is a bit challenging sometimes. Anati!"

"I am here," said Anati reluctantly, waddling slowly down the hall with weary eyes. She was dressed her usual but much too formal attire for this particular occasion, and although overdressed, Anati appeared as though she had donned her clothes in haste.

Two other members of the Plummage family poked their heads out of their respective doorways and glanced down the hall toward Monique and Anati.

"You two, be careful. Not like the last time, no?" said Monique's husband, Poullaire.

"Of course," replied Monique with a stern glance. "We will be fine."

"Pardon me. But if I may, the last time?" inquired Eldsworth.

"Later," said Monique shortly.

"Anati, is it fine if I use your…" asked Arela, Anati's younger sister, who, as with Anati and her mother, looked liked a miniature Anati.

"No," snapped Anati. "Wait until I return."

Anati then marched outside, passing Eldsworth with a purposeful stride and her bill in the air.

While Poullaire and Arela watched from the hallway, Monique and Eldsworth waved a quick good bye, closed the door and joined Anati outside. Together they took swiftly to the air, flying fast toward Doctor Lochswyn's.

❖   ❖   ❖

Millybeth readied herself for the challenge of rousing her family. Upon entering the bedroom a familiar site greeted her. Lillybeth was strewn, wings outstretched, on her back, across their bed with her mouth wide open and snoring loudly. Hackleberg was similarly indisposed, although slumped in a chair next to the bed. There was a diagram held in one wing, folded across his belly, and a pair of reading glasses hanging off one side of his bill, which was opened wide as he snored noisily, seemingly with his whole body. The cacophony they created together could be heard outside even as Millybeth approached on the footpath.

"This," she mumbled to herself while looking over her husband and daughter, "will not be easy."

Millybeth tapped on Lillybeth's shoulder.

"Lillybeth, time to go," she said softly.

Lillybeth rolled onto her stomach and began mumbling something unintelligible.

Millybeth tapped Lillybeth again and raised her voice, "We have to take Hinsberth this morning, and we must leave now before the whole Farm awakens."

Lillybeth opened her eyes, but quickly shut them again. Keeping her eyes closed, she turned onto her side… rolled to the edge of the bed… put one foot on the floor… then the other… and very slowly stood up. Almost, but not quite. She stood sagging forward, waiting for instructions.

With Lillybeth on her feet, Millybeth began the laborious effort of awaking Hackleberg.

"It is time to go, we have to take Hinsberth to Mister Fowler's," Millybeth said loudly into one ear as she nudged her husband on the shoulder.

Despite her prodding, Hackleberg only managed to open one eye, and only for an instant. Lillybeth sleepily joined in the effort. She grabbed one of Hackleberg's wings and gave it a good yank, which managed to shift Hackleberg's weight and he suddenly slid down out of the chair and plummeted to the floor with a loud thump. Finding himself on the floor was enough for Hackleberg to open both eyes, and he slowly gained his feet. As he rose he extracted his reading glasses from the side of his bill.

He glanced at Lillybeth, then at Millybeth, and seeming satisfied with his bearings he asked, "What day is it?"

"It is time to go!" Millybeth declared again.

"Go where?" asked Hackleberg.

And then his eyes slowly widened as he began to recall the Transporter and the plan for Hinsberth.

"Lillybeth!" Hackleberg exclaimed.

"Right here," said Lillybeth. She was now standing nearly upright, but with her eyes cinched shut and having wandered so close to Hackleberg he did not even realize she was there.

"The Transporter! We must take it to Doctor Lochswyn's!" exclaimed Hackleberg.

That they needed to deliver the Transporter to Doctor Lochswyn's had not been considered in Hackleberg's otherwise mostly well thought out plan. There were only the three of them, and he had designed the Transporter to be carried by no less than four adult flyers. Hackleberg knew flying the Transporter with Lillybeth, being so much smaller than he and Millybeth, would most likely result in some unexpected behavior during flight.

"Well — we will have to make due," he announced with some trepidation.

Turning to Lillybeth he said frankly, "You will have to put forth some effort to keep up with us. We will try to fly slowly and take the front, where most of the work will be."

Lillybeth nodded. She was becoming more alert. Her tired eyes widened as she began recalling what they needed to do, and the importance of the plan for helping Hinsberth.

Racing against the sun, the three ducks darted outside and into Hackleberg's workshop to retrieve the Transporter. They pushed and pulled and yanked the contraption out of the workshop and quickly attached the connecting straps to the corners. Then, after observing Hackleberg's demonstration, Millybeth and Lillybeth poked one wing up through their harnesses, then the other, and pulled them down over their heads, until they came to rest tightly around their middles. They connected the ends of the straps leading from the Transporter to their harnesses, and, at least according to Hackleberg's design, they were ready for flight.

Lillybeth was attached to one side at the rear. Hackleberg hoped all would go well if Lillybeth managed to keep the rear half of the Transporter elevated, while he and Millybeth did the hard work of flying the front into the wind.

They were ready to take to the air.

"Are you *certain?*" asked Millybeth, fidgeting nervously with her harness.

"Not entirely," replied Hackleberg with his eyes fixated on the sky. An instant later he suddenly shouted, "Three... two... one... GO!"

The three ducks took a step or two and flapped their wings with every bit of strength and speed they could muster, and in a spiralling cloud of dust they slowly rose into the air. But even flapping with all their might they could not manage much altitude. As they went, Lillybeth, performing her best impression of a hummingbird, was being pulled around to the rear as the corner without an attached flyer sunk downward and flapped in the breeze. Hackleberg and Millybeth beat their wings as hard as they could, but the weight of the Transporter was swiftly taxing their strength. The straps connecting them to the Transporter were stretching downward, pulling Hackleberg and Millybeth toward each other as the Transporter sank under them like an overloaded boat taking on water. They were flying so low they were barely clearing the tall spines of grass, and the rear edge of the Transporter was dangerously close to scraping the ground.

Lillybeth put all her effort into keeping the rear elevated and out of the foliage. A vivid vision of running themselves heads first and Transporter second into the Mayor's Office suddenly came into her mind's eye, and she tried to overwhelm the image with the furious effort of flying.

Slowly they appeared low in the sky over The Pond, scraping the tree tops, and after heaving the sagging Transporter above the rooftops of the neighboring homes, they immediately dropped, crashing hard into Doctor Lochswyn's backyard, shaken and breathless.

"That went well," noted Hackleberg, brushing himself free of herbs.

Millybeth only gave him a stern look. Knowing Hackleberg as she did, she was well aware he likely considered their short awkward flight and crash landing a rather successful test.

Lillybeth was pulled forward as they fell and went face first into the dome, and was thus cushioned and none the worse for wear. Like her father, seemed to be oddly pleased with the Transporter.

❖   ❖   ❖

CHAPTER 5

Not moments before the Transporter crashed into Doctor Lochswyn's backyard, Eldsworth had alighted with Monique and Anati, and they were in the spare room in fervent but muted discussion with Marista and the doctor, considering what to do should anything unexpected happen during the voyage.

Doctor Lochswyn had only just completed her preparations, having her satchel and two bags packed with remedies and reference books and a healthy reserve of the secret ingredients for her own special porridge.

With the loud thud and cloud of dirt rising from the rear yard, the conversation came to a sudden halt as they went to investigate.

Hackleberg greeted them with a dusty, quirky smile, which struck an unlikely chord between pride and being glad to be alive. Millybeth only presented a relieved grin. Lillybeth merely poked at the Transporter dome.

All eyes swiftly turned from the flyers to the contraption which lie mostly unburied in Doctor Lochswyn's now former herb garden. Millybeth directed an apologetic smile to Doctor Lochswyn. Lillybeth took no notice and continued poking her wing into the dome to make sure it still had its firm but forgiving structure. When Lillybeth was sure the Transporter was in good order, she hopped off and started toward the door with the intention of checking on Hinsberth. But when she caught sight of Anati, she felt her stomach go to knots and her throat seize, and being exhausted she had little reserve left to quiet them, so she instead sat down to rest.

Doctor Lochswyn, Marista, Eldsworth, Monique and Anati went curiously toward the Transporter, intending to help brush off the dirt and examine the contraption thoroughly. Doctor Lochswyn grew a curious expression they had not seen before. As she gazed upon the Transporter, her eyes belied an anxious excitement. She could barely contain herself as she examined the inside of Lillybeth and Hackleberg's invention, where she was to fly with Hinsberth.

"There is certainly enough room," she announced to no one in particular, poking her head inside the flap where one could gain entrance to the dome.

As everyone examined the harnesses and questioned Hackleberg about the efficacy and safety of his design, Lillybeth rose to her feet and slipped inside the doctor's office.

In the patient room, Lillybeth noticed Hinsberth had not moved. He was as she had last seen him, lying flat on his back. It was as if she had never left. His shallow breathing and burning hot skin dampened Lillybeth's hopes. "He is sleeping, why does he not heal?" Lillybeth thought to herself. She could not fathom how his illness could go on and on without end, without any improvement.

With light steps she waddled across the room, gathered some fresh ice from the ice box, and soaked a clean towel in cold water. After replacing the melting ice and setting the cold towel over Hinsberth's forehead, she quietly slid her wings into her satchel and slowly pulled out Hinsberth's sweater. She had washed and neatly folded the sweater, and having placed it in her satchel it had not left her side since she found it propped upon sticks. Lillybeth carefully spread the sweater over Hinsberth's blankets and tucked the sleeves underneath.

Startled by footsteps, she turned to see Doctor Lochswyn and Marista step through the doorway. Marista recognized the sweater immediately, and she knew what Lillybeth had done. She went over to Lillybeth, reached down with her large wing and patted her gently on the head. Doctor Lochswyn thanked Lillybeth for being so kind to replace Hinsberth's towels and ice, which was one more step on her long list to complete before departure.

Since words could not proceed past her throat, Lillybeth simply nodded and waddled outside to help with the Transporter.

❖   ❖   ❖

The Smythes worked diligently to ready the Transporter for another, and hopefully longer, flight. They brushed away the dirt and dust from the crash and secured the harnesses. Monique helped when needed. The sun was climbing higher into the sky; it would soon clear the hills and trees to the east and Doctor Lochswyn's neighbors would be rising along with it. Time was short.

Eldsworth went to the patient room to help Doctor Lochswyn and Marista carry Hinsberth from his bed. Doctor Lochswyn had in her possession blankets with handles woven into the corners for carrying injured patients. She brought one to Hinsberth's bedside, and while Marista and Eldsworth gently lifted Hinsberth, she swiftly spread it flat under him. And then, gazing over the sleeping Hinsberth, before lifting him for the short walk to the Transporter, Doctor Lochswyn, Marista and Eldsworth shared a silent, anxious glance, for they knew not what might lie ahead.

Lillybeth came waddling into the garden after conducting a thorough inspection of the Transporter, but she stopped suddenly in mid-step, overhearing Monique and Anati in a contentious discussion regarding the flight.

"No, I do not want to fly the whole distance," Anati declared defiantly.

"You will fly with me. And out in front of Lillybeth, you know she is exhausted," retorted Monique. "Besides, you do not know how far it is, do you?"

"I do not have to know. My wings are sore and I feel sleepy. You awakened me much too early," Anati replied stubbornly. She turned her bill to the air.

Monique folded her wings in a sign of frustration.

"I say again — and not one more time, you are *not* going to be carried with the doctor!"

Lillybeth felt her stomach claw its way into her throat as she realized Anati was trying to demand her way into traveling inside the dome with Doctor Lochswyn and Hinsberth. She closed her eyes and tried to pretend she was not listening to the conversation, for she felt as though she were intruding. She waddled behind the Transporter, out of sight, and sat down.

Monique and Anati continued on spouting words of a disagreeable sort until Hackleberg decided he might be able to resolve the situation with a technical justification.

He stood facing the Transporter and began thinking aloud, well within hearing distance of Monique and her petulant daughter, "Yes... I see. During the test flight, we seemed to be overburdened with weight. I seemed to have perhaps made a miscalculation or two... The transporter is heavier than I anticipated. The weight is the determining factor. For the flight we must keep the Transporter as light as possible."

There was a silent pause between Monique and Anati, and then finally Monique announced, "I think *that* settles it. If you travel inside, perhaps the doctor cannot carry everything she needs. You *will* fly in front of Lillybeth."

Without recourse, Anati stomped off and sat down alone in the garden.

Lillybeth heard everything from her hidden perch behind the Transporter, and she quietly thanked her father under her breath, wanting very much to rush over and wrap her wings around him. However, she did not want to do or say anything which might have Monique or Anati believing she had been eavesdropping again, even though with the volume of their conversation, listening in was thoroughly unavoidable. Lillybeth had the sense Monique and Anati did not think very highly of her, and she did not wish to provide any further supporting evidence for their, in Lillybeth's rather thoughtful opinion, errant judgement of her character.

❖   ❖   ❖

The morning sky was brightening noticeably as the final preparations were made for departure. Marista and Doctor Lochswyn came outside and Marista suddenly announced in a hushed voice, "My Hinsberth is ready!"

"We need to go now!" added Doctor Lochswyn anxiously, as she glanced upward into the glimmering sky.

Doctor Lochswyn was quite cognizant of the need for secrecy, as like Monique she remembered the old rift — a chasm of some kind between the Mayor's Office and Mister Fowler, and consequently the Mayor's Office had historically discouraged precisely what she and her accomplices were about to do.

Finally they were ready to depart and Doctor Lochswyn crawled into the dome to arrange her things in preparation for receiving

Hinsberth. Then she, Marista and Eldsworth swiftly and noiselessly returned inside the house to retrieve Hinsberth. As they waddled quickly down the hall to the patient room, Doctor Lochswyn happened to glance out the front window and spotted a visitor approaching on the footpath. In an instant she recognized the brisk and stiff gate of the visitor, and she froze in panic.

"*Quillypom*," she whispered, pointing toward the window.

Marista's eyes popped wide and she hurriedly turned and scuttled back toward the rear of the house to let down the shades and cover the windows. She slid her wing back and forth under her bill, motioning to everyone outside to keep silent, but her signal was met only with confounded expressions. In frustration Marista whispered out a window, as quietly as she could with her otherwise booming voice, "*Quillypom!*"

Those outside froze, unsure what to do. From inside the house the Transporter was in plain sight. They hoped with the blinds closed Quillypom would not notice anything amiss.

Millybeth and Hackleberg silently wondered if Quillypom would be able to make a connection between the Transporter and a journey to Mister Fowler's even if she were to spot it. Although they thought it would certainly be best to avoid having to find the answer. Explaining the presence of the Transporter would certainly require an elaborate fib, and if they were found out, it would likely finish their family's already precarious relationship with the Mayor's Office.

Eldsworth remained in the patient room watching over Hinsberth, and after drawing the shades over all the windows with a view toward the Transporter, Marista slowed her pace, took a deep breath and calmly went down the hallway to join him.

Doctor Lochswyn brushed the dust off her feathers, straightened her attire and attempted to exude an air of calm professionalism to hide a discomforting mixture of excitement and panic. She proceeded quickly to the door to answer for Quillypom.

Quillypom knocked once upon the door and Doctor Lochswyn immediately swung it open. Quillypom was taken by surprise, her wing still in midair.

"Ah, good fortune I have this morning. You were evidently passing by the door just as I arrived," stated Quillypom while lowering her wing.

"Yes, indeed. A good morning… certainly. Lovely weather, would you say?" inquired Doctor Lochswyn nervously. With her extensive interest and training in medicine, neither interpersonal manipulation nor broad scale deception were part of her conversational repertoire.

"So, are you feeling quite well?" she asked of Quillypom, and then quickly added, "Not that you look ill, mind you, of course."

Not sure what to make of the doctor's unusual behavior, under the brim of her rather formal looking hat, Quillypom's feathered brow came to furrow.

"Well, I am not feeling my best. I have no desire to complain but I seem to have come down with a bit of a bug. Unusual at this time of year I know, especially with the fine weather we have had lately. But I am not feeling quite myself," explained Quillypom.

"Really?" replied Doctor Lochswyn. And catching Quillypom's quizzical expression she added nervously, "I mean — and, for — for how long has this been going on?"

"Perhaps a few days. That little Lillybeth has come to my office — more than once. I wonder if she brought along a bug of some sort."

"Doubtful. I have seen Lillybeth, although, not recently mind you. But the last time — yes, she came to visit Hinsberth. I can assure you she seemed quite well," replied Doctor Lochswyn. She was obviously anxious. She fumbled over her words.

"Might I come in?" inquired Quillypom impatiently. "I prefer not to discuss such matters in the doorway."

"Oh! Yes, of course. My apologies. The room over here is free."

Doctor Lochswyn waved a wing for Quillypom to proceed into the spare patient room and she closed the door behind her.

With Doctor Lochswyn's many years of experience she knew Quillypom may not really be ill, but might rather just be needing someone to talk to. But the doctor was nearly in a state of panic as she became ever more aware of her complete inability to carry on meaningful conversation while trying to conceal the plan for taking Hinsberth to Mister Fowler's.

Marista and Eldsworth could hear Quillypom and Doctor Lochswyn's voices emanating from the spare patient room, and they also sensed the plan was in danger, for Quillypom was undoubtedly astute enough to detect when someone was trying to hide something from her, and she was being very deliberate in her speech to Doctor Lochswyn. Quillypom nevertheless believed the doctor possessed a highly refined character, and was most likely just having an out-of-sorts day.

Doctor Lochswyn and Quillypom nestled down upon the pillows in the spare room, and Doctor Lochswyn swiftly resorted to her standard set of patient questions to sway her thoughts away from the plan and determine precisely what Quillypom might be needing.

An odd silence descended over the house, only punctuated by

Doctor Lochswyn and Quillypom's voices, as everyone else waited impatiently for what they hoped would be a brief conversation. For every moment that passed, the probability of departing unseen grew smaller, and Marista and Eldsworth had no desire to wait yet another day.

Marista held the least patience of all, and Eldsworth had to take hold of her wing to keep her seated. Marista's tolerance for anyone interfering in her plans, especially if those plans regarded her family, was next to nought, and the consequences could be abrupt and unpleasant. Eldsworth knew, however, that this was a particularly sensitive circumstance for Quillypom, for a trip to the Doctor is not of anyone's concern excepting doctor and patient, and a confrontation with Quillypom was not in anyone's interest.

Presently, the door to the spare room slowly opened, and while still in ardent conversation, Doctor Lochswyn escorted Quillypom to the front door.

After a brief moment, Quillypom departed, coddling a small package from which wafted the aroma of the more potent ingredients resident in Doctor Lochswyn's mysterious porridge. Doctor Lochswyn casually closed the door after Quillypom made her way through the garden.

Upon hearing the door latch a great sigh of relief wafted over the house, and Marista hastily rose to her feet and marched intently down the hall to the rear door.

"Get ready!" she whispered in a piercing voice.

Marista threw open the window blinds and returned to the patient room to retrieve her son. Those in the rear yard scrambled to prepare for take off. Hackleberg and Millybeth immediately harnessed themselves to the Transporter. They were ready to leave the ground.

Taking hold of the blanket beneath him, Marista, Eldsworth, and Doctor Lochswyn ever so gently raised Hinsberth from the bed and carried him down the hall and out the rear door. In short order, Marista and Eldsworth shuttled Hinsberth into the Transporter, and Doctor Lochswyn crawled inside as Hinsberth's parents carefully tucked him in for the journey.

Once settled beside Hinsberth, Doctor Lochswyn gave a reassuring nod to Marista and Eldsworth.

"He will be fine. I will make sure of it," she stated in a confident tone.

Eldsworth closed the flap door while Marista kept a pair of worried eyes fixated on her son. Doctor Lochswyn tied the flap down on the inside. Marista and Eldsworth waddled swiftly to the rear of the Transporter, and recalling Hackleberg's instructions, they put one wing through, then the other, and pulled the harnesses over their heads. With the harnesses wrapped tightly about their middles, they tugged and pulled to make sure everything was fast and secure.

With those carrying the Transporter ready for take off, Monique, Anati and Lillybeth sprinted a short distance through the garden. They beat their wings as silently as they could manage and ascended into the air. They flew low in a tight circle, just above the doctor's office, waiting to lead the others to their as yet unknown destination.

Hackleberg immediately counted down, "Three... two... one... GO!"

Marista, Eldsworth, Hackleberg and Millybeth began beating their wings furiously, sending aloft the sound of brushing wings and a swirl of dust.

CHAPTER 5

With great determination, the four flyers beat the air in a frenzy of feathers and the Transporter gradually rose from the ground. Doctor Lochswyn had to steady herself and Hinsberth inside. Despite the precariousness of the situation and the gravity of the journey for Hinsberth and his family and friends, Doctor Lochswyn found herself unable to keep from grinning. Through the Transporter window she watched her house drop out of view as she and Hinsberth were carried higher and higher into the sky.

THE TRANSPORTER

"They lowered themselves and the Transporter into the scalloped gap between a dense maze of branches and leaves extending down to the forest floor below."

ONE PROBLEM AT A TIME

MONIQUE, ANATI AND LILLYBETH flew determinedly out ahead of the Transporter. They followed Monique as she recognized familiar landmarks leading to where Mister Fowler and his friends had settled. Even though she had traveled to Mister Fowler's more than once with her mother, it had been a number of years since the last visit and the landscape had certainly changed. The trees were taller than she remembered, and were more dense in some places and less dense in others, but she believed they would find their way.

Millybeth, Hackleberg, Marista and Eldsworth were putting forth tremendous effort carrying the Transporter; their strength was fully taxed by the weight. Doctor Lochswyn kept close watch on the flyers from inside the Transporter. She noted how hard the flyers were working and hoped the journey would be shorter than anticipated. She was especially concerned when they passed over the thick groves of forest, for at times a safe landing spot was nowhere to be seen. If for any reason they were forced from the sky, the result could undoubtedly be harmful to herself, her patient, the flyers and the Transporter, perhaps leaving them with the daunting prospect of covering long distances by foot while carrying the feverish Hinsberth.

As she reluctantly agreed, Anati flew in front of Lillybeth so Lillybeth could fly with relative ease in her air stream. This Lillybeth considered a generous gift, since having had so little sleep she was rather fatigued. Anati, however, was still spiteful over having been barred from traveling in the Transporter and for being told by her mother to fly in front of Lillybeth to lighten her load. Lillybeth could sense Anati's disgruntlement, and the two of them had not exchanged a word since Anati had arrived at Doctor Lochswyn's. Anati had no idea how upsetting this was for Lillybeth. Lillybeth still wished to salvage the opportunity for her friendship, but always being short for words when her stomach seemed, at the most inopportune times, to gobble them voraciously, she had not yet figured out how to approach her. And importantly for Lillybeth, there was the rather discomforting issue of Anati's curious interest in Hinsberth; something Lillybeth could not even consider without having to calm her stomach and control her breathing.

❖ ❖ ❖

Monique was not certain of exactly when she realized she was lost. "Oh, no!" she thought to herself in a panic. Was she headed in the right direction? There was nothing familiar in the present landscape. Where were they?

Suddenly short of breath, she took a quick backward glance at the condition of the flyers and the Transporter. "So far... no problems", she thought to herself, but this brought little comfort. As they flew on, she became more and more distraught. What had she done? Her eyes roamed swiftly over the ground ahead. She looked for a safe landing spot, but saw only trees. She turned to Anati.

When Anati caught her mother's gaze she knew immediately they were in some degree of trouble, for Monique's emotions, as long as her face could be seen, were never much of a mystery.

Presently, they were soaring over dense forest and a suitable landing site for the Transporter was nowhere in sight. Monique reluctantly decided to continue on in the same direction until a large enough clearing could be found for landing. She imagined having to announce the rather unfortunate and embarrassing news that her memory had apparently failed her, and the notion was accompanied by an immediate, sickening queasiness in her stomach. What if she had led them out into the wilderness, only to endanger Hinsberth's health? She had only been trying to help. But now she believed she was failing those who put their trust in her. Perhaps, she hoped, a quick rest would allow her to clear her mind and reclaim her bearings. Mister Fowler's was not all that far away, she remembered, although it was somewhat intentionally hidden. It would perhaps be even more so now; the trees were decidedly more thick and numerous than she remembered.

Lillybeth caught sight of the worried glances passing between Monique and Anati. Anati, like her mother, had very little ability to mask whatever she was thinking or feeling, and Lillybeth began to wonder what the matter was. She found it difficult to approach Anati to ask her what was wrong, but she also thought it could be an opportunity to speak to her and perhaps make a better impression. Feeling bold for an instant, Lillybeth darted ahead and came up alongside Anati.

"Anati!" Lillybeth called out.

Anati was surprised to find Lillybeth at her side, and at first she went on as if Lillybeth was not even there.

But Lillybeth was persistent.

"Anati!" she called again.

Anati realized Lillybeth was not going anywhere for the moment and she turned her head in Lillybeth's direction.

"Anati!" Lillybeth shouted again, but this time while looking straight into her eyes and obviously already in possession of her attention.

"Yes! Whatever is it?" Anati exclaimed sharply, with some annoyance.

"My apologies, but I could not help but notice. Is there something wrong?" asked Lillybeth politely.

Anati was well aware Lillybeth was younger than herself and she did not see it as Lillybeth's place to try and fix the problems of her elders. She could only wonder about the spate of ill mannered behavior from her new acquaintance.

"Nothing is wrong, I am sure," said Anati with her characteristic upturned bill. She knew her response was not completely honest. And so did Lillybeth

"I see," said Lillybeth disappointedly.

The optimistic Lillybeth remained hopeful she might still gain Anati's trust, so in her most polite and helpful voice she added, "Well, please let me know if you should need me for anything."

Anati only nodded.

In their brief conversation Lillybeth did not feel she made much progress toward any kind of budding friendship. She sank back behind Anati, pleased that at least she had left the opportunity open.

Meanwhile, in the clear air behind Monique, Anati and Lillybeth, the flyers were becoming more and more weary, and they all hoped they would soon reach their destination. Doctor Lochswyn was watching Hinsberth closely. Despite a bit of swaying from side to side, his condition seemed unchanged. The doctor was satisfied with the journey so far.

Monique had seen Lillybeth fly up to Anati but had not overheard their conversation. She fixed her eyes on Anati and then glanced downward, wordlessly asking with her eyes for Anati to help scout for a landing spot.

On and on they flew; the forest spread thick and dense below them. Monique became more and more worried, and in frustration she considered turning around and heading directly back toward The Farm, but suddenly, a new problem arose.

Presently, Doctor Lochswyn was frantically motioning to the flyers. With eyes wide as saucers she pointed downward toward the floor in a near panic. Marista saw her and shouted something to Millybeth, who turned to glance at the Transporter and then exclaimed loudly, "Lillybeth! Something is wrong with the Doctor!"

Lillybeth turned her head to the Transporter and she could see that Doctor Lochswyn was in distress. Alarmed that something terrible may have happened to Hinsberth, Lillybeth banked hard and swiftly came up beside the Transporter where Doctor Lochswyn could see her.

"Lillybeth!" shouted a breathless Doctor Lochswyn upon seeing the small duckling through the side window, appearing as though hovering in mid air. "The bottom! Quickly! Look!"

Lillybeth swerved underneath the Transporter and inspected it closely. One of the seams near the center of the floor was beginning to spread, forming a wide gap. The threads were unraveling fast and waving freely in the wind.

Lillybeth's heart jumped.

She darted past the Transporter and came up alongside her father.

"The seams — at the center — they are coming apart!" she shouted at the top of her voice.

Hackleberg cringed.

Ever since they finished the final assembly, in the back of his mind, a faint but persistent notion that he had forgotten something had been tingling on the edge of his consciousness. He had returned more than once to check all the elements; platform, straps, harnesses. He had observed Lillybeth tugging and pulling and did not notice anything amiss. How could he have forgotten one of the seams? Something so basic, so fundamental? Being fastened to the Transporter, Hackleberg was not in a position to assess the immediacy of the danger or to concoct a fix.

"The *seams*!?" Hackleberg shouted. "Are you *sure*?"

Lillybeth nodded, and was struck suddenly with an idea. Hackleberg watched in dismay as she abruptly darted up beside Anati.

"Lillybeth!" he called out.

Anati's bill had become more level, her eyes seemed to have widened and she had a worried look Lillybeth had never seen before.

"What is happening back there?" Anati asked anxiously as Lillybeth came into view.

"The Transporter. There is something wrong with the floor. It is coming apart!" exclaimed an exasperated Lillybeth.

All at once Anati descended into panic. Shaking her head she exclaimed, "Oh no! No, this is not good. Not good at all!"

"But I have an idea," said Lillybeth in a breathless voice but trying her best to sound confident and reassuring.

"But it is worse than you know," declared Anati fatalistically.

"Why, what am I missing? What do I not know?" pleaded Lillybeth.

Anati lowered her voice so her words would be for Lillybeth alone, and told her in a trembling whisper, "We are lost!"

"I see... Well — one problem at a time," said Lillybeth, trying to remain calm.

She reminded herself of the advice she had given Hinsberth before taking off on their search for the edge of the sky, a bit of advice she had incidentally conjured up on the spot: When exploring the unknown, the important thing when facing danger was not to panic. Lillybeth plunged a wing into her satchel, dropping fast in altitude as she did so, and pulled out an old rusted compass, to which was attached a long, thin strap. She flapped hard and rose back to Anati's side.

"How are you feeling?" she asked.

"What do you mean?" replied Anati in bafflement, confused as to why Lillybeth would suddenly wish to probe her emotional state, especially given the circumstances.

"Your energy? Do you feel strong?" asked Lillybeth firmly.

"Yes. I mean... I am not tired. Yes — I feel fine for flying," Anati stammered.

"Good! Might I ask you to drop back, below the Transporter?" asked a suddenly focused Lillybeth.

Anati glanced over to Monique to have her mother's opinion on collaborating with the ill-mannered Lillybeth. At this point Monique was open for anything, and she nodded to Anati and shifted her eyes to the Transporter, silently telling her to follow Lillybeth's instructions.

At once Anati dropped back and came up underneath the Transporter.

Marista and Eldsworth were not aware of what, precisely, was happening. They had seen Doctor Lochswyn's sudden panic but only Hackleberg, Lillybeth, Anati and the doctor were aware of the cause. With great trepidation they watched as Anati and Lillybeth flew tightly together under the Transporter. They knew something must be terribly wrong.

Lillybeth fell rapidly as she fumbled about with the compass. She plunged a wing into her satchel and pulled out a large needle. She had to flap hard and fast to regain altitude and, flying up beside Anati, they soared level with one other beneath the Transporter.

Doctor Lochswyn was frantically going from one window to the next, trying to see what was happening. She could only see Monique out ahead of the Transporter.

"Lillybeth!" she called.

"Right here!" came a voice from below.

Doctor Lochswyn could breathe again.

Lillybeth tied the compass strap loosely around the feathers of her wing, and she turned her gaze to Anati.

"Might I ask for you to fly a little lower? A little less altitude?" Lillybeth asked with a focused voice.

"Why! What are you going to do?" inquired a perplexed Anati as she made a slight descent.

"Hold steady! I am going to flip onto your back!" replied Lillybeth simply.

"What!? No! Wait!!" Anati shouted in a panic.

And as she was protesting the idea, Lillybeth abruptly dipped one wing downward and kicked herself up and over, landing mostly on Anati's back as Anati flapped her wings wildly while trying to hold her position.

Lillybeth swiftly maneuvered herself to the middle of Anati's back.

"Quickly! Up toward the seams! I can't reach!" Lillybeth shouted as she was bobbing up and down with each beat of Anati's wings.

Marista and Eldsworth watched the two ducklings with eyes popped wide. Had Anati and Lillybeth lost their minds?

Anati was strained to the limit, beating her wings in an all out effort, for it was all she could do to maintain altitude with the weight of Lillybeth on her back. She breathlessly tried to hold fast under the gap in the seam. Lillybeth worked quickly. She wove the compass strap around the gap, pulling it tight with every loop. Soon she had used the full length of the strap, and although a small hole remained, she tied it off in as tight a knot as she could manage. Just then she and Anati fell away, tumbling far beneath the Transporter. Anati had rapidly hit the depths of exhaustion. She dipped to one side and Lillybeth rolled off her back and flapped fast to come up beside her.

Lillybeth exclaimed excitedly, "I believe that may do it!"

For the first time in memory Anati was at a loss for words. She was not sure whether she should be angry, frustrated, or surprised, or even appreciative of the audacity and unpredictability of her new acquaintance.

Regarding Anati's silence, Lillybeth immediately concluded she may have angered her, and she broke the silence with the hope of avoiding an agonizing reticence, "Thank you Anati. I will remain here and make sure the repair holds. If you wish you may want to go on ahead," she suggested politely.

Anati nodded. Without a word she hurried ahead to her mother's side.

Lillybeth worried she had once again managed to offend Anati in some manner. For a long moment she stewed in frustration. Why could she not break through to Anati?

After Hackleberg noticed Anati had returned to flying beside Monique and Lillybeth seemed in relative calm under the Transporter, he sighed in relief. He knew the two ducklings must have concocted at least a temporary fix for the seam. He gestured to Doctor Lochswyn to tell her all was well. With Hackleberg's signal, Doctor Lochswyn collapsed to the floor, exhausted from the excitement, and no longer grinning over the prospect of being carried in flight.

Marista and Eldsworth were still unsure of what all the fuss was about, but they noticed Doctor Lochswyn was no longer gesticulating in panic and concluded that whatever the problem was, it must be solved, at least for now.

❖ ❖ ❖

Anati pondered Lillybeth's idea of taking one problem at a time, and as she flew beside her mother she wished to confirm her suspicions, "We are lost, no?"

Monique gulped her pride and replied, "Yes — But do not remind me, I had almost forgotten."

Anati sent a bewildered glance.

Monique continued to speak, in short phrases punctuated by some erratic flapping of wings, as if she became lost in thought between her words and consequently was forgetting how to fly: "Not lost completely — We can always turn around and return straight back to The

Farm — But what a waste — So much effort, by everyone."

Anati understood her mother felt responsible for the present predicament. She had been the one to suggest taking Hinsberth to Mister Fowler's and now she could not remember where it was. Being already quite some distance from The Farm she did not wish to turn around; the entire endeavor would then seem to have been futile and foolhardy. Monique knew time was of great import for Hinsberth and his family and friends. Hinsberth had to be better. Soon.

Although she had always sought to be involved in whatever was happening on The Farm, Monique rarely had a wing in precipitating events, and she knew she was now uncomfortably out of her realm of experience. Her daughter knew it too.

"Do you think I should tell the others?" Anati asked in a hushed voice.

"No, not yet. I was hoping to land first. I think it would be harder for everyone to hear the news in the air, especially without a landing spot in sight. And perhaps, maybe I will recognize something familiar; some hill or tree or stone — and then we will be on our way," Monique replied in a wishful fashion.

Anati generally agreed with her mother's reasoning, it would certainly be discouraging for the others to know they were lost, but waiting too long to tell them might make the situation even worse. There had to be a glade nearby, the forest could not go on unbroken forever. Anati glanced behind her to assess the flyers. They seemed rather focused and determined. Her mother was right. It would not do to break their spirit. She looked at the Transporter and wondered just how large a clearing they would need for a safe landing, then she put her eyes to the ground and began searching intently for a suitable spot. Anati flew silently beside her mother; she peered ahead over the endless verdant sea of forest.

Suddenly, Anati recognized a narrow gap in the canopy which almost certainly marked the path of a brook winding its way through the forest. She hoped there might be a sand bar or a broad meander large enough for a landing.

Anati's voice abruptly cut across the sky, "Look there! Water! Maybe a spot, no?"

"Yes! Yes, I see it! We will veer downward, just a little," stated Monique.

Monique turned to follow the gap in the trees, and the rest of the flyers adjusted to her change in direction. It was not long before Monique and Anati sighted a small glen which seemed large enough for the Transporter.

Hackleberg and Millybeth noticed the quick drop in altitude as they descended toward the hole in the tree tops, but they did not see any sign of habitation. It was certainly not what they had been expecting. Why were they descending? With the absence of buildings of any kind, they thought if this were Mister Fowler's, the stories about the proclivity of this place for healing Hinsberth would seem to have been greatly exaggerated.

Lillybeth, knowing they were lost, suspected Monique was leading them to a brief landing to rest their wings before beginning the long, disappointing return to The Farm. Although Monique had forgotten where Mister Fowler had settled, Lillybeth was very much hoping Monique would spot something familiar and recover her memory. She suspected Monique held a similar hope; she had not yet given up, and perhaps this was why she had not yet told anyone of the problem.

CHAPTER 6

As they slowed into a steep descent, Lillybeth flew out from beneath the Transporter and soared high into the sky. She intended to circle around so the flyers could prepare for what appeared to be a rather difficult landing; they would need to approach slow and steady over the tree tops with the Transporter and then drop rapidly into the glen. As Lillybeth rose into the sky, the view to the horizon spread ever wider, and she peered deep into the distance for any sign of a settlement hidden in the trees, indeed, for anything unusual or out of place.

To her complete surprise, she saw something.

Far in the distance, in the sky below her, just above the tree tops and flying fast, Lillybeth spied a familiar shape. She had to focus to be sure her eyes were not playing tricks, or her imagination was not putting into the sky something which was not really there. But the svelte shape and the brisk and nervous manner of movement offered but one conclusion.

Lillybeth darted down to Monique and came up between her and Anati. Her eyes were round with excitement, and without a word she pointed her wing toward the small shape skimming above the tree tops some distance away. Following Lillybeth's wing out into the sky, Monique's eyes suddenly popped wide, and she dipped so Anati could see as well.

Doctor Lochswyn and the flyers saw Lillybeth descend fast from out of the heights and speed up ahead. They noticed the sudden change from a slow turning descent into a veering ascent in the opposite direction.

"What *are* they doing?" Doctor Lochswyn muttered to herself, watching out the front window. The flyers were equally curious.

"The Mayor's Messenger! What is *she* doing out here?" asked Monique. She reasoned aloud: "She works in the Mayor's Office and I have a hunch they know precisely where Mister Fowler has settled. Maybe, Mister Fowler and The Farm are not quite so far apart after all."

"That is what I thought too, as soon as I saw her," said Lillybeth. "Where else could she be going? There is not anything out here, nowhere to go, nobody to visit, is there?" she asked Monique.

Monique shook her head.

"I say we follow her," suggested Anati.

"I agree!" Lillybeth exclaimed at once with enthusiasm. She was happy to have a chance to side with Anati.

"We will follow her, certainly. But we must remain hidden. If she is traveling to Mister Fowler's, it may be that not everyone is being honest with us back on The Farm," said Monique.

Monique, Anati and Lillybeth banked in unison and descended to fly fast just above the tree tops. They had to fly swiftly as the Messenger was now only a tiny speck in the distance, and with the Transporter they were going to have some difficulty keeping her in sight.

By this time Millybeth and Hackleberg were rather confused as to what was happening with the three flyers ahead of them. Given their daughter's penchant for unintentional mischief, they wondered... she had ascended high into the sky... she had spoken to Monique... they were now changing course... what could Lillybeth have said to her?

They banked hard to follow Monique. The flyers curved across the sky until they were following behind the Messenger, but at a distance they hoped sufficient to remain unseen. Millybeth, Hackleberg, Marista and Eldsworth struggled mightily to gain the speed necessary to remain close to Monique, Anati and Lillybeth.

Monique's hopes grew. As long as the Messenger did not look behind her, maybe they were on their way.

❖   ❖   ❖

Quillypom was sitting in her office studying the instructions Doctor Lochswyn had placed into the package of ingredients for making her unusual but potent porridge. In addition to the neatly ordered instructions, the package held several pouches of herbs and spices, each twisted round at the top and bound with a tiny ribbon. Doctor Lochswyn had also given her a collection of small measuring cups and an ancillary note reminding her to be precise with the amount of each ingredient and the sequence of each step.

Quillypom went through the steps one by one, and having warmed a pot of water, she had just returned from the stove down the hall. With her pot of water at the precise temperature and holding a small spoon in her wing, she was ready for the next step. She read again the instructions and examined her collection of ingredients. After raising each bag in turn to her eyes and scrutinizing the label over her spectacles, she looked up from her desk in consternation.

"Peppermint. No peppermint," she announced aloud.

She very deliberately set the small spoon down on her desk, rose from her chair and proceeded to depart from her office by creaking open the heavy wooden door. After striding strictly down the hall with a stern gaze fixed forward, she went outside and directed herself determinedly toward Doctor Lochswyn's.

Arriving at the doctor's office she rapped on the door in her usual pattern of three precise and evenly spaced knocks, and waited.

Quillypom heard no movement inside the house, which she thought surprising, for she knew Hinsberth and his parents were in all likelihood still inside, in addition to Doctor Lochswyn. She waited impatiently for a few moments and then rapped again, more forcefully this time. Still she received not a sign of anyone coming to answer and she leaned over to one side, far enough to peer into the window of the patient room. She could barely see into the darkened room, but there was sufficient detail to notice the bed appeared flat. No one was present. She rapped one final time on the door, and still without an answer, she turned round and marched in a huff back to the Mayor's Office.

After only an instant she halted in mid-step, suddenly recalling Lillybeth and Hinsberth's arrival on The Farm after their ill-fated adventure. And she wondered…

She would send someone to check, she thought to herself suspiciously, whether the Smythes and the Smerkingtons were still present on The Farm.

Quillypom swiftly returned to her office. She wasted not a moment, she scribbled and stamped a request on a piece of rather official looking stationary. She then briskly strode down the hall and turned into a side room. She silently presented the request to a member of her staff, clad in the formal attire universal to the Mayor's Office but presiding over a much smaller desk. He accepted the request and after a quick read, he nodded. It would be done. Quillypom turned and marched back down the hall, but instead of returning to her office, she continued up a small flight of stairs, coming to face the weighty, polished and well-hewn wooden door marking the entrance to Mayor Swellington's office. She entered without knocking, and closed the door solidly behind her.

❖   ❖   ❖

The Messenger could still be seen in the distance as a dark speck against a faint backdrop of haze, for the moist exhalation of an ocean of trees hung low over the forest. Monique, Anati, and Lillybeth flew fast to keep her in sight, but the hitherto slight breeze had become a headwind and the flyers and the Transporter were falling behind. With the change in wind came a change in the mood of the sky. The temperature fell by degrees and clouds were moving in, spreading broadly over the vistas before them.

The flyers fastened to the Transporter were needing rest. Marista's corner was rising above the others as her companions slowly sank under a growing fatigue and Marista's powerful wings and determination held her side aloft. Doctor Lochswyn held Hinsberth steady in the center of the Transporter as she and Hinsberth were angling away from where Marista was attached. Despite Marista's efforts, they were slowing down.

"We are going to lose sight of her!" exclaimed a worried Anati, as she strained to keep sight of the distant and speedy Messenger.

"How much further?" Hackleberg called out in a breathless voice, but without enough volume to overcome the wind and reach Monique. The fatigue was nearly overwhelming. His wings burned.

Millybeth shook her head. Neither she nor Hackleberg had any idea as to where they were going, for there did not appear to be anything resembling a settlement for as far as they could see.

Monique, Anati, and Lillybeth were intensely focused on the tiny dot of the Messenger, but all at once they noticed something rather odd in the forest ahead of her. The great boughs of the high trees were swaying slightly with the wind, and there was a strange spray of light, a faint shimmering in the tree tops as if the leaves had all turned to mirrors. The darkness of the clouded sky over the horizon contrasted sharply with these reflections of light, and when a beam occasionally swept into their line of sight they could hardly look upon it. As they flew distracted by the scene, the Messenger suddenly dropped into the trees, a short distance before the ring of mysterious, shimmering lights.

"Mister Fowler's, no?" said Monique.

Lillybeth and Anati glanced at each other excitedly.

By this time Millybeth and Hackleberg had also seen the peculiar glow in the forest up ahead, and the sight lifted their spirits. Perhaps they had at last reached their destination.

"Look! Up ahead!" Hackleberg shouted, turning his head to throw his words into the wind, to be carried back to Marista and Eldsworth. Eldsworth swiftly rose to be level with Marista as he strained to look forward beyond the Transporter.

As they approached, they could see the light spraying about the tree tops and a ring of bright, fixed beams reflecting downward toward the forest floor.

As the trees encircling the glow of light came slowly into view, the flyers could see wooden platforms of varying size, larger toward the ground and smaller toward the sky, supported from below by thick wooden planks they ringed the trees up into the heights. Smooth, polished mirrors were mounted here and there on trunks and branches, all coordinated to reflect sunlight downward to the forest floor. The whole assembly swayed with the wind.

"We really must land! Do you see a spot?" an exhausted Hackleberg shouted loudly to Monique. Like everyone else he was astonished by the scene ahead, but he had not the energy left to take it in.

Monique, Anati, and Lillybeth slowed to approach cautiously, and were soon rejoined by Hackleberg, Millybeth, the Transporter, Marista and Eldsworth.

Hackleberg's inquiry went unanswered.

Something had taken their attention.

Closing in on the sunlit glen, the circular gap opened before them, and upon clearing the tree tops they looked down with eyes popped wide in astonishment. Far below was an enormous dome roof, as big as The Pond. It seemed to be hewn from a single, gigantic piece of wood, so tight were its seams, so careful its construction. The massive roof was punctuated here and there by enormous circular skylights which glowed ethereally when struck by the shifting beams of sunlight reflected from above. Long, leafy vines spattered with lush, white blooms wound their way over the dome from ground to sky. On the forest floor, a ring of trellised pathways, under the shadows of flowering vines and dense, leafy foliage, led away from the dome to dwellings beyond. Between the dwellings the grounds were laced with terraced gardens of colorful herbs, flowers and vegetables. Residents of this remarkable place could be seen scattered about on the forest floor and in the trees, huddled together on the wooden platforms, all were wide eyed in amazement as they noticed the clutch of flyers approaching skyward dragging a curious contraption.

Hackleberg spotted an opening to the forest floor just beside the massive dome, almost directly beneath them. It appeared nearly the size of the flattened patch the Transporter had made in Doctor

Lochswyn's herb garden. He glanced over to Millybeth, who had spied the same opening, and she nodded in approval, hopeful for an opportunity to swiftly return to earth.

Hackleberg called to Monique to get her attention, and pointed to the ground with one wing to convey his intent to land. At once Monique, Anati and Lillybeth soared higher into the sky, circling up and over Mister Fowler's, as the flyers ever so slowly eased the Transporter downward beneath the tree tops. Beating their wings with every last bit of energy they could muster, the flyers lowered themselves and the Transporter into the scalloped gap between a dense maze of leafy boughs extending down to the forest floor. On the ground below, a large number of onlookers had gathered and were busily scurrying about, curious to meet the unexpected visitors and clearing the way for them and their cargo to land safely.

As they descended, the gap narrowed as tree branches encroached more and more around the edge of the glen, and the flyers had to move closer together. The currents of air fanned by their rapidly beating wings stirred aloft clouds of dust, hampering their sight.

Suddenly the Transporter tipped dramatically; Eldsworth's line to the Transporter had become entangled in a spindly branch waving about in the wind. He was torn to one side and unable to descend.

"Help!" he shouted at the top of his voice.

Doctor Lochswyn, her equipment and Hinsberth slid uncontrollably. Doctor Lochswyn tried her best to keep the ailing Hinsberth from sliding into the wall and becoming buried in a mass of blankets and ice, and to block, with wings and feet, her medical devices which in an instant had become dangerous projectiles.

Marista saw what had happened to Eldsworth and immediately

shouted with her booming voice, "GO UP!"

Hackleberg and Millybeth felt the weight of the Transporter suddenly shift through their harnesses. An instant later Millybeth was pulled downward as everything inside the Transporter keeled over. They heard Marista's command to climb, but they were too low, too depleted.

Lillybeth, Anati and Monique dove in fast, but they could not react in time.

The Transporter and the flyers suddenly crashed to the ground with a thud. Eldsworth, still caught high in the branches, was flapping in a frenzy, hovering with the weight of the Transporter threatening to pull him down through the narrow opening.

Those on the ground rushed in.

"Help us!" shouted Doctor Lochswyn in distress.

Without thinking, Monique suddenly darted down and came up behind Eldsworth at high speed. She threw her body into him, freeing him from the branches. He and Monique hurled through the air… Until when at the limit of the strap Eldsworth was yanked rudely to earth. Monique went on in an uncontrolled tumble, finally striking the ground awkwardly and rolling to a stop.

The newcomers were instantly surrounded by residents of Mister Fowler's. Anati and Lillybeth alighted together and with Marista, they ran to the Transporter to check on Doctor Lochswyn and Hinsberth. Millybeth and Hackleberg were uninjured, and they quickly disconnected from the Transporter to assist Eldsworth and Monique. Several residents of Mister Fowler's had surrounded the injured flyers, and were reaching out to try and help them from the ground.

Eldsworth was stunned, shaken and bruised, but thankfully without serious injury. Monique was slowly trying to push herself up; she was splattered with dirt, bruised, sore and had scrapes on her wings and legs.

Marista, Anati and Lillybeth arrived together with several residents at the Transporter and they scrambled to get inside.

Doctor Lochswyn, still in shock, was busily checking over Hinsberth, and carefully pushing him back toward the center of the dome. She rearranged the cold towels and ice packs, which by this time had little chill to offer. When she had finished, she examined Hinsberth thoroughly and methodically for any sign of injury before opening the Transporter door.

"I am fine... I am fine," Doctor Lochswyn repeated flatly to the helpers converging on the Transporter; for at the moment she had only concern for her patient. Coming to, she pleaded, "Please, we need ice. I need my patient taken somewhere — we need ice."

Anati and Lillybeth squeezed into the Transporter and grabbed as much as they could hold of Doctor Lochswyn's books and supplies. As the ducklings came out, Marista squirmed inside and huddled anxiously over Hinsberth, checking him over even more thoroughly than the doctor.

"I believe he is fine... Yes, he is fine," Doctor Lochswyn told Marista in as reassuring a manner as she could muster under the circumstances.

Eldsworth, supported under his wings by residents of Mister Fowler's, limped uneasily toward the Transporter. Anati and Lillybeth, with wings full of medical bits and bobs, gave him sympathetic glances. He proceeded to join Marista and Hinsberth inside.

With the dust still settling, several more residents of Mister Fowler's quickly arrived with ice, towels, blankets and a pair of small trolleys for carrying the injured. Monique was finally able to sit up but did not at all mind the opportunity for her aching body and limbs to be carried and tended to.

Those from The Farm began moving slowly, along with their helpers, toward the colossal dome. As they went under the edge of the massive roof, they looked around with wide eyes at the wondrous scene greeting them. They were deep in the forest and surrounding them, stretching into the distance in every direction was the veiled darkness beneath the dense canopy of trees. But everywhere around the dome, the reflected sunlight shone brightly, bathing all in a warm light as though open to an unhindered summer sky. The many skylights embedded in the smoothly polished, pale wood ceiling flooded the dome's interior with light, and the floor was everywhere even more lush with life than the forest beyond.

High in the distance, at the soaring apex of the dome ceiling were three colossal skylights, and in the pollen heavy air their shafts of light spread like fingers of warmth, fully illuminating the intricate landscape. Flower and herb gardens dotted the floor, defining a maze of footpaths crisscrossing in every direction. Hanging gardens grew thick and lush in large round bowls hung from the tall ceiling. Long tendrils of flowering vines swept down to the floor. Scattered about were many intimate, gently curving pools of water with still, mirror like surfaces precisely level with the floor. The pools connected the gardens; their waters ran through a series of narrow, brick lined canals. Over the larger pools arched intricate wooden bridges. The prolific life, bright light, clear, mirror-like pools and flowing water — which provided an ever present, gentle burbling sound — bestowed upon the whole scene an agreeable feeling of abundance.

The skylights were arranged so the spaces beneath them were bathed in unique shades of light, and the visitors from The Farm noticed the color of light was indicative of the activities taking place beneath them. Brighter and warmer areas were amassed centrally under the high ceiling for spirited activities such as working, preparing and eating meals, and large gatherings. Here older residents were chatting loudly and the younger ones were playing and running about. The cooler and dimmer spaces were located around the perimeter of the large central hub. Here some residents were resting by themselves and others relaxing in small groups. Near the dome walls the space was more sheltered. Thick slices of polished wood hung low, there curving shapes were drilled through in beautiful scrolling patterns, shining in spots of light on the ground.

Small dwellings were scattered about on the floor under the vast roof, and toward one of these the Farm ducks and their helpers slowly hobbled. While onlookers studied the visitors, those from The Farm went along silently with bills agape in astonishment. Marista and Eldsworth's hopes for Hinsberth were enlivened considerably as they pondered the sheer achievement of what they found themselves immersed in. Anati and Lillybeth waddled closely together, beside Hinsberth and his parents, pointing out different details to each other, and aching to be able to run out and explore.

As they neared a large building covered with earth and striped with pathways through the gardens planted over its sloping roof, they came to a stop, and only the visitors and those carrying the injured continued on. The bright red entrance door was suddenly opened by a shorter duck, with an intelligent expression and busy, jittery mannerisms whenever she moved. She was clad in a snug uniform trimmed with lace, and wore a small locket round her neck. As she stood on the threshold she offered directions to those inside. They could hear those inside rushing about with excited voices, apparently working in great haste to prepare accommodations for the ill and injured.

Doctor Lochswyn recognized a fellow practitioner of medicine immediately, and she opened her bill to speak, but was cut short as the duck at the door quickly inquired with a speedy voice, "Did you receive the ice, towels, and the cold water?"

"Yes, thank you. You have been very kind," answered Doctor Lochswyn sincerely.

"Oh, I am sorry. I forgot to introduce myself. I am Doctor Tauffenshufter, and inside are my assistants, Doctor Durmlint and Doctor Wichsluff. Now please, do bring them in," Doctor Tauffenshufter requested, waving the newcomers and their helpers inside.

Marista and Eldsworth quickly carried Hinsberth through the wide doorway into the well stocked room and placed him down gently on the nearest of several beds. They were followed immediately by Doctor Lochswyn, Anati and Lillybeth, and then Millybeth and Hackleberg. Hackleberg was distractedly wandering about as he tried to study the design and construction of everything in sight.

Four helpers carried Monique inside and put her on a second bed, separated from Hinsberth's room by a smooth, rounded wall. Eldsworth's helpers directed him toward a third bed, but he raised a wing and nodded politely. "Thank you. I am sincerely grateful for every bit of help but I believe at the moment I will not need a bed," he announced. "Please, my son..."

Doctor Tauffenshufter looked at Hinsberth curiously. She then turned her gaze to Doctor Lochswyn.

"Fever?" she asked at once.

"Yes. Several days, constant temperature. He's been unconscious most of the time," answered Doctor Lochswyn.

"Contagion? Any others infected?" inquired Doctor Tauffenshufter.

"None," replied Doctor Lochswyn.

With an accelerating pace Doctor Tauffenshufter continued questioning Doctor Lochswyn, who became ever more detailed in her replies, and soon the two doctors were discussing Hinsberth's condition, treatment and history at such a rapid pace and with such technicality that everyone else in the room grew silent while trying to follow them.

Marista and Eldsworth were holding Hinsberth's wings and looking down at his warm but silent face. As the doctors spoke, they looked into each other's eyes, both thinking perhaps Monique's idea was as inspired as they had hoped.

Doctor Durmlint, Doctor Wichsluff and Anati were tending closely to Monique. The doctors were questioning her to find out how and where she was injured. And Monique, although having only a few bumps and scrapes, had one wing draped loosely across her forehead and was conveying to the doctors, in a breathless and writhing fashion, the horrible pain she was enduring and how she had come to her injuries in a highly gesticulated, lengthy and dramatic portrait of her heroic effort in saving Eldsworth from a certain and untimely end. Anati stood at her mother's side, holding her wing. She rolled her eyes each time Monique began to retell the tale, to anyone who happened to pass by.

❖　❖　❖

CHAPTER 6

Back on The Farm, the day was ending for Quillypom, and as she assembled her things to retire to the private wing of the Mayor's Office, a tepid knock came onto her door and she wearily announced permission to enter. The door opened and one of the staff waddled briskly over to stand stiffly by her desk.

"Yes?" Quillypom requested for him to speak.

"The Smythes and the Smerkingtons are not present. Doctor Lochswyn's location is also unknown," he stated mechanically.

"I see," said Quillypom. She took a deep breath and slumped back in her chair, as if in an attempt to relieve a great weight. She turned her gaze to the windows.

"The Messenger. She has also not returned," he added gravely.

Quillypom sighed, and her eyes drifted off into the distance, as if probing the horizon, waiting, or perhaps yearning, to see something unexpected on the approach.

"Thank you," she said distractedly, and waved him to the door.

MARISTA

"What are you doing? Where are you going?"

CHAPTER 7

ANOTHER DISTANT LAND

DOCTOR LOCHSWYN and Doctor Tauffenshufter were embroiled in discussing Hinsberth's condition for such a time that their assistants needed to offer them food and water. But eating and drinking did not dampen the intensity of their deliberations. They stood close, fervently exchanging ideas and opinions regarding potential treatments. As they spoke, Marista, Eldsworth, Hackleberg and Millybeth sat together on a wooden bench, listening with hope to the unbroken stream of words echoing through the doctor's office and, when needed, helping to tend to the ailing Hinsberth.

The conversation between Lochswyn and Tauffenshufter had begun with short, concise exchanges, however, it was not long before the discussion had grown in detail, animation and technicality. Presently, the conversation was winding down, honing in on a course of treatment.

"Viral?" suggested Doctor Tauffenshufter.

"Maybe," replied Doctor Lochswyn.

"Bacterial?"

"No."

"Toxin?"

"Perhaps."

"Are you certain?"

"No. But we must try."

"Yes?"

"Yes."

While the doctors deliberated inside, Lillybeth and Anati had waddled outside together. They sat down side by side on a small rock wall surrounding a tiny flower garden just outside the doctor's office. With their wings flopped on their laps and legs dangling loosely over the edge, they gazed upon the delicate spray of color arrayed before them, but no words were spoken, for they were worn thin by the events of the day.

Anati knew her mother was a bit bruised but otherwise fine, and she was merely enjoying the attention of the doctors and staff. She felt no need to remain in the patient room. But still she shuddered each time she recalled seeing her mother tumble to the ground.

Lillybeth was feeling useless. They had brought Hinsberth, at some risk, all this way, and she hoped with the help of Mister Fowler's doctors he would soon recover. But now there was not anything she could do to help. She was deeply troubled over her unfulfilled promise to free Milchester and the others; there was an urgency in Hinsberth's voice when he had asked for her to free them, and so far she had not even determined Milchester's identity — although she was certain he was not a resident of The Farm. Lillybeth worried that Hinsberth would be very disappointed to know she had broken her promise.

After sitting together in reticent silence, peering into the garden and pondering the day's events, Lillybeth suddenly inquired, "Do you know of anyone named Milchester?"

CHAPTER 7

For a moment Anati looked up at the enormous ceiling arcing high above them, and then she simply replied, "No." She lowered her eyes to the flower garden and asked, "Why?"

"Something Hinsberth asked me to do; the last time I spoke to him. He asked for me to promise to help someone named Milchester," explained Lillybeth. "But I have not found anyone with the name Milchester, at least not on The Farm."

"I have never heard that name before. When *was* the last time you spoke to Hinsberth? He has been asleep for some time, no?"

Lillybeth looked down into the flowers, "Hinsberth awakened early one morning, a couple of days ago and he told my father he wanted to speak with me. My father asked the Mayor's Office to send the Messenger to our house, and after she gave us the message we all went to Doctor Lochswyn's. That morning was the last time we spoke."

"Why did he ask you? Does *he* believe you know this Milchester? Maybe he was delirious," Anati speculated.

"He seemed well aware of what he was saying," replied Lillybeth. "I do not think he was delirious."

"But why did he not ask his father or mother to help this Milchester, or the Mayor or Quillypom? They have much more ability than you or I to figure things out and make things happen."

Lillybeth felt awkward in trying to answer Anati's question, for she did not find Hinsberth's reasoning very compelling. Although as she thought about it she did feel the need to straighten her shirt. She floundered in her thoughts and then offered a more agreeable explanation, "Maybe you are right. Maybe Hinsberth believes I know Milchester, and he also believes I will be able to help."

"But why would he think that?" asked Anati.

"I — am not sure," sputtered Lillybeth. "He — was — struggling. His words could only be so few."

"Maybe he does not know you so well," Anati replied flatly.

"I think — he knows me — well enough," stammered Lillybeth, but not without an air of uncertainty.

Lillybeth again found her words jumbling about before reaching her bill. Having her older and elegant acquaintance probing her friendship with Hinsberth was fomenting the most unpleasant heat in her head and tumult in her belly.

"Yes, maybe so," Anati replied, in a satisfied manner.

Into Lillybeth's thoughts came the notion Anati knew what she was doing. Lillybeth wondered: had Anati noticed how she became flustered whenever talking about her friendship with Hinsberth? Could this be why Anati continued to advance the subject? Feeling uncomfortable and unable to find a reason to excuse herself, Lillybeth began searching for an urgent change of topic.

❖   ❖   ❖

Inside the doctor's office the staff were busily conversing with Doctor Lochswyn and preparing Hinsberth to be lifted from the bed and carried away.

"What are you doing? Where are you going? Where are you taking my Hinsberth," Marista asked in such a firm voice that everyone in the doctor's office froze for a moment.

"We think Hinsberth may have been exposed to some kind of toxin, and — we have an idea," replied Doctor Lochswyn calmly. "They have a pool here, and they can fill it not only with cool water to help the fever, but whatever mixture of remedies we believe Hinsberth might respond to. In addition to soaking him in the pool, we wish to try and hydrate him as much as possible, to help wash away unwanted bugs or substances," she explained reassuringly. "But of course, they will not try any treatment without your permission. Do you and Eldsworth wish to proceed?"

Marista looked at Eldsworth, and they both nodded in agreement.

"We trust you," Marista said to Doctor Lochswyn, reaching out and taking a firm hold of her wings.

Doctor Lochswyn turned to her colleagues and nodded. They were free to prepare Hinsberth for Doctor Lochswyn's and Doctor Tauffenshufter's experimental treatment. The staff began talking quietly amongst themselves. Doctor Lochswyn scribbled notes onto a small paper pad as she spoke with the other doctors. As she had hoped, Doctor Lochswyn was learning many new things, and she was proving to be an encyclopedic source for her collaborators. They often sought her advice and opinion. The medical staff were especially attentive when Doctor Lochswyn, with great enthusiasm, began presenting her ideas on optimal dietary practices, their applications in treatment, and most importantly, the constituents of her special porridge. Doctor Lochswyn explained how she consumed exactly three bowls at regular intervals each day, in very precise amounts, although on this particular day she was very much at risk of upsetting her dietary rituals.

Four members of the medical staff positioned themselves at each corner of Hinsberth's blanket, and they slowly raised him off the bed. They carried him round the wall past Monique, and through a window lined hallway to the rear of the doctor's office.

Seeing them pass, Monique sat up and rose from her bed, and

although her legs, wings and head were wrapped over with bandages, she waddled quite normally behind them, the apparent benefactor of a remarkable recovery from her heroic endeavors.

The rear of the doctor's office was a large, open room encompassing two small pools. Gauges and switches were mounted on one wall to control the water flow and temperature of the pools; the outside wall was almost all glass, and the view and the light lent a warm, comforting ambience.

Doctor Wichsluff was the resident expert on operating the pools, and at once he set about explaining, in great detail, the mechanisms and their operations to Doctor Lochswyn, who from time to time was either nodding her head or jotting down notes as he spoke. Doctor Tauffenshufter removed Hinsberth's sweater and gave it to Marista and Eldsworth for safekeeping. She then removed the blankets and ice and wrapped Hinsberth in a thin, gossamer gown. She and Doctor Durmlint took Hinsberth under his wings, and slowly and gently lowered him into the pool, until only his head remained above the surface. Hinsberth did not wake, nor did he stir. He seemed almost lifeless. An air of disappointment fell over the room.

Along one wall of the room were banks of cabinetry, and above them were shelves supporting many glass jars filled with various remedies. Doctor Lochswyn and Doctor Tauffenshufter examined the jars closely, and every now and then they would extract some of the contents. Soon the recipe was complete, and feeling time was vital, they swiftly mixed the ingredients together and placed the final mixture into a large sachet. Doctor Lochswyn tied it securely using a long reed of an unusual sort. It was ready.

Wasting not a moment they slowly lowered the sachet full of

antidotes into the water with an attached bit of twine as if it were an enormous bag of tea, and it sank beneath the surface. The contents began to disperse languidly into the pool, marked by swirling clouds of aqueous purple smoke.

Doctor Lochswyn turned to Eldsworth and Marista, who were quite clearly ready to understand the secrets of Hinsberth's treatment: "We will need to submerge him in the pool with the sachet at regular intervals. Doctor Tauffenshufter and I believe we need to repeat this procedure for the remainder of the night and tomorrow, along with sufficient quantities of ice and water. We will have to see how he responds. If he improves, we will continue the treatment until he awakens. If he does not improve, we will have to consider other remedies. Although, I believe you should know that we seem to be running short on other courses of treatment. But I can assure you we will not cease in our efforts to see Hinsberth well."

"Thank you," offered Eldsworth. He paused. "But please, tell us — do you believe my son will become well again?" he inquired in a solemn voice.

Doctor Lochswyn looked into Eldsworth and Marista's eyes. Their desperation was undeniable.

"We will do whatever we can," she replied.

It was not the answer Eldsworth and Marista had hoped for. They sat down together to watch and wait on an arc of wooden benches propped up on small stone pillars which curved around the two pools. Monique also limped over and sat down, gingerly, next to Eldsworth.

"Thank you," Eldsworth whispered to Monique. "For the bump and for thinking of Hinsberth; for sharing the idea to come here."

"Please, there is no need to thank me. I only hope Hinsberth becomes well, and I am honored to be helping in some way," said Monique as she watched Hinsberth soak in the glowing purple pool.

Monique recounted the events of the day and was struck by a sudden feeling of surprise over what she had done. She regarded how her idea had given a measure of hope to Eldsworth and Marista. She *did* only wish for Hinsberth to be well. Over the aching from her injuries, a pleasant, warm feeling washed over her.

In the doctor's office the newcomers from The Farm kept vigil over Hinsberth, waiting together in hopeful silence.

❖   ❖   ❖

In the faint light of an aging evening, Quillypom and the Mayor sat opposite each other across a long, heavy wooden table. Slowly and rhythmically they dipped their spoons into a pair of soup bowls. Quillypom had again followed the precise instructions given to her by Doctor Lochswyn, and the Mayor was duly impressed with the aroma of the results. Unfortunately, Quillypom did not possess the ingredients in sufficient quantities to brew enough of the savory mixture for the two of them, although she had serendipitously discovered the needed peppermint in a neighbor's garden. As a result the Mayor was rather disappointed at having to indulge himself in what remained of the previous night's meal.

Their meals as of late had more often than not been silent affairs. Quillypom was increasingly preoccupied and the Mayor seemed even more despondent at the end of the day than usual.

Although the hour was late, there came a surprising, sharp rap at the door. Someone was unexpectedly calling from their personal entrance at the rear of the house.

"Should I answer?" asked the Mayor gruffly, with some annoyance at the timing of the unwelcome interruption.

"No," said Quillypom. "Let me see who it is — probably someone needing approval for a permit or other minor concern. Surely an item to address tomorrow. I will take care of it."

And with that Quillypom rose from her seat, left the room and went down the short hall to the door. Peering through the window, Quillypom recognized the square hat and svelte shape of her personal Messenger.

Quillypom nervously unlatched the door and whispered, "Quietly."

"Apologies for the lateness of my arrival," the Messenger whispered, and she held silent for a moment. She shifted her eyes from Quillypom and disappointedly added, "They were not there."

"I see," said Quillypom, and after a slight pause during which a look of tired worry flashed across her face, she added formally, "Thank you, Messenger."

"Thank you," said the Messenger quietly; her usual response to almost anything Quillypom said.

"No — really — Thank you, *Lottiebury*," whispered Quillypom sincerely.

It was the first time Quillypom addressed her by name instead of title, and Lottiebury gave a slight, nervous smile, and then she swiftly turned and waddled away into the darkness.

"Who is it?" bellowed the Mayor from down the hall.

"All taken care of," Quillypom announced back into the house, and she closed the door and returned to her porridge.

❖   ❖   ❖

A world away from The Farm, in the confines of an austere, stifling metal box, Milchester slumped against the side of his cage. He shifted about, trying to rest his aching legs. It had been days since Hinsberth disappeared, and Milchester had all but discontinued eating. Each day he committed to eat sparsely, just enough to remain his current size — to stop growing. But he did not want to become ill, for he knew those who were ill were taken, never to be seen again. Each day he struggled, food had lost its appeal and eating had become a chore. One of the pigs nearby, whom he had heard breathing heavily during the night and eating frequently during the day, had been taken. Now only silence dwelled within the empty cage.

As much as he could, Milchester endeavored to escape into the worlds of his dreams by imagining stories to tell himself, but after many fitful, sleepless nights and days of little food, he was uncertain as to whether he had descended into delirium; unsure which of his memories were real and which were only dreams. Was Hinsberth *real?* Had his mind been deceiving him? When he began to doubt, he would close his eyes and recall the tales Hinsberth had told him. He remembered how Hinsberth and his friend Lillybeth had gone out that very morning on a grand search for the edge of the sky, and as he did so, he imagined again how it would be to soar swiftly in the clear air... to see into forever... with the brilliant sun warming his face... with a gentle wind flowing over his skin... he could feel his ears pushed back by the cool breeze of a brisk flight... and then he would look down... far below he would see the rich and beautiful hues of a rain soaked earth...

Perhaps he was already there.

Milchester opened his eyes. He slowly looked around at what he could see of his tiny cage; only the dark, dull bars of metal and the cold and indifferent mechanisms for food and water. He closed his eyes tightly. Once more he pushed back the tears, and he ventured onward to another distant land.

CHRYSALIS

*"As the night wore on, excepting the slight burble of flowing water,
Chrysalis fell silent, as if lying in wait for the coming light of dawn."*

CHAPTER 8

FOR THE ONES HE LOST

HUDDLED TOGETHER IN SILENCE upon a bench beside the pools in the doctor's office; Marista, Eldsworth, Millybeth, Hackleberg and Monique waited, hoping for a sign, some hint of Hinsberth overcoming his illness. At steady intervals he had been submerged into the water. Presently he was lying in bed, seemingly unchanged. Doctor Lochswyn and Doctor Tauffenshufter had before each immersion recreated their medicinal sachet and lowered it slowly into the water. With each new sachet came a strong scent which permeated the room. The familiar aroma was undoubtedly reminiscent of the ingredients from Doctor Lochswyn's porridge.

By this time night had settled in and the great dome ceiling was all aglow, faintly reflecting beams of light directed upon it from lanterns scattered about the gardens beneath. The faint, silvery light made it seem as if the moonlight somehow found its way through the opaque roof. Throughout the dome, brighter lights dangled here and there; shining toward the floor they created small and inviting nooks. Strands of tiny bulbs were strung through the bridges, reflecting magnificently in the still pools of water. Similar strands of light wound through the vines dangling from the hanging garden bowls and through the trellised arcades enclosing the stone footpaths.

Lillybeth and Anati had left their perch on the garden wall after the sun dipped below the horizon. As darkness fell, the lights began to shine and the pair of ducklings could not help but wander about, exploring the odd but delightful experience of being enclosed but having the impression of being outside on a beautiful summer evening, in an immense garden bathed in a resplendent moonlight and dotted with fireflies frozen in flight.

While roaming the gardens Lillybeth began to forget about Anati's more pointed remarks and she merely enjoyed exploring the sights with her new acquaintance.

Inside the doctor's office, Doctor Tauffenshufter sat down with the visitors. She and Doctor Lochswyn had just settled Hinsberth in bed after his latest immersion in the pool. Doctors Durmlint and Wichsluff, without other patients to attend to, also came and sat down beside the visitors and readied themselves to retire for the night.

With the rooms cleaned, remedies and implements stowed away and nothing left to do for Hinsberth but watch and wait, Doctor Tauffenshufter finally had time to learn more about these visitors who had made such an unusual entrance into their home.

"So, what brings you here to Chrysalis?" inquired Doctor Tauffenshufter.

"Chrysalis?" asked Hackleberg.

"Yes, that is what we call this place," answered Doctor Tauffenshufter.

"We came here for poor Hinsberth. We thought this was where Mister Fowler lived and I thought he might be able to help. My mother, many years ago, had helped him and some of his friends on The Farm," Monique explained.

CHAPTER 8

"Ah, so you are from The Farm?" asked Doctor Tauffenshufter.

"Yes," replied Monique. "I remembered Mister Fowler from when I was young. He was quite involved with developments on The Farm. I thought he, or one of his colleagues would certainly be able to help Hinsberth, and when I mentioned this to Doctor Lochswyn and Marista and Eldsworth, they felt the same. Hackleberg and Lillybeth, the young one who was here — she is outside with my daughter — they built the Transporter which we used to carry Hinsberth here. The landing was not quite as we expected, no? But it worked... mostly."

"Yes, I wondered about the — the Transporter, you called it? It looks like something we might have invented here. How did you come up with that idea?" asked Doctor Tauffenshufter curiously.

"It was Lillybeth," answered Hackleberg.

Hackleberg explained how Hinsberth had become ill, and how Lillybeth had encountered some helpers in a field who eventually carried her and Hinsberth to The Farm on a similar invention.

"They were almost certainly from here," said Doctor Tauffenshufter. "This is Mister Fowler's place, in a sense. He began designing it many years ago while still on The Farm. He and his friends and their families came here to try and manifest his designs, to build a place hidden from humans. They wanted to be self sufficient so they would never have to migrate. As you know those who settled The Farm were all Migrators at one time. On their travels they would stop and stay at The Farm, as they passed over, twice per year. At some point the humans had all departed, and they began to stay there year round. There was plenty for them — food and shelter — and other friendly creatures, who importantly did not mind them being there."

"I remember hearing this story from my mother," said Monique.

"Sometime after they settled on The Farm, the Mayor and Mister Fowler had a disagreement, no? And that is when Mister Fowler left The Farm to come here."

"I have not heard anything about a disagreement with the Mayor. I have known Mister Fowler for many years, and he never mentioned the Mayor of The Farm as a reason for his decision to come here. I think it was the nature of the forest here which was the pull of this particular spot. It is deep and dense enough to be hidden. He has always been concerned about the humans. He believed The Farm was too exposed, that at some point they would return."

"So, why do you call this place Chrysalis?" Millybeth interjected with some curiosity.

"Those who first began building here desired to give it a name. They wished for others to come and settle, so they wanted an appealing name and they believed 'Cocoon' was too stuffy. Chrysalis sounds much more appealing, don't you agree? Most everyone likes butter-flies, so there you have it."

"If I may ask, why was Mister Fowler so concerned about humans?" inquired Hackleberg. "They left us so many amazing things on The Farm. I have learned so much from studying their artifacts."

"I am not entirely certain. I have heard many different explanations over the years. But someone once told me that he lost one or more of his family — along the migration routes there were places where humans would wait for them. They would do the most terrible things to them, taking them out of the sky. I do not really know any more than that," explained Doctor Tauffenshufter. "My family came to Chrysalis when I was young and I never flew in the migrations. Even after being here for so long, I am still amazed at what they have done."

CHAPTER 8

As she spoke, Doctor Tauffenshufter turned to gaze out through the windows at the immense but peaceful, faintly glowing interior of Chrysalis, and she added quietly, "If the story is true, I think he did all this… all of it… for them, for the ones he lost."

Those from The Farm sat in silence, contemplating what Doctor Tauffenshufter had revealed to them. They were not fully aware of their own history; life had been abundant on The Farm for many years and was perhaps taken for granted. Beyond the row of large windows loomed the massive and achingly beautiful monument called Chrysalis, and before them Hinsberth was immersed in the warm pool of purple-hued water. For them, the world was now a more intricate place.

❖   ❖   ❖

Lillybeth and Anati were waddling swiftly around the outside wall of Chrysalis on a stone footpath which wound its way along the edge. The path was nearly concealed under lush archways of boughs and leaves; so dense was the foliage that it was easy to imagine one was winding along endlessly through some vast, unexplored forest while never leaving Chrysalis. The ducklings stopped every now and then to notice the small details placed in the unexpected nooks and crannies sprinkled throughout Chrysalis; a colorful mosaic of tile, an arrangement of rounded, polished stone, or even an overgrown insect chomping a train of holes in a lush leaf. As they crouched down and watched the insect slowly working its way across a broad green leaf, Lillybeth's ears suddenly caught a familiar call, coming from somewhere off in the distance.

"Did you hear that?" whispered Lillybeth with eyes growing wide.

"Hear what?" asked Anati.

"I thought I heard someone call my name," answered Lillybeth.

"There may be other Lillybeths here, no?" suggested Anati.

Funny, Lillybeth thought. She had always considered herself to be the only Lillybeth around. Her eyes widened further. What wondrous things could she do if there were more of her?

Lillybeth's thoughts were suddenly interrupted, for she heard the call for any listening Lillybeth repeated, only much more distinctly. Whoever was calling for her had come closer.

"What should we do?" inquired Lillybeth. "That voice does not sound like my mother or father, or anyone else I know."

"We could hide here in the plants, or — maybe someone needs you for something important," Anati reasoned aloud. "Maybe... something terrible has happened and they need us back at the doctor's office!"

Lillybeth thought for a moment. Was Anati right? Had the doctor's office sent someone out to retrieve her and Anati? Had Hinsberth been cured? Perhaps someone overheard her talking, and had figured out who Milchester was, and was frantically trying to tell her! Or maybe supper was ready.

"I think we should find out who is calling us," declared Lillybeth.

"Calling *you*," corrected Anati.

The two ducklings crawled out of the dense wall of branches and leaves and onto one of the more brightly lit footpaths. They glanced around to see if anyone appeared to be searching for them. Not seeing any particularly suspicious looking suspect wandering around calling for Lillybeth, they hopped together off the mossy footpath and onto a small bridge arching over a gently curving pond. For only an instant they peered at their reflections in the absolutely still, mirror-like water, until...

"There she is!" they heard someone shout.

Lillybeth and Anati looked up from admiring their reflections and quickly glanced around. Suddenly, rounding the ornate topiary marking the entrance to the bridge came a pair of older ducks. They came running up to the ducklings, and suddenly one grabbed hold of Lillybeth and whisked her into the air.

"Filipa!" Lillybeth shouted with joy.

Filipa handed the young duckling over to Pommelstom, who wrapped her in his wings.

"And who is your beautiful friend?" inquired Filipa.

"My name is *Anati*," Anati replied, with great emphasis on articulating her name.

Lillybeth grinned widely, not only because she had been reunited with Filipa and Pommelstom, but also because Anati did not object to being called her friend.

"How did you find us? How did you know we are here?" Lillybeth inquired with great curiosity.

"We heard some of our neighbors talking and we saw a strange contraption as we were arriving home this evening. When we heard that residents of The Farm had arrived with a very ill duckling, and after we saw that clever design sitting outside, we immediately thought of you and Hinsberth," answered Pommelstom.

"You live here?" asked Anati.

"Yes, this has been our home for many years," said Filipa. "We love it here. Anyway, when we arrived at Chrysalis and heard the news, we went at once to the doctor's office, and we could not believe Hinsberth was there. We were so worried about how deathly ill he was when we found him and brought him back to The Farm. We were really hoping he had fully recovered by now."

"Doctor Lochswyn is certainly quite capable, but having the whole staff helping Hinsberth… Well, I am glad you brought him to Chrysalis. Anati, your mother has a good heart, for thinking to bring Hinsberth here," said Pommelstom.

"Thank you," said Anati graciously.

Pommelstom's words struck a chord with Anati. Since early that morning, which now seemed ages ago, until now, Anati's view of her mother had changed dramatically. And as she considered the matter, Anati realized her mother had begun to act a little strangely ever since she had that sudden idea to help Hinsberth.

Pommelstom continued, "Oh, by the way, your parents would like for you to return to the doctor's office. It is becoming late, and Doctor Durmlint would like to prepare some accommodations for you and your parents for the night."

"Thank you both. It is very kind of you to help," said Lillybeth sincerely.

"You should thank Doctor Durmlint, when you see him," Filipa suggested.

"I will. But I meant to thank you — for helping find Hinsberth. For flying us to The Farm. I never had a chance… I saw you leave through the window at Doctor Lochswyn's house," explained Lillybeth. "I wanted to thank you and to say good-bye. I was not sure I would ever see you again."

Filipa was touched by Lillybeth's sentiment. She would have liked to stay on The Farm for a while, but perhaps Lillybeth was too young to understand. "We are both sorry we had to leave without saying goodbye," she stated with sincerity.

"But now we meet again. And if you would have us, we would like to accompany you back to the doctor's office," said Pommelstom.

"That would be more than fine, since neither I nor Lillybeth can remember where it is," said Anati.

"Perfect," said Filipa.

And off they went.

❖   ❖   ❖

That evening, after a lengthy but hushed conversation and a small hearty meal for Lillybeth and Anati, Filipa and Pommelstom bid farewell to those from The Farm and the remaining staff at the doctor's office and departed for the short journey home. They lived just outside the walls of Chrysalis, with other members of their family, in a small house at the end of one of many arcaded walkways.

Lillybeth was happy to have seen her friends again, and Anati was happy to have made some new ones. The duckling's parents enjoyed the conversation with these new acquaintances who seemed genuinely interested in life on The Farm. Before departing, they all planned to awaken just before sunrise and meet at the doctor's office to check upon and help with Hinsberth.

Doctor Durmlint had promptly arranged accommodations for the visitors to stay in for the night, a task made simple since many of the residents who lived near the doctor's office had their doors permanently open for families and friends of patients. Doctor Lochswyn and Doctor Tauffenshufter had arranged to take shifts for the night, preparing the sachet and administering Hinsberth's treatment. Marista and Eldsworth elected to stay with Hinsberth and sleep at the doctor's office. Both because they could not leave Hinsberth's side and to help the staff whenever they could. Doctor Durmlint was happy to give them pillows and blankets and to make sure they were as warm and comfortable as possible. Doctor Durmlint and the rest of the staff considered them all their patients, for they understood the strain they had been under with Hinsberth's illness, and that family and friends also needed to be properly taken care of.

Millybeth, Hackleberg and Lillybeth took a few tired steps to the door of a nearby home, wherein they were greeted and led by an elder couple to a comfortable and cozy spare room at the rear of the house. After only a minute or two, the Smythes had drifted off to dreamland.

Monique and Anati made the same tired walk, only a little further on to another home where a young family lived with their duckling's grandparents. Settling quickly into their temporary home after a long, eventful day, they were soon deep in slumber.

As the residents of Chrysalis drifted off to dream, the lights in the dome dimmed, until only the faint, silvery glimmer of moonlight remained. As the night wore on, excepting the slight burble of flowing water, Chrysalis fell utterly silent, as if lying in wait for the coming of dawn.

FILIPA

"... it was not a place we felt we should stay..."

A LONG NIGHT ENDING

THE BRIGHT RAYS OF THE RISING SUN sprayed morning over the sky. Dawn reflected warmly onto the forest floor, enveloping Chrysalis in a soft glow. With the beginning of a new day, five weary ducks waddled tiredly toward the doctor's office. Hackleberg knocked on the door, and they were greeted by a very sleepy Doctor Lochswyn. Together they shuffled into the back room to wish Marista, Eldsworth, and Doctor Tauffenshufter a good morning and to check on Hinsberth, but Doctor Tauffenshufter was still deep in slumber. Hinsberth was in bed with Marista and Eldsworth at his side; his feverish sleep unbroken.

Distant rolling clouds hung above the horizon and caught the sunlight, which wavered between brightness and shadow, slowly oscillating as if Chrysalis itself was breathing heavily, struggling to wake from a long night.

The Farm ducks draped themselves about on the arc of benches, except for Lillybeth and Anati, who sat on the floor together before the wall of large windows. Transfixed by the ever shifting light, they looked out into Chrysalis, and whispered to each other quietly, deciding on new places to explore. Few Chrysalis residents had arisen at so

197

early an hour, and the ducklings watched them waddle unhurriedly over the footpaths.

Monique gingerly lifted her bandages to examine her scrapes. She grimaced as she did so, clearly feeling a bit tender after the events of the previous day. Millybeth and Hackleberg leaned against one another after taking their seats, and in no time they returned to dreamland after wishing everyone a good morning.

Doctor Lochswyn struggled with wakefulness, she knew Durmlint and Wichsluff would be arriving shortly, and afterward she could take some greatly needed rest.

Doctor Lochswyn went quietly round to the front room to retrieve some hot water and mix her morning bowl of porridge. As she prepared to measure out her ingredients she heard a knock at the door. She placed the small bag of herbs she held in her wing lightly upon a shelf and waddled over to open the door. Filipa and Pommelstom were waiting on the threshold. Doctor Lochswyn quietly shuffled them inside and without a word led them to the back room where everyone had gathered.

"How is Hinsberth?" Pommelstom asked with a hushed voice.

"We wanted to stop by and check on everyone before we have to leave for the day," Filipa added.

"Still asleep," noted Doctor Lochswyn wearily. With her puffy, tired eyes, she was for the first time beginning to show some diminution in her seemingly imperturbable optimism.

"Do not worry, he will be fine," said Filipa encouragingly. "Between you and Doctor Tauffenshufter, I am sure whatever ails him will not for much longer."

Doctor Lochswyn smiled graciously for the sentiment, but her sullen expression suggested she was no longer quite sure.

Filipa and Pommelstom waddled into the back room and joined those watching over Hinsberth. They seated themselves beside Hackleberg and Millybeth, who both raised an eyelid to acknowledge the newcomers. Lillybeth and Anati rose to their feet and waddled over to their friends. With hushed voices they asked Filipa and Pommelstom about the many intriguing places they spied around Chrysalis.

Doctor Lochswyn finished preparing her porridge and sat down beside the loudly snoring Doctor Tauffenshufter. The scent of her porridge wafted over the room, no corner was immune to the tantalizingly sweet aroma.

Outside, the sunlight burned brightly. Chrysalis had awakened.

Marista had not left Hinsberth's side; she held his wing and gently caressed his forehead. Eldsworth slumped tiredly against Marista; his heavy head drooped forward, and every now and then he awakened with a start, only to quickly drift again into slumber.

Suddenly a loud knock cracked the silence, startling everyone in the room, for Eldsworth had fallen and his forehead struck the frame of Hinsberth's bed. Marista had suddenly stood up, causing Eldsworth to fall. Her massive form stood silent and motionless. She still held Hinsberth's wing. Eldsworth rubbed his head. He looked up at Marista and saw the tears streaming down her face. She was looking down upon Hinsberth with a broad, tearful grin. Eldsworth immediately pushed himself up and the tears came fast. Before him was Hinsberth, his tired eyes wide open, staring up at Marista. Hinsberth shifted his gaze to Eldsworth, and he smiled.

They were immediately beset upon by Doctor Lochswyn and

CHAPTER 9

Doctor Tauffenshufter — the latter of whom had been jolted awake by Eldsworth's collision with the bed frame — and then Millybeth, Hackleberg, Monique, Filipa, Pommelstom and finally Lillybeth and Anati. Hinsberth's eyes slowly traced over the assortment of family and friends. Lillybeth and Anati struggled to see what was happening, to see around the much larger bodies before them.

Doctor Lochswyn swiftly prepared to take Hinsberth's temperature, to see if his fever had finally broken. Doctor Tauffenshufter came fast with ice and water, to have them at the ready for the undoubtedly parched duckling.

But they stopped suddenly. To everyone's surprise, Hinsberth opened his bill, and said, in a weak, dry voice, "Lillybeth?"

Doctor Lochswyn and Doctor Tauffenshufter turned around, but Lillybeth was nowhere to be seen. Hackleberg, Millybeth and Anati stepped aside and Lillybeth came forward. She waddled hesitantly up to Hinsberth's bedside. Hinsberth smiled again as he saw his friend appear, and Lillybeth, straightening her shirt and choking back tears, smiled in return.

Hinsberth managed a single, wispy word, "Milchester?"

Lillybeth broke down into a blubbering mess, even worse than before. As she sobbed, Millybeth and Hackleberg put their wings over her tiny shoulders, and blinded by tears, she tried to explain: "I tried. I went to the Mayor's Office... I tried hard but I — I could not keep my promise," she sputtered.

Devastated, Hinsberth began to weep, and he spoke with a barely audible voice, "He helped me. He had nothing, but he gave me whatever he could. I am here because of him."

"I am so sorry," Lillybeth cried.

"Thank you — thank you for trying," Hinsberth said slowly.

Marista wiped his tears.

Hinsberth turned his head away and continued to weep, and the doctors silently motioned with their wings, wanting everyone away from Hinsberth so he could rest.

But all at once, Lillybeth recalled the blanket of straw... the makeshift saucer bowls... the voices... the barren, lifeless land... the sharp buildings. Milchester, she thought, with her eyes popped wide in disbelief, must have been in that awful place.

"MILCHESTER!" Lillybeth suddenly blurted through her tears.

With the excitement of discovery, she stood firm as Doctor Lochswyn was gently trying to brush her back toward the benches.

"Wait!" Marista commanded with the boom returning to her voice. "Who is Milchester? Who is it that helped my son?"

Filipa knew what Lillybeth was thinking. She spoke up from the back of the room, "When we found Hinsberth he was already unconscious with fever. He was under a blanket of straw, slumped against the side of a building of metal. Some empty cups were at his sides, a few still with food and water. We were not paying too much attention; we were so relieved to have had actually found him, and he was *so* ill, we knew we had to fly him back to The Farm. At the time we assumed *he* had covered himself and had made the cups before falling asleep. There were many voices in the building behind him, but it was not a place we felt we should stay; we all thought perhaps the place itself had made him ill."

Hinsberth was squirming, trying to speak again. Eldsworth was attempting to calm him and make him rest, but suddenly Hinsberth spoke defiantly with every ounce of conviction he could muster,

"Milchester helped me. We must free him! We must free them all!"

Marista took a deep breath, making her already substantial presence even larger, and she set her eyes on Eldsworth and then on Lillybeth. The intensity of her gaze was enough for them to know as far as she was concerned her son's request would not go unfulfilled. Marista waved for everyone except Eldsworth, Doctor Lochswyn and Lillybeth to return to the benches. There was no hesitation. She turned to Lillybeth.

"You made a promise to my son, yes?"

Lillybeth nodded.

Standing tall, pushing her flower forward and flaring her massive wings to splay them on her hips, she boomed, "Tell me what you need."

MONIQUE

"There is something —
something of great importance we wish to discuss with you."

MY HEART TELLS ME EVEN MORE

LILLYBETH SHRUGGED HER TINY SHOULDERS and told Marista, "I — am not sure what I need," and then she wiped away her tears. She had little idea how to go about freeing Milchester. What *would* she need? And how could Marista help? Millybeth and Hackleberg could see Lillybeth was overwhelmed, and they wrapped her in their wings so only Lillybeth's head was above the mesh of feathers.

Marista decided to let Lillybeth rest, and she turned to notice Hinsberth looking upon Monique and Anati with an unknowing expression. She realized they had yet to be introduced, "This is Monique and her daughter Anati," she explained to her son, "They came to us with the idea to bring you here."

"Thank you," Hinsberth said wistfully. He was still distant. His thoughts were with one far away.

"We are only glad to help," said Monique.

Monique and Anati were surprised by what they heard from Filipa, they were not aware of the details of Lillybeth and Hinsberth's misadventure and how Hinsberth had become ill; they had only overheard the news of the ill duckling through conversations with others on The

204

Farm.

Presently an aching silence fell over the room. No one was quite sure what to say, it was clear Hinsberth was not in any condition to be further upset.

Marista shooed everyone besides Hinsberth and Eldsworth into the front room. Hinsberth needed rest and to take in a bit more food and water to help his strength. Eldsworth remained with Hinsberth to help him eat and drink. Once they were alone, Hinsberth turned to his father and asked, "Where are we?"

Eldsworth quietly explained how Monique and Anati had come to Doctor Lochswyn's with the idea to bring him to Chrysalis. He described how Lillybeth and Hackleberg, after discussing the idea, had remained up all that night working on an invention to allow them to safely carry him on the journey. He recounted the flight... the crash landing... how helpful those residing in Chrysalis were in bringing him to the doctor's office... and how the staff and Doctor Lochswyn had come up with a plan to treat his illness. And finally, he told Hinsberth how thankful he was to each and every one of them, since as a result he was now speaking with his son.

❖   ❖   ❖

In the front room, the Smythes, Monique, Anati, Filipa and Pommelstom stood in an arc facing Marista.

Lillybeth knew Marista wanted to know the details regarding how Hinsberth had been found and how they may be able to help this mysterious fellow named Milchester.

"The Mayor's Office," she unexpectedly stated.

Lillybeth's announcement prompted skeptical expressions all

round. She quickly added, "I will need to go to the Mayor's Office. Quillypom will help us free Milchester, she helped me look for him on The Farm."

Filipa and Pommelstom, once again forgoing the day's tasks, glanced at each other with some trepidation. They turned to Marista.

Pommelstom began, "What Hinsberth has requested will not be easy. In the place where we found Hinsberth there were several large buildings, and there were so many voices we could barely hear each other speak. The air was foul. There seemed far too many in not enough space. No one was outside. When we first flew over, the scene was so disagreeable we tried to distance ourselves as fast as we could. It was Lillybeth who spotted Hinsberth's sweater. He had set it out as a beacon pointing skyward — very clever on his part."

Marista nodded, as if the last point were to be expected.

Filipa continued, "The buildings were made by humans. Trying to free those trapped inside may be difficult and dangerous. I cannot recall anyone ever having tried such a thing before."

"Difficult or not, my son has his reasons. He does not come up with such ideas without thinking them through. If he believes we should free them, then we should free them. Especially this Milchester. I want to know more; we will discuss this again," Marista said in an authoritative tone. For the moment she wished to return to her son. She turned and went to join Eldsworth and Hinsberth.

Lillybeth glanced around. There was an air of uncertainty in everyone's eyes. Anati was standing next to her, and Lillybeth recognized in her expression not only uncertainty but a hint of fear.

"What is it?" asked Lillybeth in a whisper.

"What are we going to do?" asked Anati.

Anati had seen her mother bumped and bruised just in bringing Hinsberth to Chrysalis. She felt no desire to voyage into even more dangerous circumstances.

"I thought we had come here only to help Hinsberth. And now he is feeling better, no? So what are we going to do now? What must we do with this Milchester?"

Lillybeth pondered over Anati's question, it seemed a good one to ask. But in order to figure out what to do for Milchester, Lillybeth knew she needed to know more from Hinsberth. She had made her promise to free Milchester, and having not done so, she believed she had already disappointed him. On her own, she had not even been able to discover who Milchester was. But Hinsberth was now tired and upset, and she thought for the moment it was best to keep her questions to herself and to let him rest.

"I am not certain what we will need to do. But when he becomes better, I will ask Hinsberth," Lillybeth whispered to Anati. "I am sure he will be able to tell us how to free Milchester," she added confidently.

Anati nodded but she was still worried.

As everyone stood in silent contemplation over what to do next, Doctor Durmlint and Doctor Wichsluff suddenly entered the room and, in noticing the somber mood, Doctor Durmlint announced in a cheerful manner, "A good morning to everyone, it is a wonderful day outside."

"It is indeed," Millybeth agreed. "Hinsberth has finally awakened! And, he has eaten a little."

The new arrivals grinned upon hearing the news and were noticeably pleased, but also a little befuddled over the otherwise solemn mood, for they knew not of the plight of Hinsberth's friend. Nevertheless, the newcomers were excited to see Hinsberth and together everyone proceeded to the back room. Eldsworth and Doctor Lochswyn were seated on either side of Hinsberth, and with the much needed food and water, Hinsberth's eyes had become more present and alert.

Hinsberth turned his head to all those coming to visit him; they were glad faces with eyes happy to see him awake and on the mend.

But Hinsberth's expression was unexpectedly one of determination, and his weak, raspy voice suddenly filled the room. He spoke into the air, slowly reminiscing over Milchester's lonely life of captivity and his inevitable fate, his inescapable destiny. He revealed that Milchester had never once known a friend and until Hinsberth had given him one, he had no name. He described the cruelties Milchester experienced and the pain of immobility he endured. He recalled the profound imagination Milchester expressed and the generous heart and kindness he demonstrated, without ever having experienced such things himself. It was indeed Milchester, Hinsberth revealed, who had given him straw to keep him warm... had constructed and given him the makeshift cups of food and water... and had kept himself alert through the night; trying to keep Hinsberth safe with his voice. Hinsberth choked as he spoke of the admiration he developed for his friend, for despite the irrevocable nature of his confinement and the cruelty of his fate, in a defiance indicative of only the strongest of character, Milchester held fast to the embers of a burning hope.

Hinsberth paused a moment to regain his strength. He took a deep breath and spoke once more, "And he is only one. We must multiply Milchester by a thousand."

Anguished faces gazed blankly upon the floor. Bills hung loosely. Eyes were reddened. Hackleberg held Lillybeth, the mystery of Milchester was no more, but never could she have imagined...

Marista and Eldsworth were overcome with pride and despair. Like his mother, Hinsberth always had strong concerns, anchored by the unswerving civility his father had instilled in him ever since he broke free of his shell. He had lived a comfortable life, and the degree of shock and dismay which beset upon him at encountering the plight of Milchester and his fellows was felt by all in the room.

Doctor Lochswyn and her colleagues stood stoically, as problem solvers with an expertise in medicine and health, Hinsberth's revelation of who the mysterious Milchester was left them speechless. To them, the intentional deprivation of life and health was unfathomable. Everyone realized Hinsberth's request did not regard a mere reciprocity for the kind help he was given one night by a generous soul, but was instead a call to eliminate an incomprehensible suffering, and at this, Lillybeth was overwhelmed. The magnitude of what she had promised Hinsberth was starkly apparent, it was much beyond freeing someone from an idea or some awkward situation on The Farm; it was something beyond which her talents for invention and unintentional mischief seemed particularly well suited. She would need help. The daunting task facing them would undoubtedly require the effort of many. And, as far as Lillybeth was concerned, there was only one way to organize many.

"I must go to the Mayor's Office," Lillybeth asserted once again, breaking the somber silence.

Millybeth turned to her daughter.

"From what Hinsberth has told us, this problem is beyond even the Mayor or Quillypom," she stated distantly.

CHAPTER 10

Hackleberg thought aloud, "Even if we approached the Mayor or Quillypom; I am not sure what they might be able to do. We know they are both quite diligent in addressing the affairs of The Farm, but this is indeed different. What might motivate them to address this problem? I must admit it seems so remote from the daily concerns of The Farm."

"I agree, Quillypom and the Mayor have not been concerned with anything beyond The Farm for quite some time. Even this place, Chrysalis, they have discouraged from visiting. But look around, it seems a big mistake, no?"

"Milchester said they take them when they grow large enough. How much time does he have?" Millybeth inquired of Hinsberth.

Hinsberth paused a moment.

"I — I do not know. His voice was rather tense when he spoke of it. I do not believe we can wait. Please, I know it may be difficult. But anything is possible. We must free them," he pleaded.

With this reply, Lillybeth felt the pressure mounting. She stood tall, puffed out her tiny chest and tried to make herself look as authoritative as possible. "I must return to The Farm," she announced firmly.

"The Farm? Now?" queried Hackleberg in surprise.

"I am going to visit Quillypom," replied Lillybeth decidedly. She was presenting her best impression of being final and stern.

"Quillypom? I really do not believe she can help," declared Monique.

"We think she can help, without question," retorted Pommelstom. Filipa nodded in agreement.

"So do I," said Lillybeth defiantly.

She suddenly found it strange that she was in the position of defending Quillypom, but some part of her still felt... what was it...

sympathy for her?

"Yes, what are you going to have her do?" inquired Anati with a hint of cynicism.

Lillybeth faltered in her stern, decisive manners, for Anati taking a position against her was surprisingly hurtful. After the time they had spent together exploring Chrysalis, Lillybeth believed they had become close friends.

But this was too important. She had promised Hinsberth. Milchester and the others had to be freed. Lillybeth sent her reply with conviction, in a voice everyone could hear, "I am going to ask her to convene the Council."

All eyes turned upon Lillybeth, and feeling the heat of many a skeptical gaze, she desperately wished to hide behind the nearest piece of furniture.

Hinsberth cracked a smile, and thought to himself, she really is an odd duck, indeed, perhaps odd enough to make it happen.

"You cannot convene the Council. The Council only meets to make decisions on problems of importance to everyone on the The Farm, problems beyond the reach of the Mayor's Office. This problem is not so important to The Farm; everyone can go about their daily lives, working, talking, doing whatever they do without even knowing of poor Milchester. Besides, I am not certain ducklings are even allowed to make a request to convene the Council," stated Monique. "I have another suggestion. We came to Chrysalis because we believed Mister Fowler could help Hinsberth, and with some luck this turned out to be true, thanks to the fine doctors here. The problem with this Milchester may also be something we should present to Mister Fowler. As we can all see outside these windows, he and his colleagues certainly have the ability to solve a problem."

"Thank you. But it is not without a great deal of effort, I can assure you," added Filipa.

"*I* think we should do both. *You* go to Mister Fowler and I will go to Quillypom. I am going to convene the Council," Lillybeth announced firmly, her face crunched into a formidable expression.

Marista, who had been listening silently, offered her opinion, "I think Lillybeth is right. We do both. The situation with this Milchester, it is intolerable. In fact, it makes my stomach turn about in my belly to think about it. I trust you," she said, turning to Lillybeth. "And if anyone gives you any trouble, *any* trouble at all, please be sure to send them to me."

Marista then turned to Monique, "You have good ideas and you have helped us so much with Hinsberth. I think you are certainly right, we need to meet with this Mister Fowler and talk to him. This problem is big and complicated. I think we will need all of the help we can find, and we need to be quick about it."

"Do you know how to convene the Council? You seem fairly sure of yourself about this," Hackleberg inquired in an aside to his daughter.

"I do not know, but I am sure Quillypom does," replied Lillybeth.

"What makes you so certain Quillypom will do your bidding?" Millybeth inquired.

"Just a thought," quipped Lillybeth.

"Well then. As Marista said, you must be certain to let us know if you think you need any help," said Millybeth as she crouched down to meet Lillybeth's height.

But the distance of far-flung possibility had already returned to Lillybeth's eyes; her restless imagination had turned to planning for the formidable task ahead.

Millybeth and Hackleberg shared a concerned glance. They knew their daughter's rather far fetched plan, if possible, would take time. The ebb and flow of requests through the Mayor's Office, the operations of The Farm and the convening of the Council had never been regarded as particularly speedy or simple affairs. They knew they must leave immediately for The Farm, for some distance away, the very life of an unknown, generous soul might depend on it.

"We are leaving now," Millybeth announced. "We can't wait."

Hackleberg turned to Filipa and Pommelstom, "The Transporter. Please make sure it is well taken care of. For now, we must leave it here."

"Do not worry yourself," said Pommelstom. "It will be under the best of care."

Before turning away, Hackleberg gave he and Filipa a grateful glance.

Millybeth, Hackleberg and Lillybeth, under the pressure of time, swiftly bid everyone farewell. Those remaining behind wished them luck, for they knew they would likely need it. In an instant the Smythes were outside, waddling swiftly toward the edge of Chrysalis to take to the sky. Lillybeth turned her head and held her eyes on the doctor's office as they went.

"He will be fine," said Millybeth reassuringly as she glanced down upon her daughter.

Lillybeth turned her gaze forward, and then as they moved beyond the great dome of Chrysalis, up into the blazing blue sky.

Surrounded by beams of light, they took swiftly to the air. Spiralling up above the tree tops, they turned about, reversing the course of their arrival to fly back toward The Farm. They hoped they were not missed.

❖   ❖   ❖

After watching the Smythes depart, Monique turned to Filipa and Pommelstom, "So, how do we find Mister Fowler? We thought this was his place, but without question it has become much more than that."

"He is often busy. There are Migrators coming from all over and he meets with them to find out what they know. I have to say, he has become rather more scarce than in the past. His age is perhaps imposing the need for more rest. But sometimes I see him, just wandering around Chrysalis alone, especially in the evening. Filipa and I will see if we can find where he is spending his time these days," replied Pommelstom.

"We have to go now, but we will be back this evening to see how Hinsberth is doing, and in the meantime we will try to arrange a meeting between all of us and Mister Fowler," added Filipa.

And with that, Filipa and Pommelstom bid farewell and departed to begin their work for the day.

Anati, feeling a great deal of trepidation with the Smythes having left so suddenly for The Farm and the tense, sombre atmosphere, inquired of her mother in a whisper, "When are we going home?"

Monique had pondered over that very question, for she had initially only wanted to help Hinsberth. But there was something about Chrysalis, and Hinsberth's revelations which made her feel needed, involved. It would seem wrong, she thought, to leave now, and let the others confront the problem of Milchester without her. And she certainly preferred Anati to be there with her. Nevertheless, she was beginning to miss Arela and Poullaire. Perhaps, she thought, she and Anati could return home and bring them both for a visit to Chrysalis. Although, there was still that pesky issue of the rift between Mister Fowler and the Mayor's Office.

"We will see," Monique said finally to Anati. "I think for now we are still needed here, no?"

"Maybe," replied Anati uncertainly.

Anati's thoughts had turned to Lillybeth and how she was usually sitting by herself, deep in thought. Lillybeth was certainly curious, but despite her initial impression, Anati was beginning to admire Lillybeth's unencumbered ways and her seeming disregard, or perhaps total unawareness, of those implicit rules almost everyone else seemed preoccupied with, even if only unconsciously. Anati thought she could also be of help if Lillybeth was having to sway enough influence to confront a problem of the size Hinsheidt described. Perhaps, Anati thought, she was needed as well.

The doctor's office fell silent as imaginations roamed widely over the morning's revelations. Without knowing precisely what to do or how to do it, their minds drifted freely over the possibilities, and with their recent history, large scale disaster was a frequent theme. But at the moment, while sitting in the doctor's office in Chrysalis, they could only wait in hope for evening, for Filipa and Pommelstom, and with luck, for Mister Fowler.

❖   ❖   ❖

Inside the Mayor's Office, Quillypom sat wearily in her chair as yet another long, laborious day came to an end. For a moment she stared without expression at the pile of papers on her desk, which as she thought about it, seemed almost as tall as it had early that morning. The frequent, impatient rapping on her door had finally ceased and she leaned back in her chair and turned her eyes, as she had caught herself doing more and more often, to the window, to gaze out upon the distant horizon. The sun was setting, and the sky, burnt here and there with fiery wisps of cloud, was blazing in the brilliant hues of sunset. She pondered the beauty of the sky and became lost in the slowly changing scene beyond the walls of her office. But suddenly Quillypom was pulled back to the immediate by an insistent and familiar pattern of knocks on her solid office door.

"You may enter," she announced, quickly grabbing one of the papers out from the nearest stack and holding it in front of her with both wings.

The door opened and the Mayor entered, slowly crossing the room with hard and deliberate footsteps.

"I spoke with one of the assistants today," he announced flatly while seating himself.

"Yes?" inquired Quillypom, without any genuine interest.

"Well, apparently the Smythes, the Smerkingtons, the doctor, and Monique Plummage are all unaccounted for. For the second day, mind you. One of the doctor's neighbors — who recently reported some missing peppermint — also reported seeing a most unusual sight: several flyers taking off with a large object in tow, leaving from behind the good doctor's house," explained the Mayor with a hint of condescension. "Doubtlessly carrying the young Hinsberth," he added.

"I see..."

"There is probably little doubt at this point regarding their destination, would you agree?" inquired the Mayor.

"Little."

"Yes, I am glad you think so. I would like to add one more item for your consideration," the Mayor said as he raised his gaze to the wall over Quillypom's head. "A neighbor of the good doctor also mentioned in passing the arrival of the Messenger last evening, sometime after sunset. This particular neighbor had also seen the Messenger leave from this office earlier in the day, in full flight, to an unusually high altitude for any destination on The Farm."

The Mayor's eyes flashed at his wife.

"I see," said Quillypom. "And does this particular neighbor do anything besides watch the comings and goings of this office?"

Quillypom knew the Mayor was prodding her about the Messenger, and she was not about to let herself be drawn into any kind of argumentative trap.

With the Mayor still silent in thought, Quillypom took the initiative, "The Messenger is sent upon any number of deliveries each day. She could have returned and departed several times over the course of the day, without anyone bothering to notice or track her activities. When and where she goes is the concern of this office and this office alone."

The Mayor looked at Quillypom with suspicion, she had mounted a forceful defense, a little too forceful, in his opinion. Quillypom knew he thought he was on to something. He seemed as though he were slowly piecing things together.

Once again Quillypom turned her gaze to the window, where the sky was beginning to sink from fiery rose into a featureless dull grey,

CHAPTER 10

as the last burning rays of sunlight were extinguished by the horizon. The Mayor's eyes held steady, focused on the wall above Quillypom's head. With a skeptical air, he was clearly lost in troubling thoughts.

As the light dimmed in Quillypom's office, the uncomfortable silence had the better of her, and finally, she turned to face the Mayor, and with a grave expression, she stated in a hushed voice, "Welshley — I want them home."

The Mayor's eyes instantly fell upon his wife and a pained expression washed over his face. He rose stoically from his chair.

"Time to close. Shall we?" he said sternly, and at once he turned and lumbered toward the doorway.

Quillypom disappointedly gained her feet and went slowly to the door. The day had ended. They retreated to the rear of the house, into their private quarters.

❖ ❖ ❖

After sharing the evening meal at the doctor's office, Doctor Durmlint and Doctor Wichsluff bid goodbye and returned to their families on the outskirts of Chrysalis. Marista and Eldsworth huddled around Hinsberth, who was becoming restless, after so much time spent unconscious he was aching to move his stiff limbs. With full bellies, everyone was becoming fidgety and impatient waiting for the return of Filipa and Pommelstom and news of a possible meeting with Mister Fowler.

Monique in particular was rather anxious to see Filipa and Pommelstom. The day was now old and the gleam of sunlight outside was softening; Chrysalis was bathed in the inviting glow of dusk. The light played upon the lush hues of the gardens and reflected magnificently in the pools and ponds.

Monique was enraptured by the beauty of the transformation taking place beyond the large windows and she suddenly had an idea. She whispered to Anati, "We should go."

"Go where?" asked Anati.

"Out."

"Out where?"

"Out there, in the light."

Anati glanced out the windows. Her eyes widened.

"Ah. Yes!" Anati agreed wholeheartedly.

Anati was quite content to spend her time wandering around and absorbing the nuances of Chrysalis, and for an instant, she was missing Lillybeth.

"Excuse us. We will be back soon. Just going out for a moment," Monique announced.

As Anati was even more impatient than her mother, both she and Monique were hoping Filipa and Pommelstom would return while they were out exploring.

Mother and daughter waddled outside the doctor's office and gazed upward in awe at the colossal ceiling of Chrysalis. Warm shafts of faintly amber light beamed down through the immense skylights, setting the landscape ablaze. Monique and Anati quite fancied most anything of an agreeable aesthetic nature, and they went eagerly out along the trails to ascend one of the arched bridges. There they perused their surroundings with great excitement, as if surveying the tasty treats of a candy shop. They stood on the bridge for a time, leaning over the ornate rail, peering into the far reaches of Chrysalis, trying to decide where to go next.

Distracted by the landscape, they took no notice of the approach of another admirer of the scene onto the bridge. He was an elder duck with a pair of very worn looking spectacles lying across his bill. He wore an undersized brown vest, a diminutive tie around his neck, and a pair of wrinkled old shoes which matched his vest. He waddled slowly up the arc of the bridge; with every step his feet scuffled lightly against the smooth wooden planks. He came to a stop just beside Monique and stood in silence. He placed his wings out to rest himself on the rail and watched the light play upon the intricate landscape spread wide into the hazy distance.

Monique was startled when she noticed a fellow admirer of Chrysalis had suddenly appeared at her side, but then all at once she was pleased to have one more spirit with which to share the all-too fleeting moment.

"It is beautiful, no?" she asked of the newcomer, with her eyes still fixed upon the scene.

"Yes, undoubtedly," said the elder duck. "If one could live permanently in the glow of dawn and dusk, one would indeed be most fortunate."

"Ah, yes. Without question," agreed Monique. "I think it a shame, we become busy, doing this and that, and we mostly miss these brief times, these small opportunities each day."

Anati nodded in agreement. She and Lillybeth had been trying to explore everything they could in Chrysalis, for fear they might miss something worthwhile, or perhaps even extraordinary.

"It is beautiful," she stated whimsically while admiring the reflection of the hanging gardens in the still water which lay like a great mirror beneath the bridge.

"Beauty. It is a sign, an impression, that tells us when we have done something right," the elder duck declared.

"What do you mean?" asked Monique.

"When we see things — things that we regard as beautiful, they contain some character, such as symmetry, or harmony, and they have these properties because deep down, they are as they were meant to be, without disruption. When we interfere with things and we create ugliness, it is because we have made mistakes, we have not read things deeply enough, and we have been either unwise or careless," he explained, and while still peering out over Chrysalis, he continued, "It is harmony, in the relationships between things, so that one thing supports another in a beneficial manner, and is in turn supported by it, that beauty comes forth. Take this bridge, the pools, the gardens and the light. They might be beautiful when viewed by themselves, but together, in this particular arrangement, they become even more so, as though beauty were fundamentally related to their organization, to their relationships. Relationships are beautiful. Friendship is beautiful. Love is beautiful."

Monique leaned forward over the rail. For as long as she could remember she had many thoughts, thoughts which always struggled to come to the surface, always searching for the befitting words to find their expression. Her thoughts had never come forth with much coherence — they were always jumbled — but as the elder duck spoke she felt them rising once again, only to pause just beneath the surface, and as they did so, she recalled the many long conversations with her mother, for she also struggled with finding the precise words to express her ideas, and eventually found her painting much more beholden to the task.

CHAPTER 10

After a long silence spent watching the landscape slowly fade into silhouette, Monique offered a piece of the puzzle in her mind, "I have often thought about these things — about what you are describing. When I was young, my mother, she would talk about composition, the ideas behind her imagery, things that she always found hard to put into words. My mother... She was a painter."

"I know," said the elder duck. "I miss her dearly. And if she were here, I know she would have asked me to say to you what I have just said."

Monique was struck silent for an instant. Regaining her composure she asked, "How do you know my mother?"

"Upon seeing you on the bridge, I thought this evening's stroll had most certainly taken a strange turn. I believed I had somehow shifted back in time. If I may say, you look just like your mother," and he bent backward to look directly at Anati, "And you look just like her mother, but much smaller, of course."

"Mister Fowler?" Monique asked.

Since it had been so long she did not recognize his appearance, but the combination of a philosophical nature and dry sense of humor were unmistakable.

"Please, if I may ask, call me "Chaffy". I am much too old for formalities," he replied.

Monique was happy to fulfill Chaffy's request, and as she considered it, other ideas came into her mind. She thought about how young ducklings, Lillybeth being a notable example, seemed oblivious to the formalities Chaffy referred to; the notions of titles, of status, or prestige, and so it seemed with the older ducks, at least with her mother and Chaffy. They seemed comfortable with themselves. They were not motivated to adhere to the implicit rules of any particular social milieu. Only those trying to find their way, those in the middle who were perhaps unsure of themselves seemed bound to the unwritten rules of the social game. Not that the younger and elder ducks were wayward or impolite, but like Lillybeth or Chaffy, they seemed to possess a certain freedom of thought and action.

"Monique," Chaffy said to get her attention, and Monique was at once surprised he remembered her name. "Please take your time and explore Chrysalis. Look around, but not as if in simple admiration. Look deeply, absorb what you see. You will see your mother's thoughts, her beliefs about the beauty of life. Many years ago, she helped me to design this place. Some things, some ideas are beyond the power of words, and she left her message here, for everyone to read and understand, to be inspired by, to enjoy. Part of her is here, for as long as Chrysalis remains here."

Monique and Anati looked silently over the landscape while listening to Chaffy. Monique could do nothing to stop them, her cheeks were soon wet with tears.

"When we create something, we manifest our ideas, our view of the world becomes inherent in its design. In a place such as this, it is as a painting, or a sculpture, writ large upon the earth. The selection of the materials, its shape, the careful details of its construction, represent how we feel about ourselves and our place in the world, and also how we value those who build it, those who will look upon it and those who will live in it. It is a collection of messages, of signals, in addition to a place. It is not just a structure to provide shelter, it is a place for gathering, eating, playing, resting. In essence, for living."

Monique did not know how to respond. She agreed with Chaffy's

CHAPTER 10

words and ideas, for he seemed to have a penchant for describing her thoughts and for finding those words which she herself had struggled with over the years. She was glad Anati was listening, as she also seemed to be silently mulling over the ideas Chaffy was so freely offering. As Chaffy spoke, Monique could not decide on whether he was still conveying the ideas he had shared in conversation with her mother many years prior, for they seemed distantly familiar, and listening to him brought forth memories of her youth.

As Monique pondered over Chaffy's final point regarding gathering, playing and living, her thoughts suddenly turned to Milchester, and she turned to face Chaffy.

"Chaffy, if I may ask, might you join us in returning to the doctor's office?" Monique inquired in a hopeful tone. "There is something — something of great importance we wish to discuss with you."

"Certainly. I would love to. I was meaning to go there as soon as I had a moment to myself, outside of my usual evening stroll of course. I heard there were visitors from The Farm who had arrived with an ill duckling. News does spread fast around Chrysalis. I like to think it has something to do with the acoustics of the dome, but, I believe the reason in fact resides elsewhere. I have wanted to see how they have been coming along, I do miss having visits from The Farm. They are all too rare."

Chaffy turned from the bridge rail and politely waved his wing to let Monique and Anati lead the way. Together, they waddled off the bridge and proceeded on toward the doctor's office.

❖   ❖   ❖

At the doctor's office, Doctor Lochswyn was preparing to leave first thing the following morning. Hinsberth seemed to be progressing and Doctor Tauffenshufter could certainly administer the remaining treatments before Hinsberth would be ready to return to The Farm. Doctor Lochswyn did not want to leave her office unattended for too long; being the only practitioner of medicine on The Farm, everyone agreed she should return as soon as possible. She inquired for some assistance flying back the supplies she had packed in the Transporter, and Marista, Eldsworth, Monique and Anati volunteered to carry whatever she had to leave behind when they too were ready to depart for home. Doctor Lochswyn and the Chrysalis staff all agreed to try to visit one another frequently and share the knowledge gained through their work.

As Doctor Lochswyn packed her belongings, Marista and Eldsworth were in fervent but hushed conversation over the feasibility of a rescue. They felt indebted to Milchester and were quite disturbed by what Hinsberth had told them. It was clear how deeply Hinsberth had been effected by Milchester's plight. There were pigs on The Farm, and every now and then the ducks and pigs would happen upon each other and say hello, or even stop and ruminate together over the weather or any particularly notable event. Marista and Eldsworth could not at all imagine the pigs from The Farm trapped as Milchester was. To them it seemed an impossibility.

A sudden rap on the door echoed faintly through the room, and Eldsworth eagerly offered to go and answer. He waddled up to the front and opened the door, and was immediately happy to see Filipa and Pommelstom. They were accompanied by two other large ducks similar in dress and appearance.

"Eldsworth, this is Bardslow," Filipa said as she pointed to the duck on one side. "And this is Bentlby," she said as she pointed to the other.

"I am certainly very pleased to meet you both," said Eldsworth. "Are you medical staff? Friends? Patients?"

"They are my brothers," replied Filipa, before Bentlby or Bardslow could open their bills.

"My apologies. I did of course see the resemblance, but did not want to mention it, just in case."

"They were working with Pommelstom and I for part of the day, and we told them about this morning — what Hinsberth had said. They are interested to meet with everyone, to see if they can help," Filipa explained.

"Well, we are all rather pleased to hear that. Your desire to help means a lot to us, I can assure you," Eldsworth said to Bardslow and Bentlby. "Everyone is still waiting in the patient room — the one with the pools — except Monique and Anati. They decided to venture out and explore the surroundings, and I really cannot blame them. It is a fascinating place you have here."

Following Eldsworth back into the patient room, Filipa quickly introduced everyone to Bardslow and Bentlby. She mentioned how they were also intent to set up a meeting with Mister Fowler to discuss the plight of Milchester and his fellows.

As Filipa was speaking, another rap on the door interrupted the conversation and again Eldsworth swiftly excused himself. He soon returned and behind him came Monique, Anati and an elder duck who entered the doorway and stopped, letting his eyes slowly wander over the room.

Eldsworth swiftly dispensed with the introductions, "Mister Fowler, this is Marista, my wife, and Hinsberth, my son."

Upon meeting him at the door, Mister Fowler had asked Eldsworth to please call him Chaffy, but formality was a deeply embedded part of Eldsworth's nature. Chaffy was quick to appreciate the character of his well mannered acquaintance, and he let him proceed with the more formal introduction.

Chaffy went over to Hinsberth.

"I am certainly happy to hear you are feeling better," he said with some enthusiasm.

"Thank you," said Hinsberth politely.

"If I may say, please do not thank me. Thank Doctor Lochswyn, the medical staff, and your family and friends who helped bring you here, with some effort and clever engineering I understand. I was excited to hear residents of The Farm had come to Chrysalis, and even more so when I learned of the circumstances and that some of us here were able to help," Chaffy explained.

"On the subject of helping," came Filipa's voice, "We have learned of a problem."

"Yes?" asked Chaffy. "It is not Hinsberth? You *are* doing fine?" he asked of Hinsberth.

"I am fine — feeling a bit better," Hinsberth confirmed.

"No, it is not Hinsberth, but rather something Hinsberth has discovered. Perhaps related to what made him ill," said Filipa.

While Chaffy listened closely, Filipa and Pommelstom swiftly recounted the tale Hinsberth had told them that morning. As he listened, Chaffy began looking off into the distance. He held his wings behind him. He made his way over to the windows. His normally informal manner became awash in a seriousness he displayed only when in deep concentration over something which was truly troubling.

CHAPTER 10

When Filipa and Pommelstom had finished recounting Hinsberth's tale, Chaffy stood silent. He gazed out over Chrysalis.

"We must free them," Hinsberth insisted in a raspy voice.

Chaffy was obviously moved by what he heard, but did not turn from the window nor speak, and everyone remained silent, frozen, waiting with anticipation.

Then he turned to face the group.

"First of all," he began, "I would like to say this Milchester is a laudable character, and it sounds as though we are indebted to him for helping young Hinsberth. But a thousand? Filipa, Pommelstom, are you certain?"

"There were three buildings. If they were indeed full, given their size, at least many hundreds, maybe a thousand or more. It is difficult to make a precise guess, having spent so little time there," answered Pommelstom.

"The greater the number the more difficult the problem, but also the greater need for action. Hinsberth has bravely brought this problem to our attention, and now it seems impossible to ignore," said Chaffy.

Bentlby spoke up, with some conviction as he always enjoyed having his opinions taken seriously, "Bardslow and I heard Hinsberth's story this morning from Filipa and Pommelstom. We think something should be done. We should at least consider helping with a plan or two for a rescue. What is happening to them… Well, we are willing to help, the four of us," Bentlby offered on behalf of himself and his siblings.

Chaffy nodded.

"Thank you, Bentlby," said Chaffy. "Your willingness to help is indeed appreciated."

He turned back to the window. Night had fallen and Chrysalis was beginning to glow.

The problem they were facing seemed enormous. A solution would undoubtedly be difficult and complicated, if not impossible. Chaffy, as had happened only once in a great while, was not quite sure how to respond, so he began thinking aloud.

"When we decided to build this place, one concern was the possible return of humans to The Farm. Of course, not everyone saw the problem in the same way. Those of us on The Farm at the time had been part of the migrations, and when we settled there it seemed a fine decision. Myself and others remained in contact with the Migrators, and we have continued to do so. In designing Chrysalis, we wished to build a place away from humans, where we could experiment and hopefully support ourselves indefinitely. We wished to have Chrysalis isolated and hidden, and be a place where anyone could come to visit, to learn or to stay. When we communicate with the Migrators, we not only let them know we are here, we also share what we know regarding the migration routes and the dangers along the way. Filipa and Pommelstom are quite active in guiding the Migrators away from where humans have been known to present a danger."

Chaffy paused for a moment.

"This problem, in order to address it, may require confronting humans, something Chrysalis has tried to avoid. Although I helped to design and build Chrysalis and have lived here from the beginning, there are no leaders here. There is no formal governance, and what would be required to help Milchester and his fellows may involve some risk. How much? We do not know. But I am uncertain as to whether Chrysalis would be willing to take such a risk."

Chaffy peered outward and everyone else pondered his words, especially those regarding the history of Chrysalis and how the residents wished to protect themselves from the outside world. What if in attempting a rescue, something went wrong? Would the humans somehow trace the effort back to Chrysalis? Or back to The Farm? With the manner in which the humans were treating Milchester and his fellows, everyone understood the potential reluctance to becoming involved. But how could they possibly leave Milchester and his companions to their bleak lives and cruel fate? For those from The Farm, there seemed only one option.

Marista broke the silence.

"Mister Fowler, you say there are no leaders here, but that may only be regarding titles. I hear how the other residents speak about you. You have respect here, and I think your words have influence. I know my son, and as I have told the others, he would not be telling his tale and asking that we do something if it were not important, and not only to him personally, he does not think that way. I see what you have designed here, what has been built, and I believe if you and the other residents of Chrysalis can create such things, than you can help us figure out a way to free Milchester and to free the others who are trapped as he is. Their situation is intolerable, it makes my stomach turn. If we cannot help them, then who is going to? Who even knows about them? Are we going to go about our days, knowing what is happening to our fellows, and in Hinsberth's case, his friend? A friend that helped him survive a horrible fever, and we will forget about him? Oh, no, I say!" she stated in a decided tone. She shook her head and waved her large wings, sending a breeze through the room.

"Filipa, Pommelstom, Bardslow and Bentlby are standing here. They have been told about what is happening and they are ready to help. I say we tell some of the others who may be able to help, and perhaps they will also decide to help."

Chaffy peered out the window as he considered Marista's argument. He had spent many years living at Chrysalis, and he was well aware of the underlying, shared ideals held by most residents. The notion of interfering in human affairs would not be enticing to them. But could they be swayed? Marista was correct. Everyone who had heard Hinsberth's tale was ready to help. Could the plight of Milchester, lost in the unknown some distance away, persevere over the desire of Chrysalis to remain distant from the outside world?

"I think you have made some valuable points. And you are correct, Hinsberth's tale has been persuasive. Filipa and her brothers are ready to help. As I mentioned before, we do not have any permanent governance, decisions are generally made by individuals. But a few residents, flying off and potentially becoming entangled in human affairs and putting Chrysalis at risk?"

Monique, with a bit of hesitancy, finally decided to speak up with an anxious voice, "I — I understand this concern. But what we discussed earlier, on the bridge, the beauty of this place, the design, the expression of life..." Monique paused a moment and then began to speak with great intensity, "How can we live with this, the awareness of its antithesis, even so close by? I think of such beauty as represented by Chrysalis, and I think — I think of what my mother would tell me. About contrast. About how things are different, and that is part of the world. Ugliness helps us appreciate the beautiful. But not this time. I say no! Because Chrysalis exists, does not mean that where this poor Milchester lives must exist. This to me is what my mind tells me, and my heart tells me even more. It tells me that we are going to free this Milchester, and as for me, I am going to help make it happen, and no one and no Council is going to do anything about it!"

Anati glanced with wide eyes at her mother. What was happening to her? She was acting strangely, but with conviction, and not for herself, not for attention. She had gone from wanting to help, to wanting to do it alone if she had to. Anati had not seen her mother like this before. Certainly, she was startled by it. She thought how her father would be beaming, happy to see her now. And even more importantly for Anati, with this new version of her mother, her sister would certainly be thwarted in trying to impose her wishes.

Chaffy, however, could feel the growing tension in the room. Monique was strong in her convictions. So was Marista. They had presented compelling arguments. But were they compelling enough?

Eldsworth suddenly inquired with curiosity, "If I may, how long do you think it would take to organize an effort to assist The Farm?"

After silently listening to the discussion, Eldsworth's question finally provoked Hinsberth to speak, "Milchester does not have time. No one is coming to take us, just because we are who we are. They will come for him. They may be taking others, even as we speak. When we look to the future, it seems distant, full of possibilities. For Milchester, the future is short. It is soon. There is nothing. No choices, only to be taken like everyone else. We think differently, because we live differently, because we were born not as one of them, not as Milchester. Our ways of doing things are designed for long times, long futures and long distances. But for Milchester, we cannot wait."

Once again Hinsberth's words threw the room into silence. As everyone pondered over what he had said, Anati's tiny voice, trembling with concern, interrupted the stillness, "What happens to them? Where are they taken?"

Chaffy turned from the window. His eyes passed over all those in the room.

"As you are aware," he began, "we are in contact with the Migrators who pass over Chrysalis twice per year. They have been observing the humans and sometimes what they see is disturbing. In many places, humans seem fine to share with us the ponds and fields, even as they use them for their own purposes. But at times, terrible things have been done. I think what Hinsberth has discovered is an example of what I am referring to. From what we have gathered, when they are taken, they do not survive. And I will say no more."

Chaffy was confirming what everyone had already suspected, but nevertheless it was difficult to hear. Anati was particularly disturbed, and she placed her head in her mother's wings. With Anati and Hinsberth present, Chaffy did not wish to reveal any of his suspicions regarding the treatment of the pigs and what they were used for. It was but one more reason for the creation of Chrysalis so many years ago, to escape the dangers of such a world, a world in which life itself was taken as a mere commodity.

After Chaffy had affirmed the mortal danger Milchester and his companions were in and Hinsberth had made everyone aware of the urgent need for action, a growing feeling of despair had overtaken the room. A feasible rescue was beginning to seem distant, complicated. Hinsberth had reminded everyone the steps they would have to take to organize themselves for a rescue were based on perceptions, on methods of doing things under particular circumstances, in a sense fabricated and unreal, while Milchester's suffering was real and immediate. What was to be done?

Chaffy noticed the increasingly dour expressions. Just a moment ago, Marista and Monique had presented impassioned arguments. But they all knew that with either Chrysalis or The Farm, progress toward a plan for a rescue might be pushed into a future which for Milchester would almost certainly be too late.

All eyes slowly turned upon Chaffy, and as he glanced around the room, he paused to look at Hinsberth, who was slumping in his bed, as if the fire inside had been doused, even if not quite extinguished, and then at Anati, who's head remained buried in the wings of her mother. He considered his ideals, his principles, not only regarding Chrysalis, but his belief in the profound mysteries and dignity of life, and how life in its high ideal should be allowed to flourish. It had been his dream, a deeply held conviction for as long as he could remember. Chrysalis was but one manifestation.

Presently, before him were members of the generation that had grown after the migrations had ended, after they had settled on The Farm. And he was amazed at how they progressed, there was an idealism, a fire burned inside them, and their standards and expectations for life were high and unselfish. Also before him were two ducklings, and he thought about the message they would receive if Chrysalis did not offer to help. He looked at Anati and Hinsberth, and he tried to confirm for himself what he must do.

In an instant, he made his decision.

"Very well, then. Filipa, Pommelstom, Bardslow, and Bentlby, I will need your assistance. We will need to find whether or not anyone will assist us in working with The Farm. We must develop a plan."

"You have it," said Bardslow. There was no hesitation.

Under his breath Hinsberth whispered, "Thank you, from Milchester."

ANATI

*"There will be a headwind coming from the direction of The Farm,
I am sure. Always at this time of year — or any time of year."*

CHAPTER 11

UPON A STRANGE PLACE

AFTER A LONG FLIGHT, Millybeth, Hackleberg and Lillybeth finally alighted in front of their home. They took a moment to survey their surroundings, and seeing that everything was as they had left it before the journey to Chrysalis, they went inside. Millybeth and Hackleberg immediately went to the kitchen and scoured shelves and cabinets, searching for ingredients to prepare the evening meal. Lillybeth flopped wearily down onto a pillow. She propped herself beneath a window to look out over the darkening landscape and steep herself in thought…

"Here, have some. It is still warm," said Millybeth sometime later, gently nudging Lillybeth's shoulder and presenting her a lukewarm bowl of aromatic soup.

"How long?" asked Lillybeth, rubbing her eyes.

"Not long, but you do need your rest," answered Millybeth.

Sitting up, Lillybeth stared sleepily into her soup. She stirred her spoon round and round slowly in the bowl and watched the spiraling swirls form in its wake. She noticed if she stirred the soup just right, the swirls would form a regular pattern, flowing smoothly, moving round as if chasing her spoon. If she stirred too slowly, there was not enough agitation, and the larger particles would lumber along the bottom, only reluctantly rolling forward. If she stirred too fast, the soup would try to lift out of the bowl, and she would have to cease her experiment before making a mess of her supper.

After some time watching the soup, Lillybeth's stomach began to grumble in protest. At once she slurped the soup in one great gulp, picking up the bowl and drinking it like a mug of frigid pond water on a scorching summer day. She wiped her bill and returned her gaze to the window, but only darkness could be seen.

Millybeth and Hackleberg were concerned about their daughter, they could see her mind grinding away. They left her alone for the moment as they tidied the house for the night, and then came back to lift and carry her to bed; once again she had silently slipped away into slumber.

The next morning, Lillybeth awakened as the first rays of sunlight streamed brightly through the windows. Millybeth and Hackleberg were also awakened as Lillybeth stirred. They swiftly rose to prepare themselves for the day; they planned to visit Hackleberg's parents, who lived just a bit further out in the rolling grasslands near the edge of The Farm. But first, they were to accompany Lillybeth to The Pond, and then Lillybeth would proceed on alone to the Mayor's Office, as she had insisted.

A quick breakfast was devoured with little formality, and with comfortably satisfied bellies, the three ducks waddled off toward The Pond, beneath a brilliant cobalt sky and the welcoming rows of gently waving grass. The breezy, light and mild air was crisp and comforting, and Lillybeth had the thought that on such a fine morning perhaps those in the Mayor's Office would be even more excited to see her than before. And perhaps, on such a day, Quillypom just might be under such a summer spell that she might even choose to fulfill Lillybeth's rather unusual request.

After a silent stroll, the Smythes arrived at the shoreline of The Pond, and there Millybeth and Hackleberg bid their daughter farewell and offered a few welcome words of encouragement. They wrapped her in their wings.

"Do not to regard the Mayor's Office too seriously," remarked Millybeth, "They have their own ways of doing things and they might seem a bit rude at times."

Lillybeth nodded her head, but she really was not sure to what, exactly, her mother was referring to, for lately the Mayor's Office had seemed most accommodating, even friendly. Lillybeth waddled alone over the footpath ringing The Pond and soon she was at the Mayor's Office. As she anticipated, even though still early morning, inside the Mayor's Office was already beginning to bustle with activity. But the door was closed.

Lillybeth spied the garden planter she had used as a stool, it lay on its side, as though it had been carelessly shoved to one side of the walkway. Lillybeth pushed and pulled the pot back through the garden and placed it in front of the door. She hopped on top and seized hold of the knocker. She stretched her wings taught over her head, and then she thumped the knocker hard against the door three times. Hopping down, she waited impatiently for someone to answer her call.

Soon the Messenger appeared, she peeked wide eyed round the door for an instant before catching sight of Lillybeth standing beside the planter. An expression of shock melted away, replaced by a faint smile of recognition.

As Lillybeth expected, when led inside she was met with rows of faces, leaning out of doors and windows. Did everyone in the Mayor's Office spend their days merely waiting around to know the identity of the latest visitor? However, this morning their expressions were not of the friendliest sort, for they seemed a little more surprised than before to see Lillybeth waddling through the doorway. As soon as Lillybeth entered the hall the faces retreated, to return to the important work of managing The Farm.

Lillybeth went directly to Quillypom's office. She thought that if anyone in the vast labyrinth of the Mayor's Office could help her, it would undoubtedly be her friend Quillypom. However, Quillypom's office door was closed solidly, and Lillybeth was unable to reach the knocker. She went to search immediately for something she could stand upon to make herself taller. But with so many doors lining both sides the hallway was sparsely adorned. Most every door was closed, so Lillybeth wandered down the hall until she found one with a thin shaft of light poking around the edge. After making sure she was unseen, she cracked the door open and peeked inside. In the tiny room were great stacks of paper; so high they seemed unstable; she imagined at any moment they might come tumbling to the ground and the sheets would scatter about propelled by a breeze of their own making. Lining the walls were cabinets and shelves and bins of various sorts, all overrun with paper and ink and other odds and ends used in the important business of the Mayor's Office. Lillybeth searched for something tall and light, something she could carry or push and stand upon. Finally, she spied a small wooden cabinet topped only by a pair of massive hard bound books. It seemed tall enough, so at once

Lillybeth decided to scramble up the neighboring stack of paper and clear the top.

It was at this moment she lost her footing. She tumbled backward into one of the lofty columns. A great swaying ensued, as if paper had turned to water, and this was followed by a great tumbling. The floor shook, trembling under the weight of the collapse. The other columns quickly followed suit, deciding at once to follow a similar course. Deafening thumps and thuds shuddered the room as the paper columns and books struck the ground and scattered into the air. Fortunately Lillybeth found herself landing softly in a cushioning pile of paper. She quickly departed from the room unharmed; fearful as to whether anyone had noticed the sudden din from down the hall.

Standing alone, trying to appear nonchalant in the hallway, she was met again with an inquisitive crowd of faces, all staring at her and seeming rather stunned. Lillybeth took little notice as her eyes went to Quillypom's door. It was open! At least partway. She quickly raced down the hall to slip into the narrow aperture. Quillypom was in her usual position, seated behind her desk, discussing something of undoubtedly great importance with another visitor clad in rather formal attire.

Quillypom's expression turned to surprise as she noticed Lillybeth standing meekly in her office. Lillybeth smiled nervously and waved a friendly if bashful greeting with only the end of her wing. Quillypom allowed Lillybeth only a quick glance, she continued to speak with her guest without pause, as if Lillybeth were not even there. Unsure what to do, Lillybeth stood silent and motionless, patiently waiting for the conversation to end. Every now and then the visitor glanced over at the duckling and then set his eyes quickly back upon Quillypom. His expression was not at all friendly, and Lillybeth grew more nervous, thinking perhaps knocking first would have been the better strategy. The volume of the conversation quieted after Quillypom noticed Lillybeth's presence, and Lillybeth concluded their words must be too important for her to hear. Nevertheless, she continued to wait patiently; it was the least she could do for Quillypom.

Finally the visitor rose from the small chair facing Quillypom's desk, and they shook wings and he departed huffily from the room. Lillybeth smiled at him as he passed, but he kept his gaze focused straight ahead, as if deliberately avoiding Lillybeth's gaze. Lillybeth thought this very odd. She wondered what they could be doing at the Mayor's Office that was so important and secretive that it might be revealed even through their eyes.

Quillypom set her eyes on Lillybeth and shook her head. Her face was stern and Lillybeth worried for a moment that she might even refuse to see her. But as Quillypom looked upon Lillybeth, she took a deep breath and her eyes softened. Without a word she waved Lillybeth over to take her seat.

Lillybeth hopped onto the chair in front of Quillypom's desk, and took up her usual position with only the top of her head and her eyes visible to Quillypom.

"Little Lillybeth," began Quillypom, shaking her head in apparent dismay. "What might I do for you this morning?"

Lillybeth shifted in her seat a little, but then she straightened herself up as much as possible, trying to look tall.

"I wish to convene the Council," she stated flatly with a rather serious tone.

"May I ask you to repeat that please?" inquired Quillypom.

"The *Council*," said Lillybeth.

Quillypom smiled. The gumption of this little duckling! Her complete unawareness of the formalities and rules regarding the operations of The Farm and the Mayor's Office were, on this visit, somehow refreshing.

"Lillybeth, the Council is only requested at particular times and for certain, important purposes. I have a set of procedures and guidelines — somewhere. You may have a copy for your household if you wish," Quillypom explained as she looked over the desktop and proceeded to open drawers.

"We don't have time for that," declared Lillybeth.

At once Quillypom discontinued searching for the booklet, and she gazed at Lillybeth curiously.

"I see. Well, what then do we have time for?" she asked Lillybeth in a condescending manner.

"To convene the Council. But we need to do it fast," answered Lillybeth.

"Lillybeth, convening the Council is a serious matter, and I do not have time to sit here and play. I have many appointments and a great deal of work to finish today, and I do not want to keep either my appointments or my tasks waiting," said Quillypom, trying to hasten Lillybeth's departure from her office.

Lillybeth pondered Quillypom's response for a moment.

"Are any of them emergencies?" she asked.

"No — there are not any emergencies, but some may be rather urgent," replied Quillypom.

"Mine is an emergency," stated Lillybeth.

"Even if it were, I do not believe ducklings can even convene a

CHAPTER 11

Council meeting. Perhaps we can discuss this another time. I do appreciate your coming to me and asking for help, but I must return to this morning's schedule," Quillypom explained; hoping to motivate Lillybeth toward the door.

"May I ask for you to check?" asked Lillybeth.

"Check what?" Quillypom replied.

"Check and see if I can have a Council meeting?" asked Lillybeth.

"I see. Yes. Certainly I can check. But under one condition. If the regulation prohibits you from convening a Council meeting, might I ask that you allow me to return to my other pressing matters?" Quillypom asked.

"Sure," replied Lillybeth simply.

Quillypom immediately rose from her chair, and went over to the giant cabinet in the corner with the solid doors hiding the three huge drawers which made the eerie creaking sound. Quillypom pulled open the middle drawer; it groaned under the heavy weight of several voluminous books. She looked over the contents for a moment, withdrew a good-sized book and then returned to her desk. She set the book down on her desk with a decided thud.

She paused to glance firmly at Lillybeth for a moment, and then opened the book. She turned to and studied a specific page, her eyes roamed intently over each word.

"Ah! Here we are," she announced.

Quillypom read. She glanced nervously up at Lillybeth. She shifted in her seat. She reread the page.

"Well?" asked Lillybeth impatiently.

Quillypom considered herself to be an honest, dedicated, loyal and diligent worker. But now she found her values in conflict; she was in a predicament. She looked into Lillybeth's deep, hopeful and inquiring eyes. Despite the opportunity to bring the present conversation to an expedient end, she decided honesty, for the time being, was the most important.

"There is nothing in the regulations — as they are written — that specifically prohibits a duckling from convening the Council. It seems only to be a common notion ducklings are not so privileged. From the actual regulations there is no such prohibition," she stated aloud, somewhat surprised herself at the finding.

"Great! Then how do we start? How do we do it?" Lillybeth inquired with a renewed note of optimism.

"We? I thought *you* wanted to convene the Council," retorted Quillypom.

"I thought *you* were certainly the one to help. We do not often do such things alone, do we?" replied Lillybeth.

"No. You are right. Not usually. Convening the Council is typically an act regarding a matter beyond individual concern, even beyond the normal operations of The Farm; something that effects us all," Quillypom explained.

"Good. So how do we do it?" Lillybeth repeated.

Quillypom slumped into her chair. She was obligated by the responsibilities of her position to provide such information to Lillybeth, indeed to any resident of The Farm, if so requested. She took a deep breath, for she knew this day would indeed be a long one.

❖ ❖ ❖

On The Farm, fact metamorphosed to rumor and spread swiftly. A Council was to be convened, and, it was being called by a duckling regarding some unspecified concern. Without any specifics, speculations over the reason for the Council meeting became wild, bizarre and of course, immensely intriguing. Under the peculiar circumstances imaginations were free to roam without bound, and they did. All the mystery and speculation regarding the meeting worked in Lillybeth's favor, as nearly everyone developed an interest in attending just to see which of the rumors might be true.

Lillybeth returned home in the late afternoon. She would have been famished but for Quillypom having provided her a generous lunch. Lillybeth was rather grateful to Quillypom; she had helped her immensely with the laborious and complicated procedures for convening the Council.

Quillypom had pressed Lillybeth on the reason for the meeting, but specifics were not explicitly required for the public announcement under the regulations, and Lillybeth did not want to offer Quillypom an inadequate abstract of Hinsberth's tale. Lillybeth held fast to the idea that she could not give a proper description of Milchester's plight in such a brief summary as allowed by the space on the public notice.

Quillypom finished the day ultimately wondering for whom the regulations were written, as Lillybeth's simple line of questioning left her without recourse but to grant her requests. In the end it seemed surprisingly easy to convene a Council meeting, in contrast to what most residents of The Farm believed.

Normally Council meetings were announced in public notices spread about The Farm for a *number* of days prior to the actual event. Lillybeth, with Quillypom's reluctantly given advice, took the expedient route of calling an emergency meeting, which bypassed many requirements for public notice. Only once before had an emergency meeting been called; when The Pond had flooded and immediate action needed to be taken to address the water and irrigation systems.

For Lillybeth's meeting, a notice was put up at the Mayor's Office on a message board hung beside the entrance door. The hastily written announcement revealed the Council meeting was to be held that very evening at sunset. Quillypom was a member of the Council, as was Mayor Swellington, Doctor Lochswyn and four others. The doctor had thankfully arrived home from Chrysalis the previous morning. Given the shortness of time for preparation, Quillypom was expedient in sending the Messenger out to notify all the Council members of the imminent emergency meeting.

Everything was swiftly prepared. The venue for Council meetings was the Old Barn, even though the roof was somewhat dilapidated and some of the structure needed repair, inside was a generous open space allowing a large number of Farm residents to gather, and an elevated platform upon which each member of the Council had a privileged seat. If the Council was asked to convene, the parties submitting the request would present the issue or proposal from a podium placed centrally on the floor below the Council platform. For Lillybeth's proposal, she would be alone, facing the Council from the podium.

When Lillybeth arrived home and told her parents about the events of the day, she was met only with silence, and bills which slowly hung ever lower as Lillybeth recounted how helpful Quillypom had been in helping her convene the Council. Hackleberg and Millybeth had only just returned from visiting Hackleberg's parents, where they had a fine time together, even though Lillybeth's grandparents had difficulty understanding why Lillybeth had not joined, as she was spending her day at the Mayor's Office for an undisclosed purpose. When

CHAPTER 11

Millybeth and Hackleberg arrived home that evening and noticed Lillybeth was still out, their imaginations had the better of them and they began to worry that yes, maybe she was indeed busily convening the Council. As Lillybeth recounted the whole convoluted process, it was as they had feared. It was not that they were entirely surprised Lillybeth had done so, but they were fearful of how she might be treated by those who considered themselves in authority. Lillybeth always thought the best of those she met, and even those she had yet to meet, and she trusted others generally. Millybeth and Hackleberg only hoped the Council and those involved in the rigid formalities surrounding it would not try to teach her to do otherwise.

❖   ❖   ❖

That morning in Chrysalis, Chaffy had arisen before sunrise. He sat in his home, a small, inconspicuous, almost hidden structure in a corner of Chrysalis draped with garden plants. He plodded through his preparations for the day, donning his usual attire, of which, like Hinsberth, he owned little else but a few identical copies. The conversation of the previous day weighed heavily on his mind. He was disturbed by what he heard, and unsure what to do.

A simple wooden stand with a single drawer stood next to his bed, and as he did every morning, he slowly opened the drawer and pulled out an old, small, framed drawing, and held it for a time with both wings over his chest. He sighed deeply. He closed his eyes. He held it tighter, and he remembered. He was in Chrysalis... and she was there. With a soft, aching smile she held out her wing, and he took hold. He could feel the warmth, it spread over the whole of his being, it spread over Chrysalis. Together they strolled languidly through the gardens, beside the ponds, over the bridge. He never wanted to leave... if only she could go beyond a memory...

After a time Chaffy returned. The tears had glistened his cheeks. He dried his eyes. And unlike every morning since he had first penciled it, he did not return the drawing to the drawer. He placed it in his pocket. He would not be alone.

Chaffy left his home, and strolled slowly down the familiar long, leaf covered walkway to the giant walls of Chrysalis.

Being early morning, Chrysalis was quiet, calm. Very few residents were up and about, and those that were seemed in a similarly thoughtful, contemplative mood. They stood in silence, entranced by a low, burbling waterfall, they sat on benches, lost in the still ponds or the languid, murmuring canals feeding life to the morning blooms.

Chaffy's destination was the doctor's office. Marista, Eldsworth, Hinsberth, Monique and Anati had already gathered there and were preparing to return to The Farm. They had to ensure the still weary Hinsberth was indeed ready for the flight home and also to retrieve and ready the Transporter to return to Hackleberg's workshop. They knew four adult flyers were required to carry it, but they had only three: Marista, Eldsworth and Monique. Anati was not quite large enough, but after discussing the matter they reasoned she could balance the empty Transporter for the flight home. If needed, Hinsberth could be attached to the same corner as Anati, and Anati was well aware of this fact.

"I will need help to fly, I cannot do it all alone," declared Anati with a feigned fatigue in her voice. "There will be a headwind coming from the direction of The Farm, I am sure. Always at this time of year — or any time of year."

CHAPTER 11

Anati believed the flight home a perfect opportunity to spend time with Hinsberth. She had wanted to be introduced to him, but so far she had had very few chances to speak with Hinsberth directly.

Presently there came a rap on the doctor's office door. A moment later Chaffy entered the room and announced, "Ah, I am very happy to see everyone doing so well. I wished to check in, just to be sure all is well. Unfortunately I cannot not stay long, as is too often the case my day is full of this and that, work and meetings. I would not trade it for anything, of course, but I do wish I had more time to spend with you. I do so miss The Farm."

Chaffy seemed unusually jittery in manners and voice, but he managed to bid a humble farewell to all. He then turned and waddled off to begin planning for whatever was to come.

Monique, Anati, Eldsworth and Marista were huddled around Hinsberth as Doctor Tauffenshufter examined him for what was expected to be the final time.

After completing the examination, Doctor Tauffenshufter smiled and said, "It does indeed seem as if Hinsberth is on his way to recovery. I am rather confident he will be able to make the flight back to The Farm." After pausing a moment to put away her things, she added, "After you return home, please thank Doctor Lochswyn for her ideas and assistance, and tell her to remember to come for a visit as soon as she is able."

Hinsberth nodded and stood up, anxious to return home and to check on Lillybeth. He popped his feet up and down, in an attempt to shake off the long days spent bedridden.

"Thank you," he told Doctor Tauffenshufter sincerely, although he felt indebted to her and the other Chrysalis doctors to such a degree that he did not believe he could fully express his gratitude.

"No need to thank us, we are only grateful we were able to help," Doctor Tauffenshufter replied, speaking for all the staff. "Please take care, and be careful with what you get yourself into."

Hinsberth waddled over to Monique and Anati and thanked them, his new friends who had come to his aid from afar.

"No, no. Do not worry yourself over such things. We brought you here to become better, it was the least we could do. We are just happy to see you well," said Monique.

Anati did not say anything, but she set her gaze on Hinsberth, and with her soft, dark, smoky eyes, she looked at him in such a manner that Hinsberth immediately felt shaky from head to toe.

But soon Marista, Eldsworth and Monique began to discuss what to do next. They decided first to ready the Transporter. Anati again presented the idea she and Hinsberth could be attached together to one corner of the Transporter, since they were without a fourth adult flyer. Anati's suggestion made Hinsberth even more nervous. He was rather unsettled by the way Anati looked at him. More than once he had to divert his eyes to less distracting sights. Staring off at nothing in particular, Hinsberth found his thoughts drifting to The Farm. Lillybeth had returned to convene the Council and he was hoping everything would go well.

Eventually Eldsworth and Monique decided Anati's suggestion was a good one, and having settled how they were to carry the Transporter they all went strolling through Chrysalis, in search of Hackleberg's contraption, and eventually they were led outside to a quaint shed spread over with garden plants. With a bit of help from a couple of Chaffy's friends, they fabricated a pair of small harnesses especially for Anati and Hinsberth. While working on the harnesses, Eldsworth and Monique recalled the crash landing, and with Eldsworth's urging, their Chrysalis friends invented a new kind of fastener for the harnesses, with a snap release for emergencies. Unfortunately, Hackleberg was not present for the proceedings; he would have enjoyed them thoroughly.

After completing their preparations, they loaded the gear Doctor Lochswyn's had left behind into the Transporter, they arranged themselves at the four corners: Marista and Eldsworth took the front, and Monique took one rear corner and Hinsberth and Anati were paired at the other.

Anati stood uncomfortably close to Hinsberth as they prepared to go aloft.

"Very exciting, to be going home, no?" inquired Anati with some enthusiasm.

"Yes, I am ready to be home. But Chrysalis is such an amazing place. I hope it will not be the last time we come for a visit," Hinsberth replied wistfully.

As he spoke Anati's alluring gaze made him uneasy, so Hinsberth turned his eyes to the sky, trying to appear as though he were assessing the conditions for flight.

"Alright, I think that is it," Marista boomed after fastening her harness. Everyone pulled and tugged and stretched their harnesses and connectors until they were satisfied nothing was indeed going to come undone. Then Marista counted down, "Three... two... one... GO!" and they bounded into the air, beating their wings with all their might they slowly rose into the shimmering sky. They ascended into the brilliant shaft of light reflected from above, leaving behind the shadowy world of the dense forest. As they rose above the tree tops they cast a small dark shadow on the vast roof of Chrysalis. With the Transporter in tow, they ascended over the green sea of forest, to begin the long journey home.

❖   ❖   ❖

On The Farm, residents were eagerly gathering in the Old Barn. Rows of seats faced the stage where the Council was to preside. The seats for the Council members had been neatly arranged in a small arc upon the stage, facing down upon the podium. Millybeth and Hackleberg accompanied their daughter on the walk to the Old Barn, and once inside, Lillybeth felt her stomach climb irrepressibly into her throat. She had not expected anything so formal in arrangement, or the large number of her fellow Farm residents in attendance. She was also surprised by the number of Council seats, she anticipated the presence of maybe only two or three members, but she counted seven. She wondered: who would they be?

Lillybeth did not pride herself on her abilities for eloquent and persuasive speech; and that was exactly what she perceived was going to be necessary to present to and persuade such a large Council and the rather extensive court of her neighbors.

When the Smythes entered into the room through the wide open barn doors, Lillybeth heard the muted discussions rise in fervor, and she wondered if perhaps many of those in attendance already knew it was she who had convened the Council, and maybe even what the reason was for doing so.

Hackleberg could sense his daughter's anxiety as she absorbed the scene.

CHAPTER 11

"Well, you certainly have quite a few supporters this evening," he said optimistically.

"Indeed," Millybeth added as she took in the room. She quickly decided some added encouragement was in order, "You will do fine. Just let them know what you have learned; what Hinsberth has told you. If there are enough kind hearts out there I do not think you will have to do much convincing."

Lillybeth was not so sure. She began to conceive of the Council meeting as just another type of expedition, and she wondered if once again she may have gone in over her head. But then she remembered her own words of advice about not panicking in the face of danger. Breathe, she reminded herself. She told herself over and over that there was no real danger here, for she only needed to convey Hinsberth's tale.

Lillybeth tried to calm herself by remembering the Council was there to help, and surprisingly, she felt a bit more relaxed when Quillypom, who had earlier in the day been so helpful, found her way to one of the Council seats. She also saw Doctor Lochswyn, who took a seat at the far end, somewhat distant from Quillypom, who was seated in the center. A short moment later the Mayor appeared and took a seat on the opposite end from Doctor Lochswyn. Lillybeth noticed Quillypom and Doctor Lochswyn had not greeted one another, and she began to wonder what might be the reason, for they normally seemed quite amiable.

Quillypom was accompanied by the Messenger, who was tightly and anxiously clutching a paper pad and pencil with both wings. Quillypom directed her to take a seat placed far off to one side of the stage, ostensibly to keep a record of the proceedings.

As the Old Barn continued to fill, Lillybeth suddenly wished Marista was with her. Marista had promised to help her if necessary, and she had a certain undeniable way with those who considered themselves to be in authority. Even the Mayor avoided confrontation with Marista. But she knew Marista was at Chrysalis with Hinsberth. Lillybeth suddenly wished Hinsberth was at her side, for he seemed to have a deep, unspoken confidence in her and was always intrigued by her approach to things, as if he knew that however unorthodox her methods, she would find a way to make things work.

Lillybeth imagined Hinsberth, Marista and Eldsworth were with her. Eldsworth, with his even keeled manners never appeared to be upset by any kind of situation, he always maintained his focus. As the room filled to capacity and beyond, Lillybeth tried to remember all the characteristics she admired in her friends and family, and she planned to draw upon them if needed.

Presently, with the volume of the chatter in the Old Barn reaching a fever pitch and the Council members now arrayed in their seats, the Mayor finally stood and faced the assembly. The Old Barn, with the exception of Mayor Swellington's distinguished voice, immediately fell silent.

"Good evening, everyone. I am pleased to see so many of you could attend this Council meeting on such very short notice, and I am sure you are all more than curious as to the nature of this *emergency* meeting. It is not often the Council is convened, and I must say a meeting has never been called with the particular characteristics of our gathering here tonight. For it is true that only one here in attendance tonight is aware of the purpose, although we have been notified in no uncertain terms that this purpose is of a most dire and immediate nature. If I may remind everyone, the regulations require silence while the requestor and the Council are speaking. Now, and without any objections, the Council members are ready to receive the proposal."

Having completed his brief introduction, the Mayor set his authoritative gaze down upon Lillybeth. Being completely unfamiliar with the expected course of the proceedings, Lillybeth was still sitting nervously with her parents. The Mayor suddenly seemed impatient and motioned for her to approach the podium.

Lillybeth's legs froze for a moment as she felt the heat of a thousand eyes focus upon her. She closed her own eyes, and remembered her promise to Hinsberth. She felt her mother and father's wings on her back, gently nudging her to stand up and make the now seemingly perilous journey to the podium. Lillybeth took a deep breath, and she thought of Marista. She recalled Marista's habit of pushing that giant red flower over her brow to let everyone know she was rather serious and that disagreement could come at a penalty. Lillybeth imagined she had such a flower; in her mind's eye she lifted her wing and pushed it forward over her brow, and as she did so, she set her eyes alight with a piercing conviction. She furrowed her brow with determination and she contorted her face in an expression which could only be a warning to those who would attempt to block her path. As she slowly rose from her seat and began to focus on gaining the podium, all the imagining and facial contortions swiftly became tiring, so she fell back to her usual approach of trying to relax, breathe, and take one step at a time.

Waddling to the podium, she heard the rise of muted speculation echo through the assembly, and she thought about how those watching her had probably expected her to be carrying some notes, or a big official looking book — something of consequence. But Lillybeth brought nothing but herself and her satchel of adventure gear, of which not one item would assist her regarding this particular task. Oh well, she thought to herself, it is too late to satisfy other's expectations. She ignored the chatter.

Lillybeth arrived at the podium with no papers, no notes, no prepared speech. The podium was much too tall for her to see over, so she stood to one side.

She quickly decided to follow the Mayor's lead.

"Hello everyone. Hello Council Members. As the Mayor said, you are probably wondering why I convened the Council this evening. Some of you are probably aware of how Hinsberth had recently fallen ill with fever which lasted for several days. You may have heard that he and I went on an expedition, and that we had unfortunately become separated by the weather. Hinsberth became injured, ill and grounded after we were separated. While on the ground, he wished to explore about and came upon a strange place..."

As if in a dream, Lillybeth somehow spoke with a flowing eloquence. She told the assembly how Hinsberth discovered Milchester. She described how his new friend helped Hinsberth survive a devastating fever, for had he not kept Hinsberth hydrated, nourished, and protected with straw, Hinsberth might not have survived the night. She conveyed her own memory of the forbidding place where Milchester was held captive. She told them of Milchester's desperate life of confinement, the frightful conditions and terrible suffering he and his fellows endured, and the horrific fate which was to befall them.

After her tiny voice had echoed alone through the unusually silent barn, Lillybeth drew her story to a close, revealing how there were

CHAPTER 11

perhaps a thousand others who shared Milchester's plight. A round of audible gasps ushered from the assembly.

"Milchester or any one of his companions may not have much time. Or any time at all. It is for this reason I believe this to be an emergency. Thank you for letting me speak."

Lillybeth suddenly found herself bereft of any more words, so she immediately turned round and looked for a place to sit down behind the podium, but nothing presented itself. She stood in place waiting for whatever was to come next... and she waited... and waited.

A stunned silence gripped the assembly.

Not one of the rumors had even come close to the actual issue presented by Lillybeth, and no one knew what to think, or could fathom what was to be done about it.

The Council members were equally struck silent, only Doctor Lochswyn knew of Hinsberth's story, and seeing the other members fixed firmly in their seats, she slowly rose to her feet and broke the burdensome silence.

"Thank you, Lillybeth."

She then returned to her seat, expecting the Mayor or someone else to begin speaking. But another long reticence ensued and Lillybeth feared she may have overdone something once again. With a growing sense of desperation she glanced around for a nearby place to sit down and take herself out of sight.

The Mayor, although unsure of what to say, nonetheless felt obligated to begin the discussion, so he slowly and very deliberately rose from his seat. He could only think to ask, in his deep, flowing voice, "Do any of the Council members have a question for the requestor?"

Silence.

Not receiving any response but a row of anguished expressions, the Mayor continued, "I, for one, would like to know what exactly does the requestor expect to be accomplished?"

Lillybeth, quickly surmising that she was the one who was being referred to as the "requestor," moved closer to the podium to respond to the Mayor's question.

"To free Milchester, and all the others," she answered.

A raucous mumbling began at once in the assembly, as it was certain no one knew exactly what Lillybeth's request might entail.

"Does the requestor have any idea as to how that might be accomplished?" inquired the Mayor.

Lillybeth replied, her voice quivering with a little uncertainty, "We would have to find out how they are trapped, and come up with a plan — to make a rescue."

"And what obligation does the Council have to consider such a plan, and the resources it might involve?" inquired the Mayor.

"Obligation?" asked Lillybeth.

"Yes, obligation. What obligation does The Farm have to these pigs?" inquired the Mayor with a serious tone.

Quillypom shifted in her seat. She knew what the Mayor was trying to do, and she did not agree with it. Despite the interruptions Lillybeth had imposed upon her work, as Quillypom looked from her privileged seat at Lillybeth — the same Lillybeth who had earlier sat so innocently in her office arranging all of this and now stood bravely before the Council without regard to herself — she felt an undeniable soft spot for the duckling. But Quillypom bided her time, for she knew Lillybeth, with her most curious nature, could hold her own against those who were unaware of her unique ways and hailed from the often rigid and myopic world of the Mayor's Office.

"The *obligation*, please," insisted the Mayor.

"They are suffering," replied Lillybeth.

"No, no. What jurisdiction, what obligation of a legal, formal nature does The Farm have regarding these pigs? You have done your research, I assume?" asked the Mayor again, as if he thought Lillybeth did not understand the question.

"We do not have time for that," said Lillybeth.

Several muted chuckles echoed through the assembly.

"They are suffering *now*," added Lillybeth firmly.

The chuckles stopped.

"They are being taken as we speak."

The Mayor was becoming flustered.

"So we have no legal, jurisdictional rules? No rules, no regulations, no procedures to cover any sort of action in this regard?" he asked looking around at his fellow Council members.

In response came only shaking heads and befuddled expressions. This was new.

"There is *no* precedent for this request. The Council has never before been requested to take an action outside the legal boundaries and jurisdiction of The Farm."

Lillybeth stood silent.

The Mayor repeated his statement, only louder this time, "There is *no* precedent."

Lillybeth quickly surmised the Mayor was expecting her to respond, even though he was not framing his statement in the form of a question.

"That is fine. I do not think we need one. After we do it we will have one for later," she replied simply.

The Mayor paused a moment, confused but thinking fast. He was entirely unsure how to proceed, for this unusual request had no formal structure, it was completely outside of what had come before, and there seemed to be no procedure or criteria for evaluating its legal merit.

To end the awkward moment, Quillypom slowly rose from her seat. "The requestor is correct. Precedent is not a requirement for a proposal to the Council," she stated flatly.

The Mayor did not like having to concede this point to a duckling. He swiftly thought of a new line of reasoning. He felt as though this little duckling was trying to publicly mock his authority with her unusual statements and emergency proposal, and he sought to change his tactic. Thinking he would undermine her credibility, he took a deep breath, and paused a moment.

He then began to speak, slowly, quietly, in an authoritative tone, "This proposal is indeed unique, and I respect the concern for our fellow creatures and the fact this issue has been brought bravely before the Council. However, might I remind the Council the requestor has a history of troubling the operations of The Farm and in particular the Mayor's Office with unprecedented activities."

The Mayor stood tall and began to stride slowly back and forth before the seated Council members. He continued to speak in a very precise and deliberate manner, slowly building his intensity, "The requestor, as we will recall from the previous summer, went off rather recklessly with her father in a large, and if I may say, hastily constructed gondola attached to an enormous red balloon, which ascended into the sky above The Farm and then drifted for some distance into a remote region, whereby the Mayor's Office was forced to distribute a small ransom to, need I say, a group of rather unruly badgers, in order to have them safely returned to The Farm. And only a short time later, if we remind ourselves, there was the submersible, if we recall, in The Pond. She and her father set out to explore the depths, and after they released from the, shall I say, loosely constructed scaffolding, they sank like a stone, and it took us the better part of a day to assemble the ropes and pulleys to dredge them up. Luckily they had at least thought to use a hose to the surface or it could have been much worse..."

To his satisfaction, Lillybeth cringed at the mention of the latter, and the Mayor continued on, more loudly, building to a crescendo, "And the rocket, its engine tested along The Pond front, the exhaust of which set fire to the Mayor's Office, taking several days to repair. And finally, the requestor's own activities in flying off into a storm and losing her companion are what resulted in the discovery for which she now wants The Farm to pick up and fix for her!"

Upon finishing his monologue, the Mayor ceased his pacing, and he puffed himself up, standing tall in the center of the stage. He gazed down in condescension at tiny Lillybeth, believing he surely had her on the defensive, and awaited her response.

Lillybeth stood silent.

"Well?" asked the Mayor.

"Do you have a question?" asked Lillybeth.

"What do you have to say about it?" asked the Mayor.

"About what?"

"What — I — just — said," stated the Mayor slowly and firmly with a growing frustration.

"Do you have a question about the proposal?" asked Lillybeth. "They are still suffering," she added.

Lillybeth had not been taken in. The Mayor hoped to draw her into an embroiled debate over her credibility, but she had kept her focus on the task at hand. The Mayor, however, remained motionless, standing tall in the center of the stage, in yet another moment of awkward silence.

"Thank you," said Lillybeth.

The Mayor looked uncertainly over the assembly, unsure of what to say. His words had abandoned him. He turned round to face the rest of the Council. They looked back at him with a few forced smiles, and then they very subtly motioned him toward his seat, recommending he sit down and avoid any further embarrassment.

Quillypom suddenly broke the impasse.

"Do any other Council members have questions for the requestor?" she queried in a loud voice. After the proposal was presented, the normal procedure for a Council meeting was to call for questions from the Council members, and then from the assembly.

"How many? Exactly how many would we need to rescue?" a Council member inquired.

"At least hundreds, perhaps a thousand or more," Lillybeth replied.

A collective gasp again emanated from the assembly. A thousand? How could they ever hope to rescue so many?

Lillybeth stood patiently, awaiting more questioning, but almost everyone was at a loss for words. It was certainly true there was not a precedent for what she was proposing. The chatter in the assembly slowly grew in volume.

"Any more questions from the Council?" Quillypom inquired over

CHAPTER 11

the din.

Her inquiry went unheeded.

"If I may," said Quillypom firmly, "what is being asked of the Council and The Farm would require significant planning, effort and resources, and according to the requestor's account, must be accomplished in the most expedient fashion. With this in mind, are there any additional questions?"

"If we were to decide to do this," one of the Council members began, "How would we do it? What exactly would a rescue entail?"

"The Council meeting is only to decide whether to move forward with the proposal. If a majority of the Council votes to move forward, we would then begin planning how to carry it out," answered Quillypom.

Quillypom could not believe she was explaining the next step, as she did not think Lillybeth would have ever come this far. But here they were. She could tell the Council had been strongly moved by Lillybeth's account, and were rather unsure how to respond.

"Very well then," announced Quillypom, "the Council will yield to the assembly for questions."

Lillybeth grew tired of standing beside the podium. To her, the course was fairly clear, there were perhaps a thousand or more fellow creatures suffering under intolerable conditions. "Free them!" she thought.

"Where they are being held, it is under the control of humans is it not?" someone asked from one of the back rows.

"Yes," replied Lillybeth.

There was another pause. And the chatter began again, only more loudly this time.

"Quiet please," ordered Quillypom. "Any other questions?" she asked.

"How are we to decide anything regarding this proposal when no one has any idea on how to accomplish it?" asked a skeptical voice from the assembly.

"We will look at the feasibility if it is voted upon and approved," said Quillypom. "Might I ask for questions to be directed to the requestor?"

"May I sit down?" asked Lillybeth, holding one of her feet by the opposite wing. "My feet are sore."

Over time a few more inquiries were made, and Quillypom had to quiet the assembly more than once. The questioning eventually came to an end as the Old Barn echoed with muted discussion.

Quillypom was ready to move to the next step: to call for a vote of the Council regarding Lillybeth's unique and by this time rather controversial proposal.

"According to established procedures, it is now time to call for a vote of the Council," Quillypom announced firmly over the din.

She arose wearily from her seat and waddled slowly to the center of the stage, to the spot where the Mayor had earlier made his unsuccessful attempt to intimidate Lillybeth. She held before her in both wings a very official looking form to record the vote.

"All those in favor of the proposal please raise your wing," she requested flatly.

With Quillypom standing before them, six Council members remained seated on the stage. From these, three wings went up.

"Very well. All those not in favor of the proposal, please raise your wing," requested Quillypom.

Three other wings rose into the air. The Mayor, sporting a smug expression after seeing only the three votes in favor, stretched his massive wing swiftly to a lofty height.

In an instant Quillypom's stomach turned all to knots. With six votes counted the result was a tie; she would have to cast the deciding vote. She glanced at her husband, who had made no question of where he stood on the issue, as he had tried to make quite clear with his attempts to humiliate Lillybeth and with his wing reaching skyward while smugly voting not in favor. He had always expected, even demanded, and took for granted that Quillypom would go along with and support his positions and policies. The Mayor expected her support even when he took a position merely out of spite, instead of opting for what might have made sense under the existing policies and regulations. For at times it seemed he even went against what the residents believed The Farm ultimately stood for.

As she stood center stage, all at once Quillypom felt her head flush with heat, and she began to feel a little wobbly, her legs a little unsteady. Was it anger? Or frustration? She was not sure. She had been working far too often, for far too long. She wished she could sit down. Rest. Quillypom glanced over her shoulder behind her. She saw little Lillybeth, patiently waiting beside the podium. It was taller than she. At that moment she seemed so small. Lillybeth was standing there, popping up one leg and then the other, weary of being on her feet, seemingly oblivious to her placement of the whole of The Farm and Quillypom in particular into such an untenable conundrum. Quillypom turned to face the Council again, and she let her eyes wander over each and every one of them. Suddenly she felt an immense pressure and she could not help herself. She turned once again to look back at Lillybeth, but this time she saw someone else standing in her place, someone most dear to her, another young duckling, just as she was not so very long ago. Overwhelmed in anguish and confusion, she tried to turn her head quickly to face back to the Council, but the world spun and overcame her, and she collapsed hard to the floor. As the crowd gasped, the Council rushed from their seats to her aid.

"Filipa," Quillypom whispered, and she lost consciousness.

HACKLEBERG

"How did it fly? Did you have any trouble?"

WHAT HAS HAPPENED HERE?

L ILLYBETH STOOD FROZEN IN PLACE, she had seen Quillypom collapse not too far in front of her, and for an instant she thought it was yet another bizarre act in the strange rituals of the Council. Doctor Lochswyn was quick to come to Quillypom's aid, and she was holding Quillypom's head with one wing and was busy checking her breathing and other signs. Mayor Swellington knelt down beside her. The agonized expression Lillybeth had sometimes seen washing over the Mayor's face was now ever present as he held Quillypom in his wings.

The assembly was stunned, hushed, many of them were standing, stretching their necks, trying to see what was happening.

When Lillybeth began to grasp that Quillypom was in real difficulty, she readied herself to bound up onto the stage, but the wings of Millybeth and Hackleberg came over her shoulders from behind and held her.

"Let Doctor Lochswyn work, she can do without too much distraction right now," Millybeth told her daughter.

Lillybeth stood next to the podium and watched as the Council members huddled around Quillypom, picked her up and swiftly carried her away, with Doctor Lochswyn holding her head and watching her closely. They proceeded out the barn door toward Doctor Lochswyn's office.

"What is going to happen to her?" asked Lillybeth with great concern over the wellbeing of her friend.

"They are taking her to Doctor Lochswyn's, and as you know she will be in the best of care," replied Hackleberg.

Those in the assembly were unsure what to do, some of them began to wander outside and drift in the direction of the doctor's office. Many others remained standing over their seats.

Lillybeth looked over the crowd. She suddenly became aware she had no idea what was going to happen to her proposal. She understood a vote had been taken, and from the raising of the wings the result appeared to be a tie. She, like everyone else, did not know whether the even vote meant her proposal had been passed or rejected.

Lillybeth imagined if the proposal had passed, she would be very excited for when Hinsberth arrived home. She would be able to tell him that she had finally made a modicum of progress regarding her promise. She did not want to consider the other possibility, for Lillybeth knew she would have to try again, with a larger effort when Quillypom was well again. But what would she do if Quillypom remained ill for days or weeks? By then, she thought, it could be too late. As she looked around at the disorganized, slowly dispersing crowd; at the shambles of her efforts, she hung her head and tried to hold back the tears.

The Smythes stood together. They watched the assembly disperse and it slowly became clear that the issue would not be resolved that evening.

WHAT HAS HAPPENED HERE?

Presently Lillybeth heard her name, called out above the voices in troubled speculation. She glanced around for who had called for her, and she again heard her name, this time more loudly and in a familiar voice, and she turned to see Monique, Anati, and Hinsberth quickly emerge from the entrance to the Old Barn.

As they approached, Lillybeth saw how close Anati was to Hinsberth, and the sudden wave of joy at seeing her friend turned into a slight sinking feeling.

Monique came directly up to Millybeth and Hackleberg.

"My! What has happened here?" she inquired with astonishment. "Everyone is scattered outside, and looking worried. They told us the Council was meeting in the Old Barn. Well, we knew what that meant." She smiled at Lillybeth. "And now everyone is out, talking about Quillypom. Please tell us."

"Lillybeth convened the Council and made her presentation, which, if I may say so, went rather well, and they were taking a vote on whether or not to approve the proposal. The vote was tied, and Quillypom was preparing to cast the deciding vote. She seemed a little distraught. I saw her glance at Lillybeth. She looked heartbroken. And then she fell. It was terrible, we were all shocked. Luckily, Doctor Lochswyn was on the stage with the Council and she began to take care of her at once."

Monique, Anati and Hinsberth listened closely to Millybeth's depiction of the evening's events with their eyes widening. Monique placed the end of her wing over her bill and gasped as Millybeth revealed what had happened to Quillypom. They were all quite stunned by the news, for as distant as Quillypom's personality often seemed, they were rather worried for her.

271

"I am so sorry," Lillybeth said to Hinsberth dejectedly, her head hung low, her eyes reddened. "I tried as hard as I could. But I do not know what is going to happen now."

"Please do not apologize," said Hinsberth. "You could not have done anything about what happened, and we can hope that things will still work out. I really appreciate everything you have been trying to do."

Lillybeth was grateful for Hinsberth's sentiment, but between the way Anati was looking at him, how close she was standing at his side and the disaster which had befallen her Council presentation, her normally energetic nature had abandoned her to await in hope for more favorable times. She gazed at the floor and waited to depart for home.

"Maybe there will be some kind of announcement from the Mayor's Office later tonight, or in the morning," Monique offered hopefully.

Millybeth and Monique exchanged a few more words, and then Monique suddenly recalled something she wanted to tell Hackleberg.

"Oh, by the way, we have returned the Transporter," she announced triumphantly. "We flew it all the way from Chrysalis and left it just outside your workshop. Marista and Eldsworth will be here soon, they hoped to be doing you a favor by tidying it up so it would be easy to move. Of course, they are very grateful to you and Lillybeth for building it."

"How did it fly? Did you have any trouble?" asked Hackleberg, always keenly interested in the efficacy of his inventions.

"It was fine. No troubles," Monique replied, which pleased Hackleberg immensely.

And then with animated wings forming the shape of each part, she told him of the modifications by the Chrysalis ducks. This gave

Hackleberg, although certainly tempered by the evening's events, quite some excitement.

After Monique finished her descriptions she announced to everyone, "We must be going now." Although she wanted to remain with her new friends, Monique was missing Arela and Poullaire and was eager be home. She suspected Poullaire and Arela had probably attended the Council meeting, but they must have missed them in the chaos and confusion.

As they bid farewell to everyone and turned to leave, Lillybeth watched as Anati bent over and gave Hinsberth a tiny peck on the cheek.

Hinsberth's stomach went to knots and a debilitating nervousness washed over the whole of his body. A crushed Lillybeth, felt her stomach, heart and everything else under her skin collapse into her feet.

As Monique and Anati turned and waddled away, Hinsberth stood speechless. In addition to the usual loss for words when around Lillybeth, he did not know how to try and explain Anati's behavior and not seem as though he were making up stories. He only stewed in his frustration.

As Monique and Anati disappeared into the darkness, Marista and Eldsworth suddenly appeared. While Hinsberth and Lillybeth stared sullenly at the ground, Marista and Eldsworth began immediately with the questions, asking Millybeth and Hackleberg for details regarding what had happened. They had overheard the news in bits and pieces as they waddled toward the Old Barn, and were desperate for an unbroken account.

Marista noticed the despair on Lillybeth's face, and she spoke to her in a calm voice, "Do not worry. I am sure all of this will work

CHAPTER 12

out. Hopefully it is not serious for Quillypom, just feeling a bit faint, perhaps from too much work."

Marista glanced at her son, and at once took notice of his sullen and silent expression. She quickly gathered something else besides Quillypom's collapse had transpired, but she was not at all sure what.

As passersby saw Hinsberth, many offered well wishes, and he was surprised by just how much of The Farm seemed to know he was ill. Eldsworth quickly thanked those who offered their sentiments, but like Marista he noticed both Hinsberth and Lillybeth seemed to be taking Quillypom's fainting and the demise of the Council meeting exceptionally hard. Hinsberth seemed to be staring at the ground to avoid looking at Lillybeth, and both he and Marista immediately decided it may be best to part and let everyone go home to have a long night's rest, and then meet again in the morning to determine what to do next.

The Smythes and Smerkingtons waddled down the footpath together in a disappointed air, and they solemnly parted ways where the footpath forked toward their respective homes.

As Millybeth and Hackleberg prepared for sleep, they quietly discussed the days events and their daughter's unusual and sudden deflation. A devastated Lillybeth flopped into her bed, and uncharacteristically buried her head in her pillow.

THE DIGNIFIED PIGS

"As the tale wound to an end, the pigs, who were normally never short for words, stood silently, with expressions mixed of confusion, anguish and despair. The ritual of their morning discussion had never taken on such a solemn air."

CHAPTER 13

URGENT MATTERS

HINSBERTH LAY WIDE AWAKE even before the sun had drifted above the horizon. He was sad and disappointed over the failure of Lillybeth's Council meeting. He was frustrated over how long it was taking to organize The Farm for a rescue; how much time might Milchester have left?

He recalled the events of the previous evening, and how what he believed was merely a friendly gesture from Anati had deeply effected Lillybeth. In frustration he continued to remind himself that he should have said something... anything... to Lillybeth.

Presently Hinsberth struggled to pull himself out of bed. Although tired, he was determined that today he would put forth whatever effort was needed to right things with Lillybeth and to move, help or no help, toward freeing his friend.

❖   ❖   ❖

Lillybeth had arisen before dawn. She lay awake; her eyes wide open. Her thoughts and dreams through the night had alternated between themes of dejected, suffocating sadness and disappointment and vexation. Perhaps, she thought, Anati was only thanking Hinsberth for something he had done or said. Hinsberth is rather polite and help-ful, she reminded herself, and Anati and her mother certainly have a penchant for being close to others, it seemed a natural part of who they are. But how could she be certain there was nothing more? Had Anati attached herself to Hinsberth? Lillybeth could not be certain. But at least one thing was indisputable, today she had to make prog-ress toward fulfilling her promise to Hinsberth. She had failed to dis-cover who Milchester was. Her presentation to the Council ended in disaster. After a string of calamities, she feared Hinsberth might be growing ever more disappointed in her. She knew Hinsberth would never say such a thing to her or mention it aloud in company, he was too kind for that. But she had to do something, and not only just for Hinsberth, but for Milchester and his companions. They had to be freed, and fast. She had to find a way to rescue them, but she needed help. How much more time might Milchester have? How many had already been taken? The thought of how much time it would take to organize The Farm made her head boil. She cinched her eyes shut and concentrated hard on the problem. She agonized over what she could do, alone, to help. Not a thing came to mind. Certainly, she would have to find out how Quillypom was doing. She needed her friend. Quillypom was the only one who understood the strange rituals of the Mayor's Office. Only she could organize enough help to have any chance of rescuing the pigs.

As she tossed about in her bed, two stratagems suddenly jumped out from the tangled web of her thoughts: First, she would go to the pigs on The Farm. She would tell them of Milchester and his fellows, and ask for their help. As she considered the idea, Lillybeth felt certain they would not refuse. For on occasion she had spoken to the pigs when out exploring; tracing along the fence beside the cool pool of mud where the pigs so often wallowed during warm summer days. At least to her, they were always quite amiable. Second, she would go to Chrysalis, on her own if necessary, to retrieve Mister Fowler and bring him to The Farm. He commanded a great deal of respect and all who knew him regarded him as quite knowledgeable. Lillybeth reasoned that if she had the support of the Farm pigs and Mister Fowler, perhaps she could win over the Council members who had voted against her, excepting, of course, the Mayor. As she pondered over her plans, Lillybeth decided she would first have to know how Quillypom was feeling and the final result of the Council voting. Before anything else, she would have to visit Doctor Lochswyn's and the Mayor's Office.

Lillybeth hastily popped out of bed with a renewed determination, and she quickly threw on her clothes and satchel and waddled into the front room. She found her parents there, already set to take their early morning meal out into the fresh morning light. Millybeth and Hackleberg's eyes traced across the room as their daughter strode past and, without a word, quickly departed out the door. They shared a worried glance. Lillybeth was quite obviously in one of her rather focused moods and likely not amenable to questioning.

"Be back soon?" Millybeth called out with a hopeful tone.

"Yes," replied Lillybeth.

And with that she continued swiftly on toward the doctor's office. She arrived in little time, rapped on the door and waited impatiently. After a brief moment, Doctor Lochswyn appeared in the open doorway. She looked weary but she smiled warmly when she saw that it was Lillybeth who had come to call.

"I am very sorry, Lillybeth. I know you are here to see Quillypom, but she has requested not to have any visitors," Doctor Lochswyn informed a suddenly disappointed Lillybeth.

"I really *must* see her," pleaded Lillybeth.

"She has asked that I not let anyone in to see her, and I must follow the wishes of my patients," Doctor Lochswyn explained.

Lillybeth stood firmly in place, refusing to leave.

"Please, Lillybeth. I know Quillypom appreciates your concern…"

"Heleen — please, let her in. It's alright," came a familiar voice from the patient room.

A surprised Doctor Lochswyn slowly stepped aside. She held the door open for Lillybeth.

Lillybeth waddled down the short hall and turned to enter into the patient room. She paused before the doorway, startled to see the normally bustling Quillypom lying where she had for so much time watched Hinsberth struggle with illness under blankets and ice. Quillypom, however, was not covered with ice; only a thin blanket. She looked tired and her usual forthright manner was subdued. Only Doctor Lochswyn was with her and Lillybeth wondered where the Mayor might be.

Quillypom turned to look at Lillybeth, spotting her little head peeking around the doorway.

"What may I do for you?" Quillypom inquired, without her usual terse manner and seeming more sincere.

"I wanted to find out how you are doing," replied Lillybeth.

Quillypom gave her an unexpected smile.

"I can always count on you, can't I? Whether in my office or here; always my little visitor."

279

CHAPTER 13

At first Lillybeth hesitated to enter the room, but there was a calmness about Quillypom that made Lillybeth feel she was free to approach her, and she slowly waddled up to her side.

"Thank you, for all your help," said Lillybeth.

"It has been my pleasure," replied Quillypom.

Lillybeth wanted to ask Quillypom if she could help her once again, but Quillypom seemed so tired and so peaceful compared to when she would visit her at the Mayor's Office. Lillybeth kept her request to herself, it seemed what Quillypom needed most was rest.

"I hope you are well soon," Lillybeth said sincerely.

"Thank you, Lillybeth," said Quillypom. "When I am well again, I wonder if this time you can do a favor for me?"

"Sure, anything."

Quillypom smiled softly, and she reached out and took hold of Lillybeth's wing.

"Take me to Chrysalis," she whispered.

"I will."

Quillypom closed her eyes and turned her head away from Lillybeth. Doctor Lochswyn quickly waved for Lillybeth to come to her in the doorway.

"She needs her rest," whispered Doctor Lochswyn. "But I think your visit meant a lot to her."

"Thank you for letting me in," said Lillybeth, and she shuffled out the front door, stood for a moment, took a deep breath, and set off in the direction of the Mayor's Office.

❖   ❖   ❖

The journey to the Mayor's Office was short, and as she came up to the door and looked around for her planter, her heart stopped. The fire in her spirit was instantly doused. For before her was the most unwelcome greeting she could imagine — a notice was tacked just to the side of the door, on a sheet of very official looking paper, its message was printed in large, bold, final, absolute letters:

"NOTICE: IN REGARDS TO THE COUNCIL MEETING AND VOTE OF LAST EVENING, SINCE NO REGULATIONS HAVE BEEN ESTABLISHED REGARDING THE FAILURE OF ONE OF THE COUNCIL MEMBERS TO VOTE, THE MAYOR HAS DETERMINED THE ISSUE TO BE WITHIN HIS JURISDICTION AND TO CAST THE DECIDING VOTE. THE MAYOR HAS VOTED TO DENY THE PROPOSAL ISSUED BY THE REQUESTOR."

It was signed at the bottom in even larger letters, "Sincerely, Mayor Swellington."

On the opposite side of the door another notice was posted:

"NOTICE: IT HAS COME TO THE ATTENTION OF THE MAYOR'S OFFICE THAT UNAUTHORIZED TRAVELS AND ENGAGEMENTS HAVE BEEN MADE WITHOUT REGARD TO ATTAINING OFFICIAL APPROVAL FROM THIS OFFICE. CONTINUATION OF SUCH ACTIVITIES WILL BE INVESTIGATED."

This notice was also signed with a hastily scribbled, "Sincerely, Mayor Swellington."

Lillybeth's innards plummeted to become a jumble in her shoes. The fire she had awakened with was snuffed out, only weakly smoldering embers remained.

In disbelief, Lillybeth had to read the notices again. Her bill hung wide open. She had not misread. It was true. The Mayor decided to vote, twice! The flames only just doused began to be fanned by an abrupt feeling of outrageous injustice. And as she steamed in front of the Mayor's Office, her belly caught fire. Lillybeth decided she and Hinsberth and Milchester and all the others would not be denied, they would not be ignored and left alone to their fate. She turned and marched stormily away, waddling with determined steps toward where the pigs of The Farm made their home.

❖   ❖   ❖

Immediately after Lillybeth stepped away from the grounds of the Mayor's Office, another small, waddling shape approached. Hinsberth came up to the front door. Hardly able to miss it, he immediately spotted the large, glaring notice. He read its hastily written message, and his bill flopped wide. Stunned, he readied himself to give a good, hard knock on the door, but as he raised his wing, he saw the second notice.

Hinsberth was outraged.

With the knocker just out of reach, he picked up a large stone and hammered it against the door.

After what seemed to be an inordinate amount of time, the door slowly opened, and the Messenger peeked her head round the opening. She held yet another notice. She paused a moment, and then reluctantly displayed it to Hinsberth. It read simply:

"THE MAYOR'S OFFICE IS NOT ACCEPTING VISITORS UNTIL FURTHER NOTICE."

The Messenger then tacked the notice to the door, in full view just below the knocker.

"Sorry," she said with apologetic eyes and shrugged her shoulders. Hinsberth heard a voice inside. "I must go," she said anxiously, and she gently closed the door.

Hinsberth was generally regarded as a very polite and sophisticated sort, but he, like most, had his thresholds. The heat of his long fever returned, only this time it was fueled by outrage over what he believed were gross injustices and a lack of concern and compassion for the suffering of Milchester and his fellows. A seething Hinsberth stormed off down the footpath in the direction of Lillybeth's. He knew he had to tell her immediately of this disheartening discovery.

Millybeth and Hackleberg were out front of their house as Hinsberth came storming up the path.

"Hinsberth!" said Millybeth. "Glad to see you out on this fine morning."

"I must speak to Lillybeth," Hinsberth stated, still furious but trying his best to be polite.

"I am sorry Hinsberth. Lillybeth left early this morning. We thought she was off to meet with you," said Hackleberg with a sudden concern.

"But I have not seen her; she did not come to my home," said Hinsberth. He immediately began thinking about where she might be, and he quickly concluded she had probably set off for Doctor Lochswyn's or the Mayor's Office. But he had not seen a sign of her at either of those destinations, so he began thinking of other places Lillybeth may have planned to go so early in the day. All at once a great fear washed over Hinsberth. Perhaps, he thought, Lillybeth had already been to the Mayor's Office, and knowing her as he did, he worried she may have waddled off to partake in some drastic activity only she would ever think of.

He had to find her.

Always a little nervous around Lillybeth's parents, Hinsberth bid them a swift farewell. He turned and waddled quickly down the footpath toward the clearing where he and Lillybeth had taken off on their misadventure. Once out of sight of Lillybeth's home, he quickly darted down the trail and took off into the still morning air; for there was no faster way to find her than from the sky.

❖   ❖   ❖

Lillybeth went with heavy, determined steps down the footpath toward the pigs home. Finally she came up to the old fence between the trail and the deep, muddy pool for which the pigs of The Farm held a certain reverence.

A quartet of pigs was present, facing each other, standing on the harder ground beyond the sodden mud, and from the volume of their voices they were evidently in very fervent conversation. Excited to find her quarry, Lillybeth promptly ran, flapped her wings and took off into the air. She tumbled over the fence and alighted with a barely audible splat on the soft ground. At once she waddled up to the conversing pigs.

"Pardon me," Lillybeth said in her most polite manner.

The closer of the pigs was startled to hear the little voice coming from behind, and he turned, looked down and saw tiny Lillybeth on the approach.

"Excuse me," Lillybeth said again, louder this time, trying to capture the pig's attention.

"Yes?" the rather large pig rumbled in an inquisitive tone.

The other pigs also went suddenly silent and turned to look at the duckling who had just interrupted their morning conversation. Each day after the morning meal, the four friends invariably gathered to discuss the latest gossip from their mysterious and secretive sources on The Farm.

"Hello, my name is Lillybeth. I need to talk…" said Lillybeth fervently.

"Did you say 'Lillybeth'?" the giant pig interposed. "Well, if I may, allow me to introduce myself. My name is Swinston, and I am certainly pleased to meet you."

Swinston was a substantial pig, and his voice resounded with a deep, aristocratic air, each word flowed effortlessly into the next, so the boundaries between were barely distinguishable.

Lillybeth felt tiny and inconsequential addressing this particular group of Farm residents who were all much larger than she.

"Yes, Lillybeth," Lillybeth replied to Swinston, with a tone attesting to the fact that she did not believe her name was at all relevant to the important subject she desperately wished to introduce.

"Well, little one. As you may know, news does travel fast around The Farm. We have heard about you and the Council meeting held last evening in the Old Barn. Poor Quillypom, quite a shame. How is she doing by the way?" inquired Swinston. His companions shook their heads in sympathy at the mention of Quillypom's mishap at the Council meeting.

"She is resting," replied Lillybeth. "She is a rather tired; she works very hard on many important and urgent matters. And she is quite helpful when one needs to accomplish something."

"Yes, quite helpful," said Swinston dubiously. "She is doing fine then?" he asked of Lillybeth in a curious manner, as if trying to confirm for himself Lillybeth was indeed being truthful.

"Yes, fine. Doctor Lochswyn is taking care of her, but it is really not why I…" said Lillybeth.

"Good, good," interjected Swinston.

"Swinston!" Lillybeth snapped sharply, trying to begin the conversation again, "I need to talk…"

"Well, pardon me and my complete lack of manners," Swinston suddenly interrupted, apparently unaware of Lillybeth's ardent attempts to speak. "It has regrettably slipped my mind to introduce you to my rather distinguished group of associates."

Swinston pointed to each of his companions in turn with his front leg and announced their names, "Lillybeth, may I present Abselard, Babeth and Quenelope. Everyone, may I present Lillybeth."

"The-e-e Lillybeth?…" said Babeth. "She is a bit smaller than I imagined."

"A bit smaller, yes. Indeed she is," confirmed Quenelope.

Lillybeth was confounded, her size seemed utterly irrelevant.

Abselard remained silent. Abselard was also a very large pig, perhaps a little leaner than Swinston, and his expression was more contemplative. He did not speak as much as Swinston, but rather seemed content to assimilate whatever was said, sometimes looking as though he was mumbling to himself about his own conclusions regarding the topic of conversation. Babeth and Quenelope were both slightly smaller still, and Babeth had a calm, almost wise expression, and her head was covered with a large brimmed and brightly colored hat. Quenelope had a similar hat, perhaps a little less gaudy but still rather colorful, and her nose was always slightly upturned. She liked to talk while looking downward at the others, and was much more terse when speaking, at least much more so than Swinston.

Lillybeth was eager to have the formalities dispensed.

"Very pleased to meet you," she said quickly, with some annoyance at her inability to breach into the conversation.

"Why, *this* is certainly unusual," announced Babeth. "For here we have the very Lillybeth who convened the Council for the ducks last evening. "Most unfortunate result, I should say."

"Yes, most," agreed the group in unison.

Lillybeth raised her little voice, "So you know about the Council meeting?"

"Yes... yes," the pigs replied in unison with heads nodding all the while.

"Then may I assume you are aware of why the meeting was convened?" inquired Lillybeth curiously.

"Well, on that matter, I must say, we have not heard a gratifying amount. And I believe I can speak for the four of us in that regard," said Swinston, turning his eyes upward and trying to recall any detail. "Yes, I cannot remember having heard even a smidge about the reasons for the meeting."

The others nodded in agreement.

Swinston glanced skyward again, as if to try and recall something more on the topic, but this time continued looking upward and he squinted, and grew a rather curious expression.

"Well surprise — surprise. If I may say, very strange weather we are having today. It seems to be raining ducklings!"

Lillybeth looked up and was startled to see Hinsberth descending from the clear morning sky to alight next to her.

"Lillybeth!" Hinsberth called loudly as he neared the ground. "Lillybeth!"

Lillybeth turned her eyes away from Hinsberth to keep her focus on Swinston. She was still hurt by how Anati was acting toward Hinsberth, and Hinsberth's seeming acceptance of it. Her loudly speaking stomach told her the situation was very disagreeable, and whenever Hinsberth was present, she had not yet found a way to demand it act otherwise.

"Have you been to the Mayor's Office?" Hinsberth asked breathlessly.

"Yes," said Lillybeth flatly. Then she quickly changed the subject. "Everyone, this is Hinsberth," she announced.

The pigs gasped. They could not believe this morning's fortune, having both Lillybeth and Hinsberth before them.

"I cannot believe what he is doing!" said Hinsberth in a loud voice and with uncharacteristic fervor.

"Ah. Yes. Mayor Swellington. Sometimes thinks he owns the whole Farm," declared Swinston.

The other pigs again nodded in solemn agreement.

"Might I inquire, what, precisely, has he done?" asked a very curious Swinston.

"It is not important," Lillybeth quickly announced. "What is important is what I have been *trying* to tell you. About the Council meeting; why I convened the Council. We must have your help," stated Lillybeth, in as forthright a manner as she could manage.

"Our help?" asked Babeth with great curiosity.

Hinsberth remained silent for the moment. He quickly pieced together what Lillybeth was likely planning in speaking with the pigs of

The Farm this particular morning.

"Yes, your help," confirmed Lillybeth.

And finally having the attention of her hosts, she began to tell them of Milchester and the reasons for convening the Council. Hinsberth added the details, but they tried to keep it brief.

The pigs could tell the ducklings were in distress and felt pressed for time. As the tale wound to an end, the pigs, who were normally never short for words, stood silently, their expressions went in turn from confusion to anguish and finally, to despair. The ritual of their morning discussion had never taken on such a solemn air.

Swinston, clearly stunned and uncharacteristically upset, cleared his throat and broke the somber silence, "And you ducklings — you plan to free them?"

"Yes," said Hinsberth.

"All of them," added Lillybeth.

"You are going to need help," said Babeth, her eyes reddened and shaking her head in dismay. "You cannot possibly do something like this, just the two of you."

"We do have help, from Chrysalis, from Mister Fowler," said Lillybeth.

"Ah. We know of Chrysalis, and Mister Fowler of course. One of the first ducks on The Farm. A very fine gentleman," added Quenelope, and everyone nodded in agreement.

"Unbelievable. I had heard the Council meeting was regarding an unusual circumstance, something beyond The Farm. But I would never have suspected," said Abselard, who was clearly shocked and dismayed by what he had heard from the ducklings. "I say we begin arrangements at once."

Swinston and the other pigs sat down with a far off look in their eyes.

"They will need to be taken care of. They will need food, and shelter. We will certainly need to prepare," Swinston thought aloud, his smooth voice had become a bit choppy.

"Yes, I considered that. Please, there may be little time left. We need your help," pleaded Lillybeth.

"You have it. Unquestionably," boomed Swinston at once, coming back on his feet. "We will need to be in contact with the surrounding settlements far and wide. We must coordinate with them, to take them in. From what you described, they may be in terrible health, needing care. As you know we have our own Council. You can be certain, if what you are telling us is true, I can assure you there will be no objections to an immediate plan for action."

Swinston thought for a moment, and then he continued, "Lillybeth, please return to us this evening. I will have something for you, something that, if we can ask for your help, will need to be flown to the surrounding settlements. They will need to prepare."

"Please, if I may ask, we need to be quick about it," said Hinsberth. "We have already spent too much time. Before another can be taken…"

"Agreed. But one more thing," interjected Swinston with his deep voice rumbling, "If you decide to convene another Council meeting, let us know. We will be there."

Lillybeth and Hinsberth thanked them all for graciously allowing them to interrupt their morning routine, and for their offer to help. They also let them know they would indeed return in the evening, to retrieve the document Swinston said he would prepare. Then the pair of ducklings flapped over the fence and dropped to the ground. They faced each other on the footpath.

Lillybeth did not look directly at Hinsberth; she let her eyes wander about the landscape, and then she set about observing the rather interesting activities of a pill bug just beyond her feet.

Hinsberth was not quite sure what to say to her. He was by nature imperturbable; only with Lillybeth would he lose his words, and only with Anati would he become unnerved. Hinsberth found both conditions resulted in unwanted complications.

Lillybeth, without a word, eventually turned and waddled past Hinsberth up the footpath. Hinsberth immediately followed her.

"Where are you going?" he inquired.

"Chrysalis."

"Of course," Hinsberth thought. The Mayor had implicitly prohibited travel to Chrysalis. Where else would Lillybeth want to go?

Lillybeth thought about what Monique had said about the disagreements, the rift between Chrysalis and The Farm. Lillybeth believed the rift was most likely between Mister Fowler and Mayor Swellington. She was not particularly fond of such insensibilities. She knew how many residents felt about Quillypom, and after several unscheduled appointments with Quillypom, Lillybeth believed these opinions unfounded. Hearsay had little value.

But without Quillypom, the Mayor seemed to become ever more rigid. Lillybeth needed a plan and she knew Chrysalis must be part of it.

Presently Hinsberth was waddling fast behind Lillybeth, who seemed intent on keeping at least one step ahead so he could not gain her side on the narrow footpath. Lillybeth was heading toward the clearing, to take to the air for Chrysalis.

"Wait!" shouted Hinsberth. "Lillybeth!"

But Lillybeth continued on, ready for flight.

Hinsberth stretched forward and managed to grab hold of Lillybeth's wing. She stopped in mid-step.

Hinsberth did not let go.

Lillybeth turned, and they stood together for a moment with their wings touching. Lillybeth's heart slowed. For an instant the seething frustration she felt over what the Mayor had done faded away.

As they stood together in silence, another duckling approached marked by the sound of her tiny feet gently scuffling along the path.

Anati rounded a bend in the trail and stopped suddenly. Before her she saw Hinsberth and Lillybeth standing side by side, holding each other.

"I am very sorry," she said, thinking she had intruded on a private moment. "I did not mean to interrupt."

Hinsberth let go of Lillybeth's wing, and they began shifting their feet and nervously letting their eyes wander about.

"I *am* sorry," Anati reiterated.

Lillybeth and Hinsberth shared a befuddled glance over Anati's continuing apologies.

"There is no need to say you are sorry, it is really not a problem for you to be here with us. We were just trying to figure out what to do next, about the plan," explained Hinsberth.

"No, no. I am sorry about other things... the way I have treated you," said Anati. "I can see it is not my place."

Anati felt lighter as she spoke. She thought of her mother and how she had changed, from her desire to help Hinsberth to her time at Chrysalis. Anati believed she had changed along with her. She watched her mother and had followed suit. She decided it was time for her to consider her own ideas and passions. Anati never felt comfortable as the subject of attention and she felt she needed more time to be alone. Anati knew of things she wished to explore, things she could not put into words. But maybe, she thought, through painting, like her grandmother, or through something she had yet to discover. And at the moment, she needed her friends.

Hinsberth, although still feeling a sudden wave of anxiousness whenever looking into her eyes, felt rather relieved over Anati's words. While he certainly did not at all mind being kissed, he was not always sure what to think about Anati's intentions. He was very grateful to her and her mother for what they had done for him, and he did not want to do anything to offend her and upset their friendship.

Lillybeth also felt relieved. From the time they had met, Lillybeth was hoping to have Anati's friendship. They enjoyed their time together exploring Chrysalis. And although she had not been able to express her thoughts to anyone, Lillybeth could never quite understand why Anati could not see how important Hinsberth's friendship was to her.

The three ducklings stood pensively for a moment. Lost in their thoughts they were unsure what to say to one another, but somehow they all felt just a little more at ease.

However, they could not escape the ever growing pressure of time. They had to act. Now. And Lillybeth in particular was not in the mood for waiting.

"We must go to Chrysalis," Lillybeth declared suddenly. "Will you come with us?" she asked of Anati.

As Anati opened her bill to answer, Hinsberth quickly explained what they had found tacked to the front of the Mayor's Office; the double vote, the ambiguous message regarding unauthorized travel, and the fact they would not meet with anyone for explanations or elaboration, or, it appeared, for anything else.

Anati listened to Hinsberth with great disappointment, and a fervent burning sensation in her belly. She had to repress the desire to go immediately to the Mayor's Office and let them know of her rather pointed opinions on the matter.

Lillybeth added to Anati's disgruntlement by describing her visit with Quillypom at the doctor's office. Without Quillypom, Lillybeth explained, it would be impossible to accomplish anything at the level of the Mayor's Office. "What else could go wrong?" Anati asked herself. She quickly decided to join her friends on their journey, "Yes, I will come to Chrysalis with you. But we must be quick. I must return before nightfall. I told my mother I would only be out for a moment. I was only coming out to look for the two of you."

"You came looking for us?" asked Lillybeth.

"Yes," said Anati. "I did very much want to apologize. I had trouble with sleep last night thinking about it. But when I came to your home, I found only your parents outside, eating and chatting. They told me they did not know where you were, but they believed you probably went to see Hinsberth. So I started down this path. Fortunately I came upon you here, no? Or I might have been wandering around all day. I would never have thought you went to Chrysalis on your own."

With the apparent good fortune of encountering each other on the trail, the three ducklings wished to take advantage of whatever luck they might still have and leave for Chrysalis immediately. With time running out for Milchester and the pigs, they swiftly clambered up the footpath to the clearing, and with a brief, fast run, they launched themselves into the air on the path to Chrysalis.

❖   ❖   ❖

The news of the notices posted at the Mayor's Office spread quickly, mixing sourly with the somber mood that had descended over The Farm after the demise of Lillybeth's Council meeting. Many contentious debates and divisive opinions arose between friends, families and neighbors over what Lillybeth had revealed and what, if anything, should be done about it. Quillypom's health had become as much a topic for discussion as Hinsberth's had been. Many on The Farm believed the Mayor had overstepped his bounds and was taking advantage of Quillypom's absence; most had no idea what the unauthorized travel notice was referring to, but one thing everyone could agree on was that any feasible plan for a rescue would require a large, coordinated effort, at least at the level of the Mayor's Office. Quillypom was The Farm's resident organizer and she was stricken with an unknown illness, and the Mayor's Office was refusing visitors. Even for those on The Farm who believed it necessary, the hope for a timely rescue of Milchester and his companions did indeed seem dim.

❖   ❖   ❖

Marista and Eldsworth were out for a morning stroll when they encountered a small group of friends near the Mayor's Office.

"Oh! Good morning!" Marista exclaimed.

Her greeting was met only with gloomy faces.

"What is happening here?" she inquired with concern.

CHAPTER 13

"Haven't you heard?"

"Heard what?" asked Eldsworth.

"The news."

"What news?"

Marista held her wings out, motioning for her friends to reveal whatever it was that seemed to be so noteworthy.

When informed of the notices, Marista was incensed. She puffed up her chest and flared her wings on her hips. Eldsworth, always alert, grabbed hold of her to prevent her from storming off to the Mayor's Office.

"This is unbelievable!" Marista exclaimed while trying to free her wing from Eldsworth's grip. "The Mayor cannot do that. Milchester, and Chrysalis? He is not going to be telling us where we can go, or who we are going to help."

"Perhaps there is another explanation," Eldsworth offered with his characteristic restraint. "Maybe… the Mayor… is trying to reduce the burden on the staff. After all, Quillypom is absent and there is no shortage of work to be done," he suggested optimistically.

"Oh, yes. You are very diplomatic. But you know as well as I the Mayor has something else in mind," retorted Marista. "He is only acting out of spite toward poor Lillybeth and the pigs, just to show he is still in charge!"

Marista did not maintain any secrecy regarding her thoughts on the Mayor's motives. From his years of experience, Eldsworth knew there was no convincing Marista of any other interpretations of the Mayor's intentions than the one she already held. But he suddenly became concerned about how the ducklings might respond to the news.

"Are the Smythes and Plummages aware of the Mayor's decisions?"

he asked at once.

Even though he was trying to maintain an outward appearance of calm and diplomacy, Eldsworth felt the issue had passed beyond the threshold of his personal sensibilities; he believed Lillybeth and Hinsberth had put forth very respectable efforts toward organizing a rescue, and that they were not being given the appropriate level of consideration. For Eldsworth, a conversation with the Smythes and Plummages regarding some support for their ducklings appeared to be in order, and doing so would at least for the moment deter Marista from marching off to the Mayor's office.

"I suggest we should go at once to Millybeth and Hackleberg, or Monique and Poullaire, to see what we may be able to do together regarding the decisions of the Mayor," reasoned Eldsworth.

"Yes. Poor Lillybeth. She will be crushed to hear the news."

"So will Hinsberth."

"And Milchester."

"And the pigs."

A long reticence ensued.

"Well, it is not the time to stand around," Marista suddenly declared. "Eldsworth and I are going right now to see the Smythes and the Plummages."

Marista was not one for patience. She was worried about her son, and she felt the need to do something, to take action. Marista and Eldsworth bid a quick farewell and they immediately turned and set off toward Monique and Poullaire's home.

Marista and Eldsworth strode as fast as they could out to the edge of The Farm, finally ascending the steeply sloping hillside graced by the embellished facade of the Plummage's house.

CHAPTER 13

After rapping on the door, they waited. There was a fine view of the surrounding hills, darkened here and there with the occasional rolling shadow from the few passing clouds. Hearing the door open, they turned to see Monique greeting them with a big, warm smile.

"Ah! So good to see you!" she exclaimed. At once she stepped aside, bowed slightly and waved her wing in a long gracious arc, as if to sweep her friends inside. "Welcome to our home."

Marista and Eldsworth waddled into the foyer. Marista marveled for an instant at the unusual sculptures placed about the room in their artfully placed, dramatic displays. Then she set her gaze on Monique and forthrightly announced the reason for their visit, "Have you heard what the Mayor has done?"

"No, I have not heard anything. What has he done? What would he be doing without Quillypom?" Monique asked. "She is still at the doctor's, no?"

"Yes, she is still…" Eldsworth began.

"With Quillypom out and ill, the Mayor decided he could cast Quillypom's vote!" Marista interjected, raising her wings in exasperation. "And of course, he voted against Lillybeth!"

Arela came bounding down the hall.

"Anati went to see Hinsberth!" she said with a giggle. "She is not here."

"Who is there?" bellowed a piercing, sharp voice from the rear of the house.

Poullaire suddenly appeared with earnest steps, striding down the hall toward the visitors. He looked as though he had only just awakened and had hastily dressed. He wore a small beret over his rather ruffled feathers, a light brown vest which looked like it had seen too many years, and oddly, a pair of Monique's brightly colored foot covers.

"Who had voted?" he asked firmly with an agitated tone.

Poullaire never missed an opportunity to offer his opinion. Always touchy and passionate, he was rather vocal on any issue involving the Mayor's Office, or most any concern of importance to The Farm.

Eldsworth feared what might result from his wife and Poullaire becoming embroiled in a discussion about the Council vote, so he quickly took the initiative before Marista could offer an answer, "The Mayor has apparently decided to cast Quillypom's vote. And he voted 'no', naturally," he said in a very calm and soothing manner, for he had an idea of what might be coming next.

"WHAT?!" exclaimed Poullaire in disbelief. "Why, he has no right to do so. He, like everyone else, has *only* one vote on the Council. ONE. Not two. This is outrageous!"

Poullaire waved his wings around wildly, and his voice was close to shouting. Eldsworth cringed as Poullaire ranted, "And it is unacceptable! Unacceptable! I say we go down to that office right this moment and tell him that he cannot do what he believes he has done. We need to organize an immediate manifestation!"

"We just came from The Pond and many are there already, discussing the matter," Marista noted.

Arela was giggling again, this time at her father. When he was agitated, she found his mannerisms rather amusing.

"Have you talked to Millybeth or Hackleberg?" Monique asked with concern. "If she has heard about this, Lillybeth must be terribly upset."

"We planned to go there next," said Eldsworth.

CHAPTER 13

"Anati went to see Lillybeth," Arela added at the top of her little voice and flopping both wings forward as if making a very important point, and trying to make sure she was noticed.

Monique turned to her youngest daughter. She bent down to be face to face with her and asked, "Well, my little one. Did Anati go to see Lillybeth, or to see Hinsberth?"

"Both," said Arela with big, excited eyes.

Poullaire calmed a bit.

"Yes, I think what Eldsworth suggested is a good idea. We should speak with the Smythes. We must organize a resistance to this violation of the Council. Quillypom would know, for certain, if what the Mayor has done is even allowed by the regulations. Is she well? Has anyone visited her?" he inquired.

"No," said Eldsworth. "As far as we know, no one excepting Doctor Lochswyn has seen Quillypom. We have not heard anything regarding her condition."

"So. You are coming with us to see Millybeth and Hackleberg?" queried Marista.

"Yes," replied Poullaire. "I am not going to stay here and do nothing. *Something* must be done."

"Arela, you are coming too," said Monique, waving her daughter back to retrieve her things.

Arela excitedly bounded back down the hall and into her room. A short time later she returned draped from head to toe with sacks, bags and a satchel brimming with toys, eating utensils, a pair of maracas, and a butterfly net, anything she thought she may need for the voyage.

Monique stared at her in bewilderment.

"I do think we need to do something. But Quillypom is the one who would be able to check the regulations. If there is a mechanism to address this problem, she will know what it is. As far as we know she is still at Doctor Lochswyn's," Eldsworth thought aloud.

"Maybe Quillypom is there, but do you think she will do anything? Will she challenge the Mayor?" asked Monique.

"If there is something we can be certain of, it is that Quillypom always upholds the rules," stated Marista.

"Quite right," said Eldsworth.

Monique and Poullaire nodded in agreement.

"Well, for me, there is only one way to find out for sure. And I intend to do it. Shall we?" asked Poullaire, waving intently toward the door.

And out they went.

Marista and Eldsworth, waddling closely behind Monique, Poullaire and a bouncing Arela, noticed Poullaire was still wearing Monique's foot covers. They smiled and did not feel a need to say anything. As Poullaire strode purposefully down the trail, his ruffled appearance seemed befitting of his irreverent and feisty mood.

ELDSWORTH

"The Mayor posted a notice warning that unauthorized travel would be investigated... he was almost certainly speaking to us."

CHAPTER 14

A CERTAIN PATH

QUILLYPOM WAS SITTING UPRIGHT IN HER BED in the doctor's office, sipping a steaming hot concoction of Doctor Lochswyn's own secret blend of tea. Doctor Lochswyn had presented the tea in a large wooden cup which Quillypom held close with both wings. She savored the warmth, and for a long moment she only watched the steam billow from the tea. The ephemeral clouds of vapor rose into the air, spread out and disappeared, diffusing the sweet, aromatic scent over the room.

The rest and being far removed from the pressures and concerns of the Mayor's Office had Quillypom feeling better. She was becoming restless as her busy nature returned, but Doctor Lochswyn insisted she remain in bed and rest until fully recovered. She knew Quillypom was depleted, having spent far too many days working for far too long. Doctor Lochswyn was also quite certain, although she had not yet mentioned it, that something besides her work was preoccupying Quillypom and only making worse the effects of her condition.

"How do you like the tea?" Doctor Lochswyn asked as she entered the patient room. She noticed Quillypom had not moved at all; she seemed transfixed by the clouds and the scents and from the look in her eyes, her thoughts had wandered far into the distance.

Doctor Lochswyn had just finished her morning dose of porridge, and the smell had diffused through the house, mixing sweetly with the more subtle aroma of the tea.

"It does have a most appealing scent. But I have not yet had a chance to taste it. Lost in my thoughts for a moment, I suppose," replied Quillypom vaguely.

Doctor Lochswyn was pleased with Quillypom's response. She believed if it took Quillypom most of the day to drink her tea, she was on a certain path to recovery.

"Feeling better then?" queried Doctor Lochswyn softly.

"Yes. I would say so," replied Quillypom. "Not as sleepy. Vaguely more pep, perhaps."

"Very good. I am glad to hear it," said Doctor Lochswyn. "Might there be anything else?" she inquired in a curious tone.

"Anything else?" asked Quillypom quizzically.

"Yes. Is there anything you may wish to talk about? You seemed to be thinking about something when I came in. I thought perhaps I was interrupting," Doctor Lochswyn explained nonchalantly.

"No… no. Nothing I am aware of. I was only thinking for a moment — of everything, not of anything in particular," replied Quillypom, with an air of melancholy she peered down into the translucent blackness of her tea.

Doctor Lochswyn stepped slowly over to Quillypom's bedside. She pulled over a small stool, and sat down. Quillypom looked away, toward the window. After sitting silently for a moment, Doctor Lochswyn began to speak in a soft, almost soothing voice: "Many years ago, after I first became interested in healing, I had a patient come to me. He was very elderly, and very ill, so much so his condition began to impress upon me a disappointing awareness of the limits of my own knowledge and practice. He seemed very aware that he might not have much time left here with us. He had a large family, and they were always coming and going and staying for a time to visit, sometimes just to sit silently by his side. He always smiled when he saw them. It always brought him joy to have visitors, no matter how ill he may have felt otherwise. Sometimes the young ones would play, running and bouncing around the room. I would try to calm them, but he would stop me. He told me how he found their play... their excitement... their *life* especially comforting. Over time, he could see how frustrated I had become over my inability to cure his illness, and very late one evening, as his family slept, I was sitting at his bedside, just holding his wing, watching him breathe, wishing for something which had proven beyond my means. I felt completely lost, helpless. I did not feel there was anything more I could do for him. After a time he opened his eyes, and he must have noticed the expression on my face, because he began to speak, as if trying to comfort me. He told me he had lived a long life, and that he was happy. He was happy to see his family. He was happy to see me every day; he considered me a close friend, and he said he greatly admired my caring and diligence. And then he told me he wanted me to know about something — something he had learned over his many years of life. He told me about the Edges of Things. He meant not the edges of those things we can hold and feel and touch, but the edges that form between us; between families, between friends, between neighbors, between us and those we do not know, those we have never met, or never will. He told me of the edges we create inside, bounding what we believe we can achieve, bounding what we believe we can do. He said these edges, all of them, are not real. They have only been taught to us, and they creep upon us insidiously. We are mostly not even aware of their presence, but we can feel them; sometimes appearing hard as stone when we try to cross them. He said our challenge was to see these edges for the illusion they are, to jump over them, to plow through them, or to watch them crumble effortlessly to dust with a simple turn of thought. He explained how he had only become truly aware of the mythical nature of the Edges of Things after a long, full life. He wanted me to know this, he said, because passing beyond the edges allowed him to heal his family, to end old grudges and renew strained friendships, and to free himself from the perceived bounds on what he could accomplish. All these things had made him happy, and freed him from regret. He told me he knew he would be leaving us soon, but he was quite certain he was only crossing another edge, and that it too would ultimately prove illusory."

Quillypom listened intently to Doctor Lochswyn's story, and when she had finished, she turned to her and said sincerely, "Thank you, Heleen."

She knew Doctor Lochswyn was intelligent enough to know there was far more to her diagnosis than overwork, and she was aware Doctor Lochswyn was trying to help her in her own and very appreciated manner. Nevertheless, even though Quillypom had her defenses deployed, Doctor Lochswyn's words had made their mark. Quillypom understood the message, and strangely enough, her thoughts turned almost immediately to Lillybeth. Of course, Quillypom thought, that little Lillybeth! She was almost, or as close as anyone could imagine, edge-less. Quillypom, who had once again been exhausting herself in trying to fight back tears as Doctor Lochswyn spoke, suddenly developed a wide grin, and the teardrops fell freely into her tea even as her smile grew wider. She knew what she had to do. Lillybeth, the Council, Milchester, Filipa, Pommelstom, Bardslow, Bentlby, Chrysalis and the Mayor; Quillypom decided she could no longer have anything more to do with holding forth edges.

❖   ❖   ❖

The Plummages, with the exception of Anati, and the Smerkingtons, with the exception of Hinsberth, arrived at the Smythe's home. A sudden cacophony whirred away from the side of the house. Huddled together, they slowly, cautiously went round to have a look. The doors of the workshop were closed.

"Hello!" shouted Eldsworth.

His call apparently went unheard. No one answered.

"Hello!" repeated Eldsworth, more loudly this time but in unfortunate synchrony with a sudden, deafening screech and grinding crunch; the sounds of heavy machinery giving its last futile breath, before everything fell into silence.

"HACKLEBERG!" boomed Marista.

Almost immediately the workshop door opened and Hackleberg appeared. He was all in grease and dust, and a feeble puff of smoke escaped through the top of the doorway. Millybeth also appeared in the doorway, coughing, her clothing splattered all over with grease, in her wings she held the remnants of what may have at one time been some kind of mechanical device, but was now a twisted corpus of metal, springs and wire.

Seeing the confounded expressions held by his newly arrived friends,

Hackleberg said simply, "The Submersible."

"Oh. Yes, of course," said Eldsworth in surprise, and they all nodded in apparent comprehension, but merely out of politeness.

Millybeth and Hackleberg looked at Arela and the haphazard collection of odds and ends which covered her from head to toe. They also noticed Poullaire's rather odd pair of shoes, and they thought perhaps the confusion was mutual.

Marista and Poullaire did not want to become distracted by Hackleberg having a chance to expound on a typically long winded explanation of what he was doing and why it may have gone awry, so they seized the opportunity and began to explain the reason for their visit.

"So, have you been to the Mayor's Office?" Marista asked bluntly.

Poullaire, with his passionate manner, could not help interjecting before either Millybeth or Hackleberg could respond, "The Mayor, do you know what he has done?"

Hackleberg and Millybeth replied in unison, "No, and, no."

"What has the Mayor done?" Millybeth inquired curiously, knowing very well the answer would soon be dramatically revealed, even if she had not.

"He has voted twice! He voted again, against Lillybeth. Can you believe it!?" steamed Poullaire with a renewed sense of disbelief and flailing wings.

Millybeth and Hackleberg shared a disheartened glance.

"Technically, I do not think he can do such a thing," said Hackleberg, clearly disappointed, both about the vote and his ailing machine. He immediately wondered how this news might effect Lillybeth and Hinsberth.

"Technically or not, the Mayor's decision seems wrong to me. But has anyone seen Lillybeth? Does she know?" asked Millybeth, her thoughts had also gone quickly to her daughter and how she might take the news. She already seemed tired and sensitive, such news could not help matters.

"We have not seen her," said Monique, shrugging her shoulders.

Arela raised her voice again, "Anati went to see Lillybeth. And she went to see Hinsberth."

This announcement was naturally followed by a brief round of giggling.

"Lillybeth left early this morning. We thought she was going to see Hinsberth," said Hackleberg.

"Hinsberth also left this morning, a bit early for him. We assumed to see Lillybeth," said Eldsworth.

"As we all know, my precious Arela has generously informed us that early this morning Anati left to visit Lillybeth *and* Hinsberth. They must all be together somewhere, no?" suggested Monique.

Millybeth and Hackleberg looked at each other with eyes full of trepidation. They knew their daughter well enough, and they immediately wondered if Lillybeth and her friends had already discovered what Marista and Poullaire had just told them.

"Do you think they know?" asked Monique. She suddenly felt anxious. Had the ducklings done something rash? She could see Millybeth and Hackleberg were rather concerned about something as yet unmentioned. For Millybeth and Hackleberg were in silent consideration over some possibly worrying answers to the question: What might Lillybeth, Hinsberth and Anati be doing right now if they knew of the Mayor's decision?

"The double voting is not the only item of concern," said Eldsworth. "The Mayor posted a notice warning that unauthorized travel would be investigated; I think he intentionally left it ambiguous. But he was almost certainly speaking to us."

"Monique and Anati were very pleased with their journey to Chrysalis. If Chrysalis is what the Mayor is referring to, he has no right to tell my family they cannot return. And what does investigate mean? He is not going to tell me or my wife and daughter where they can or cannot go," said Poullaire in a speedy manner, with passionate conviction and another does of elaborate gesticulating.

Millybeth and Hackleberg's pulses were rising. If Lillybeth did go to the Mayor's Office, and if she had seen the notice, where would she think of going? Undoubtedly, she would go to Chrysalis.

"What is it?" asked Marista, noticing the looks on Millybeth and Hackleberg's faces.

"Suppose Lillybeth, Hinsberth or Anati had been by the Mayor's Office and read the notices, or had fallen into conversation with someone on the way to wherever they were going, and were told of the notices. If Lillybeth knew about the implied prohibition on traveling to Chrysalis… well, knowing my daughter, she can be a little strong minded, and she just might have decided to go there. Not out of spite, mind you. But if the notion was in her head, the notice would have confirmed it for her," explained Millybeth.

Hackleberg nodded and added, "Yes, that is exactly what she would do."

Poullaire, a bit surprised, asked, "So you think that Lillybeth would have convinced Hinsberth and Anati to go to Chrysalis?"

Monique knew Anati may not have resisted such a suggestion, and her expression turned from deep concern to deeper worry.

"Yes, if they are not here on The Farm, they have probably left already," said Hackleberg.

Marista also cringed. She knew that if Lillybeth expressed the idea that going to Chrysalis would help free Milchester, and given the disappointment and injustice Hinsberth would certainly feel over the notices, he would almost certainly not have objected.

Poullaire saw the change in Marista and Monique's expressions as they considered Millybeth and Hackleberg words, and with their subtle nods of recognition that the ducklings may have already departed for Chrysalis, he did not need any more affirmation.

"Anati went to see Lillybeth and Hinsberth. She is wherever they are." Arela offered in consolation. She looked up at the distraught faces ringed high above her, and this time she did not giggle.

**DOCTOR
TAUFFENSHUFTER**

*"The ducklings called loudly as they approached the dome,
"Doctor Tauffenshufter! … Doctor Tauffenshufter!""*

SO THAT THEY COULD BE FREE

ANATI, HINSBERTH AND LILLYBETH flew swiftly toward Chrysalis, spying the spray of light in the middle of the forest some distance away. A moment later they dropped into the trees and alighted just outside of Chrysalis.

Once on the ground, they scrambled inside and glanced around for anyone who might know the whereabouts of Mister Fowler. A few Chrysalis residents were scattered about waddling here and there, and a few more were standing or sitting and chatting quietly beside gardens and ponds.

They called out to a resident who had taken notice of the three ducklings bounding into Chrysalis, distracting him for a moment from watering a small garden. He at least seemed a little curious about the newcomers.

"Hello!" exclaimed Anati in a friendly manner. "Excuse me, but if I may ask, do you know where we may find Mister Fowler?"

"Oh, yes, Mister Fowler. Let me think… Let me think… I cannot remember seeing him wandering around this way lately. I know he enjoys his morning walks. If he is here I would suspect he may be on the other side of Chrysalis, over there, beyond the apex," he said, waving with his wings toward the far end of the dome.

"Thank you," said Anati, and the ducklings quickly turned and set off for the apex.

Taking a winding path along the maze of stone footpaths curving their way through the gardens and crisscrossing the interior of Chrysalis, they finally arrived at the center, in the brilliant light beneath the apex of the great ceiling. Looking around, they were not at all sure where to go next.

"Where is the doctor's office?" Hinsberth suddenly asked.

"Good idea," said Lillybeth.

"Excuse me," Anati called out to another resident who was busily netting insects out of a pond. "Pardon me for asking, but might you be able to direct us to the doctor's office?"

"Certainly. The directions on the ground can be confusing. So instead of giving them to you, do you see the amber hued skylight, third one down?" he asked, pointing to the roof. "The doctor's office is directly beneath it. Just follow the sky."

"Thank you!" said Anati excitedly.

The ducklings went fast down a winding path, over bridges, through gardens and under the arcaded walkways. Finally they came upon a small terrace with three earthen buildings, planted from top to bottom with flowers and herbs, and they quickly recognized one of them in particular as the doctor's office, for the bright red door was open and a patient limped away with a cane and a cast on his leg.

The ducklings called loudly as they approached the dome, "Doctor Tauffenshufter! ... Doctor Tauffenshufter!"

The door of the doctor's office opened wider, and Doctor Wichsluff's head poked out, looked around, and spotted the ducklings. He then quickly popped back inside, and as the trio came to the front entrance, Doctor Tauffenshufter was there with a wide smile to greet them.

"Hinsberth! Anati! Lillybeth!" she exclaimed excitedly.

She was very delighted to see the ducklings, especially with Hinsberth seemingly in such good health.

The ducklings were out of breath after crossing Chrysalis as fast as they could, and they needed a moment to recover.

Finally a breathless Anati managed to speak, "Doctor Tauffenshufter, we need to find Mister Fowler."

"Well, he is not here, of course. He only visits if he is ill, or someone close to him. I have not seen him since he stopped by before you left for The Farm," explained Doctor Tauffenshufter.

"If we may ask, we need to find him quickly. Might you help us?" inquired Anati hopefully.

Hinsberth and Lillybeth stared up at Doctor Tauffenshufter with pleading eyes. Looking down at the three of them, she could hardly refuse.

"What is this regarding?" asked Doctor Tauffenshufter.

"It is an emergency!" exclaimed Lillybeth.

"They refused to help us. At The Farm, they voted against saving Milchester!" added a still seething Hinsberth.

"Oh, my..." said Doctor Tauffenshufter, suddenly seeming quite concerned. "I am not sure Mister Fowler could help on such short notice. It could take him many days to organize something here at Chrysalis."

"Please. We need to speak to him," pleaded Anati.

Doctor Tauffenshufter regarded the urgency in the duckling's faces,

315

and she turned back into the dome to notify the staff she was going out and would return as soon as circumstances would allow.

She then returned swiftly to the doorway and stepped outside, to stand with the ducklings.

"Now, let us see if we can find him," she said while glancing around for a place to start. "If he is here, he obviously cannot be too far away."

The four ducks strode down the nearest trail, and Doctor Tauffenshufter asked everyone they encountered if they had seen Mister Fowler. But after asking a number of residents, not one knew of his whereabouts. Finally, just as they were beginning to lose hope, they met a resident who had seen Mister Fowler the previous evening on the arch bridge, alone and watching the lights. At least they knew he was probably still in Chrysalis. They continued down the path until coming across a resident waddling swiftly in the opposite direction.

Doctor Tauffenshufter stopped him.

"Excuse me, have you seen Mister Fowler?" Doctor Tauffenshufter asked suddenly.

"Chaffy? No. I have not seen him. But earlier today, some Migrators arrived… and I think they were intending to meet with Chaffy and a few others, over near the hub. There are three buildings beside the seating areas. If they are still in their meeting, they may be there," he said.

With the best lead they had received so far, Doctor Tauffenshufter quickly led the three ducklings on a winding trail to the seating area under the very apex of the dome, and then, looking off to one side, they saw the set of three buildings, all similar in appearance to the doctor's office.

"Well, all we can do is try each one," suggested Doctor Tauffenshufter.

"Wait! I think I can hear them!" said Hinsberth excitedly.

They quickly proceeded to the only dome from which the sound of voices emanated, and listened closely for a moment.

"Yes! That is definitely Mister Fowler!" exclaimed Doctor Tauffenshufter in a fervent whisper. Even she was a bit surprised they had found him.

The windows of the dome were open but the door was closed. To everyone's surprise, Lillybeth immediately strode over to the door, opened it and went inside. There she saw a group of five ducks, one of whom was standing and pointing with a long stick at a very large diagram, which looked like a view of Chrysalis from above. The others were seated closely around a long table, facing the diagram.

"Mister Fowler?" Lillybeth inquired of the speaker.

"Yes little one?" the startled speaker replied with more than a little surprise. "I am Mister Fowler. But please, call me Chaffy."

"I must talk to you," Lillybeth declared firmly.

Chaffy made a reassuring glance toward the ducks around the table, and then he turned his gaze back on Lillybeth.

"I am flattered that you so urgently wish to speak with me. But at the moment I am now busy with this other rather mundane preoccupation. If I may ask, might you return just a bit later, please?" Chaffy asked politely.

"No! It is an emergency!" declared Lillybeth emphatically.

The meeting attendees looked amused, but Chaffy saw something in Lillybeth's eyes that made him take her quite seriously.

"I see..." Chaffy began. He paused briefly. "Might I inquire into the nature of this emergency?"

"I need your help," stated Lillybeth.

CHAPTER 15

"Help?" asked Chaffy.

Anati and Hinsberth waddled through the doorway, and Chaffy recognized them immediately.

"Milchester..." he whispered under his breath.

"I went to the Council for help. But the Mayor voted against it. Milchester needs us, and we have to go now," pleaded Lillybeth with distress in her voice. She came to the front of the room and stood directly before Chaffy.

The meeting attendees shifted in their seats, they were not at all sure what to make of such an unusual intrusion. Chaffy raised his eyes from Lillybeth to those seated around the table. He then looked over at Anati and Hinsberth, who were standing just inside the doorway. Their faces were etched with undoubtedly desperate but still hopeful expressions that they would soon have some kind of answer, some way forward to rescue Milchester and his companions — something that now seemed almost out of their grasp.

Chaffy hesitated only an instant.

"My deepest apologies," he suddenly announced, returning his gaze to the befuddled attendees. "I know this may seem entirely unusual. But if I may ask, I would be most appreciative if you could offer me a bit of time with our young visitors here."

The ducks at the table glanced at one another, uncertain what to do. After a brief moment, they spontaneously rose from their seats and went outside.

"Thank you, and my apologies again," Chaffy offered as they departed. Finally the last one out gently closed the door.

As the meeting attendees huddled together outside, they looked around for something to occupy themselves with, and fortunately they were greeted by a gregarious Doctor Tauffenshufter. She apologized repeatedly for the interruption, and then generously proceeded to try and hold their attention by offering a general lecture about the history of Chrysalis and her medical practice.

Inside, Chaffy announced, "Now you three have my complete attention."

The ducklings suddenly went silent.

Chaffy continued, "If I recall, we were to develop a plan to assist The Farm if any action were to be taken regarding a rescue. You are now telling me The Farm has chosen to take no action. They have *rejected* a rescue?"

The ducklings nodded.

"This places us in a most difficult situation, does it not?" thought Chaffy aloud.

"It does," answered Lillybeth. "But for Milchester it is much worse."

"Undoubtedly," said Chaffy. "While some here have volunteered to help, we do not have enough volunteers to attempt a rescue by ourselves."

"Come to The Farm," Lillybeth interjected suddenly with a serious tone.

Hinsberth and Anati glanced at one another, surprised at Lillybeth's request. Hinsberth then turned to look upon Lillybeth, seeing her standing there, her eyes gazing up at Chaffy, and for the first time this day, he smiled.

Chaffy was taken aback, but Lillybeth was rather serious and was looking deeply into his eyes.

"I have not been to The Farm in quite some time..." Chaffy said distantly, and his voice drifted off.

CHAPTER 15

"You must come to The Farm," Lillybeth pleaded again.

Chaffy glanced down on Lillybeth, but his eyes were even more distant.

"We can send Bardslow and Bentlby from Chrysalis. They can fly together, to where Milchester is trapped. They can tell us what to do to free them," said Lillybeth. "You can come with us to The Farm. I know they will listen to you."

Chaffy was still lost in his thoughts, he had not considered returning to The Farm for a number of years.

"Please," pleaded Lillybeth. "Please, for Milchester."

Hinsberth and Anati stood silent, watching Lillybeth and Chaffy. They could see Chaffy was deep in thought, and that there was something beyond Lillybeth's apparently simple request he was taken by. Something distant yet powerful, perhaps beneath Chaffy's awareness, where he was fighting to keep it.

Lillybeth stood patiently, waiting for an answer. She could also see Chaffy was seriously considering her request, but something unsaid was holding him back.

"Please!" Lillybeth pleaded again.

Chaffy looked down into her eyes.

He took a step back. He looked away.

After a long moment, with the ducklings waiting hopefully, Chaffy turned his head up and began speaking, slowly, quietly and as if to no one in particular, "We came here to build this place. I wanted to build something, a place where anyone could come, distant from humans, distant from danger. The Farm was too close. Too many artifacts, traces of them were everywhere. They would come for them. Maybe only a matter of time…"

"Why?" Lillybeth asked. "Why can you not go to The Farm now? What is there?"

Chaffy stood in silence. He seemed pained. Unsure. Then he began to speak with a voice distant in time; he seemed to be struggling with his words, "It was many years ago, during the last migrations, after we had begun to settle on The Farm. We had flown, every year from one place to another, to avoid the weather — the winter — when food became scarce. We went to find areas of shelter. Again and again we flew, and one year… they… took her. They took her from me, right from the sky…"

Overcome, Chaffy paused. He tried to gather himself. He took a deep, sorrowful breath. "What is there? Memories. My memories are there. I came here to build Chrysalis, for her. To make something as beautiful as she was. And for the others, so that they could be free, never having to experience what I have. They can come and live, and they are safe. And for the others still flying, we tell them where to go. They come here to share where the dangers are, for all to avoid them."

Chaffy finished speaking, but the burden of the years spent burying his memories proved too much, and he covered his face in his wings. Lillybeth waddled to Chaffy and wrapped her wings around him as far as they would reach, and she held him as tightly as she could.

Anati and Hinsberth were deeply moved by Chaffy's recounting of the past, and for the moment they were beyond words. They stood motionless as Chaffy wept into his wings, and Lillybeth embraced him with all her might.

Doctor Tauffenshufter eventually entered silently through the door and saw Chaffy weeping and Lillybeth trying her best to comfort him. Anati and Hinsberth were still frozen just inside the doorway. The meeting attendees were becoming impatient, but Doctor Tauffenshufter waved for them to remain outside.

Finally Chaffy wiped his eyes of tears. Lillybeth let her wings fall, and Chaffy patted her on the top of her head.

"I am so sorry," said Lillybeth. "I did not mean to…"

"No need to apologize, little one," Chaffy interjected. "It has been too long. I certainly needed that."

Still drying his eyes, Chaffy began to think aloud, "Now where were we? Ah yes. The Farm. And Milchester. And the Council. I see. Yes, I will go to The Farm. But at this very moment, we must find Bardslow and Bentlby. Doctor Tauffenshufter, would you mind asking my guests to return?"

"Certainly," replied Doctor Tauffenshufter.

The four attendees soon swiftly reentered the room.

"My apologies again, but I am afraid our meeting must be adjourned until further notice," Chaffy quickly announced.

The attendees were startled by this news, but their respect for Chaffy's judgement was palpable, and they offered no objections. They filed out of the room and waddled off together, huddled tightly, in grave, speculative discussion.

❖   ❖   ❖

At once Chaffy marched outside and the three ducklings and Doctor Tauffenshufter waddled swiftly to keep up with him. They left the central area under the apex and then followed under a trellised arcade to a small wooden workshop with a steeply pitched roof, draped in vines just beyond the Chrysalis dome. Chaffy entered, noting several ducks seated round a table inside. The walls were covered with diagrams, displaying various parts of Chrysalis from sundry perspectives.

"Might you be able to tell me where Bardslow and Bentlby are at the moment?" Chaffy inquired hastily.

"Yes. They went to meet with Pommelstom and Filipa under the apex, to plan for tomorrow," replied one of the seated ducks.

"Thank you," quipped Chaffy.

And with this information he quickly darted off again, switching from one path to another, in a complicated route lined with gardens and ponds which he seemed to have memorized, not a misstep was made.

Finally, they arrived under the apex, where, awash in sunlight, many residents and visitors were seated, all chatting away. Quickly glancing around, Chaffy spotted his quarry, seated around a small wooden table in the warm glow of a shaft of sunlight reflected from high above.

Chaffy waddled directly up to the table, quickly followed by Anati, Hinsberth, Lillybeth and Doctor Tauffenshufter, whose curiosity would not yet let her return to the daily routine.

When Filipa saw Lillybeth and Hinsberth she immediately jumped from her seat and bounded over to embrace them, a duckling in each wing. Not wishing to leave anyone out, she buried Anati in both wings.

"I am so happy to see all of you. And everyone looking so healthy," Filipa declared, standing upright with a wide grin.

"No time for sentiment," stated Chaffy. "I think we have exhausted ourselves already."

Everyone at the table looked at Chaffy confoundedly, but their confusion faded quickly as they remembered just who was speaking.

CHAPTER 15

"Firstly, and if there are no objections, however odd it may seem, I am going immediately to The Farm with these three ducklings. Secondly, Bardslow and Bentlby, if you recall our discussion about assisting The Farm with the rescue of a thousand distressed pigs, it appears some events have transpired at The Farm and they have been unable to organize any sort of plan. I want you two to fly over where Hinsberth discovered Milchester and his companions, and I want you to figure out how we might be able to free them. We will need to know about building materials, layout, possible paths of entry and exit, both for ourselves, and for the pigs. You may need to enter one or more of the buildings, we need to know by what manner they are confined. Oh, and by the way, please do stay out of the water and be careful what you touch."

"When?" asked Bardslow.

"Now," said Chaffy.

"I am going too," declared Pommelstom.

"So am I," added Filipa.

The four siblings immediately rose together from the table and without even a quick goodbye strode along the walkway toward an archway to the outside, to leave Chrysalis and take to the air.

"How will they know where to go?" asked Doctor Tauffenshufter.

"Filipa and Pommelstom have both been there, and they never forget. The Migrators told us of their destination when it was first laid down on the bare ground. We know where it is, but until Hinsberth had explored it on the ground, until he met this Milchester, we did not know its nature," Chaffy explained.

He turned to the ducklings.

"Now, shall we?" he said, waving them down the path to exit

Chrysalis.

Doctor Tauffenshufter watched as Chaffy and the three ducklings waddled away, round a bend in the trail and out of sight. She remembered the conversations at the Doctor's Office, and not without some worry, she wished them well. She thought about The Farm, and how she would like to visit, perhaps one day soon.

Chaffy and the three ducklings swiftly waddled outside, and beneath a shimmering sky they immediately took off into the air, climbing fast. Once clear of the trees, they banked hard and darted away toward The Farm.

❖   ❖   ❖

The duckling's parents and Arela were huddled together just outside Hackleberg's workshop.

"Do you think we should check to see if they are still here on The Farm?" asked Eldsworth. "If we fly we should be able to cover the grounds rather easily."

Millybeth and Hackleberg considered Eldsworth's suggestion. But they both knew if Lillybeth had become aware of the Mayor's ruling on travel, they were almost certainly at Chrysalis.

"Perhaps, at the moment, we should not draw too much attention to the fact we are searching for the ducklings. The Mayor, I should think, might be rather upset to know his notices were being ignored so quickly," Millybeth suggested.

"I am not worried about the Mayor," said Marista defiantly. "But I would like to know the whereabouts of my son."

"I think we should go back to The Pond," recommended Poullaire. "If they are still on The Farm they will show up there eventually."

"Yes, if they are here and on any of the trails between our homes, they will pass The Pond at some point, either coming or going," agreed Monique.

Millybeth and Hackleberg decided Poullaire's idea was a good one, for even if their daughter and her friends had travelled to Chrysalis, they were likely to return before nightfall.

"Agreed. But wait here a moment," Millybeth suddenly announced.

She and Hackleberg went into their home to quickly gather some food and drink, and they packed what they found into a small basket. Offering some food to their friends was the least they could do under the circumstances, for they were once again feeling a little responsible for yet another round of unintentional mischief.

With a bit of nourishment in tow for what was expected to be a long afternoon, Millybeth, Hackleberg, Marista, Eldsworth, Monique, Poullaire and a bouncy Arela waddled off quickly toward The Pond. Coming out of the undergrowth bordering the trail and onto the The Pond's sandy beach, Marista and Eldsworth noticed the crowd gathered outside the Mayor's Office had grown considerably.

In observing the Mayor's Office, every now and then they could see the Messenger, glancing with some concern through a window at the growing number of Farm residents settling around The Pond. It had been many years — since the big flood — that so many residents had spontaneously gathered in one place. The Mayor, however, had not been seen by anyone, and his opinions on the matter could only be a matter of speculation.

Poullaire nodded his head in approval when he noticed the large number of his neighbors scattered about The Pond. For him, a little disruption in the course of the normal routines of The Farm was a much too rare occurrence.

Finally they all sat down, finding a comfortable spot under the shade of a large tree, and settled in. While watching the activities around The Pond, their eyes frequently found the footpaths leading in from the trees to the sandy beach. They also glanced skyward every now and then for any sign of a trio of ducklings on the approach.. and they waited.

❖   ❖   ❖

On the edge of consciousness and frequently lost in sleep, Milchester dreamt he was flying. Without body, over the earth he soared, the clumps of cloud beneath him shining brightly in the brilliant sun. In his dreams, he was home.

He had not eaten in days, and his hopeful nature was spending its last. Of the defiant fire of optimism he had once held, only small embers still dimly smoldered. He no longer knew if his friend was merely a dream, and he had resigned himself to living solely in his imagination, and in his dreams whenever sleep greeted him. For now sleep was his only friend, its gentle approach would relieve him of the pain in his body, the despair in his mind, and the loneliness in his heart.

For they had come, harshly restrained him and wrapped a length of cold tape grimly around his belly. Milchester knew he would soon be taken. It was the inevitable fate of his companions, and he was beginning to succumb to the fact it was the inevitable fate for himself.

Presently, something caused him to stir.

He opened his eyes for an instant. But he could no longer bare to see the cold bars of his captivity, and the numbing noise of his surroundings faded into the distance as he drifted once more into a fitful sleep. His body slumped feebly against the side of his cage.

High above Milchester, in a place he had no privilege of sight, on the burning metal roof of the building which defined the edges of his world, four shadows arrayed in a diamond shape suddenly appeared. The shadows traced swiftly along its length, accompanied by the subtle sound of brushing wings waving ever so quietly through the stifling air, beneath the ambient noise. The shadows soared off the roof and onto the desolate ground, and for some time they traced out great circles around the buildings. With each circle the shadows grew in size and moved more tightly together. There was no other noise, only the delicate sound of feathers pushing aside air. Then, for a time, only three shadows circled. The fourth soon reappeared, and the dark shapes completed a final broad sweep over the barren earth. All at once the shadows darted swiftly away from the buildings, and they quickly and quietly disappeared into the trees, in the direction from which they had come.

CHAFFY

*"Reputations are always easier to be had when one has
no opportunity to fail them."*

329

CHAPTER 16

EVEN FROM A DISTANCE

OCTOR LOCHSWYN WENT OUTSIDE to gather an additional batch of ingredients for porridge. Quillypom was resting silently, sitting upright in the patient bed, looking out the window and taking in the beauty of the softened light; coming through the doctor's garden it seemed to have gathered unto itself the hues of leaf and flower. She could not see the horizon; the view out of the window in the patient room was shadowed over with leaves, and what might otherwise be seen was kept hidden by a wall trees.

Nevertheless, Quillypom found herself looking outward, drawn by a faint hope of seeing something in the distant sky...

Quillypom turned her gaze back to the porridge Doctor Lochswyn had prepared for her after she spoilt her tea with an abundance of salty tears. With her spoon she plied through the thick, lumpy porridge. She examined the porridge closely and wondered why it always seemed to smell and taste so much better when Doctor Lochswyn prepared it. What secrets did she hold? Even after several attempts and following the instructions exactly, she failed to duplicate the porridge at home. As she considered the possibilities: better ingredients, the sequence of mixing, or maybe even the type or quality of bowl or spoon, she was startled to hear Doctor Lochswyn stumbling through the front door. For a moment she heard not only the creaking sound of the door, but a great many voices flooding in from outside.

"How are you feeling?" Doctor Lochswyn inquired, a little breathlessly. She held several large bags of ingredients tightly under her wings.

"Better. The porridge helps, certainly. I can only wonder what you do to it? Mine does not come out nearly so inviting," answered Quillypom.

Quillypom paused for an instant, but before Doctor Lochswyn could formulate a proper answer, she added hastily, "I hate to bother, but what is happening outside? Is there some sort of meeting taking place?"

"I am not exactly sure," replied Doctor Lochswyn. "There has been a crowd forming out by The Pond since early this morning. They seem to be discussing something important, but I did not stop to gather their reasons. By the way, these ingredients need to be stored fresh, in a timely manner."

Doctor Lochswyn was trying her best to be evasive on the subject, knowing Quillypom would not be able to restrain herself from wading in on any issue of importance to The Farm, and she knew Quillypom might easily reverse her restful progress toward recovery.

"If you will pardon me, I will return in a moment after I settle my ingredients," she stated nonchalantly, and she went off quickly down the hall.

Quillypom strained to listen to what was happening outside, but Doctor Lochswyn's home was not short on quality, and nothing intelligible could be heard. In a short time, Doctor Lochswyn poked her head round the doorway and attempted to continue the conversation regarding the proper and exact preparation of her uniquely formulated porridge.

"Yes, yes. I see," replied Quillypom, and she tried to bring about a hasty end to the subject. "I think I have it now. Yes. Fairly certain."

"But the trick is —" interjected Doctor Lochswyn.

"Heleen, I appreciate your efforts. And I can tell from them there is something of importance occurring outside your door, something you would prefer I stay out of, for my own sake," Quillypom explained. "But I can assure you I am feeling fine, certainly much better than I was, and I can also assure you the messages you have given me have not fallen onto deaf ears. So let me offer you a compromise. If you would be willing to return outside and investigate what issues have prompted the discussion, I will promise not to return to work for at least several more days, and to remain indefinitely on this diet of yours, until you tell me to do otherwise."

Doctor Lochswyn considered Quillypom's proposal for a moment. At first blush it seemed reasonable. But she did not generally have to negotiate the course of treatment with her patients, and she felt she had to weigh Quillypom's concerns over knowing what was happening outside against her not knowing, and to determine which may cause her the least amount of harm.

After pondering the balance between these imperatives, Doctor Lochswyn offered her own compromise, "I will accept your terms — if, what I find I judge not to be in the best interest of your health, you will accept your not knowing."

"Agreed," said Quillypom, somewhat reluctantly — she was not quite certain what Doctor Lochswyn was implying.

With a sealed agreement, Doctor Lochswyn departed from the patient room and proceeded outside. She glanced around at the many familiar faces, but then she spied off in the distance and under the shade of a large tree, the Smerkingtons, the Plummages and the Smythes. She noticed they were without their ducklings and appeared to be waiting for something. Doctor Lochswyn went round The Pond until coming up to where this curious clutch of her neighbors were eyeing the sky.

"Hello everyone!" she called.

"Oh! Hello Doctor Lochswyn! It is so, so good to see you!" Marista exclaimed, always elated to see friends and family, the latter of which she now considered Doctor Lochswyn to be a member.

"I am very glad to see everyone out here enjoying the day," said Doctor Lochswyn. "Is Hinsberth around and about?" she asked curiously.

"No. But of course he is around here on The Farm... somewhere," said Marista in a loud voice, and then she continued in a whisper, "We think he went to Chrysalis."

"Chrysalis?" whispered Doctor Lochswyn in surprise.

"The Mayor," Poullaire interjected loudly, "he has decided that he can tell us where to go. I think many of the others out here agree with me, that he has no such right."

"But why did Hinsberth go to Chrysalis?" whispered Doctor Lochswyn.

"We are fairly certain it was not his idea," stated Millybeth. "Lillybeth may have found out about the notices at the Mayor's Office, and she is not usually one to follow such pronouncements, by the Mayor or otherwise. And we suspect Anati is with them, and it all has something to do with the Council meeting."

"What notices? And the Council meeting?" asked Doctor Lochswyn. "I thought everything was still unresolved?"

"Ah. So you have not heard, no?" asked Poullaire. "That Mayor, he voted twice! He thought since Quillypom fainted he could cast her vote, and he voted against poor Lillybeth. Can you believe it!?" Poullaire again seemed ready to boil over, as he did each time he revealed this particular piece of news. He waved his wings around wildly whenever the subject arose. Arela stepped up to her father and sat on his lap. She waved her butterfly net. This seemed to calm Poullaire for the moment.

"He put notices beside the Mayor's Office door, and as you might expect the news has already spread far and wide. I think some of our neighbors here are a little upset about the Mayor's actions, even if they are of one mind or another regarding the rescue, they are not at all happy about the Mayor. I think they do not believe he can override the Council as he seems to think he can," explained Monique.

Doctor Lochswyn was busy concentrating, trying to remember everything she was hearing, and trying to imagine how Quillypom might take the news. After Monique had spoken Doctor Lochswyn felt she was in a rather difficult quandary. The decisions of the Mayor were making even those who were not present at the Council meeting indignant. She had no difficulty believing Quillypom's reaction might be much worse. A setback in her health would almost certainly result.

"Well, I believe what the Mayor can and cannot do is well described within the rules and regulations, in the records Quillypom possesses and maintains in her office," said Doctor Lochswyn, hoping to ameliorate some of the agitation.

"Ah. And that is why he is doing it, no? Because Quillypom is your patient, and not in the office," said Monique. "By the way, how is she doing?"

"I appreciate your concern, Monique. As you know, that information is strictly for myself and my patient," answered Doctor Lochswyn.

"Yes. Sorry, I should have known better than to pry," said Monique. "But I think she is certainly the one to clear up this mess, no?"

With Monique's words Doctor Lochswyn was beginning to feel as though she were in an even tighter dilemma with Quillypom. Informing her of what was going on outside now seemed a matter of legal importance. Yet the situation would almost certainly be upsetting for Quillypom. Doctor Lochswyn was torn. She chatted a bit more but she was mostly distracted thinking of Quillypom, so she quickly bid everyone a good day and turned to slowly waddle back to her home.

Opening the door, she paused for a moment, trying to conceive a strategem for conveying the news she had gathered to Quillypom in the most favorable manner possible. After giving it due consideration, she reasoned that any potential approach was equally unlikely to be met with success. For Quillypom, there was nothing favorable about anything Doctor Lochswyn had discovered.

Doctor Lochswyn came ever so slowly around the doorway to the patient room, with a feigned and anxious smile.

"Well?" asked Quillypom impatiently. "What did you find?"

Doctor Lochswyn considered herself to be honest, but she was rapidly weighing the importance she placed on always being truthful with always acting in the best interests of her patients.

"Please," pleaded Quillypom, as she waited impatiently for Doctor Lochswyn to reveal her precious secrets.

Doctor Lochswyn drew a deep breath, and she began to speak in a very optimistic tone, "Apparently the Mayor has recommended that unauthorized travel be discouraged."

"Is that all?" asked Quillypom dubiously.

She followed her query with a deep breath as she attempted to repress any appearance of agitation.

"He... also cast your vote for you," Doctor Lochswyn announced quickly, framing the Mayor's action in such a manner as to make it seem a favor.

Doctor Lochswyn watched as Quillypom's brow furrowed. She quickly donned an apparently calm demeanor. Inside she was indignant.

"Anything else?" asked Quillypom thoughtfully.

"Well... he.... closed the Mayor's Office to visitors until further notice," said Doctor Lochswyn, closing her eyes tightly with the pain of revealing this final insult to Quillypom's sensibilities.

Quillypom tensed and turned to the window. She recalled her decision regarding the future after hearing Doctor Lochswyn's story about The Edges of Things. She thought of Lillybeth, not only of the warmth she had begun to feel toward her little visitor, but about her edgeless nature. She regarded her personal beliefs about what was possible, and of the boundaries she believed she could not pass. For everyone's sake, she concluded, she would have to go beyond, into the unbounded world Lillybeth had so innocently and unwittingly shown her.

"My apologies," Quillypom said as she turned to Doctor Lochswyn.

"For what?"

"I am afraid I may have a temporary setback in my progress. But there is something I must do, and if all goes well I may leap ahead in the course of my treatment," answered Quillypom. "It is a risk I must take."

"I understand," said Doctor Lochswyn in solemn disappointment. She tried to hide it, but she was very worried for her patient.

Quillypom slowly rose from the bed. Her energy remained low but her spirit was determined, and she straightened her attire, put on her coat, waddled down the hall, and gingerly departed out the front door.

Doctor Lochswyn watched with concern as Quillypom passed by and left the calm confines of her home to the outside, hoping that whatever was to come, Quillypom had made enough progress to find her way home.

❖   ❖   ❖

A wave of surprise and a rise in the fervor of the chatter swept through the crowd beside The Pond as notice was made of Quillypom departing from Doctor Lochswyn's, and of her slow but steady waddle down the footpath toward the Mayor's Office.

Quillypom went up to the front of the house, and she paused, taking time to read the notices. She stood up for a moment, and then she turned, and went through the gardens leading to the rear of the house and her private entrance.

The crowd quieted, only the incessant giggling of Arela, the whispers of burbling water and the faint rustling leaves could be heard.

Quillypom slowly drew open the door and entered her home.

"Welshley?" she called.

There was no answer.

Being met with silence, Quillypom stepped lightly down the hallway toward the office wing of the house. The office was unusually empty. From out of nowhere the Messenger appeared, looking even more uptight and anxious than usual. She motioned subtly with the bottom of one wing, pointing Quillypom to where the Mayor could be found. Quillypom silently nodded with grateful eyes and then she turned and went to her office. She opened the solid, heavy door, which creaked and strained and moaned as it opened, to find the Mayor seated in her chair; his wings spread over the piles of unfinished work covering her desk. He sat frozen, motionless, his eyes drawn distantly through the window to the horizon, as if waiting, perhaps yearning to see something.

"Welshley?" whispered Quillypom.

The Mayor turned slowly and set his eyes upon Quillypom, but said not a word.

❖   ❖   ❖

After Quillypom passed into the Mayor's Office, the crowd outside erupted again into vigorous speculation. But soon a new excitement fanned the ever more feisty assembly as four flyers were seen in the distance, fast on the approach. As they flew closer, it became apparent there was one adult accompanied by three ducklings. The crowd quickly made way as they descended rapidly out of the sky to alight near The Pond.

As they made their descent, a voice from the crowd exclaimed "Oh, my!" and the words echoed loudly around The Pond.

"Its Chaffy!" another voice announced in astonishment, and the crowd erupted as the news spread wide. Everyone rushed toward the new arrivals, waddling swiftly to the landing site from all over The Pond. With the sudden din of noise, the nearby homes had their doors and windows thrown open. Everyone watched and waited. Never before had one returned after so long.

The parents of the wayward ducklings were stunned to see them arrive in the company of Chaffy. Poullaire picked up Arela and Millybeth and Hackleberg forgot their picnic basket as they all darted as fast as they could toward where the ducklings alighted.

Lillybeth, Hinsberth and Anati were caught in the throes of the crowd, and they had to deftly weave their way out to the edge to take a moment to breath after the fast flight.

Everyone gathered round Chaffy. Those who remembered him were especially overjoyed to see an old Farm resident return after so many years. Tears were not scarce. Chaffy was overwhelmed by the reception, but for a moment the greetings faded into the distance as his eyes followed along the trail to the place he and one other once called home. He fought back tears, both from a flood of memories and the joy of seeing old friends. He never stopped reminding himself he was on a mission, to do whatever was necessary to see Lillybeth and Hinsberth's request fulfilled. Chaffy was smothered; embraced by a number of old friends, he shook the wings of new acquaintances who had no idea who he was, but could see that he was rather well known and equally well regarded by the older residents.

Doctor Lochswyn had left her door ajar after Quillypom departed, and she saw the flyers arrive and the reaction from the crowd. She stood in the doorway, and watched Chaffy make his way through the gathering. As Chaffy glanced around, eventually his eyes met hers, and he smiled and immediately turned to advance toward Doctor Lochswyn's home. He and a group of friends, assorted acquaintances and curious onlookers arrived at the front gardens, and then Chaffy requested he be able to go forth alone. He waddled up the path and onto the small porch fronting Doctor Lochswyn's house, and coming up beside her, he asked if they could go inside.

"Certainly," she replied.

They went inside together and Doctor Lochswyn gently closed the door.

"I just need to breathe a little," said Chaffy, wiping his eyes. "I was not expecting such a reception. How did they know we were coming? Or did we land in the middle of a celebration of some kind?"

"Not exactly," said Doctor Lochswyn. "I think they are a bit upset over the Mayor's decisions."

"Ah, I should have known. One can always hope, though. I thought maybe I had developed a bit of a reputation here on The Farm during my absence. Reputations are always easier to be had when one has no opportunity to fail them," Chaffy offered with a slight grin.

"That is probably true. But in your case, I am not so sure," replied Doctor Lochswyn.

"Well, I promised myself I would focus on what I need to accomplish here," said Chaffy.

"I assume that your task has something to do with Lillybeth and Hinsberth?" asked Doctor Lochswyn.

"Yes, but more specifically, with someone named Milchester," answered Chaffy.

"That will not be so easy," said Doctor Lochswyn. "We seem to be in somewhat of a predicament here on The Farm at the moment."

"I can certainly see that," said Chaffy peering out the front window. "But I believe it will not last much longer."

"Really?" asked Doctor Lochswyn.

"Yes," said Chaffy.

❖   ❖   ❖

Anati, Lillybeth and Hinsberth were suddenly surrounded by and smothered under the wings of their parents and Arela as they wandered aimlessly through the growing assemblage around The Pond.

"Chrysalis?" Hackleberg immediately asked Lillybeth.

Lillybeth nodded.

"After reading the notice?" asked Millybeth.

Lillybeth nodded.

"You know the Mayor was discouraging travel there?" Eldsworth asked Hinsberth.

"Yes, but we had to go. For Milchester," replied Hinsberth.

Eldsworth felt as though he should remind Hinsberth about the importance of adhering to the rules and regulations of The Farm, but he understood that in this case an issue of greater importance was being served, and he said nothing more about it.

Poullaire swung Anati into the air and announced loudly, "That is right, you have shown the Mayor who is really in charge, and her name is Anati."

Anati grinned widely, and Monique smiled and said, "Yes, there are certainly times when you have to do what you think is right. We do not worry too much about the Mayor, no? After all, Marista is standing right here."

CHAPTER 16

Marista stood tall.

"What is going to happen now?" asked Anati.

"Look around. I do not think anyone knows. Chaffy went to Doctor Lochswyn's, and Quillypom went to her home. I think now we wait," answered Marista.

"We do not have time to wait!" Lillybeth announced anxiously.

"We must do something now!" exclaimed Hinsberth.

❖ ❖ ❖

"Welshley?" Quillypom repeated. "Why did you do it?"

The Mayor looked at Quillypom, but still he said nothing. He seemed stern, but he was wearing down. He was not so sure now, he felt uncertain, confused, a tinge of doubt skirted over his every thought. He needed the authority, to be there for The Farm. He knew The Farm would not function without someone in charge, someone to make sure everything was running smoothly, someone to make decisions when they needed to be made. But creeping into his thoughts was another, that making the right decision was better than merely making one, and he thought in this case, perhaps he had... No, he reminded himself. He had made the decision, and that was that.

"Welshley, please. Talk to me," pleaded Quillypom.

By now it was late afternoon, and the sun drew lower in the sky. Through the row of windows gracing the outside wall of Quillypom's office, the last rays of sunlight spread across the sky, the gleaming fingers of light and shadow streamed off into infinity above the horizon.

The Mayor turned to the sky. He did not want to face her. He did not want to face his decision any longer. He felt weary, more weary than ever, and he looked up into the distance once again.

Quillypom stood patiently, facing her husband's back. She would not leave him.

"Welshley, I still love you," she whispered.

The Mayor did not say anything in return, but he suddenly began breathing heavily; he seemed to be in some kind of trouble. His breath was catching. Short quick breaths. He was taken by something, and he leaned forward, almost falling wearily toward the window.

"Welshley, what is it? Tell me, PLEASE!" Quillypom demanded in a panic.

Quillypom quickly stepped forward to come up behind him. She placed a wing on his back, and she leaned over his shoulder so she could see the side of his face.

Tears were streaming out of his eyes and running to the floor, and he began sobbing heavily, uncontrollably. He was staring into the sky, toward the horizon. Quillypom followed his gaze outward, and she saw them. Four of them. And she knew, even from a distance, they were coming home.

❖   ❖   ❖

Lillybeth suddenly turned to Hinsberth.

"The pigs! We must go visit the pigs!" she exclaimed loudly.

"The pigs on The Farm?" asked Hinsberth.

"Yes. Remember? We went to visit them this morning and they said they would help. They asked me to return, they said they would have something for me. We need to go visit them now!" explained Lillybeth emphatically.

"Yes, yes. I had almost forgotten," said Hinsberth, and he gave her a smile that made Lillybeth want to check the arrangement of her footwear.

Millybeth and Hackleberg glanced at each other in surprise.

"You went to visit the pigs this morning? Before leaving for Chrysalis, I assume?" inquired Hackleberg.

"Is there anything else we should know about?" asked Millybeth.

Lillybeth shrugged her shoulders.

"Well, everyone, I hope we are free of any pressing matters because it appears we are needing to go visit the pigs," Hackleberg announced.

"Nothing pressing here," said Monique.

"Or here, I can tell you that right now. This is what we are here for," said Marista.

"We leave now," said Poullaire as he lifted Arela and swung her in a wide arc up onto his shoulders. "I for one want to be present for anything. Anything that happens. Especially regarding the Mayor's decisions."

Even as Poullaire tried in vain to move Arela into a position where her gear was not flopping down in front of his eyes, Marista and Eldsworth were already waddling quickly in the direction of the pig's home. Anati, Hinsberth and Lillybeth followed close behind.

They all darted rapidly down the trail, but as they disappeared into the foliage, they did not look upward. For just at that moment four flyers swooped down from out of the sky and alighted in the same spot where the ducklings and Chaffy had arrived moments earlier.

The crowd around The Pond, and those watching from their homes, once again brought forth a collective gasp and a loud, spreading wave of speculation regarding these latest arrivals.

After alighting, the four flyers were swiftly surrounded just as Chaffy and the ducklings had been. Old friends and relatives gathered close and embraced them, one after the other, and they shook wings, often with one or two others at the same time. Tears were shed, and there were the cries of joy from having those long absent suddenly and unexpectedly returned.

But all at once the noise collapsed to a hushed murmur, as Quillypom reappeared in the garden in front of her home, her wings crossed in front of her and heavy tears flowing from her eyes. She stood for a moment, frozen in place, her gaze focused on the four ducks. Following the turning heads of those gathered around them, the new arrivals caught sight of Quillypom in her garden, and the entirety of their surroundings seemed to fade away.

Quillypom began to stride intently toward them and all those along her path spread wide, allowing her to pass. The four flyers watched her approach, their wings fell loosely to their sides, and then all at once they darted toward her, meeting her partway through the crowd, wrapping their wings around her and holding her as tightly as they could.

Chaffy and Doctor Lochswyn watched the proceedings from Doctor Lochswyn's porch. They averted their eyes for a time from what they considered to be a private moment, even if the context was undeniably public, to look at each other as Quillypom and her children were reunited before their friends, family and neighbors.

"How did you know?" asked Doctor Lochswyn.

"Truthfully, I did not. But I had my suspicions, and one can always hope for the best. They had to come here, to tell me of the results of a task I had given them earlier," said Chaffy. "At times we all need a little push. But all is not well, I see Welshley has not presented himself."

Doctor Lochswyn immediately considered Chaffy's words

regarding needing a push, and she grew a soft smile while looking upon Quillypom and her family. She knew yet another edge had fallen.

Chaffy and Doctor Lochswyn continued looking on silently together, and Chaffy waited patiently for the moment when he could approach the Swellington siblings and discuss their findings regarding the looming task ahead.

THE SWELLINGTONS

"Quillypom looked at Welshley, he was so distraught,
and she wanted to help him."

CHAPTER 17

THROUGH THE GARDEN

THE PIGS OF THE FARM who had spent the end of a fine day in careful observation of the beauty of dusk were quite surprised when up the rarely used trail beyond the wooden fence marking the boundary of their home came three families of ducks.

The manner of the duck's approach made clear to the pigs their intention was to begin a chat, and they knew a particular pig named Swinston was anticipating the return of a certain duckling named Lillybeth.

"Swinston!" called Babeth.

The morning round of conversation had long since ended, and Swinston had been indisposed the entirety of the day, having many and intensive discussions with his fellows on The Farm. Swinston considered what Lillybeth and Hinsberth had told them to have implications of the utmost importance, not just for he and his companions on The Farm, but for the pigs in all the settlements both far and wide.

"Swinston!" called Babeth again, more impatiently.

Abselard appeared, from out of a solid wooden structure which looked somewhat akin to the Old Barn but with a flatter, angled, grass covered roof. The facade was lined with painted wooden planks and rows of small paned windows, all facing the pool of soft, wet earth known affectionately as The Puddle.

"Thank you Babeth, your request has been noted. Swinston will arrive momentarily," Abselard stated as he approached Babeth, with each word running smoothly and assuredly into the next.

Lillybeth, Hinsberth and Anati rushed excitedly ahead of the rest of the ducks. Lillybeth repeatedly called out, "Swinston!… Swinston!"

Abselard turned his head slowly to see Lillybeth and her friends gathered on the other side of the fence. All at once they flapped furiously and hurled themselves over the top to land together with a thud, in a feathered clump near the massive presence of Abselard.

"Ah, yes. Lillybeth. I see you have brought a number of friends and relatives, if I may presume?" Abselard inquired.

"Yes," said Lillybeth. "They are all here to help. You remember Hinsberth, and this is my friend Anati."

"Very pleased, naturally," said Abselard, in what seemed to be a single word.

And suddenly, from out of the sky above where the pigs of The Farm made their home, it once again began raining ducks, although this time there were more of them, and larger, as the remainder of the group undertook the short hop over the fence.

"So, you are a friend of Lillybeth and Hinsberth?" Abselard asked Anati.

"Yes, they are both my friends," confirmed Anati.

Babeth drew closer to the conversation, as she wanted to be sure not to miss any potential news of importance.

CHAPTER 17

"I believe you are in admirable company," said Babeth in a stately manner. "I would not feel I had conveyed my complete sentiments if I did not tell you how word of your efforts has spread around our distinguished residents here on The Farm, and well beyond. Without exception, if I may say, those of us here believe you have undertaken a very honorable deed, and we will do whatever we are able to help."

The ducklings stood silent, not knowing quite what to say.

As the rest of the ducks arrived and gathered with the ducklings, Abselard dispensed with the formalities, "Everyone, I am Abselard. And this is Babeth, a prominent participant in our morning conversations. It was during this morning's meeting when we had the pleasure of being introduced to Lillybeth and Hinsberth."

The ducks all introduced themselves, and Abselard and Babeth greeted them openly. Swinston soon appeared, trotting closely beside Quenelope. They proceeded outward from the barn Abselard had come from moments earlier. And suddenly, before the startled ducks, a great number of pigs appeared. They came from everywhere; from behind the barn and from out of the brush and trees, all trotting in a stately manner toward the ducks. As the pigs approached, Marista and the other adults tried to stand tall, to make themselves look a bit larger.

"Swinston!" Lillybeth shouted as she caught sight of he and Quenelope.

"Lillybeth, thank you for returning as I had requested," Swinston said in his deep, smooth and flowing manner once he was within a proper distance for conversation.

The anxious ducks huddled together tightly, and as they watched they were enveloped completely by pigs. With their vast size they could not see over their hosts; the ducks could not tell precisely how many pigs had come. Engulfed by the Farm pigs, with the fence to their backs the ducks felt small, and a little vulnerable.

Swinston suddenly spoke up in his loud, rumbling voice, while glancing about at the large gathering of pigs, "They have come here to meet you, to see who it was that had come to tell us of the plight of our fellows, and to brave themselves for their release. They wish to offer their gratitude."

In unison, the pigs bowed their heads to the surprised and anxious ducks huddled tightly before them.

Ducks and pigs stood together silently for a moment, then Swinston trotted to Lillybeth, sat down and from his vest pocket, pulled out a substantial envelope of thick parchment paper, sealed with a spot of wax stamped solidly with a large hoof print. He presented Lillybeth with the envelope, and she took it into her wings.

"Very well then, little Lillybeth. You must take this message to Chrysalis with all due speed," said Swinston in a stately manner.

"Chrysalis?" asked Lillybeth, surprised.

"Yes. They will know what to do," Swinston assured her.

"Thank you," said Lillybeth graciously. Since he was too great in size to embrace, she reached out and touched Swinston gently on the outside of his front leg.

Swinston glanced down at the tiny duckling, and then raised his softened eyes to meet those of the other ducks.

Their anxiousness had departed. Unquestionably, The Farm would be a little different...

Time was short and the ducks quickly turned, flapped and flopped themselves back over the fence. Poullaire lifted Arela, who was struggling to become airborne under the weight of her gear. Lillybeth gave the envelope from Swinston to Marista, who could manage the short hop over the fence with much less effort.

Returning to the trail, the ducks proceeded immediately back toward The Pond. The large contingent of pigs watched together, silent, unmoving, until the last of the waddling shapes disappeared into the foliage.

❖　❖　❖

A short time later, the Smythes, Smerkingtons and Plummages emerged from out of the trees near The Pond. Gathering on the soft sand, they glanced around to see the grounds overrun with a large number of Farm residents. They wondered what might be happening to hold their interest. Evening was fast approaching, yet there seemed to be no loss of fervor in the assembly.

Marista spied Doctor Lochswyn and Chaffy standing in Doctor Lochswyn's garden. They were peering into the crowd; something had caught their attention.

Lillybeth suddenly pointed and shouted, "Filipa!", as she recognized from afar a familiar face amongst the many.

The outburst caught everyone's by surprise, and they looked to the spot pointed to by Lillybeth's wing. All at once they all dashed down into the crowd to meet their friends from Chrysalis, and as they came closer they recognized, to their amazement, Quillypom, surrounded by the quartet of Chrysalis ducks. They were holding each other and seemed distant from what was going on around them, simply sharing a delight in each other's presence.

"Oh my!" Marista loudly exclaimed, stopping and clasping her wings together in front of her bill. She suddenly realized what had happened. Monique held one wing before her bill, and Hackleberg, Eldsworth and Poullaire abruptly froze in place. Anati, Hinsberth, Lillybeth and Arela just continued fumbling onward over their feet, faster and faster down the hillside until they all collided together and went tumbling into Quillypom and their friends.

"Filipa!" Lillybeth exclaimed, raising her head from the dirt.

Hinsberth grinned, and Anati and Arela tried to brush themselves off. Bardslow, Bentlby, Pommelstom and Filipa grabbed wing-fulls of feathers and heaved the ducklings upright. The ducklings and the visitors from Chrysalis shared an embrace in a billowing cloud of dust. Quillypom only watched them with a wide grin, and for a long moment, she had not the slightest concern for rules and regulations.

"Chrysalis!", "Milchester!", "We have to find Chaffy!", "My maracas!" announced the ducklings all at once.

"Yes. We *do* have to find Chaffy," said Filipa, glancing over the crowd.

The duckling's parents had by this time caught up to them.

"Chaffy is over there. At the doctor's office," said Marista. She pointed the way with a massive wing. Everyone turned to see Mister Fowler was indeed standing with Doctor Lochswyn in her garden.

With time being of the essence, they hastily sped toward the doctor's office. Chaffy and the doctor watched them approach, and stepped out onto the footpath to greet them.

"Shall we?" Chaffy waved his wing, requesting Doctor Lochswyn's permission to have everyone gather in her home.

"Certainly," replied Doctor Lochswyn without a second thought.

Chaffy returned to the house and held the door open, waiting for everyone to enter. The doctor's office was soon full; the families divided themselves between the two patient rooms and the hallway between.

Quillypom was the last to enter. She hesitated for only an instant, then she determinedly shuffled past Chaffy and he closed the door behind her.

Chaffy was immediately beset upon by Bardslow and his siblings, and they pried him into the patient room to present a series of hastily drawn sketches Filipa had taken from her satchel.

Quillypom was standing in the hall, watching Chaffy and her children, and she turned to look at Doctor Lochswyn, who, using only her eyes, motioned for Quillypom to go and join them.

With their sketches arrayed on the bed, Bardslow, Bentlby, Pommelstom and Filipa were all pointing to this and that and speaking all at once to Chaffy in loud, animated voices, and Chaffy, overwhelmed and distracted, tried to take everything in.

Finally, he lifted his wings, "Please! Please, everyone please be quiet for a moment."

In the sudden silence Chaffy turned to gaze upon the sketches, spending a moment leaning over each of them. He looked them over closely, until he suddenly caught sight of Quillypom standing just inside the doorway. He turned to her, and said in an uncharacteristically soft voice, "Please — please, do come in."

Quillypom stepped closer, to stand together with her children and Chaffy.

Chaffy paused silently for a moment.

His eyes roamed slowly over everyone in the room.

"It makes me happy, to see everyone, here, together," he announced in a very sincere tone.

And then he turned his attention back to the diagrams. As he studied each one, at times he nodded his head, at times he shook it, at times he murmured, "Ah, yes," or mumbled, "That will not do, that will not do at all."

"Might I have a pencil?" he asked.

Doctor Lochswyn handed hers to Chaffy and he began to scribble symbols and arrows pointing this way and that all over the sketches. Every so often he would ask a for details from Filipa, Bardslow, Bentlby or Pommelstom about the buildings, the grounds, the doors and hinges. As he worked his way through the drawings, he began talking to Bardslow extensively, for he had separated from the others during their flight, and had entered one of the buildings through an open vent. Chaffy listened to Bardslow intently and scratched notes while Bardslow described what he had seen. As they spoke, the four ducklings entered the room with Marista.

"Chaffy?" Marista asked.

"Yes, Marista?" Chaffy replied mechanically, still lost in his considerations of what Bardslow had revealed.

"Lillybeth was given a message from the pigs of The Farm. There was one named Swinston; he requested we take this message to Chrysalis, and that the ducks there would know what to do," Marista explained.

She pulled the envelope from her satchel and presented it to Chaffy.

Chaffy glanced at the envelope. With its thick parchment and wax stamp it had an official air.

"Swinston. Yes. I remember him, he was on The Farm when we first arrived. A gentleman to the core, I would say. Might I have it?" Chaffy asked.

Marista handed Chaffy the envelope, and he took his pencil and scratched a brief message and signed it just below the seal.

"Now we need someone to take this to Chrysalis," he said placing it on the bed with the diagrams.

He looked around the room.

Everyone present was needed there, for one reason or another, to help with the plan for the rescue.

They all turned to look toward the spare patient room where the duckling's parents were happily playing about with Arela.

Filipa said quietly, "They have done so much already."

Quillypom suddenly sparked with an idea and excused herself, "Go ahead. I will take care of it."

Bardslow, Bentlby, Filipa, Pommelstom and Chaffy watched as Quillypom swiftly departed through the doorway, curious as to what she was planning.

Quillypom was at once surprised as she waddled outside, noticing the crowd had concentrated around the doctor's office. Almost everyone had seen Chaffy and the others enter the doctor's home and remain inside, and their curiosity had the better of them.

Once again the assembly parted for Quillypom to pass unhindered, accompanied by a wave of muted discussion as she made her way to the Mayor's Office and disappeared through the garden. Only a moment later, she returned outside and retraced her path. As she arrived back at the doctor's office, she was suddenly halted, being met outside the door by three large ducks, all nearly the same age as her children. Quillypom, with her great memory for detail and knowing almost everyone on The Farm, greeted each of them by name.

"Good evening, Budger, Girmalyn, Feldmith. What might I do for you this evening?" she inquired.

"We wish to help," said Budger decidedly.

Budger was a tall, broad duck with eager manners and an expression which bespoke of a serious, committed nature.

"At the Council meeting, when Lillybeth told us of the pigs, the three of us thought we should do something," mentioned Girmalyn.

Girmalyn was big and thickly built. She had kind eyes which flashed every now and then with a purposeful, almost intense gaze.

Their companion, Feldmith, stood silent, but nodded in agreement while the others spoke. Feldmith was not quite as large as Budger, but he was still a rather large duck, at least the equal of Girmalyn. He was quiet but seemed just as determined as his friends. They were going to help, with permission or not.

For a brief moment, Quillypom looked over the three of them. They would need help for the rescue, that much was certain. She could not turn them away.

"Come in. I will check to see if there is something you can assist us with," she offered.

Many in the crowd outside noticed the trio conversing with Quillypom, and then saw them enter together into Doctor Lochswyn's. They all wondered what, precisely, might be happening inside.

After Quillypom entered with the three volunteers, Doctor Lochswyn's home was almost entirely overrun with the unanticipated company.

"Everyone! This is Girmalyn, Budger and Feldmith. They have expressed a desire to help us," announced Quillypom sonorously.

There was a brief flood of introductions, which were quite suddenly interrupted by a tentative series of barely audible knocks on Doctor

Lochswyn's front door.

Doctor Lochswyn had some difficulty navigating to the doorway through the maze of visitors. She opened the door, and quite unexpectedly, there stood the Messenger.

"Yes?" said Doctor Lochswyn, expecting an envelope or package of some kind. But the Messenger just stood there, with a nervous smile, even more nervous than usual.

After a long moment, during which the Messenger only stood with anxious eyes, she finally managed to announce in her typically swift and jittery voice, "I received a message, to come here?" And as she remembered another piece of important information, she added, "From Quillypom."

Doctor Lochswyn asked the Messenger to wait at the door, then she made her way back to find Quillypom and let her know she had a message waiting for her. Quillypom immediately stood up and joined Doctor Lochswyn, and they both swiftly made their way back to the front door, at one point having to step over Arela, who was crawling over the floor looking for pigs with a maraca in each wing.

"Come in, Lottiebury," Quillypom requested, seeming a little distracted.

Lottiebury entered and followed Quillypom back to the patient room. She glanced around, everyone was crammed in the small house, sitting or standing wherever they could find an accommodating volume of space. She nervously averted her gaze when she caught sight of Pommelstom.

"Lottiebury, please sit down. Just for a moment... over there," Quillypom requested while waving to a narrow space between two cabinets packed full of Doctor Lochswyn's medicinal remedies.

The space was not quite wide enough for Lottiebury to sit, so she stood, and made herself small between the cabinets. She had to crouch slightly under a shelf that was just lower on the wall than she was tall.

In the dim glow of a single lantern, Bardslow, Bentlby, Filipa, Pommelstom and Chaffy engaged in fervent discussion, running through different ideas and strategies, urgently planning a rescue in the most rapid fashion they could manage, sometimes talking all at once. Their voices echoed through the house.

They called in Hackleberg for his mechanical expertise. They questioned him frequently. Each query received an intense flood of technical detail from Hackleberg's bill. There were many things to consider, but the agreed upon imperative was they would have to break free at the first light of dawn, still under cover of darkness, but with enough light so they could navigate near the ground.

Quillypom became lost for a moment in the discussion, and then she remembered something with a start.

"Lottiebury!" she exclaimed.

Hearing her name, Lottiebury stood up suddenly, and her head crashed into the bottom of the shelf. She emerged from her tiny enclosure with a flattened hat and gingerly rubbing the top of her head with her wings. She timidly excused her way back over to Quillypom, who had snuck a wing past Bentlby to retrieve the sealed envelope from The Farm pigs.

Quillypom looked directly into Lottiebury's eyes, and spoke to her with a firm, sincere voice, "Lottiebury, I know I have asked much of you, and at times I have perhaps seemed rude, and maybe even unappreciative of your efforts. You have never failed to deliver a message for me, even in the harshest of weather or when I have asked you to do so at the last possible moment, and you have never complained or objected or given me the slightest cause for concern. So before I ask one more thing of you, not as my Messenger, but as my friend, I want to thank you for everything you have done for me, and I want you to know how much I appreciate every bit of it."

Lottiebury was struck speechless.

She had been waiting to hear those words from someone — anyone, for all her years at the Mayor's Office. She had always put forth her best effort, but no one ever seemed to notice. But now she understood that Quillypom had indeed noticed, but had never expressed so in word or action, at least not to her, and not until now.

Lottiebury stood in an anxious silence before Quillypom, staring directly into her eyes, and she finally managed to utter a barely audible "Thank you."

Quillypom noticed the expression on her face and could tell what her words truly meant for Lottiebury, and Quillypom's own insides felt that much lighter, freer.

"If I may ask," Quillypom began, presenting the envelope to Lottiebury, "would you please deliver this extremely important message immediately to Chrysalis?"

Lottiebury accepted the envelope at once.

"Certainly," she said quietly. "But the Mayor? The notice?" Lottiebury asked anxiously, stuffing the envelope into her delivery bag.

"He will be fine," Quillypom replied assuredly. "I will see to it."

Lottiebury turned, and with her usual speed she sliced through the crowd and exited through the front door, and in an instant was off to take to the air for Chrysalis.

THROUGH THE GARDEN

Over the course of the day, the Mayor had been watching the developments outside from the windows of the Mayor's Office. Quillypom had left his side when his children alighted on The Farm, it was the first time Bardslow and Bentlby had the soil of their home beneath their feet in many years. Filipa and Pommelstom had briefly landed to deposit Lillybeth and Hinsberth only a few days before, but had quickly departed. The rift with his children the Mayor now felt as a rupturing of his very being. They were there on The Farm, not far away. He watched them descend from out of the sky. He had sobbed as he had not in years in seeing them arrive, and while watching his beloved wife leave his side to greet them, washing away the hardness of barriers he seemed unable to break.

He wondered in lonely solitude and anguish... Why could he not respond when his wife told him that she loved him?

His wife and children were only steps away, he imagined walking over to the doctor's office and barging through the door and grabbing the lot of them as he ached to do. But the crowd would certainly see him. Would they see it as weakness, or capitulation to another's demands? And what of Chaffy? He had blamed him, for so long, for his children's departure from The Farm. But what if he was wrong?

The Mayor sat motionless, staring out the only window with a view toward Doctor Lochswyn's home, lost in his thoughts. In the dimming light, he felt confused and saddened, and so deeply tired.

He let his head sink downward toward the desk...

Suddenly he felt another presence in the room. Perhaps he had fallen asleep for an instant. The Mayor sat up with a start, and turned to see Quillypom standing in the doorway. At once she came over to him, and set her wing on his back.

"Welshley," she said softly. "Please, come with me. They are here."

He rose slowly from his chair, and following Quillypom, he went outside. But to his astonishment, it was a brilliant summer day, and they *were* there. All four of them. But they were small, and young. They ran about, in and out of his legs, pulling on his feathers, begging him to chase them. They splashed him with pails of water. Quillypom laughed, and he ran after them. They giggled as he did so. He tried to catch them, but made sure to come only so close. He laughed hard as he ran. He was out of breath. It felt so good to run, to breathe. He chased his children round and round the gardens, and their laughter echoed across The Farm. He was happy. He caught Filipa and lifted her high into the air and she squealed with delight. He glanced over at Quillypom, and she smiled at him, as she used to, in the way that would make the rest of his world fade into insignificance.

Suddenly he was jarred awake. His dream had left him distant, in a surreal state, and he wanted only to return immediately to sleep, to reenter the world he once knew. He glanced out the window again. Night was descending over The Farm, the deep blue sky dimmed into darkness and the first stars had begun flickering in and out of their tenuous existence. He could see the doctor's office in the distance, its windows aglow in the warm, welcoming hues of lantern flame.

He suddenly turned round, and Quillypom was there, standing in the doorway. With a sullen, distant air he regarded her in silence. He was not at all sure what to say, but he knew what he wanted, at that moment, more than anything else, and he began to speak, wearily, as if from a great distance, "I just now remembered, so vividly, a time long past. When the ducklings were young, and we used to play. I would chase them through the garden, and we would laugh. Sometimes we would laugh so hard I thought I would need Heleen just to revive me. And I remembered how you used to look at me... and I would not care about anything, just you and I, and the ducklings... our family and our friends. That was what mattered to me. That was *all* that mattered to me."

Quillypom looked at her husband. She could tell he was breaking down, he was on the edge of giving up, of disavowing the rigid construct he had created for himself in his long quest for prestige and influence in the eyes of others.

"Welshley, we can live that time again. I am here, and our children are here. Let them come home to you. Tell them you want them here. Tell them you *need* them here. I think even now, even with what they are considering doing at the moment, they are waiting, waiting for you."

"And Chaffy?" queried the Mayor with a sullen voice, as if contemplating the crushing weight of a thousand regrets.

"Chaffy has no animosity. His world is Chrysalis now, he revealed to me what drove him away; not only the pull of his ideas, of what he wanted to accomplish, but the memories... the reminders of his life here with his wife on The Farm. It was so very painful for him. He built Chrysalis for her, he wanted to remember only her beauty, her personality, her love, and he carved it out, to have part of her with him always."

"I remember her. It was crushing, for all of us. It was then I knew we had to stay on The Farm, forever. I sympathize with his motives. But our children?" the Mayor asked solemnly.

"Just a moment ago Chaffy told me how they went to Chrysalis by way of their own choosing, and how he told them to return to The Farm. He told them The Farm needed them, that you and I needed them, and they needed us. Every day, every week, for months he would mention this again and again, but they would refuse to listen. They are stubborn, Chaffy mentioned, each one of them. And he said it is because they have strong concerns, just like their mother and father. Over time they became part of Chrysalis and made their home there, and Chaffy told me he believes it was never his place to tell them to leave, to force them to go. He does not order anyone to do anything, it is not his way. He wanted to tell you to come to them and to convince them to return to The Farm, if here is where they truly belong. But you would never return his messages. He correctly interpreted that you blamed him somehow for our children's decisions, and he found he could not get around it, if you would not speak to him."

Quillypom could tell her husband was suffering, he did not deal well with his emotions, especially regarding any notions of failure or mistake on his part. He took such notions both very seriously and very hard.

The Mayor's head sunk even further, his face cringed under the realization that he may have been wrong, about Chrysalis and especially about Chaffy. He started to think aloud, searching for the reasons behind the mistakes he might have made, where precisely he may have went wrong. "I do not know what to say. I thought it was Chaffy, and Chrysalis. Maybe filling their heads full of idealism. At the time I believed Chaffy and his collaborators departure may have had something to do with my becoming Mayor. I thought perhaps he was trying to get even with me, by influencing our children with the idea to go to Chrysalis. I am not sure — I may have misinterpreted *everything*."

The Mayor paused for a moment. And then, with the hard realization he was making, his voice became so tense he was barely able to convey it, "I may have pushed them all away."

Quillypom looked pityingly at Welshley. He was so distraught, all she wanted at that moment was to help him. She still loved him, and she could hardly bare to see how far he had sunk into doubt and despair.

"Please, understand, I am only trying to help, not to present criticism. But, Welshley, I think you are still doing it, still misinterpreting things. Look what you did to poor Lillybeth. She has the purest of intentions, she lives in a boundless world of caring and optimism. She and Hinsberth see something that is upsetting, they see suffering, something that is not right, and they pursue it. And you tried to deny them, because of how you thought everyone might look at you, whether or not you would appear strong and principled in the world you and I inhabit. I am just as guilty, I tried to impose our world onto Lillybeth's whenever she came into my office. I did not understand what I was doing, until Heleen told me a story, about the Edges of Things — about growing past the boundaries we create for ourselves, even though they can appear more real, more solid and impenetrable than the hardest of stone, in reality they are nothing, lesser than air. Lillybeth, in her own curious manner, gave me a glimpse of that world, a world without edges. Please, Welshley. Come with me, into that world," Quillypom pleaded. She reached out to her husband with a trembling wing.

The Mayor sat silently. He glanced up at Quillypom, unsure what to think, unable to sort his thoughts. His mind was a flood of doubt and regret. Then all at once, the vision of running with his children, chasing them through the gardens in the bright sunlight of a hot summer day, began to steal away his thoughts. The edgeless world his wife described; was it there? Was his dream a part of it?

He pondered Quillypom's words regarding Lillybeth. Certainly, he thought, the little duckling would not hesitate, not even for an instant. And as he considered the notion, with the rest of his body still frozen in place, still staring into the distance with his head hanging low, his wing rose, slowly, unconsciously, aching to touch his wife's, to join her in the hope of regaining something which existed now only in a memory.

Just as the Mayor's wing touched Quillypom's, they were startled to hear a rap on the door at the rear of the house, at their private entrance. The Mayor went to drop his wing and answer the caller, but Quillypom held tight.

"Please, enter, we are here," Quillypom called out loudly.

They heard the door unlatch, and then the sound of light footsteps brushing over the wooden floor, in a slow but purposeful gait.

"We are in here," Quillypom called.

After a few more steps, into the doorway came a familiar face.

Quillypom and The Mayor were stunned.

"Should you be here? Are you not still working on the plan?" asked Quillypom in surprise.

The Mayor was struck silent, he was not expecting any visitors, especially this one in particular.

"They think I stepped out for some air. As one might imagine it is becoming quite stuffy in there. I do not think Doctor Lochswyn ever considered having so many visitors running through her home," said Chaffy with a hopeful smile.

Noticing the solemn mood of his hosts, he offered to depart at once.

"I am sorry to come at such a time. I feel like I may have interrupted something. Should I go?" Chaffy asked politely, pointing himself back toward the entrance.

"No... No, please do not leave," Welshley suddenly replied.

Chaffy turned back into the doorway.

"I thought I should come for a little visit, since I am here, on The Farm. It seems we may have had some degree of misunderstanding over the years. Quillypom was generous enough for us to have discussed the subject for a time, and I thought it appropriate that we meet."

The Mayor shifted in his seat, he tried to sit up a little straighter, to be more fully present. His mind was still shuffling over his thoughts, trying to reach a conclusion of some sort, to be at rest, to be at ease.

"I agree. It seems perhaps, I may have been a little too forthright in my interpretations of certain things," the Mayor announced.

"As have I. If I have caused anyone harm, or grief, or suffering of any kind, my deepest apologies, of course. It has never and will never be my intention," Chaffy offered.

The Mayor hung his head again under the burden of what he felt compelled to admit, to himself and to Chaffy, "The fault, I must say, may reside more fully with myself, than with anyone else. From what I have been told, it seems I have been stubborn, and perhaps arrogant, believing the ideas I had formed on my own and not allowing any suggestions to the contrary, from others or even from myself. And in believing them, I may have acted in such a way as to cause unnecessary pain to all those I care most about. Chaffy, I believe I owe you an apology. A sincere apology. I am sorry. I do not know what it may mean to you now, but I feel at this moment it is all I can offer."

Chaffy never really believed he would hear Welshley admit he was wrong, or offer apologies for what he believed to be his own errors, and he was moved by the admission. He has changed, Chaffy thought. With his children finally all nearby, and seeing he had not the courage to face them, Chaffy saw the extent to which his old friend was now drowning in sorrow and regret, and at once he sought to comfort him.

"I should have come, a long time ago. I sent messages, but maybe that was not enough. I was unwilling, myself, to face my own grief, the presence of my past, here, on The Farm. Please, do not place the blame solely on yourself. I, and certainly with their stubbornness, your children, we all share the blame. You have accomplished so much here, with The Farm. It runs like a well designed machine. The residents... they are admirable in so many ways."

The Mayor knew Chaffy was trying his best to cheer him, and he thought it must be clear to him the depths to which he had sunk. He had intentionally shattered Lillybeth and Hinsberth's hopes for a Council driven rescue plan to save a thousand suffering souls. What had he become?

"I appreciate the efforts, Chaffy, and I thank you for coming here this evening. It means a lot to me, probably more than I can express at the moment. I need some time to think. But I want to promise you, and if you could do the same for me, that we will not find each other scarce, either here or in Chrysalis."

"Yes, certainly," replied Chaffy.

There was a brief moment of silence, and then Chaffy announced in a hushed voice, "I should be getting back to Heleen's. They will be missing me, and sending out a search party soon, I am quite sure of it."

Quillypom and Welshley nodded together. Chaffy turned and strode softly down the hall and departed out the rear door, letting the latch close gently.

Chaffy tried to remain concealed as he waddled back to the rear entrance of Doctor Lochswyn's home. The crowd surrounding The Pond had thinned somewhat, or perhaps there were just more of them sitting or lying down, certainly a great many remained. The homes surrounding The Pond had windows and doors open and they were glowing from within, lit warmly with the inviting flickers of candles and lanterns. Many were serving food and drink to those huddled around The Pond, waiting in the cool evening air to see what might happen next. With the surprising return of Chaffy and the Swellington children, there was continuing hope for the unexpected.

POULLAIRE

"Go! You must do it, now!"

CHAPTER 18

BEYOND THE EDGE

CHAFFY ENTERED DOCTOR LOCHSWYN'S HOME happy to have remained undiscovered. He strode up the hall to the patient room and slipped inside. Lillybeth, Hinsberth and Anati had worked themselves into the crowded room. They surrounded the table, and were pointing to the diagrams and relentlessly tossing questions about the room at Bardslow, Bentlby, Filipa and Pommelstom. The siblings did their best to answer the onslaught of queries, and they could not help but smile in amusement even though they felt overwhelmed by the demands.

"How are we doing?" Chaffy asked to anyone with an answer.

"I think we have a plan... generally speaking," offered Filipa.

The ducklings shared an anxious glance.

Bardslow, Bentlby, Filipa and Pommelstom discussed the plan with Chaffy. The exchanges were fast and detailed. The ducklings, huddled around the bed, listened intently, staring at each other all the while. Their parents were in the spare room with the three volunteers and Arela, also listening, straining to follow every word as the house became eerily silent. Doctor Lochswyn was preparing her evening meal in the only part of the house which was not overrun with guests, and the scent wafted down the hall and spread to every nook and cranny.

The exchanges between Chaffy and the four siblings slowed and finally stopped. There was nothing more to be said, nothing more to be done. They looked at one another, and suddenly a palpable tension filled the room, competing with the aroma of Doctor Lochswyn's porridge. Was this it?

"Do we have everything we need?" asked Chaffy.

They swept through a list of supplies, Filipa checked each item off on one of the diagrams.

"And the Farm pigs — the message?" asked Bardslow.

"Quillypom sent it. The message is on its way, probably already arrived in Chrysalis," answered Chaffy.

"They will be ready, then?" asked Bentlby.

"As ready as they can be on such short notice," said Chaffy. "They will have help to take them in, Chrysalis will not stand idle, I can assure you of that."

Outside, they could hear a rising din. The crowd was making quite a cacophony.

"What is it?" Chaffy called out to those nearest the doorway.

Marista, Hackleberg, Millybeth and Eldsworth rose up and went to the front door, but before they could reach it, Poullaire came quickly from down the hall, with Arela bouncing on his shoulders and Monique trailing closely behind holding out her wings in case she should slip. He threw open the door to see what was happening. There was some cheering and a round of applause, as in front of the Mayor's Office stood Quillypom and Mayor Swellington, facing the door, holding each other.

The Mayor was inscribing something on the notices. He and

Quillypom stood before them for a time, the Mayor scratching all the while with his pencil. Then they both stepped back, as if to admire the Mayor's work. Seeming satisfied, without fanfare the couple disappeared into the Mayor's Office.

In the dimming light, a number of rather curious residents waddled up through the front gardens and read the revised notices. Quillypom had swiftly performed some research and found there existed no time limit constraining when a Council member was required to vote on a proposal. However, the meeting had technically adjourned, so the tie vote had held, and the Mayor, while serving on the Council, was prohibited from casting an additional vote to break the tie. So the Council vote remained even, leaving the proposal open for appeal. The implied restrictions on travel were lifted regarding Chrysalis specifically, but upheld regarding contact with a group of unruly badgers who lived not too far away from The Farm, and whom had earlier ransomed two residents in a cited incident involving an experimental balloon.

This development spread swiftly through the crowd and the voices returned with great enthusiasm, along with a release of the tension that had been mounting through the day.

Poullaire was one of the first to arrive at the Mayor's Office. While Arela waited patiently on his shoulders, he read the notices himself. With a passionate wave of excitement he immediately turned round and bounded swiftly back to the doctor's office, and he barged into the house and exclaimed, "Lillybeth!"

Lillybeth soon appeared, followed closely by Hinsberth and Anati. "Yes?" she asked.

"I have just been to the Mayor's. He and Quillypom rewrote the notice, and you can appeal the proposal!" Poullaire exclaimed. "Go! You must do it, now!" Poullaire was not known for patience.

"Where is Quillypom?" Lillybeth queried in wide eyed surprise.

"She is still at the Mayor's Office," Chaffy shouted from the patient room, having overheard the conversation. He knew she would not leave Welshley.

Lillybeth, Hinsberth and Anati immediately departed out the front door and waddled swiftly down the trail to visit Quillypom. Arriving through the garden, they could not reach the knocker, so Hinsberth deployed a stone to great effect.

Quillypom arrived promptly at the door and threw it open knowing quite well, given the nature of the interruption, who might have come to call. She looked down upon the three ducklings who stood with hopeful anticipation before her.

"I want to make an appeal," declared Lillybeth.

"So do I," added Hinsberth.

"And I second them both," stated Anati.

"Very well, then," said Quillypom. "As the deciding vote on the Council, I wish to vote in *favor* of the proposal. All resources of The Farm are free to forward the proposal to its conclusion. I will complete the necessary documentation and other formalities."

"Thank you Quillypom!" exclaimed the ducklings in unison.

"Before you go, might I ask for something in return?" Quillypom requested.

"What may we do for you?" asked Hinsberth politely.

Quillypom stood tall, and the stern expression returned.

"Free Milchester," she commanded. "Free them all."

❖   ❖   ❖

The three ducklings immediately turned and waddled as fast as they could back to the doctor's office. Upon arriving, they burst through the door and announced what Quillypom had done for them. Chaffy, Bardslow, Bentlby, Filipa and Pommelstom all looked at each other. Poullaire, who had entered the room with the ducklings, nodded in verification.

"Well, that certainly changes things," Chaffy said.

They immediately began scratching on the diagrams, crossing things out and making new lines, arrows and lists. Tearing from one of the diagrams a list of items they knew to be present on The Farm, they asked the volunteers and the duckling's parents to go and help retrieve them.

In an instant, those gathered outside understood what was happening, and the volunteers began to arrive at Doctor Lochswyn's in droves. They wanted to help gather supplies, bring food and water, and to go and rescue the pigs directly. Time was short.

Bardslow, Bentlby, Filipa, Pommelstom and Chaffy, indeed everyone inside Doctor Lochswyn's, were suddenly busy, darting here and there and helping do whatever needed to be done. The volunteers began organizing themselves in small groups around The Pond. Those that volunteered to go rescue the pigs arranged themselves directly beside the shoreline, where gentle waves lapped lightly against the shallow banks. Chaffy and the Swellingtons darted outside, and in the light of the lanterns they carried, they and the other volunteers studied the diagrams until everyone seemed quite sure of what they needed to do.

From the nearby homes, residents nearby delivered tents and blankets and supplies, for they knew many would not sleep this night.

CHAPTER 18

They brought lanterns and the boundaries of The Pond began to glow, the light reflected as though a thousand glimmering amber stars floated upon the softly rippling water.

The Farm was suddenly alive with activity, but the ducks were not without worry over what might lie ahead, especially for those who had volunteered to fly out into the unknown.

In little time, every home surrounding The Pond had their doors propped open, and a steady stream of residents going in and out, helping gather supplies and do whatever else they could.

The stars began to hold steady as the last gasp of dusk faded to darkness and the crescent moon shown brightly. With just enough light, the flyers were grateful for the timing.

Chaffy was quickly directing the preparations using the diagrams and notes he and the Swellingtons created. Supplies were amassed near the volunteer flyers, who awaited anxiously for preparations to be completed. Bardslow and Pommelstom showed them all what to take and how to load it in their packs and satchels, and describing what to do once at their destination, and what to watch out for. With the preparations nearing completion, they were joined by the duckling's parents, and a short time later, by the four ducklings.

Working with Girmalyn, Budger and Feldmith, Bardslow saw the families approach and immediately suspected what they were desiring to do.

"Please, you cannot go," Bardslow announced firmly.

"Yes, we have more than enough flyers for the plan already," added Budger.

"Is that so?" asked Marista. "We have seen this endeavor go this far and we are not about to sit here and wait and do nothing."

Even Budger held his bill, for he, like everyone else, was fearful of trying to counter Marista.

Poullaire spoke up and his passionate voice cut through the night air, "We are going. I am personally going to take some of those pigs right out of their cages with my bare wings if I have to!"

"Budger is right. If we have too many flyers going in, we will draw attention to ourselves. The pigs may notice us, and their surprise may alert the humans. We need to remain few, and hidden. I know you want to join us, but we need for you to stay here. It will help us more if you stay," explained Bardslow firmly but sincerely.

"You listen to me right now," said Marista. "We *will* go. Maybe we will stay outside, in the trees. We can wait there. But I am not going to let all of you go and risk yourselves while we sit here. If something unexpected happens, we can help."

Monique added, "Yes. You are going for us, for Hinsberth and Lillybeth. For everyone who has heard about the pigs and wants them to be freed. We need to be there if something goes wrong. To carry things, who knows? Let us go, we will stay away, out of sight, as Marista says. Hackleberg, for example, he knows very well of mechanical things. He could be invaluable."

Bentlby was listening to the conversation.

"I will ask Chaffy," he suggested to Bardslow. "Maybe it will be fine, if they go no further than the edge of the forest."

Bardslow nodded in agreement.

"But please," he insisted, "leave the ducklings here."

Marista and Poullaire glanced at each other in sudden disappointment, for neither of them were willing to leave their ducklings behind. They would have to stay.

CHAPTER 18

Anati, Hinsberth and Lillybeth were saddened to hear they would not be going. Arela was also disappointed, she fully intended to use her butterfly net to rescue at least one pig.

Hinsberth was particularly disheartened. He hoped to finally meet Milchester, to be able to see him, to know him as not just a voice. He wanted nothing more than to be the one to pry open his cage and release him to the outside, to rid the world of such injustice and to thank him for his generosity, for maybe even saving his life.

Anati and Lillybeth could see the deep disappointment on his face.

"Do not worry. If all goes well, they will bring him here to the pigs on The Farm. Then you can see him, no?" Anati offered in consolation.

"Thank you, Anati," Hinsberth said wistfully.

He appreciated Anati's attempts to cheer him, even if not entirely successful.

Lillybeth was unsure of what to say to Hinsberth. She hoped it would only be a matter of time before the rescue was accomplished, and the pigs would be on their way to new lives. But she felt uncomfortable leaving the task to the volunteers. She had been there with the pigs, and so had Hinsberth, and certainly, she thought, their presence must offer some advantage.

Presently, Bentlby reappeared after having conversed with Chaffy.

"Chaffy said he was not going to tell anyone what they should do. You are free to go if you wish, but he suggested to please remain in the trees, out of sight, and away from the rescuers. The plan is very detailed and everyone has their precise tasks to accomplish. Everything must go smoothly for the plan to be carried out with the least risk."

The message from Chaffy provided some consolation for the

ducklings and their parents. Perhaps they could go along and help in their own small way, maybe even their presence would be enough to help the rescuers feel more safe and secure, knowing someone was watching over them.

"But please," repeated Bardslow, "leave the ducklings here. It will be too dangerous."

❖   ❖   ❖

The flyers made their final preparations and friends and family huddled around them, wishing for everything to go well, and hoping for all to return safe and sound.

Suddenly, the feverish activity around The Pond ceased, and the lightly lapping waves and leaves twisting in the breeze could again be heard, as two familiar figures appeared, approaching from the direction of the Mayor's Office. Waddling silently and huddled together, Mayor Swellington and Quillypom rounded the banks of The Pond, toward the flyers.

In the sudden silence, Bardslow, Bentlby, Filipa and Pommelstom turned their heads and caught sight of them, and they immediately stopped what they were doing and glanced at each other in uncertainty. Even though darkness had set in, it was a very public place, and seeing their father approach, they became anxious. They had not spoken to him for some time, and not one of them knew precisely what to say.

At the doctor's office, Doctor Lochswyn and Chaffy watched Quillypom and Mayor Swellington approach the flyers. They swiftly turned away from the window, to let those outside have a degree of privacy, and hoping all would go well.

CHAPTER 18

The Mayor and Quillypom came into the lantern light where their children stood side by side, so at last they could see each other's faces.

Bardslow, Bentlby, Filipa and Pommelstom saw their father for the first time in some years and were surprised at his appearance. He seemed tired, beyond his age. His posture and expression reinforced each other in conveying an air of despair.

Bardslow and Bentlby, initially seeming to become stern at seeing him approach, softened noticeably when once again in the presence of their father. For a brief moment, the Mayor and his children only looked at one another, without a word, without knowing what to say, without knowing whether to greet each other as long lost friends or as distant acquaintances with a shared past.

Then suddenly the Mayor began to speak, slowly and quietly, breaking the silence to everyone's surprise, "I fell asleep and had a dream this evening. Or at least I believed it to be a dream, but perhaps it was not. It may have been a memory. A memory that has become a dream, a dream I want to relive, over and over again. Even now it keeps repeating in my mind. And at this very moment, everyone in my dream is here. Now we are in a different time and place, but everything important to me is here.

"This evening I also realized that over time, I have done many things that have pushed this dream to the back of my mind, and buried it under goals and imperatives that my wife, my Doctor, and a little duckling have demonstrated are without merit, and I have pursued them at my loss. And for this I can only blame myself, and ask for you to forgive me."

The Mayor's children were stunned. Their father, who had always been quite stubborn in his belief that he was unquestionably choosing the right course, had admitted that in regarding the most important decisions of all, he had made mistakes, and believed it was his responsibility alone.

But they stared at one another anxiously. For the moment they had no words.

The Mayor continued on, speaking in the same quiet voice, "Now we are here, and you are about to fly off, to do something that I know needs to be done, but is nonetheless something not one of us has ever done before, and with it comes an unknown risk. It profoundly worries me, for everyone, but especially for those whom I love so deeply and can never do without."

Bardslow, Bentlby, Filipa and Pommelstom turned their eyes toward the ground. They knew what they were about to do might be dangerous, but what their father had said went straight past their focus on the endless details of preparation and into their hearts.

The Mayor stood before them, taking them in. And as he did so, for an instant he saw them as they were in his dream, as the young ducklings he had chased through the garden so many years ago. And he decided this time they would not get away. The Mayor suddenly lurched forward, he grabbed Quillypom and pulled her off her feet. He flared his massive wings, and wrapped them over the whole of his family, holding them tightly, refusing to let go. His children worked their wings free, and they reached forward and held the Mayor in a mesh of feathers. They embraced each other for the longest time, hoping with the coming sunrise and with everyone returned safely to The Farm, their dreams could begin again, together.

A calm spread across The Pond.

The preparations and activity ceased as everyone watched the

Swellingtons huddling together in the warm glow of the lantern light.

For the Mayor, the years of remorse and regret slowly dissipated into the cool night air. Finally he lessened his grip, and they let their wings fall.

"We must get ready to go," said Bardslow.

"I understand," said the Mayor. "We will be waiting for you."

"Please, you need to sleep," Quillypom told her husband. "I will wait for them."

"Not tonight," said the Mayor. "Not ever again. We will wait together."

❖   ❖   ❖

The preparations resumed in earnest.

Chaffy and Doctor Lochswyn scuffled over the sand together to stand before the flyers. The ducklings and their parents also joined them to say goodbye and wish them well. As the flyers made final preparations to go aloft, the whole assembly circled around them. They shook wings. They embraced. They hoped everyone would return safely.

Filipa, Pommelstom, Bardslow and Bentlby strapped their packs around their torsos and attached a dim light, as they were to lead the others to their far-off destination. They packed the diagrams and maps of The Farm and the surrounding lands, marked with the locations of all the nearby settlements inhabited by pigs and ducks. The other flyers donned their packs and gear, and in little time they had completed their final checks.

"We are ready to go!" Bardslow exclaimed after helping Pommelstom fix his pack. "Is everyone ready?"

"Yes," came a uniformly anxious response.

"No, wait a moment," said Budger. "My wing is caught on something…" Budger fiddled with his pack, and a moment later he said, "Sorry. Ready now."

"My light is out," said Filipa, looking backward across her shoulder. The light mounted to her pack was set firmly in place, but was as dark as the night sky.

"It is fine, we have mine and two others," said Bentlby.

"Can someone tighten my strap? It feels like my bag is about to fall to my knees," inquired Girmalyn, trying to reach around to her back.

"I have it," replied Feldmith quickly.

After a bit more squirming, everyone became quiet once more.

"Anyone else?" asked Bardslow.

His request was met with silence, although there was certainly a fair amount of nervous fidgeting.

The crowd surrounding the flyers began to part, creating an unbroken path toward the trees, skirting down the side of The Pond, a passage into the unknown.

The flyers readied themselves to go aloft. They glanced around at each other with anxious expressions.

No one had ever done what the flyers were setting out to do. The dangers involved were entirely unknown, and many in the crowd could not help but to hold their breath, and some gasped and placed their wings in front of their bills.

The tension among the flyers was palpable; etched in the expressions on their faces.

"Please, take care," Chaffy whispered under his breath.

Doctor Lochswyn reached over, and took hold of his wing.

CHAPTER 18

Filipa had volunteered for the task of counting down, and after nodding to Bardslow, she suddenly blurted out, "Three... two... one... GO!"

Together, the flyers accelerated down the passageway marked out for them by their friends, family and neighbors, and with wings outstretched and flapping hard, they began rising into the crisp night air. As the flyers went aloft, they glanced back into the warm pool of lantern light surrounding The Pond, seeing the many tears and worried faces shrinking into the distance behind them. The flyers gradually disappeared into the darkness, in total silence except for the tinkling of the metal objects they carried and the fervent brushing of their wings; each beat pushed them higher and faster into the unknown.

The ducks on the ground stood absolutely still, staring up at the sky until the three dim lights faded into the darkness over the tree tops. Quillypom and the Mayor stood holding each other, peering deep into the darkness, fixated on the spot where their children had faded from sight.

Lillybeth, Anati and Hinsberth huddled together for warmth, and in their worry, the comfort of being close. Their parents stood over them, glancing into the night sky with concern, wondering what lie ahead for the flyers.

Hinsberth felt a single tear fall down his cheek and Lillybeth, before she could catch herself, raised her wing and wiped the tear away. Hinsberth gave her an appreciative smile as he remained fixed on the dark night sky. Lillybeth looked anxiously away.

And then, they waited.

All around The Pond, tents had been pitched, lanterns burned, homes were open, and sleeping bags and blankets were scattered about on the soft, sandy soil. A few small fires were lit. There was not a single departure, and everyone slowly began settling in for a long and anxious night, waiting in anticipation for the coming light of morning.

Marista and Poullaire still pined to join the expedition; they did not agree with leaving the flyers to do the rescue alone. They continued quietly discussing the possibility of flying out to land on the ground under the nearby trees in order to watch over the flyers and make sure they were safe.

Doctor Lochswyn and Chaffy delivered blankets and pillows, and Doctor Lochswyn invited everyone over to stay in her garden, where she had placed a soft mat over a small enclosed court with a flat stone floor. The Smythes, Smerkingtons, and Plummages graciously accepted the invitation and set up their camp for the night. They settled down together, wrapped in warm blankets, and began the long, anxious wait for dawn.

Quillypom and Mayor Swellington eventually turned and waddled together away from the spot where they had been staring at the sky, and surprisingly, they also found their way to Doctor Lochswyn's, setting down together in the garden for the night. Exhausted, they quickly fell asleep, propped up against one another, utterly depleted from the course of events defining a long and memorable day, a day which they would never forget.

THE FARM & THE POND

*"The loud brushing of their wings was enough to startle some of those on
the ground nearby, and as they sat up, they saw the last of the tail
feathers fade into the darkness, leaving behind the warm glow
of the lanterns lighting the edge of The Pond."*

CHAPTER 19

TO FREE THEM ALL

THE FLYERS WERE ARRAYED IN A GREAT ARROW with Pommelstom, Filipa, Bardslow and Bentlby forming the leading edge. In the shimmering night air, the slender crescent moon and stars shown brightly. The silvery sheen of moonlight imparted just enough light; the outline of each flyer could just be seen against the pitch dark forest below and the inky purple of night above; a dozen dark silhouettes flew swiftly over the backdrop of stars. The weight of the equipment they carried and the lack of streamlined form in the shapes of their packs made flight difficult, but they remained focused, remembering the plan and playing out in their minds the sequence of tasks they needed to perform over and over again.

Silence was key. They knew as they approached their destination, they would have to try and make no sound at all, for they did not wish to startle the pigs, and they certainly did not want to alert the humans.

They cut silently through the night air, gliding whenever possible to avoid brushing their wings. Leading the way, Filipa and Pommelstom concentrated intently, they squinted hard to see ahead into the veil of darkness.

On and on they soared.

Suddenly, Filipa and Pommelstom dipped their wings in opposite directions, sending a signal to those behind that they were approaching their destination. At once the flyers felt their hearts quicken and their stomachs tighten. They strained to see what lie ahead.

And suddenly, through the distant trees they could see a sizable clearing dimly illuminated by a few faint lights, it was mostly cloaked in darkness.

Without warning, it hit them. They had heard the stifling air described, but they were unprepared for the severity of its reality. A cacophony of noise erupted into the sky. They could hear a thousand voices, but no words or conversation. The tone was solemn, distraught, full of despair.

The impact on their senses made some of the flyers falter. They were struck for a moment by the scene, by the desolation, the air, the voices. For an instant the plan slipped from their minds. But as they drew nearer, from out of the sharp buildings arrayed in the darkness, slowly coming into view just ahead, they began to discern individual voices. They heard the cries of suffering; the haunting moans of those ill and in pain, and they became emboldened once more; focused on what they were there to do. And as the lights guiding them were extinguished, the flyers began to glide until the subtle sound of air over feathers faded out into silence, drowned by the cries of the aching, the distressed and the infirm below them.

From out of the sky, the silhouettes approached, blotting out the stars, with no sound, not a whisper or a hint, like the most ephemeral of shadows. Unbeknownst to the pigs, to the humans or to the creatures in the woods, as in Milchester's dreams, they had come.

The pigs stood in darkness. The pain in their bodies, the aching in legs and hips, relieved only by sleep. During the night, some managed to escape into unconsciousness, but many could not, and they cried over their misfortune. Even those who tried to sleep often could not, the suffering about them always audible, a constant reminder of their own hardship.

If only they could move! Some of them banged their snouts repetitively against the bars, or bit at them or scraped themselves on the concrete or metal beneath them. The confinement had taken them. They had lost the soundness of mind.

In every building, high above the captives, the strangest of noises could be heard, if only for an instant. Cutting through the stifling air came the sound of metal twisting against metal. Silhouettes descended unseen from openings near the roof with the slightest brush of wings. A sound — muddled, quiet, hushed — emanated from both ends, where the doors remained closed. Before the pigs, from out of the darkness, the sound of metal grating on metal could be heard, first twisting, then rising, then falling to be caught by something near the ground.

Then came the smallest of voices, of a kind they had never before heard, "Do not move. Wait for the signal, to come at first light."

Was it a dream?

They could hear the words repeated over and over, ever so quietly, to their neighbors on either side, then proceeding further and further away.

"Do not move. Wait for the signal, to come at first light."

Pigs froze. They looked up into the darkness. Who was there?

CHAPTER 19

All night long the voices continued.

Mothers, confined in cages barely larger than themselves, unable to nest, their young separated from them by thick metal bars with only their mouths accessible for feeding, also heard the sounds of metal grinding against metal, and in the darkness the strange voices told them, "Do not move. Then take them, on your back, when the signal comes at first light."

Into the night the flyers worked furiously, trying as hard as they could to ignore the shock and dismay over what they were seeing. They disarmed cages. They removed the stays from their hinges and told the pigs that when the sun began to rise a signal would come. They worked faster and faster, for there seemed to be too many cages, and they began to fear they would not be able to reach them all before morning. But they continued on relentlessly into the night, ignoring the terrible conditions and the growing feelings of exhaustion, they worked as quickly and as quietly as they could manage.

❖   ❖   ❖

Marista, Eldsworth, Hackleberg, Millybeth, Poullaire and Monique sat in the cold night air, leaning against each other in Doctor Lochswyn's garden. Sleep was evasive. At least one of them had been awake and alert throughout the night.

Hinsberth, Lillybeth and Anati had formed a little duckling pyramid, their backs supported one another, and they were staring blankly into the dark night sky with their bills drooping open. Arela was draped, butterfly net at the ready, in Poullaire's lap. The stars previously overhead were now dipping low on the horizon; the night was growing old. It would not be long before a faint hint of morning light would begin to reveal the dark line of the eastern horizon.

"What are you thinking?" Marista asked Poullaire, whom she could see staring off into the starlit sky.

"I am wondering," said Poullaire. "Wondering what is happening, wondering if the plan is working as designed. In my experience, things inevitably go wrong. Truthfully, I am worried. What if we do not see them arriving? How do we know they are safe?"

"I agree," said Marista. "I do not think we can leave them alone, out there, trying to do the rescue all by themselves without anyone to help. If something should happen…"

"What do you want to do?" asked Poullaire quietly, not wanting to wake Arela.

"I say we do what we originally intended to do. We have had a bit of rest, the flyers have not. They will be exhausted by morning, and they might make a mistake. I say we go, and as we agreed we can stay under the trees, out of sight, just to make sure everything is fine," replied Marista, in her characteristically piercing whisper.

"I can hear you talking," said Monique, opening her eyes. "Are you sure that is a good idea? It seems as though it could be dangerous, no? What if you surprise the flyers while they are doing the rescue. You know the old saying about too many cooks?"

"I know — I know," said Marista. "But they are trying to do something that I think is too risky. I like the idea of having just a few, to sneak in. But once they have sneaked the sneaking, I think they will need help to do the doing."

"Well, even if we agree, how do we go? Everyone is asleep. What about the ducklings? Are you going to leave them here alone?" asked Monique skeptically.

"Chaffy has the map, we can use it too. It is not so very far from here. If we fly swiftly, we could be there before morning. We can bring the ducklings with us and they can stay behind, back in the trees, even further away from where we go to watch the flyers," suggested Poullaire.

Hackleberg began to stir, hearing the voices of his friends. His twitching also awakened Millybeth.

Seeing Millybeth's eyes opened, Marista asked bluntly, "What do you think?"

"Think?" said Millybeth inquisitively.

"Marista thinks we should go and make sure everything is fine with the rescue," said Poullaire.

"Part of me thinks that is a good idea. Another part thinks we may be in the way. But most of me wishes only to sleep," Millybeth answered wearily.

"Sleep, that is the problem. The flyers have been working all night. I think they could use us now," said Poullaire.

"Well, you are not going without me, no?" said Monique.

"Of course," said Poullaire. "And we are not going without our ducklings."

Marista added, "No one is going without me. And I am not going without Eldsworth and Hinsberth. This is for what my son discovered, and what that admirable character did for him, and I intend to see that Mister Milchester and whoever else is taken care of."

"If you go, you are not going without me," said Millybeth. "And that means the rest of us."

"Agreed!" exclaimed Poullaire emphatically.

"Wake everyone up. I want to be in the air!" Marista declared.

Marista and Poullaire both came to their feet, and without their support, the other ducks tumbled over to one side or another, and were rather rudely awakened by the unforgiving ground.

The ducklings stirred with the noise, and seeing everyone else standing they rose up, and with eyes still cinched tight, began to be shuffled along by their parents.

Marista stood tall, and announced firmly to everyone else, "We are going to go. I have a bad feeling, and I intend to make sure that nothing goes wrong."

Chaffy and Doctor Lochswyn barely stirred in the front garden, as the three families of ducks groggily began to prepare to ascend into the air.

Millybeth and Marista looked over at Chaffy and the doctor, sleeping peacefully with their backs together, and they smiled knowingly at each other. Quillypom and the Mayor sat in nearly the same position but on the opposite side facing The Pond.

Right near the shore was the only place free enough of encampments to allow for all of the families to take off together. The groggy ducklings stumbled along the trail in pursuit of their parents, and the whole assemblage went running, clumsily, with beating wings, down the side of The Pond and took to the air, dipping and flopping about, still not yet fully alert.

The loud brushing of their wings was enough to startle some of those on the ground nearby, and as they sat up, they witnessed the last of the tail feathers fading out into the darkness.

❖　❖　❖

As the ducklings and their parents flew fast through the night sky, the cold breeze of flight quickly revived them.

"Stay close!" called Marista loudly, her voice booming through the night.

They flew in a tight cluster with the three ducklings in the center. Poullaire knew Arela could not keep the pace; he carried her in his pack; her fuzzy head peeked out from the open lid and she wore a huge grin on her otherwise tired little face. Lillybeth helped direct them as Poullaire recalled what he had seen on the map he carefully borrowed from the wings of a sleeping Chaffy.

The first brightening was beginning to show in the eastern sky, but the stars still shown brightly, as did the setting moon. Like the flyers who had traced the same path a nighttime ago, the ducks carved out dark silhouettes against the background pattern of stars.

With dawn fast approaching, finally Millybeth spotted their destination in the distance, the few scattered lights still shining feebly could be easily seen in the predawn darkness. Not wanting to draw any attention to themselves, while still some distance away they began to glide, to make as little sound as possible. Even Arela managed to hold her urge to protest the increasingly foul scent and the strange voices. Hinsberth felt overwhelmed at returning to this place, as did Lillybeth. Anati was seeing it for the first time, and she recoiled at the scene. Her parents were equally shaken.

Not wanting to come too close, they descended rapidly to find a spot to land in the trees, to avoid being caught in the open on the bleak and barren ground.

Descending into the trees, Marista and Poullaire glanced up to see their decision to come was a wise one. To their dismay, there were several young pigs outside, squealing and making a fuss, for they had broken free of their cages, and with the flyers having shattered the door hinges on both ends of the buildings, the pigs had managed an escape. The doors were flat on the ground; the ends of the buildings were wide open. In the distance they saw Filipa and Pommelstom flying about over the squealing pigs and trying to calm them. The pigs were young enough they did not seem to understand the precariousness of the situation and the grave danger they were in.

Marista, Poullaire, Hackleberg and Millybeth spotted some of the other flyers. Their heads poking out of the ventilation openings near the roof lines. They were rapidly looking around, apparently trying to figure out what was happening.

As Marista and Poullaire made their descent, in the distance they saw a fourth building, smaller than the others, and through the windows they saw a light turn on. The door flung open.

The rescue was in grave trouble.

In an instant Marista and Poullaire darted forward, skimming over the ground toward the buildings. Millybeth, Hackleberg, Monique and Eldsworth quickly followed suit, shouting out loudly "Stay close!" to the ducklings, who took off after them, following them over the desolate ground. They quickly split into three groups, each flew toward a different building, and they descended fast into the ventilation openings where they had seen the flyers peering out.

"They are coming! The humans are coming!" they warned everyone as they entered the buildings.

In great distress, the flyers and the three families descended into the buildings, disregarding the need for silence, and the pigs, who had become ever more quiet over the night as the voices had come to them, began to panic.

"Over there! The last of them!" one of the flyers shouted to Marista, pointing to a row of cages.

The sun was readying itself to peak over the horizon, and the flyers had not yet removed all the cage stays. It was the same in the other buildings, and Marista, Poullaire and the others began noisily and without concern for secrecy to rip out cage stays left and right, and the loud clanging sounds of metal against metal rung through the air.

Hinsberth and Lillybeth flew into the nearest building, behind Marista. Marista flew to the end of the rows of cages and began tearing out cage stays with her feet while flapping hard, almost hovering in mid air.

Hinsberth and Lillybeth descended to a landing and darted across the floor, sending out a trailing shock wave of noise from the pigs.

Finally, as they neared the far end of the building, Hinsberth began to call out, "Milchester! ... Milchester!"

Milchester was asleep, dreaming. Flying. In his dream, his friend appeared, but only as a voice, calling his name. His friend was ill, in distress. He needed his help. But from his vantage point in the sky, he could not see him. There was only the earth and clouds below. But he heard it again, a call of distress. In his dream Milchester wondered... Where could he be? Was he real? Could he be real? He would never know. He began to cry, and the tears in his eyes made him blind. He knew he would never find his friend. In his dream he called out, so he would never forget, as loudly as he could, "Hinsberth!"

And in the commotion, Hinsberth heard his name, faintly, but nearby. He did not know what Milchester looked like, but he knew his voice. It was a voice he would never forget, a voice that had helped him so unselfishly when he was most in need.

Lillybeth and Hinsberth continued down the rows, darting through the darkness.

"Milchester!" Hinsberth shouted again.

The pigs they passed looked at them in a blank panic.

Finally they came to the end of the row, where isolated between empty cages, and leaning feebly against the unforgiving metal bars, was a sleeping pig. He was not as large as the others. His face looked sickly, pale, and there was a sadness which shown through even while asleep, as well as an unmistakable kindness. Hinsberth stopped in front of the cage, and Lillybeth stopped and stood beside him.

"Milchester..." Hinsberth whispered.

And suddenly he remembered where they were, and what was happening.

"MILCHESTER!" he bellowed at the top of his voice.

The pig slowly opened his eyes, as if returning from a great journey. His eyes were swollen and he could barely see in the darkness.

"Milchester!" Hinsberth shouted again, and he reached forward with both wings through the bars. "We have come! We are here!"

Lillybeth flew up and took hold of the cage stay with her feet, and she twisted it upward and flung it skyward with all her might, for it to strike hard against the back wall, hoping for it to shatter into dust.

Hinsberth's wings touched the sides of Milchester's nose, and Milchester began to sob. Hinsberth and Lillybeth also began weeping over the sight of the kind and generous spirit they knew as Milchester, seeing the sores on his skin and the filth he was surrounded by in the tiny, isolated prison that cruelly enclosed his body but could not contain his gigantic spirit and imagination.

"Hinsberth — my friend," Milchester whispered through his tears.

"You are going to be fine," Hinsberth sobbed. "Come with us."

Lillybeth flew down and alighted next to Hinsberth.

"It is open!" she exclaimed. "Set him free!"

Hinsberth grabbed hold of the cage door with his wings, and Milchester watched as the door was pulled open before him, a vision he had forever dreamt, becoming reality before his eyes.

"Hinsberth, I am so sorry. I almost forgot — you are real," Milchester said, sobbing weakly, for he had little energy left.

"We have to go!" insisted Lillybeth urgently.

The other flyers, who had been warned the humans were approaching, gave up all pretense of being secretive and were flying around wildly, pulling up the remaining cage stays and dropping them to the floor. Marista, noticing Hinsberth and Lillybeth with a particularly sickly looking pig, descended quickly to land next to them.

"We have them all! We have to go NOW!" she shouted. "Toward the door! GO!" she bellowed again for everyone to hear, pointing her massive wing toward the opening at the front of the building.

The sun was beginning to peak over the horizon.

But no signal had been given and many of the pigs remained standing in place as the voices had told them, waiting.

In the other buildings it was the same, Budger, Girmalyn, Feldmith, and the Swellingtons were flying about releasing the last of the stays. Hackleberg, Eldsworth, Millybeth, Monique and Anati were flying from one corner to another, helping mother pigs exit their cages, and mounting their children on their backs, securing those who could not hold on with straps the flyers had carried in their packs.

A few more of the younger pigs bounded out of their cages, ramming through the remaining doors and knocking them flat, so they were now all open to the outside.

"We have them all!" exclaimed Hackleberg. "Get ready to go!" he shouted with all his might, throwing his voice back into the building. He stood fast with wings outstretched, guarding a frightened mother and her babies.

"Everyone get ready! We have to go!" Filipa shouted into the last building.

Budger suddenly darted outside. He had seen Bardslow there, with the pigs who had already escaped, and to his shock and dismay he saw him harassing three humans who had run up and were trying to grab hold of the escapees. Another human appeared and started going after Bardslow with a rake, swinging it wildly.

"WATCH OUT!" bellowed Budger.

Bardslow dipped just in time to avoid being struck.

"NO!" Bardslow shouted, as he noticed another human was pushing up one of the doors in an attempt to trap everyone inside.

The other humans turned and followed suite. They seemed confused, they had noticed all the doors had been disassembled and were lying uselessly on the ground. They dropped their attempts at reigning in the few young pigs outside and began pushing up the doors.

Lillybeth and Hinsberth were trying to guide Milchester down the narrow aisle between the rows of cages to the doorway. To their horror, they could see two humans outside lifting the door. They stopped in mid-step, wide-eyed and frozen in shock, not sure what to do.

Marista saw the humans as well. At once she lurched forward, taking off and rapidly accelerating to charge ahead at full speed. She banked through the narrowing doorway and surged into one of the humans, knocking him several feet out into the dirt. Poullaire took off after the others, and the humans had to refrain from sealing the doors under the intensity of his harassment. The humans were waving around wildly, looking for tools to grab and swipe at the ducks, who flew around them, diving and swirling and shouting, preventing them from raising the doors.

But finally the humans had tools in hand; rakes and shovels, and were deploying them in such a way that the ducks could not dare approach them, for they would surely be injured, or worse. They continued to dart around and call out loudly, but their voices were not enough. The sun had risen above the horizon, and the brilliant, apricot glow of morning began to spray across the bleak ground, alighting the sterile metal faces of the buildings. The humans mechanically prepared to reseal the doors, to mount them back on their hinges.

The ducks stood frozen or hovered in air. In shock they huddled closely together and stared in the face of disaster, in fear for their lives and those of their loved ones, as the first rays of morning began to light their faces.

The humans worked quickly to remount the doors, but as they did so, the soft light of morning suddenly turned to an eerie glow. Instead of brightening steadily, the cloudless sky began to darken once more.

Turning from the darkening metal walls of the buildings before which they stood, the humans looked toward the eastern horizon, and they lowered their tools.

As they looked on into the sun, a large, dark cloud appeared. It grew swiftly. Shifting in shape, its borders changed rapidly. The humans looked on in silence, watching, as if in awe, or confusion. As the cloud approached, it grew larger, and the top suddenly took on an ominous shape. It spread over the sky in the broad anvil of an approaching thunderhead. In only an instant it grew so large it blotted out the sun. The humans began to appear anxious, afraid.

The ducks inside saw the darkness return, but they could not see what was happening. Lillybeth and Hinsberth stood in place, frozen, on either side of Milchester, waiting for the chance to run outside with him, to set him free once and for all. They saw the humans move away from the doorway, and they waited.

The massive, darkening cloud approached ever nearer and the humans became distraught. They shouted to each other loudly, angrily, their voices broken by great distress. The storm appeared to be moving as if it had a mind, a purpose, directly toward them.

The broad, spreading anvil approached menacingly, and as it did so, they could hear it. The storm was alive, and from it thundered the noise of a hundred thousand voices, a haunting sound which presaged for them an apocalyptic vision. The storm swallowed the sky, and they could see the cloud lowering, forming into a seething river of movement. And it was headed straight for them, straight for the pigs.

The humans cried out to each other, with strain and fear, and as the leading edge of the river approached, they suddenly bolted up in fright and ran, consumed with fear, as fast as they could away from the buildings.

Bardslow peered up into the darkness.

"The doors!" he suddenly bellowed.

As the storm continued its relentless approach, Filipa, Bardslow and Pommelstom took off and flew rapidly toward the doors, barreling into them to knock them to the ground once more.

"Give it!" bellowed Filipa. "GIVE THE SIGNAL!"

Just as Bardslow shouted at the top of his voice, "GO!", the river hit with a vicious blast of wind and the deafening sound of their voices, all shouting loudly in threat to anyone who would dare to interfere. Great masses flew through the buildings, in one side and out the other, and the pigs knew the signal had arrived. They burst out of their cages, running as fast as they could, enveloped in a cloud of ducks.

"Go! Follow them!" shouted the rescuers from inside.

Lillybeth and Hinsberth looked up in awe as vast columns of Migrators streamed overhead.

"Milchester! Let's go! Follow us!" Hinsberth shouted at the top of his voice.

Milchester broke his attention from being awestruck, to begin freeing his legs from the frozen and useless state they had suffered for so long. All of the pent up vigor his body instinctively demanded burst forth, and he jolted painfully forward and ran toward the open doorway, with Lillybeth and Hinsberth in flight at his sides. In an instant, he broke out into the crisp air of morning, enveloped in a dense cloud of ducks, and he ran and ran. With his friends and into freedom he ran, and he never looked back.

The Migrators flew in a gigantic, tall arc, exiting from one side of the buildings, rising to a great height, to return again to the other side, circling for as long as pigs remained inside. Huge clouds of them trailed off into the distance, across the bleak, lifeless landscape, forward into the trees, disappearing, enclosing large groups of pigs with every pass, the dust from thousands of stomping hooves spiralled skyward in the vortices from their flapping wings.

The humans looked on in fear and awe from a nearby hilltop. One had fallen to his knees. Two of them gripped their hats, holding them tightly over their chests, their mouths agape at the spectacle. All ignored completely the one who seemed to be imploring them to do something. They watched helplessly as the pigs departed, the last of them in a vast cloud of dust and surrounded so densely by ducks that only their hooves could be seen, trailing off into the distant edge of trees. The living storm dispersed with them over the tree tops, and the rising sun slowly began to brighten once more.

LOTTIEBURY

*"...I did something I was not supposed to. But after the Council,
I wanted to help, and it is all I know how to do."*

OUT OF THE AZURE SKY

HAFFY AND DOCTOR LOCHSWYN AWAKENED as the morning sun arose over the hills of the eastern horizon and spread glimmering rays over The Farm. They were startled to notice the stone court in the garden was empty. The three families who had fallen asleep there the previous night were missing, and Chaffy, who knew them well enough, suspected where to.

Quillypom and Mayor Swellington were also awakened as the sun gently warmed their faces. They sat side by side, their faces touching, facing to the east.

The sounds of life returned to The Pond as the sky grew brighter. The lanterns were doused and vociferous chatter again began to fill the air. The anticipation was palpable. At any moment, they expected flyers to return, and finally they would know whether or not all was well.

Beyond the eastern edge of The Pond loomed a large hillock, and from the summit it was possible to see all the way to the pig's home. If the plan had been successful, rescued pigs were to arrive there. Chaffy and Doctor Lochswyn joined Quillypom and the Mayor in clambering up to the summit of the hill, to see if there was any sign of the flyers. The Swellingtons were worried over their children, and they hoped that upon cresting the hill, they would receive some sign of their children on the approach. A number of others in the encampment noticed the foursome waddling intently up the hillside. They joined in the journey, and gradually a large number of Farm residents were streaming up the hillock. Reaching the crest they sat down, made themselves comfortable in the grass and rocks, and settled in to wait in anxious silence.

Chaffy and Doctor Lochswyn were especially concerned, since they knew the three families had departed, in all likelihood to help with the rescue. If anything had gone wrong...

As the morning wore on, the worry and tension mounted. Where were they? Many began to wonder if perhaps the flyers should have returned already if everything had gone smoothly. Stomachs turned to knots as the bright morning sky remained empty.

But at long last, they saw something. However, it was not what they were expecting. From out of the trees in the distance they saw flyers, but not their flyers. There was a large, seething cloud of them, skimming fast just over the canopy and winding low through the trees. They slowly emerged from the dense foliage, and started to spread across the intervening meadow in the direction of The Farm. As they did so, a large cloud of dust billowed behind them.

After a short time they crossed the meadow and skimmed low toward the pig's home. As they arrived at the edge of The Farm, the pigs began to emerge from behind the old flat roofed barn, and they stood — in a formal and dignified arrangement — and waited.

Then suddenly, the massive cloud of flyers lifted skyward, and as they did so, a large group of pigs came into view on the ground beneath them. They looked pale and exhausted. There were young pigs and older pigs and mothers with babies hanging and strapped onto their backs. They looked around anxiously, their eyes squinting at the bright sky. The cloud of flyers flew swiftly toward those watching on the hill, climbing steadily, and they soared directly overhead, putting the Farm ducks briefly in shadow, and they called down salutations from above.

The newcomers approached the Farm pigs cautiously. The Farm pigs approached them slowly, so as not to cause any alarm. As the ducks looked on, they saw the Farm pig leading the group, who even from a distance could still be identified as the gentlemanly Swinston, raise his front leg, and he touched one of the newcomers, gently, reassuringly. They could not hear what the pigs were saying to one another, but as they spoke, the other pigs from The Farm approached the newcomers, and they welcomed them. They touched together their noses, and the sides of their snouts. Those rescued slowly began to move closer, and cautiously they began to interweave with the Farm pigs, who embraced them without hesitation.

The Farm ducks watched in wonder, with great relief and a warm and deep feeling of dignity. Somehow a notion arose within them that they were witnessing something important, something beyond themselves, something The Farm had done, for no other reason than it was necessary; for them, for the pigs. A few could not help but to shed tears, as they watched the Farm pigs, with great gentleness and care, take in those who had been rescued.

The Farm ducks knew there must have been at least some success for the flyers. At least some of the pigs had been freed, and they were just now beginning new lives, right in front of their eyes as they looked on from the hilltop. But they could not help but wonder and worry. Where were their flyers? Where were those who had departed the previous night? Where were all those who were so eagerly expected?

As they watched the rescued pigs set about discovering their new home, Chaffy glanced back into the trees, and saw, skimming above the tree tops, a small spattering of dark specks, and he pointed his wing.

"There!" he exclaimed excitedly.

The whole assembly turned their gaze to follow Chaffy's wing off into the distance, and they saw the flying spots as well. Tears and gasps of relief flowed from eyes and bills, as Girmalyn, Budger, Feldmith, and the Swellington siblings came soaring up the hillside. They alighted, running up the crest, stumbling wearily into welcoming wings.

Quillypom and Mayor Swellington swiftly went to their children. They held one another and shed tears of joy and relief.

"And the others?" Chaffy asked.

"They are coming," replied a battered Filipa.

With the weary flyers in tow, the whole assembly turned to descend back down the hill toward The Pond. As they arrived at the shore, the crowd began to huddle tightly again, circling around the rescuers, Chaffy, Doctor Lochswyn and the Swellingtons, to find out what had happened.

"Look! There!" came a voice from the crowd. And before anyone else could speak, they all looked up to see six more flyers arrayed low in the sky over The Farm. They rapidly descended to a tired and hard landing near the center of the crowd next to the Swellingtons, Chaffy and Doctor Lochswyn. There was a deep, shared sigh of relief to see them arrive unharmed.

"Where are the ducklings?" asked a concerned Doctor Lochswyn.

Poullaire turned around to show everyone Arela, still nestled comfortably in his pack. Only her tiny head protruded; she was grinning widely, happy to be home. She was, however, mildly disappointed as she never had a chance to use her butterfly net.

Marista, with an uncharacteristically weary voice, announced, "My Hinsberth, he is with Lillybeth and Anati. They will be coming soon. They have their own plans, for which we will later have to join them."

The crowd gathered tightly around them, everyone wanted to know what had transpired during the rescue.

Bardslow began to speak to an audience which fell most unusually into complete silence, "At first, everything was going well, just as we had planned. There were so many of them, so many cages. We worked hard, all night long, trying to free them. The air was horrible, the conditions intolerable. The horror of it motivated us further, and we committed ourselves to freeing them all as fast as possible. It is still a blur, I cannot remember everything we did, everything we accomplished. But, things began to go wrong; cages sticking, tools breaking, the door hinges were difficult to remove." The crowd listened intently to every word, and Bardslow continued, "And then some of the pigs, the younger ones, escaped from their cages. By that time we had unhinged the doors and they knocked them down. They were squealing loudly and running about, and the sound of the doors collapsing or the squealing awoke the humans. We had not finished opening the cages, and were in a great deal of trouble. That is when Marista, Eldsworth and the others arrived. We would not have made it had they not been there for us."

CHAPTER 20

Many in the crowd were shocked and even more grateful to have the flyers home when they came to understand just how close they had come to serious danger.

Filipa then continued, "The humans came, and they tried to push the doors up. Bardslow, Budger, Marista, Poullaire, and some of the others attempted to stop them, to delay them, or else we would have all been trapped inside. But they were too strong, they had tools and they swung them at us and we could not go near them. They started to put the doors back on their hinges, and we thought that was it, that we had failed utterly, and the pigs would be trapped, just as they always have been, and somehow we were going to have to go in and rescue the flyers, and the ducklings, and everyone else."

Filipa, who was normally rather bubbly, became more subdued, and her voice broke as she recalled what happened next, "That is when — the Migrators came — many thousands of them, it must have been most of Chrysalis and everyone in the surrounding lands. We could not believe it, there were so many. They filled the sky. They frightened the humans away, they all ran off as the Migrators approached. The Migrators stormed through the buildings, a solid run of them, and helped guard and guide the pigs out. They continued flying through until every last one of them were free, and they stayed with them, directing them out into the forest, out into the surrounding settlements."

The crowd was stunned into silence by Filipa's tale; they stood motionless, imagining the scene and the danger the rescuers had just narrowly escaped.

"How — how did the Migrators know?" inquired the Mayor.

"Who? Who told the Migrators?" added Chaffy, confused.

Everyone glanced around, awaiting an answer.

"Anyone?" asked Chaffy again. "We only just planned the rescue last evening. How did they know?"

Everyone expected someone to answer, but no response was forthcoming.

"I suppose... we should most assuredly thank each and every one of the Migrators appropriately," an exhausted but somehow rejuvenated Mayor Swellington announced.

The crowd tightened around the flyers once more, wanting to welcome them back, shake their wings and thank them for what they had done, even more so with the knowledge of just how close they had come to disaster.

"Who is *that*?" a voice suddenly bellowed from the crowd, taking everyone by surprise.

They all lifted their eyes skyward, and in the warming light of the late morning sun, they spied a lone flyer on the approach, soaring out of the azure sky, wings pointing this way and that, apparently on the edge of a barely controlled fall.

"Oh my!" exclaimed a shocked Quillypom.

The crowd quickly parted to create a space for landing, and out of the air, landing hard on her feet came the Messenger, looking more haggard than ever. Her eyes were swollen and tired, her clothes tattered, and her hat hung loosely on the side of her head. To universal astonishment, she wobbled over to Pommelstom and fell loosely into his wings, and he dropped onto his knees and held her tight.

"Lottiebury!" exclaimed Quillypom. She quickly went to her side.

"Yes. Thank you," said Lottiebury in a barely audible voice.

"What has happened to you?" asked Quillypom.

She knelt down beside Lottiebury and put a wing under her head, to hold her and look into her eyes.

Quillypom sent a quick glance to an anxious Pommelstom, as he held the drooping Lottiebury in his wings.

Lottiebury was silent.

"Lottiebury," Quillypom repeated in a softer tone. She cradled Lottiebury's head in her wings. "Please, tell me. What happened?"

Lottiebury began to reply, but her nervous, speedy manner of speaking only retained its nervousness, for her speed had long ago departed.

"I delivered the message — the message from the pigs here on The Farm — to Chrysalis. But you will forgive me? Please forgive me," she asked of Quillypom.

"Forgive you? Lottiebury, I do not understand. Forgive you for what?" inquired a baffled Quillypom. "Please, Lottiebury, what did you do?"

"I delivered two messages to Chrysalis, not just the one you gave me. I did something I was not supposed to. But after the Council, I wanted to help, and it is all I know how to do," replied Lottiebury cryptically.

"What message?" inquired Quillypom.

"I took the transcript of what Lillybeth had said before the Council, about the pigs. I put it in an official Farm envelope and sealed it with the official feather stamp," Lottiebury stammered, and she paused, expecting a reprimand of some kind, but not receiving one, she continued, "And worse, I wrote something on it, something I felt they should know. I told them about the plan... I told them about the signal at sunrise... I told them that it was their chance, an opportunity. For Chaffy's wife, for all who have ever been taken, to send a message.

To send a message to the humans... to tell them they do not own us, they do not own Milchester, or the others. To send a message... to stop taking us... to stop hurting us."

For a long moment no one spoke and no one moved. Then tears came to Chaffy and he had to cover his eyes. Everyone was stunned, not only by what the Messenger had done, but how she did it, and why. Quillypom only looked upon Lottiebury, in admiration and disbelief.

"You flew, all night?" asked Quillypom.

Lottiebury nodded.

"Contacting the Migrators, using the Chrysalis network?"

Lottiebury nodded.

Quillypom placed her wings gently on either side of Lottiebury's face, and held her. Lottiebury was too depleted to return the sentiment. Pommelstom lifted her in his wings, and he buried his head next to hers. Quillypom, still stunned, managed a soft smile at Pommelstom.

"I know," she said. "It is fine, you do not have to hide it."

The crowd huddled in a solemn silence around Pommelstom and Lottiebury. Exhausted in Pommelstom's wings, Lottiebury drifted off to dream...

Into the Clouds

"They continued upward, climbing higher into the sky."

CHAPTER 21

INTO A DREAM

THE EVENING SUN LAY LOW IN THE SKY and Lillybeth and Hinsberth stood in the soft grass beside Hackleberg's workshop. The long shadows of trees and grass created shafts of light and shadow across the field as the ducklings ran through their checklists. Lillybeth donned her cap and satchel, the latter packed with a full set of gear. Hinsberth remembered the goggles and was wearing his favorite sweater, the now worn argyle sweater he had deployed as a beacon, leading to his rescue. After finishing their checklists, they decided to go through them once more, just to be sure, but soon they were joined by Anati, who was rather unusually dressed, sharing some of Lillybeth's more durable expedition attire. After ensuring Anati was fully equipped with the needed supplies, the three ducklings waddled down the footpath to their preferred spot for taking flight. Here they were to embark upon whatever adventure was to come.

They came into the clearing, and an instant later they ran a short distance, gaining speed and flapping fast. Accompanied by the sound of their small beating wings, they rose together into the air.

They spiralled upward into the clear blue sky, slowly gaining

CHAPTER 21

altitude in the shimmering air over The Farm. Toward the horizon the sun shone brilliantly, its rays lit the evening sky in tones of fiery orange and gold. Every now and then they passed in shadow as puffs of cloud passed before the sun on their relentless march to the distant horizon. The trio of ducklings flew tightly together. As they rose, they pointed things out for one another on the ground; their homes, the Old Barn, the fence and the home of the pigs, which had to be more than doubled in size with the arrival of so many new faces.

They continued upward, climbing higher into the sky.

Suddenly they entered the realm of the clouds. The water droplets collected and streaked off their feathers, over their wings and bellies. Their satchels became wet and striped where the chilled droplets laid down their tracks as they ran across and sailed off into the wind.

Inside the cloud, they seemed to be in another place; a featureless place where only the three of them were real, with all the detail in their feathers and faces. Surrounding them was a uniform grey, a sort of nothingness. Looking into the mist, the cloud appeared boundless, like the sky itself. A more subtle hue, certainly, but without form, without edges.

They continued climbing, and Hinsberth drifted toward Lillybeth until they were flying wing tip to wing tip, almost touching. Lillybeth glanced over to Hinsberth, and saw how close he had become. Her stomach quivered, but she did not try to move away. Hinsberth made sure he stayed with her, close to her side.

Anati noticed her friends moving together, but she did not mind, for she knew her heart was destined for something else…

Finally, they rose out of the mist. The deep blue sky and bright orb of the sun went in and out of existence as they sailed through the bubbling cloud tops. The vapor streamed off their backs, and their wings scooped great gobs of it and sent it skyward, where it disappeared, lost in the ocean of blue.

They flew onward, the three ducklings lost in an infinite expanse of sky in every direction; an endless playground high above the earth. But suddenly they slowed... and waited.

At a snail's pace, the ducklings flew just fast enough to maintain their present, lofty height.

And then other shapes began to appear, slowly peeling through the mist, like whales surfacing in a distant sea. First came the wings, swirling the vapor into vortices streaming off behind them. Then came the tops of their heads and backs, and then the spread of their tail feathers. A vast number of them were spread widely across the sky, encircling the ducklings. With their companions finally beside them, the ducklings began to climb again, and as they did so, the other flyers followed suit, ascending above the clouds.

Lifting into the clear blue, the ducklings looked down to see their parents surface from the mist, beating their wings with great effort, their torsos clad with the harnesses of the Transporter. As they rose, more flyers began to appear, also flapping purposefully and wrapped tightly in their harnesses; Budger, Girmalyn, Feldmith, Filipa, Pommelstom, Bardslow and Bentlby. They all toiled strenuously as they rose further into the sky. A final group of flyers; Lottiebury, Trewnslough and Hershelbaum peeled away from the mist as they struggled to gain altitude. Then all at once, everyone soared clear of the cloud tops. Their straps stretched tightly downward and disappeared into the veil of vapor beneath them. The ducklings rose a bit higher, and the flyers followed, flapping as hard as they could.

CHAPTER 21

And as they did, another, larger shape began to appear through the bubbling sea below. The vapor broke free and swirled about, first from the pointed ears, and then the large rounded back surfacing like a great beast of the sea. As the flyers pulled higher still, the top of the head and eyes appeared, along with the pinkish body. In an instant they all burst out of the cloud and into open sky, with nothing but sunlit blue surrounding them. The air was shimmering in its clarity, and Milchester looked up and around at the ducks high above him. The Transporter, its dome removed, was stretched around his middle, the straps straining but tight, leading up to the flyers. Milchester glanced down, and he saw the beauty of the distant Earth, stretching wide from horizon to horizon. The landscape was laid bare in brilliant relief, broken only by the slowly drifting shadows of the lumbering clouds. He saw the deep browns of fertile soil and the bright greens of fields and forests. He looked skyward into the endless blue, and as they left the clouds behind, Lillybeth, Hinsberth and Anati flew down beside him.

"Let's go!" Hinsberth bellowed, and the flyers began to fly faster, flapping as hard as they could.

Milchester felt the cool breeze of flight, softly brushing the skin on his face and pushing his ears gently back. His eyes watered, and he pushed his front legs out and held them, as if he had wings of his own. The flyers went faster still, and Milchester grew a wide grin, as wide as his face would allow, the likes of which he never before had, and with the accompanying feelings of joy he had never before felt. Milchester savored the feeling of wind on his skin, and he gazed in awe at the bright blue sky and the brilliant white clouds. He looked downward to the distant Earth and upward to the many friends who surrounded and carried him. It was his dream. He was happy. He was free. Finally, he was home.

And away they carried him, into the boundless sky...

❧ ABOUT THE AUTHOR ❧

A curious character interested in almost everything, R. S. Markel rediscovered, at a neither tender nor ripe age, but in that somewhere in-between state, his passion for writing and illustration, all but forgotten mainstays of the more open-ended days of childhood. The impetus was his avid book-loving daughter's sixth birthday. So enamored was she with the stories he would invent and the piles of books gathered from frequent walks to the local library that he decided to write a short story with a meaningful message to present to her for her birthday.

After finally sitting down to write, the proverbial floodgates were released. In a tireless whirlwind of inspiration, at times writing ten to twelve hours per day, in little more than eleven weeks he had written a 105,000 word novel, *Lillybeth and Hinsberth: The Edges of Things*. He has since completed a second 140,000 word novel, *Lillybeth and Hinsberth: The Essence of Things*; a sequel to the first. He hopes readers both young and young at heart will have as much delight in reading about the lives and adventures of his colorful cast of characters as the author had in writing about them.

❧ Artistic Direction ❧

Artistic direction for this book was a collaborative effort put forth by R. S. Markel and Cheryl Lynn-Collier Markel. The art for both the cover and interior were drawn over the course of several months by R. S. Markel primarily using a .5 millimeter mechanical drafting pencil on high quality sketch paper. Once satisfied with his work, the completed drawings were scanned at 1200 DPI and the digital versions were turned over to Cheryl Lynn-Collier Markel. Using the Adobe Creative Suite software package, she modified and formatted the artwork for print. The text was set in 12-point Adobe Garamond and 14, 17 and 20-point Trajan Pro. The book and cover were designed and print formatted by Cheryl Lynn-Collier Markel.

http://www.rsmarkel.com